Jo Thomas worked for many years as a reporter and producer, first for BBC Radio 5, before moving on to Radio 2's *The Steve Wright Show*. In 2013 Jo won the RNA Katie Fforde Bursary. Her debut novel, *The Oyster Catcher*, was a runaway bestseller in ebook and was awarded the 2014 RNA Joan Hessayon Award and the 2014 Festival of Romance Best Ebook Award. Her follow-up novel, *The Olive Branch*, is also highly acclaimed. Jo lives in the Vale of Glamorgan with her husband and three children.

You can keep in touch with Jo through her website at www.jothomasauthor.com, or via @Jo_Thomas01 on Twitter and JoThomasAuthor on Facebook.

Readers can't resist Jo Thomas's feel-good fiction:

'Romantic and funny, this is a great addition to any bookshelf' *Sun*

'Warm and witty . . . Well worth a read' Carole Matthews

'Sun, good food and romance, what more could you want?' *Heat*

'Captures the essence of France from the vineyards and chateaux to the glorious sunshine' Cathy Bramley

'Perfect for those who dream of a new life in the sun!' *My Weekly*

'An utterly charming read full of rustic romance and adventure' *Woman* magazine

'Set in a beautiful landscape with lovable characters, it's a lovely story and a real page-turner' *Candis* magazine

'Best read with a glass of Prosecco. Salute!' *Bella*

By Jo Thomas

The Oyster Catcher
The Olive Branch
Late Summer in the Vineyard

Digital Novellas
The Chestnut Tree
The Red Sky At Night

Jo Thomas
Late Summer
in the
Vineyard

headline
review

First published in paperback in 2016 by
HEADLINE REVIEW
An imprint of HEADLINE PUBLISHING GROUP

1

Cataloguing in Publication Data is available from the British Library

ISBN 978 1 4722 2372 2

Typeset in Caslon by Avon DataSet Ltd, Bidford-on-Avon, Warwickshire

Printed and bound in Great Britain by Clays Ltd, St Ives plc

Headline's policy is to use papers that are natural, renewable and recyclable
products and made from wood grown in well-managed forests and other
controlled sources. The logging and manufacturing processes are expected
to conform to the environmental regulations of the country of origin.

HEADLINE PUBLISHING GROUP
An Hachette UK Company
Carmelite House
50 Victoria Embankment
London EC4Y 0DZ

www.headline.co.uk
www.hachette.co.uk

For Dad.
A classic vintage with unique character
that stays with you forever.

Dear Reader,

Bonjour! Bienvenue! Hello and welcome to my latest world in *Late Summer in the Vineyard.*

I love France. As a child, I holidayed in France every year with my family, mostly in the Ardeche region, the Rhône Valley and, later, further south in the Côte D'Azur. Funnily enough, I later discovered that they are all big wine regions! My parents adored the French way of life, as I do; the food, the wine, the markets, the language . . . and the manners. I love the way the French greet each other. As a teenager, I went back to the French Riviera and found myself a job there, waitressing in a restaurant on a campsite. I spent long, hot, sunny days and balmy nights serving *steak-frites* and *plats du jour* to holidaymakers. It was a fantastic time in my life.

These days, I visit France because a couple of my friends did the very thing I dream of doing. They found a house, fell in love with it and moved out to Castillon-la-Bataille, about an hour's drive from both Bordeaux and Bergerac, and they started a new life and business. They run writer's retreats and courses so, lucky for me, I get to go and write in this wonderful place, which is just down the road from the beautiful Saint-Émilion. It was here that, like the grapes on the vines, the idea for *Late Summer in the Vineyard* began to grow. Who would move here, to the historic wine country, and why? They'd have to know all about wine, wouldn't they? Or else they'd have a heck of lot to learn . . . just like Emmy Bridges – the heroine in this novel. I hope, like a good vintage, you'll enjoy it, remember it and tell your friends. Àvotre santé!

Jo x

Acknowledgements

A big, big thank you to my friends Janie and Mike Wilson who made a life-changing move and bought a house in France, in between Bordeaux and Bergerac, where they now run writing and painting courses and writing retreats (www.chez-castillon.com). It's because I started to visit them that I began to get to know the area, and I've loved watching their business go from strength to strength. If you're looking for a course or want some time away to write, look no further. It is a beautiful place on the banks of the Dordogne and set in amongst the vineyards of south-west France.

Thank you, Janie, for organising our trip to the wine school at Saint Emilion and our wine-blending evening with a professional wine maker, the early morning swims, tea, cheeky glasses of rosé and of course for all the many early morning emails.

Big thanks to Basil and Julie at La Maison de la Riviere for talking me through the wine-making process and helping me understand it. They have a fabulous gîte and B&B there (www.lamaison-riviere.com).

And thank you, Basil, for putting me in touch with Nick at Château de Claribès, who showed me round his fabulous organic vineyard and *chai* and helped me out with my wine-making queries. Do have a look at their website: www.claribes.com. Any discrepancies in the wine-making process in this book are entirely of my own making!

And a huge thank you to David Headley from Goldsboro Books who was a fabulous companion and help to me on my last research trip. You were brilliant!

And big hugs and thanks to wonderful friend and travelling companion Katie Fforde and my Chez Castillon writing buddies for all the support, fun and friendship.

Prologue

I can feel the big, brown envelope, full of odd coins – copper, silver and gold – weighing down the bag on my shoulder. It feels like the weight of the world as I tentatively step through my open front door, heart banging, mouth as dry as sand.

I hear a strange voice from the front room: 'Just look for anything that might sell for a few quid.'

My heart lurches and I instinctively draw my shoulder bag closer to me, gripping it tightly with both hands as my worst fears are confirmed and I see the big, broad shoulders in a worn leather jacket filling the space in the middle of the living room. The wearer picks up a framed photo of my mum from the mantelpiece and studies it.

'There's not much here worth anything,' he tells my dad.

'It's the memories that count,' I hear Dad say in a thin shaking voice.

'If you could just put your hands on some cash . . . I could drive you to the cash point, if you like,' the man says, putting the picture back.

My cheeks burn with rage. My heart beats so loudly in my chest and a noise like a train in a tunnel whooshes in my ears blocking out any other sounds. How dare he? The cheek of it. A burglar in broad daylight, offering a chauffeur service!

I look from him to my dad, terrified and pale, sitting in his chair, just like he had all those years ago. A filthy dark night sixteen years ago, to be precise. Only back then, it was a man and a woman in black police uniforms standing in front of him, delivering in gentle, even tones the devastating news that would change our lives for ever. I remember their kindness and the concern in their eyes. Not like now: some low-life chancer in our home, helping himself to whatever takes his fancy, by the looks of it. But Dad looks just as terrified now as he did then, and my thundering heart squeezes and twists.

'What about jewellery or medals . . . Premium Bonds, stamps, even?'

Dad shakes his head.

I slide the heavy bag off my shoulder, careful not to let it fall to the ground with a thud. With effort I raise it above my head, aiming it at the mountain of man with long wavy hair picking over the ornaments along the mantelpiece.

'Hey!' The word is out of my mouth before I can even think about the consequences.

'No, Emmy, just leave him.' Dad puts out a shaking hand, clutching a piece of scrunched-up paper, as I attempt to swing the weighty bag at the back of the intruder's head, but my aim falls short because the bag's so heavy. I let it fall to my side and step up to the giant of a thug.

'Emmy, leave it!' Dad says again, but I ignore him.

'What the hell d'you think you're doing in my house? Get out!' I shout.

'Your house?' The burglar replaces an Ikea candlestick and turns to me, looking like Hagrid from the *Harry Potter* films:

huge bulk of body, ruddy cheeks, slightly sweating forehead and a beard you could knit a jumper from. 'I was under the impression it was Mr Bridges' house,' he says in a hard local accent, and I get a sudden flicker of recognition. His voice, his eyes . . . I shake my head, determined not to be distracted from getting this chancer out of our house.

'Oh, what? And that makes it OK, does it? To go around robbing old men's houses in broad daylight?' I'm bouncing with anger now, all my earlier nerves running for cover. I can't believe he hasn't made a run for it.

'I'll go up here,' a smaller, wiry man with a missing front tooth appears, walking past the front room from the kitchen, pointing a pen and holding clipboard. Oh God! There's another one.

'Hey,' I shout, pointing at him. 'What the . . . ? You! Get out! I'm calling the police.'

'Any chance of a cup of tea, love?' he replies from halfway up the stairs, and now my patience is stretched like a piece of well-chewed Hubba Bubba.

'Get out!' I shout again, dropping the heavy bag at my feet, picking up a cushion from the settee, aiming it and throwing it at him. He bats it off with one arm and Hagrid laughs.

'Emmy, leave it. Let them do what they have to do,' Dad tries again, attempting to stand but failing, weak with the shock.

'Emmy?' Hagrid frowns suddenly and looks at me. 'Emmy Bridges?'

I notice a roll of orange stickers protruding from his jacket pocket and that he's stuck some on the television, the

DVD player and the old piano that hasn't been opened in years.

'What do you mean, let them rob us blind in broad daylight?' I say to Dad, and then turn back to Hagrid. 'And how do you know my name?'

'I'm sorry, love, I should have told you.' Dad shakes his head, beaten.

'Told me what?' I fold my arms and frown at Hagrid, who really does seem vaguely familiar.

'I can't believe it.' Hagrid suddenly grins broadly. 'It's Graham . . . Graham Bingley.'

I shake my head. 'I'm sorry, do I know you?'

'Graham Bingley. We were at primary school together. You took me home that day that I got picked on by Louis Tudor and his mates. They took my cookery homework. Mini sponge cakes. They crumbled them up, chucked them on the floor and stamped on them. Then they started on me,' he says more quietly. 'You were walking home with your mate, Layla. You came running across the park, told them to bugger off. You put your arm round me and walked me home. My mum was so grateful.'

A vague memory starts to wind its way into my mind.

'She made me make more cakes and brought them round as a thank you.'

'Yes, I remember,' I say, nodding. 'So you went on to become a career burglar, terrorising old men. She must be really proud.'

He laughs again. 'No, actually, I'm a . . .' He looks at his hands for a moment. 'Mum died, a year ago.'

I say nothing but swallow hard, feeling my cheeks flush.

'I'm giving this up, actually. Off to college. You're one of my last jobs,' he says brightly.

I let out an exasperated sigh. 'I'm sorry, I'm still not getting this.' This man is robbing our house and I'm getting sucked into a schooldays catch-up. I look at Graham Bingley, baffled, and then at Dad.

'He's a bailiff, love. He's come to mark up what they can take if we don't pay off the mortgage arrears.' Dad flops back in his worn green wing-back chair. 'He's just doing his job.'

Graham Bingley grins at me, waiting for my delighted response.

I can hear the other man walking about upstairs, in our bedrooms, mine and Dad's, whistling as he rifles through our drawers. I shut my eyes. This can't be happening. I mean, we've never got any money but I had no idea things had got this bad.

'I just got a bit behind, love. My savings ran out and then . . . well, I just couldn't stretch what we had coming in.'

'Why didn't you ask me for more, Dad?'

'I couldn't, love. You already give me nearly everything you earn.' He drops his head into his hands. I turn back to the bailiff.

'Graham,' playing on our schooldays connection now, 'please . . .' I hold out a hand towards Dad, imploring the big man.

Graham's smile drops and he looks as if he's thinking very hard. I hold my breath.

'Look,' he says finally, 'I just have to take them something . . . anything. Can you make the last payment?' He picks up and holds out a clipboard with some figures in red on it and with a sharp intake of breath I read the list of missed payments. I look at him, shaking my head slowly.

'To be honest, like I say, there's not a lot here of value,' he says gently. Then he looks at me very seriously. 'If you don't do something, they'll take the house, Emmy.'

'What? They can't!' I reel back. 'This is our home.' I look around the 1950s three-bedroom semi that has been my family's since I was in secondary school.

'But you don't own it. You still have a mortgage. They can,' he says, more like a gentle giant now. 'Look, like I say, I'm leaving the job, going to catering college. Mum passing over made me realise, you've got to go out there and grab life.' He gives a little grin as if I'd understand. 'Let me take them back something, then I'll put the paperwork to the bottom of the pile, buy you some time so you can start to get a handle on this.' He glances from Dad to me, and I realise I have to take this offer. It's that or they'll be back for the house in next to no time. I nod quickly.

'Thank you,' I stammer.

'What can you give me to take back to the office?' He looks around for something of value.

I think about the money in my bag, for the collection I've just organised in the office for another worker, Candy, and her new fiancé's engagement. Trevor, my boss, always gives me the job of looking after the collection and then buying cava and cakes on the way into work on a Friday.

'How much would we get for this?' the wiry colleague comes in and holds up Mum's jewellery box. 'There's nothing in it of any value. Oh, hang on . . .' He opens the drawer at the front and pulls out my mum's gold wedding band and I can see Dad wince.

'That's Dickie. Here's with me,' Graham says, seeing my shocked face. 'Look, anything you can give me, I can get this lot off your back, just for a bit. It's the least I can do. You saved my arse that day after school. Made me realise I wasn't going to let myself be bullied again. I'd like to give you a chance, too. I'd hate to see you and your dad have to leave.' He looks at Dad.

'Here,' I reach for my bag and, with shaking hands, hand him the collection envelope. 'Take this.' I can't believe I'm doing this.

'Put it back, Dickie,' Graham says firmly. Dickie goes to argue but, with one look from Graham, changes his mind, drops the ring back in the jewellery box and takes it back upstairs.

'You sure?' Graham checks with me about the envelope.

'Wait!' I grapple in my bag again for my purse and pull out my last tenner. 'And this.' I empty the last of the coins from my purse into his hand.

'OK,' Graham nods. 'I mean, it doesn't really come close on what you owe, but it's something. I'll give them this, and then this,' he waves the notice with red lettering all over it, 'I'll put this to the bottom of the pile. Should buy you a couple of months, three at the most . . .'

'Thank you,' I hear my voice say though it doesn't sound like me.

He heads for the door, his shoulders practically touching the walls either side of the hall. He calls to Dickie to leave.

'Bye, Emmy. It was nice to see you again,' he says, turning, and then smiles and shakes my hand. 'And good luck.'

'And you,' I say as relief washes over me, followed very quickly by a cold, chilling feeling.

I wrap my arms around myself, standing protectively at the front door. I watch as his blue van drives off over the speed bumps down the road. Graham holds up a hand to wave.

Suddenly I feel like my world is teetering on a cliff edge. I have to make sure they don't come back again. I have to make this right. But I have no idea how, no idea at all.

Chapter One

'*Madame, Madame!*' I shout, and wave my arms around like I'm at a Take That concert, trying to attract Gary Barlow's attention in the midst of thousands of other possessed fans. The midday sun beats down on the back of my head, making me dizzy and reminding me I'm in south-west France. A small town called Petit Frère, to be precise, on the banks of the Dordogne. It's a long way from Bristol Airport, where I started out first thing this morning with my boss's words still ringing in my ears,

'I'm giving you one last chance, Emmy. I mean it, don't blow it.' And I don't intend to, believe me.

'*Madame!*' I call again, perspiring in my non-crease navy suit, waving and then pointing to the old, worn, leather purse left on the bench beside the fountain in the middle of the square. But the old lady just glances round at me, glares and hurries on. The fountain is spouting water into the pool at its feet, but even its gentle splashing doesn't make me feel any cooler. Just beyond the fountain there is a sandy boules pitch, right by the riverbank where a leaning weeping willow brushes its boughs across the surface of the fast-moving water. There are benches either side of the pitch, and three old men in short-sleeved shirts are sitting on one under the shade of a plane tree. Around the outside of the square are shops, including a *boulangerie* – a baker's – and an *épicerie* with fruit and vegetables laid out under a green and white sun-bleached awning. People are buying their lunchtime loaves and the warm smell of bread is wrapping itself around me. There's a busy café too, with round silver-topped tables outside and men in overalls smoking, and drinking small cups of coffee and glasses of cream-coloured, cloudy liquid.

I look around hopefully for someone to come to my aid and help give the purse back to the old lady. But everyone seems just to be staring at the four of us like we've arrived from another planet and, quite frankly, that's how it feels.

The woman had stopped at an empty bench by the fountain to rearrange her shopping between her two baskets, distributing the weight more evenly, no doubt. She'd put down her purse whilst doing so and then left it behind on the bench.

I look towards the *épicerie* for help, hoping someone's seen what's happened. An assistant is busy serving a young mum with a toddler in a pushchair. She hands the child a big round peach and they all coo in delight when the child takes it and bites into it with relish.

I can smell the ripe strawberries on the table outside from here. Why don't strawberries smell like that back home? In fact, everything about here smells different. The hot coffee, baking bread, even the tobacco smoke from the café and the hot sun on tarmac roads. Every breath tells me I'm in France, even if I still don't quite believe it yet myself.

I hold my hand up against the early September sunlight, looking in the direction of the old lady as she hurries up through the square, snatching quick glances over her shoulder, deftly side-stepping shoppers and disappearing between lunchtime gatherings. She's nearly out of sight.

'*Excusez-moi, Madame*,' I call again, waving, still holding one arm over my eyes against the blinding sun. '*Vous avez oublié votre* . . .' I rack my brains, reaching into the dark recesses of my mind for the right words. But GCSE French was a long time ago and this is the furthest I've travelled since going on holiday to West Wales with my best friend, Layla, and her family. This is south-west France at the beginning of September and, quite honestly, it's the last place I expected to be right now, with the last group of people on earth I'd want to be here with.

My three work colleagues look at me and shrug. We all work at the same place, but not together. Not until today, that is. A carefully selected group of Cadwallader's call centre employees . . . and me. We'll be living and working together for the next twelve weeks. Which right now seems like an eternity. A pang of homesickness twists my guts.

Cadwallader's is run by Trevor Cadwallader. Trevor lives and breathes the world of telesales. He runs the telesales for small companies: knitwear producers in remote Scottish islands, a client shipping cleaning products from a warehouse in Weymouth. Trevor will sell anything, for a cut.

Making sales makes Trevor happy. We have a brass ship's bell by Trevor's desk we have to ring when a big order is secured. Trevor likes to keep a happy and motivated workforce. At the end of every week there's usually a collection round the office for something or other: an engagement, a hen party, a stag party, a wedding. Trevor sends someone out to buy cakes, cava and a voucher. It's always for the same people.

Last week it was Candy and Dean's engagement. Dean and Candy are the golden couple at Cadwallader's. Top selling agents, both of them. I think this will be Candy's fourth engagement collection. I'm thirty-five and I've never had an office collection. But frankly, I'm just lucky to be holding on to my job. If it hadn't been for a stroke of luck – if that's what you can call it – I wouldn't be here at all. These twelve weeks are a training course for the four of us to be the sales team for a small wine company who have signed up to Cadwallader's. I know nothing about wine except for what's on special offer each week at my local supermarket. All I know is, I need a miracle bigger than the loaves and fishes to get me out of the mess Dad and I are in right now, and this could just be it. If I can't pay off those mortgage arrears we'll lose the house. I can't afford to mess this up.

I watch the short, bent old lady, dressed head to toe in black despite the scorching sunshine, turn and scowl at me once more before quickly opening the door to her small battered Renault Twingo, putting her baskets in, getting in after them and starting the engine.

A voice in the back of my head tells me not to draw attention to myself. Not to get involved. I'm here for work and I need to fit in. But I can't just let her drive off without her purse.

I take a deep breath.

'Madame,' I call again, and rush over to the bench, pick up the shiny, worn purse and wave it, trying to catch her eye. Then I run towards her, still waving, round the fountain and up the square. The stares from the café follow me and my cheeks burn.

'*Vous avez oublié . . . vous êtes . . . vert vieux dame et vous êtes . . . le sac, je pense*,' I stutter as she throws me another scowl through her open car window, then spins the steering wheel and shoots out of her parking space at speed, past me and on to the road by the river, past a war memorial, over a humpback bridge and out towards the neighbouring town, set on a hilltop in the distance.

'I think,' says Nick, in his public school accent, coming to stand beside me, 'that you just told her she's forgotten that she's an old green bag!' Nick's in his early thirties, usually works in advertising for tourist guides and maps, and frankly sounds like a bit of a know-it-all. Candy, standing behind him, snorts and laughs like a hyena, and Gloria, the fourth member of our party, looks visibly embarrassed by my *faux pas*, dips her head shyly and steps into the shadows of the plane trees.

'Shit!' I can see it's going to take a while for my French to come back. I turn slowly and look around at the staring eyes of the men in flat caps, sipping pastis and smoking outside the café. So much for not drawing attention to myself.

Double shit, I think. 'Now what am I going to do?' I say, mortified. I look down at the battered purse. My feet have barely touched French soil and I'm already getting involved with other people's problems when I should be keeping my head down.

'Maybe,' Gloria says, stepping out of the shadows, 'you could see where she lives. She'll need her purse. I know I would.' This is the most Gloria has said to me since we arrived. Possibly in her mid-fifties, she's wearing a short-sleeved cotton dress, her cardigan over her arm, her handbag across her body, and carrying a small battery-operated fan, which is permanently directed at her face. She looks hot.

I can't help but wonder why Gloria is here. Maybe she's been sent to keep us all in order. God knows, it looks like we need it.

'Don't be long.' Nick looks down his nose and through his big round glasses. 'We need to have lunch and meet at the Featherstone's offices, back there by two.' He points down the road by the river. 'Look.' Down a side street opposite the church, tables are outside on the pavement beneath a red and white awning. The tables are covered in matching checked tablecloths and are laid with knives and forks and tulip-shaped glasses. It looks wonderful, and I can just picture a lovely shady lunch there. Then I remember I really can't afford to go eating out in restaurants. I'm here to earn money, not to spend it. My heart dips in disappointment as we go over to look.

'*Es-car-gots . . .*' Candy reaches up and puts one hand on her large-rimmed sun hat as she peers at the blackboard on the pavement outside, then has to tug at the front of her floral dress, which is straining at the seams and struggling to keep her big, round bosoms from rising up like dough balls.

'Wassat?' She screws up her nose and then looks to Nick, who momentarily looks terrified by the struggling bosom and takes a step back. Then he throws back his head and laughs loudly, like a fog horn, attracting more looks from the café and from a single diner, sitting outside the restaurant. He's eating hungrily and drinking from a large wine glass, which now has just an inch of wine in the bottom. He's dark-skinned, with dark, unkempt hair and a bandana round his head. An earring dangles from his ear. In a sleeveless T-shirt under an open shirt, he doesn't look like he's dressed to come out to eat. He's friendly with the waiter when he brings him more bread to dip into the deep brown sauce on his plate. My stomach rumbles, reminding me I haven't eaten since Dad insisted on the two Weetabix I had this morning before I left home. I'm glad he did.

'Snails!' Nick finally tells Candy, and her mouth drops open in horror. Nick's laughter and Candy's shriek makes the lone diner look up again and then smile, before tucking back into his bread and sauce.

'No, really? Beurgh! It's true? They really do eat snails?' Candy's face screws up and Nick rolls his eyes and shakes his head. 'Disgusting,' she adds with finality.

The knot of homesickness twists in my guts again. But however hard this is going to be, I have to stick it out. Twelve weeks isn't that long, I tell myself. A demon voice in my head tells me that it's actually three months and I squeeze my eyes tightly shut, telling it to go away. It's just twelve weeks, I repeat. I open my eyes again to the bright light. Why then does it feel like a life sentence? And why am I worrying about whether or not I'm going to make it out the other side?

My phone trills. I grapple for it amongst the papers in my bag, and fall on it, desperate to hear a voice from home.

'Hello, Dad? Yes, everything's fine,' I say as the homesickness twists tighter. 'I'm having a great time,' I lie, trying to sound bright. I don't tell him I've just insulted an old woman,

I don't know the other sales agents, and if they knew who I was they'd hate me, anyway. I don't fit in and I want to come home.

'That's good, dear. Don't worry about me. I'll be fine. This is a great opportunity for you. Trevor must think very highly of you.' I can practically hear his heart squeezing.

'Oh, no, nothing like that, Dad.' I turn away from the others, who are still discussing the lunch menu, and walk towards the river. Two swans gently circle the weeping willow. 'Let's just say I was in the right place at the right time.'

'Well, make the most of it.' I hear a catch in his voice and it's my heart that squeezes now.

'I have to go, Dad,' and that catches in my throat, too. 'I'll call tonight.'

'Don't you worry about me,' he says again. But I do as he hangs up with a clatter.

A huge tennis ball forms in my throat and bobs up and down. I go to push the phone back into my bag, alongside my copy of the bailiffs' bill, and the electricity bill I picked up off the mat this morning. I sigh deeply. I have no idea what we're going to do. If only I could get a chunk of cash together; pay off some of the arrears. A mad thought grabs hold of me and I pull my phone back out and scroll through my contacts. My thumb hovers over my sister, Jody's, number and just for a moment I wonder whether to press the button and make the call. But thinking about Dad's voice, how frail he sounded, I decide against it.

Dad hasn't worked for years now. It's just him and me at home. Jody lives in Cheshire. We don't see much of her –

well, actually we don't see her at all. She married young, a promising footballer. Until he was injured on a skiing holiday. Then he went into business. Like I say, we don't see her, or her boys. I think that's what hurts Dad so much. She's happy and settled, and that's all I ever wanted for her. But we haven't spoken in a long time. A lot has changed since the skiing accident. I've tried to put the past behind us, but looking down at these letters filling my bag, my head, my heart, I can't forgive, I just can't. I feel a surge of fury on Dad's behalf bubble up in me.

I shove the phone deep into my bag, scrunching down the brown envelopes. Fired up by life's unfairness, I march towards the shop from where the old lady came with her shopping.

'Where are you going?' Nick calls after me.

'To ask in the shop if they know where she lives.' I march into the shop. '*Um, excusez-moi . . .*' I hold up the purse but have no idea what I'm going to say next. 'The old lady, she's forgotten her purse,' I say slowly in English with a slight French inflection, and feel really stupid.

'Ah, Madame Beaumont,' says a short, rotund man, wearing a green and white apron. He nods and then shrugs, pulling his mouth back into a grimace.

'Yes, it's her purse. I will take it to her,' I reply loudly, walking my fingers across the palm of my hand to demonstrate.

The shopkeeper picks up a wooden box of flat, white peaches and walks past me, their perfume taunting me as he takes them to the table outside the shop.

'It's OK, I'm not deaf, just French,' he says dryly, turning to look at me through his thick milk-bottle-bottom glasses.

'Oh God, I'm so sorry.' My cheeks burn with embarrassment again. Candy, who has followed me here, snorts with laughter again, and my shoulders droop again.

'You are on holiday?' The shopkeeper asks in stilted English, as he gets another box of peaches. The smell of them makes my stomach roar this time and my mouth actually water. A tall, wiry woman frowns as she rings money into the till and then barks orders at a younger woman with a dark ponytail, sweeping up at the back of the shop.

'Oh, no, we're here to work, for three months,' Candy fills him in. It's just twelve weeks, the voice in my head corrects her. 'We're with Featherstone's. We're sales reps, here to learn about the wine and then sell it back in the UK,' she tells him.

The tall woman practically snorts.

'Then, *bonjour*. I am Monsieur Obels and this is my wife, Madame Obels. This is our daughter, Isabelle, who works in the shop,' he says by way of formal introduction. 'Welcome.'

Candy cuts straight to the chase, with no such formal introductions.

'Actually, can you tell us where would be a good place to eat?'

The shopkeeper looks bewildered, having obviously exhausted his English phrases.

'Isabelle?' he calls, and beckons. The younger woman smiles and steps forward to answer.

'Well. There's Le Papillon, just on the corner on the square; they do three courses at lunch, with wine for twelve euro. A lot of the workers go there.'

'Three courses with wine? For lunch?' Candy squeaks.

The younger woman nods and Monsieur Obels takes the broom from her and leans on it, nodding.

'Of course,' she smiles. 'Or there is the café next door. They have a more . . . tourist menu. Omelettes, croque monsieur, chicken wings.'

Madame Obels tosses apples from a nearly finished box into a full one. Big green and red apples, like cricket balls.

'What's a crap monsieur?' Candy grimaces and Isabelle laughs. The rotund shopkeeper looks as bemused as his wife.

'Actually,' I cut across Candy with urgency, 'I need to find the lady I was just telling you about. The one who was just in here. She left her purse.' I hold it up.

'Oh, Madame Beaumont,' Isabelle nods sagely.

This time Monsieur and Madame Obels both raise their eyebrows and turn down their mouths disapprovingly.

'She lives out at Clos Beaumont, on the road between here and Saint Enrique, the next town, up the hill.' Isabelle looks to her father for confirmation. He nods.

'I'd like to get it back to her,' I tell her.

'You won't get any thanks from her,' Madame Obels joins in, and sniffs disapprovingly.

'She doesn't speak to anyone really,' explains Isabelle.

A man in a suit comes into the shop and they all turn their attention to him, shaking his hand and kissing both cheeks.

'From Featherstone's . . .' Monsieur gestures to us by way of explanation and then says something in French about the purse I'm holding and the man, in the cream trousers held with a leather belt, nods.

'*Monsieur le Maire*,' Monsieur Obels introduces him to us and the man shakes our hands.

'I understand you're looking for Madame Beaumont to give her back her purse,' he says. 'You won't get a reward,' he goes on, smiling widely. 'She doesn't mix with local people, let alone visitors.'

I'm a little taken aback. Madame Obels picks up the empty apple box and sniffs loudly again. 'It goes back a long way.'

'You can leave it here, if you like,' Isabelle offers with a shrug.

It's my turn to frown. 'I don't want a reward. I want to give her back her purse. She'll need it.' I feel hot and bothered as I turn back to Isabelle, who seems more help than the others. 'Could you just tell me where to go? Actually, could you write it down?' I ask her.

'I'll draw you a map,' she says, and Monsieur le Maire agrees this is the best plan. She takes a pad and pen from behind the till and draws a little sketch. I take the paper and thank her.

I know that I'd want someone to do this for my dad if he left his wallet behind.

I look down at the old, cracked leather purse and take a deep breath.

'OK, I'm going to go and give this back to her,' I inform the others, now gathered here and looking at me like I'm crazy. Madame Obels tuts and Monsieur turns away. Monsieur le Maire shrugs with a knowing smile. How could they be so uncaring?

'Just make sure you're back by two. You don't want to

blow it on your first day,' says Nick, arching an eyebrow.

He's right, of course. The last thing I should be doing on my first day here is scouring back roads for a house and a woman I've never met, and who may or may not thank me. I look at Madame Obels, who sniffs again, and with it my hackles rise higher. I may not know where this old lady lives, but I know I have to try to find her.

Chapter Two

I can't believe that only two days ago I was standing at the cash machine just round the corner from work, watching it slowly whirring out my last tenner. Yesterday I was clinging on to my job by my fingernails and now I'm here. I look around the town square as I turn to walk down towards the wide, fast-moving river. The trees along each riverbank bend their long branches into the water. Birds dip in and out of the trees, or dive across the river like little bomber planes. Swans gather and mingle serenely. There is the occasional splosh in the water, and I'm thinking it's a fish but it's too quick for me to see.

I really do feel like pinching myself. When we arrived first thing this morning we were met at the airport by Jean François, or Jeff, as he told us to call him.

'*Bonjour, bienvenue*,' he said, helping us with our cases, before rattling away, partly in French, partly in English, in a thick accent, very, very quickly. I could just manage to pick out the odd word, but between us we worked out he worked at Featherstone's in *la cave* – the cellar – with the wines. He was 'a vintner', he said, grinning and showing dark purple teeth, responsible for the settling of the grape juice and the fermentation of the grapes.

'*Les raisins!*' he exclaimed. 'Ze grapes!' and laughed. As he drove us at speed from the airport, he talked, gesticulating with one hand, the other on the wheel. Sometimes he swapped them, and at some point I think he may have been talking with both hands off the wheel. Gloria sat next to him, nodding shyly but saying nothing, holding her fan close to her face for the entire journey.

Nick, Candy and I were squashed into the back of an ancient Renault covered in dents, our cases on our laps, and Candy's spilling over on to everyone else's. As we left the town and Jeff slewed the car, together with us and our cases, along roads that became country lanes, small patches of vines began to appear, squeezed in between buildings. Even the roundabouts had vines growing on them! Then the closer we got to our destination of Petit Frère, the more vineyards there were. Rows and rows of twisted trunks, with large leaves and big bunches of grapes on them. Dotted along the sides of the road were big cream and terracotta-roofed properties, with ornate gates and majestic evergreens in the gardens.

'*Les châteaux*.' The big wine houses, Jeff told us. Then he pointed to a beautiful town on the hill ahead.

'Saint Enrique, throwing its shadow over the smaller town at its feet,' he said, gesticulating as if he were playing an elaborate game of charades. 'Where wine lovers flock and tourists pay over-the-top prices when they could come to Petit Frère and have better wine,' he said passionately. 'Taking from us here . . .'

'A bit like whoever took my engagement collection!' Candy piped up.

'Terrible,' Nick said, tutting. 'Who'd stoop that low?'

Gloria dipped her head lower.

My toes curled. My cheeks burned. I wondered, just for a second, whether to say something, get it out in the open, but decided against it, determined to put everything right in the end. I knew I couldn't let them find out who I was: Emmy from cleaning products, the one who'd 'borrowed' the office collection last week. I needed to keep my head down and stay out of their way.

I stared out the window, taking in the light brown soil, the rows of vines reaching far across the fields with the occasional tractor travelling up and down the rows, spraying the crops. I noticed, too, rows of cypress trees standing tall at every point on the skyline.

Jeff swung his old Renault through the town, past the church and the fountain, giving a wave and a shout through his open window to friends sitting outside a café. He drove towards the river before veering off to the left and continuing along its banks, slowing briefly before swinging the car in through big stone gateposts and pulling up on a white gravel courtyard with a crunch and shower of little stones.

Finally we arrived at Featherstone's Wines, where Colette, the office manager, met us and introduced herself while Jeff deposited our cases in the courtyard. I looked around as if I were The Doctor's assistant emerging from the Tardis, not knowing what to expect. Jeff bid us '*au revoir*', wishing us a '*bon après-midi*', before disappearing off with a toot of the horn and a wave through the window.

All around the courtyard I noticed old, but smartly converted one-storey barn buildings that had been turned into a shop, offices, and a winery by the look of the barrels I could see through the open doors.

There was an old and twisted wisteria tree right in the middle of the courtyard, with seats around its trunk, giving off a heady perfume in the heat of the day.

Opposite the offices and shop was a smart house, made from cream stone. There were long-paned windows along the front with neatly tied back bright white net curtains. Grey and white stone pillars stood either side of the grey front door. This, Colette told us, as she showed us to the *gîte* at the back of the house, was where the Featherstone family lived part of the year. The *gîte* was a smaller building attached to *la grande maison.* It had a small garden with a white metal table and chairs, next to a smart brick barbecue, and looked out on to the river. The *gîte*, Colette told us with lots of hand signals, and speaking slowly and loudly, was used for holidaymakers wanting wine tours in the season.

But for the next twelve weeks it was to be our home.

Candy was like a sprinter out of the starting blocks as she raced in through the *gîte* front door, ignoring the shabby chic living room, with its imposing stone fireplace, dark leather settees with soft grey throws draped over the arms, a big-screen TV and music system. This place had been done up like an interiors magazine set: rustic meets modern. Not like the rest of Petit Frère, which was exactly how I'd expected a traditional French town to look.

Beyond the living room was the kitchen with a round table and chairs in the middle of the room, whitewashed dresser on one side with terracotta fruit bowl, full of apples and oranges, and a big gilt-edged mirror on the far wall. The place smelled overwhelmingly of lavender furniture polish. Candy had raced up the white-painted stairs, doing a quick recce of the rooms, before bagging the biggest twin at the front for herself. Then she had noisily banged her case up the stairs, taking paintwork with it.

Gloria and Nick looked at each other with amused, raised eyebrows and then we all followed her. Whilst Candy was already unpacking her clothes all over the floor, we looked around the other rooms and then congregated on the landing.

'How about you take the smaller double at the front, Gloria?' Nick bossed us around, but actually I was quite grateful. Decision making never was my strong point. 'Is that all right with you, Emmy?'

'If you're sure,' Gloria said quietly.

'Fine,' I said, overbrightly.

'I'll take the attic room,' Nick said, pointing to a narrow flight of stairs, 'and you can have that one.' He indicated the single room at the top of the stairs, with a small en-suite under the eaves. I could see why Trevor had picked Nick to come on this course. He had us all organised and happy, the perfect gentleman.

It took Candy some time to decide what to wear before we headed into town for lunch. It was easy for me: I'd brought the only summer clothes I had in my wardrobe, a couple of pairs of knee-length cut-offs I'd customised from jeans I'd bought in my favourite charity shop round the corner from work. It supports a local dogs' home where I help out every now and again with dog walking. I'd love a dog but I can't have one while I'm out at work all day and Dad wouldn't cope with the walking.

I get most of my T-shirts in the shop, nipping round there in my lunch break when they have new donations in. I've brought my favourites with me, my faded and worn Nelson Mandela one, a Stereophonics one, my Take That one from after Robbie left the first time around, and another with the dogs' home logo itself. I've got a couple of ones I've tie-dyed and my absolute favourite Live Aid one, even though I was only four when it took place. And my 'I love Portugal' one. It has holes it in now, and I've patched it with denim that doesn't match. But I don't care. I love that T-shirt. It was my Mum's. I live in T-shirts – the bigger the better. They hide the fact that I've got practically no boobs and I'm pear-shaped. And as I'm only five foot three they always cover said bottom. Apart from T-shirts there's a pair of trainers I bought from the charity shop for dog walking. And the suits I bought from the big supermarket on the outskirts of town, as my boss, Trevor, told me to. 'Be like the others, like Candy, be more business-like,' he said to me before I left. I was determined to do that, even if it maxed out my credit card. I bought the two suits and had my curly blond hair cut into a manageable short bob. Only problem is, instead of being manageable, it seems to have gone even curlier. One of the new suits I was wearing and finding unbearably hot. The other was packed. I had certainly brought a micro wardrobe. Unlike Candy, who seemed to have brought an entire one.

'Is that all you've brought?' Candy had sneered at the airport. My case was dwarfed by her large case on wheels, which matched her travel bag and make-up bag. I'd only brought my mascara, eyeliner and lipstick. I don't really wear that much make-up.

'Travelling light,' I'd told her. 'I plan to buy what I need while I'm out here.' That was a lie. Any wages I had coming my way would have to go straight into the bank account back home to start chipping into the mortgage arrears. There wouldn't be any money left over for shopping.

I slipped off my black waist-length jacket and put it over my arm, revealing a short-sleeved cream blouse I'd bought at the same time as the suit, catching my little silver necklace as I did. It's a tiny silver curvy letter 'E' I had from Mum when I finished my A levels. I can remember my mum's proud expression when I opened the box and held it up. I patted it back down now, and wished I could have slipped my sparkly flip-flops on, another of my charity shop finds, but instead stuck to the new court shoes instead, to try to give the right impression. Then I attempted to tie my wilful hair back, but it was too short. I tried to pin it in at the sides, but it just sprung out from different places, refusing to comply, and I kept having to tuck it behind my ears.

Nick had changed and was suitably dressed in light chinos, deck shoes and a light pink polo shirt with the collar turned up, a lightweight sweater draped around his shoulders. Gloria was wearing a large, voluminous kaftan-like dress and a huge sun hat and big sunglasses, hiding any expression, fanning herself. She looked like a woman on holiday. But this wasn't a holiday, I reminded myself, it was work. I blew out my hot red cheeks, remembering the promise I'd made to myself and Trevor that I wouldn't mess this up.

Of all the sales agents at Cadwallader's, I am the very last person he would have chosen to send here. When I arrived at the call centre yesterday morning without the usual Friday cava and cream buns, Trevor called me into his office.

'What do you mean, no cream buns?'

'I . . . I . . .' I stammered, and then blurted out, 'I had to borrow the collection money.' Much as I would have liked to have come up with an excuse, I couldn't. I've never been very good at lying.

'What?' Trevor loosened his tie, outraged. 'They'll have your guts for garters out there,' he pointed to the sales room beyond his office window, 'if they find out you've nicked the office collection. This isn't like you. What's got into you?'

'It was important, an emergency.' My dad's face, pale at the prospect of losing his home, came into my mind.

'Oh, Emmy, what am I going to do with you?' Trevor ran his hands down his face. 'Your sales are terrible. Listen to this.' He pressed play on his iPad, and out of a loudspeaker came a recording of me making one of my weekly sales calls to one of my regular customers, asking how he is, asking how his wife is getting over her varicose veins operation and him telling me about his bumper runner bean crop this year. As the call went on Trevor covered his face with his hands and bent lower and lower on to the desk until it was resting there.

Humiliation burned my cheeks and my protests caught in my tight throat. Then fury flared up inside me.

'Mr Jones didn't need any more cleaning products. I wasn't going to push them on him just to help me get some figures on my sale sheet.'

'But that's what we're here to do, Emmy, sell things.' He looked up, exasperated.

'He has an animal sanctuary. He needs all the help he can get,' I argued back. Sometimes I sent him end of lines and free samples with his order, but I wasn't going to tell Trevor that.

'What exactly am I going to do with you, Emmy? You haven't sold a thing all week.'

I knew I should just be quiet, but my mouth kept going, arguing my point.

'But I just don't think we should encourage our customers to buy stock they don't need,' I protested. 'Surely it's better to sell something to someone who wants it. You shouldn't force people into parting with their hard-earned money, you know.'

'But that's the point, Emmy, we're here to sell stock. If we don't sell, we go out of business. You're too . . . what's the word? Too kind.'

I began to panic. What if this was it? What if he was fed up of giving me warnings to step up my game? What if he really was going to sack me?

'Please, Trev, I really need this job. I need the money right now.' Although my basic wage was very basic, it was better than nothing. 'I'll try harder, I really will.'

'You can't let your emotions get in the way. You have to visualise your goals in life. What do you want for yourself? A new car, a holiday, a penthouse apartment down the Bay? You need to be more like some of the other agents. You're bright. Look and learn from them.'

'Trevor, I'm thirty-five.' I looked at him incredulously.

Most of the agents at Cadwallader's, like Candy and Dean, and Candy's best friend, Harmony, are still in their twenties with all of life's steps to take. All I wanted was enough money to pay off my mortgage arrears and the electricity bill. With Dad being at home all day, it's a big house to heat. Too big for the two of us really, but that's how it is.

'Well?' he asked. 'There must be something?'

How could I tell him? The thing I'd love is so far from where I'm at. I want to be like the other women here, like my sister, climbing up life's ladder, getting engaged, married. Share my life with someone. Start a business together – a B&B by the sea, maybe. Be like my best friend, Layla. We used to work together, but she's running a seafood restaurant in West Wales now, The Lobster Pot. It's beautiful there. I really miss her. But she's found her place in life and someone to share it with. I'd like anything rather than having to phone people up and try to sell them more of what they already have or don't need. More than anything, I'd like a family of my own, children. But time is running out for me on that one. Right now, it's just me and Dad, and what I really want is for the red bills to stop falling through the door. I just want to stop worrying about the electricity being cut off before my pay cheque comes in and that I can keep the bailiffs from taking the house on my pathetic basic salary.

'I'm just not sure how many more chances I can give you, Emmy. You practically talk your customers out of spending any money,' Trevor said.

'Only if they don't need anything. I can't take their money off them if they don't need it,' I blurted out again, kicking myself and shooting myself right in the middle of my foot at the same time.

'We're a call centre, selling stuff!' Trevor looked to the sky. 'And once the other agents discover what you've done with the office collection . . . you don't help yourself, Emmy. You don't try and fit it.' He's right. I never have fitted in here.

'I really think, Emmy, if you don't think you can sell, and from your recorded sales calls I'd say you do struggle to sell . . . well, then,' he shrugged.

Oh, no, here it comes, I thought. He *was* going to sack me. I felt myself go hot and then freezing cold. Clammy. He looked at me, his shoulders still shrugged apologetically.

Suddenly the office door burst open. One of Cadwallader's best-selling agents, Harmony from 'next day delivery flowers and chocolate boxes', poked her thickly made-up face in and shrieked like a teenager on a fairground ride.

'Oh my God! Trevor, I really need to talk to you!' The air had filled with thick, cloying perfume, making me cough. Harmony is loud, brassy and orange, much like her best friend, Candy.

'Harmony, I'm in a meeting,' Trevor shouted back, throwing his hands up again. Harmony ignored his dismissal and carried on.

'Trev, it's no good, I can't go to France! I'm having my teeth veneered next week. They've had a cancellation. If I miss my appointment I'll have to wait months, and Debbie in double glazing is getting married in three weeks. I've got to have them done by then.'

Trevor clutched his head and squeezed. Trevor often

clutches his head. He held his biro like a cigarette and loosened his already loose, brown tie.

'What? You can't back out just like that! You're leaving for France in the morning. It's all booked. This new client could take this company to another level. I'm putting my best agents on this team. Harmony, please! Don't do this to me. I've promised them four of my best-selling agents to train up. Don't do this. They could take their business to Dickie Danbrooks and I'd have to make cut-backs, lose staff.' He threw me an apologetic look. 'Besides, there's a bloody great pot of gold waiting there for the best-selling agent,' he tried to appeal to her.

'Sorry, Trev. Not my problem.' Harmony looked me up and down. 'It's a no-brainer,' she said and, with that, left again, stopping only to greet a man I hadn't seen before arriving in the open-plan office with a huge smile, skirting around him closely and expertly on her high heels, whilst smoothing down her short skirt over her round hips. He smiled back pleasingly as she sashayed her way back to her desk, turning just before she reached it, fiddling with the pink ends of her white-blond hair, to throw him another killer smile, which he returned.

'Where were we?' Trev tried to refocus, head in hands.

Right now, 'a bloody great pot of gold' was exactly what I needed, I thought to myself. Or even a small one, for that matter.

'Like I say, if I can't start making more money, I can't afford to keep everyone on, especially those not paying their way.'

The door knocked again.

'Oh, for God sakes!' Trevor threw his hands up and I turned to see the man Harmony had just circumnavigated and my stomach did an excited flick-flack. I can see why Harmony was so pleased to see him.

'Charlie!' Trevor jumped up, recognising the visitor and going into jovial-host mode, waved him in and put out a hand to shake.

'Not interrupting anything, am I?' Charlie, the new arrival asked, looking from Trevor to me, and my tongue twisted itself into a knot like a Twister lolly. He was wearing a smart dark blue suit that slightly strained over his biceps and shoulders as he stretched out a hand to shake Trevor's. Under his jacket was a blue and white checked shirt, with silver wine bottle cufflinks. His face was tanned and lit up when he smiled; the bright white of his eyes sparkled. His dark hair was short, neat at the sides, stood up straight on top and had a slight glint of product in it. My stomach did another excited flick-flack, over and all the way back again. Not tall, but what did that matter with a smile like that and eyes that bright?

'No, no, nothing we can't finish later, eh, Emmy?' Flustered, Trevor dismissed me.

I went to stand, feeling like I'd had a stay of execution whilst awaiting sentencing.

'Just popped in to check you're all ready for the morning. I'm heading off back to the Featherstone's office in France this afternoon. Just wanted to make sure you had all the agents in place and ready to go.'

'Yes, yes, of course.' Trevor clutched the edge of his desk.

'Glad you think you can do this,' said Charlie. 'Danbrooks'

is a much bigger operation but I could see this means a lot to you. Don't let me down.' He cocked his head, winked and gave another cheeky grin. I felt a crackle of electricity rocket through my body as his sparkling green eyes, flecked with light green and gold, stared straight at me, so I could see they had a ring of darker green on the outside. Like an emerald-green lagoon you see in holiday brochures, you just want to dive into. They were mesmerising. His intense stare made me feel like I was the only person in the room. Embarrassed, I dragged my eyes away and looked at the floor. Trevor reached for his e-cigarette, looking flustered. He looked through the glass of his office towards Harmony with an imploring look.

'Everything is OK, Trevor, isn't it? I mean if you don't think you can raise the team . . . I know you're a small company.'

From her desk Harmony shrugged a sorry and I could see Trevor's shoulders slump.

'Yes, yes. No problems . . .' Trevor was suddenly like a drowning man looking for a passing branch. 'I just wasn't expecting . . .' He laughed nervously. 'Emmy and I were just finishing up on some sales figures . . . um . . .' He pointed to me and trailed off, and I suddenly felt very guilty. He did give a lot of people jobs, even when they weren't bringing in the revenue. Me included. He was a bit of a softy really. Anyone with my disastrous track record should have been sacked years ago. But Trevor had kept me on, moved me from department to department. I wish I could help him now, repay him for his faith in me. But what could I do? I couldn't even hang on to the office collection.

'Emmy. Hi.' Charlie leaned forward and put out a hand to shake mine as my stomach did that flipping thing again, like an Olympic gymnast going for gold.

'Hi,' I tried to reply with my twisted tongue, shaking his smooth hand.

Trevor cleared his throat again and tugged at his loose tie.

'Charlie is our new client, very big new client. He's bringing a lot of new business our way,' said Trevor in his telephone voice, but I could see he was feeling very nervous by the way he kept tugging at his collar. He was playing for time.

'If all goes to plan,' Charlie corrected Trevor with a smile, and something told me that this was very much a testing of the waters.

'Charlie is taking over Featherstone's Wines from his dad and is looking to expand, not just sell to single customers on the phone, but to move into restaurants, shops . . .'

'Supermarkets, hopefully,' Charlie added. 'Cadwallader's agents will be learning about the wine in France before coming back here to fly the flag and train up more staff as sales increase. It could be win-win for us all.' He beamed at a now visibly sweating Trevor.

Of course I knew about the new client and the trip to France. Trevor was always on the lookout for new clients, and Charlie Featherstone's deal had been the talk of the office. It wasn't something I was ever going to be in the running for, not with my sales record. This was for the high-achieving agents.

'Are you one of my new sales team?' Charlie asked, and I looked up and around to see who else is had come into the office.

'Oh,' I stammered and started to wave away such a silly idea. They would never let someone like me go.

'Actually,' Trevor said quickly, 'Emmy's just leaving.' I gathered my bag and turned back to Trevor. He had a look of panic about him. This was his biggest client yet and he was about to lose him because Harmony, who had been booked to go for months and talked endlessly about matching outfits with Candy, had now just pulled the rug from under his feet. Could I really leave Trevor drowning like this?

'Actually . . .' I said slowly, my head shouting, *What are you doing?* and my heart saying *Just do it!* I took a huge breath. Trevor and Charlie both looked at me, waiting on what I was about to say. 'Yes, yes, I am. I'm one of your new sales team and very much looking forward to it.' I put out a confident hand to shake his, whilst the voice in my head screamed in panic. Trevor's face fell in horror and then he started to nod slowly, looking at me in disbelief and then finally with a strained smile.

'Yes, I'm . . . er . . . just checking Emmy's passport details and reminding her to be at Bristol Airport tomorrow morning, first thing.' He looked at me wide-eyed as if trying to give me all the details telepathically.

'Great.' Charlie threw me another killer smile, showing off his white teeth, and my insides felt like they'd been microwaved. What had I just done? Was Trevor going to kill me? I had to do something. I couldn't let him sack me. I needed to save my house, mine and Dad's. And at least this way Charlie Featherstone wasn't going to go to Dickie Danbrooks. He had to be pleased, didn't he?

Although, a moment before I was in the middle of being

sacked, Trevor smiled at Charlie, then took me by the elbow and showed me the door, whispering in my ear, 'Bristol Airport first thing in the morning. I'll email you details. I'm giving you one last chance, Emmy. I mean it, don't blow it!'

I stepped out of the office. 'And Emmy,' Trevor called me back and I turned to him. He swallowed. 'Thank you,' he said briefly, and I breathed a sigh of relief. I hadn't got it totally wrong then. And at least this way I didn't have to face all my colleagues when they discovered I'd spent the office collection.

I had a lot to thank Trevor for, and I was determined not to let him down.

Chapter Three

Whoever first said 'It's just like riding a bicycle,' should try it themselves sometime. Who'd have thought that just twenty-four hours after leaving Trevor's office, and hanging on to my job by the skin of my teeth that I'd be standing in the road, next to the Dordogne, sweating in my cheap suit trousers in the midday sun, court shoe poised on a pedal?

I've been lent a bike. Nothing fancy, thank goodness. Just a bog-standard lady's 'sit up and beg'. It comes with the *gîte* we're all sharing. It was Gloria who remembered the bike and suggested I go back for it. We were shown it when we first arrived, when Colette, Featherstone's office manager, met us with a definite look of scepticism in her boldly made-up eyes. Colette looks like Dolly Parton. Dyed blond bob with a pink streak, blue mascara over her brown eyes, tight-fitting garish pink T-shirt with plunging neckline and rhinestones. She was wearing a tight denim skirt and tassel-trimmed ankle boots. She offered me the keys to the Featherstone's cream and burgundy Citroën van, but I shook my head by way of explanation that I didn't drive and took the bike instead.

I haven't ridden a bike since I was twelve. And frankly, I'm not sure which one of us is more rusty, me or the bike.

The others have decided to buy two baguettes, ham, tomatoes and bottled water. They're now sitting at a wooden bench and table, on the grassy riverbank, just across the road from Featherstone's, as I attempt to take my first few turns on the bike's pedals. Having ditched my jacket and covered my face and arms in factor 50, I'm perched on the tiny saddle.

Quite frankly I'd like to be sitting on the riverbank too, but I have to find this purse's owner.

I try to push forward steadily and take my foot off the ground at the same time, but it takes a few attempts and I'm very aware I've now got an audience behind me. I had no idea it would be this hot here. I take a huge breath and push down on the pedal, hard.

Suddenly I'm off. The wobbling front wheel seems to be mostly pointing forward in the direction of the road ahead.

A gentle incline in the road allows me to get both feet on the pedals and start to turn them, occasionally checking the brakes, well, quite a lot really. I daren't turn round or call back to the others. I have to just keep going.

'Be back for two. We're meeting at the winery with Charlie Featherstone and his wine man,' calls Nick, and I can barely hear him as the wind starts to whistle in my ears. But I do know he's said Charlie's name. Charlie, whom I met yesterday at the Cadwallader offices. Him with the smart dark hair, those two-tone green eyes and the wink! My stomach fizzes with excitement.

The road is worn, full of dips and bumps, and dusty in the dry heat. It catches in the back of my throat. But I'm moving! Well, side to side, violently, before crashing into a grassy bank. Thank God it was the grassy flower-strewn bank and not the riverbank. I pick myself up and reposition the bike, pointing in the right direction, when there's a loud hooting noise behind me, making me jump. I stop and turn, and see that my colleagues do seem to be containing their laughter, just. Down the middle of the river, flying just above the water, are two huge white birds, honking as they go. That's not something you see in Cardiff city centre every day. I suddenly feel like I'm in another time zone altogether. Life is going on at home. Dad will be watching *Pointless* or one of the many other TV quizzes he loves, and I'm here, in boiling hot, dusty France with a huge expanse of river just a stone's throw from where I'm staying, and surrounded by fields and countryside on the other side. It's surreal. I can't believe I'm here. I should really be thinking how lucky I am, instead of getting hot and cross. I reposition the bike and poise my foot on the pedal. I push off again and focus on the road and my front wheel, which is veering violently left and then right again.

I reach the entrance to the bridge where the trees thicken either side, throwing the path into darkness. I can hardly bear to look as I wobble to and fro, and find myself squeezing my eyes tight shut as I go up and down, my stomach following, and I head away from the river up a shady lane towards Saint Enrique, the place Jeff seems to think is Petit Frère's overbearing, overpriced, bullying neighbour. My legs already ache.

A small farmhouse, Isabelle Obels had said, called Clos Beaumont. She said I wouldn't miss it, the last house out of Petit Frère and before Saint Enrique. No other houses around it at all. A stone farmhouse up a lane with old gateposts that I'd see on the roadside. But Isabelle hadn't mentioned it was going to be uphill all the way.

On either side of me are fields now, with row upon row of vines. They have bunches hanging from them like little bags of marbles and big green leaves like dinner plates. There is a different coloured rose at the end of each vine, which is strange. I thought roses were a British thing. In some fields they are red, some yellow. Every now and again there is a splash of vibrant bright yellow: a field of large sunflowers nodding their big yellow heads, like dinner plates, in the early September breeze. There's definitely more of a breeze up here. And there's a smell in the air of herbs, mixed with summer sunshine. Wow! If you could bottle that smell . . . It seems to lift my flagging spirits. I pedal faster, and the faster I go, I discover, the more of the breeze I feel and the more of that tangy, sunshine smell fills my lungs.

But suddenly, as I turn a bend in the road, there's a large tractor coming towards me and, just like earlier, I'm in the hedgerow with the bike on top of me instead of the other way round. The driver calls to me in French but I have no idea if he's asking if I'm all right or shouting something rude at me. I pick up the bike, dust myself off and set myself back on the road again after a couple of false starts. I do hope this won't take much longer. I have to be back by two. I look at my watch. I must remember to move it on an hour. My stomach roars again. I wish I'd taken some bread and ham from the picnic the others were having before I left them.

As I was leaving Petit Frère I passed pretty little houses with verandas covered in brightly coloured flowers, neatly tended vegetable plots with fat, white geese and chickens pecking away in well-fenced runs. I passed a noisy campsite where holidaymakers are enjoying the last of the summer holidays and then suddenly, nothing. Now there are no houses at all, just this lane – more like a dirt track in parts – the vines and the occasional nodding sunflower field. Let's hope I find Clos Beaumont soon. In the distance I can see the town of Saint Enrique on a hilltop: a church steeple at the top and sand-coloured stone walls and houses spreading out from it like a bridal gown, down to the town's stone wall at the foot of the skirt, where there are huge houses, standing proud, showing the world their finery.

There isn't another farmhouse in sight. All I can see now is the road starting to incline steeply uphill again. I'm halfway up when I have to get off and push. I'm sweating and panting, and frankly I don't think I can go any further. My lungs feel like they've had the air ripped out of them. More tractors pass me but I'm grateful for the whoosh of air they bring as they pass. I finally make it to the top of the hill. Saint Enrique still looks a distance away. The road has flattened out. I turn back to see the Dordogne like an inky line through the middle of the vines and in the distance the bridge just before Featherstone's. At least it'll be downhill all the way back. But I don't think I can go on. I stop and contemplate turning back when I feel the weight of the old lady's purse in my pocket pushing against my thigh. I can't turn back. I have to just try to go on a little further.

Rounding another corner I see two crumbling stone gateposts and feel a little skip of hope. Either side of the gateposts there is a low, crumbling wall, overgrown with ivy.

Big round moss-covered stones sit where they have fallen in long grass, either side of the wall and at the foot of the posts. I'm in the middle of nowhere, away from the town Petit Frère and nowhere near Saint Enrique yet. There is a cooling breeze up here that I'm grateful for. Behind the gateposts, through the trees, I can see a sorry-looking farmhouse. I'm not even sure it's inhabited.

I push the bike up the track, the smell of lavender and wild herbs even stronger here.

'Hello! *Bonjour!*' I call, leaning the bike gently up against the wall of the house, and little pieces of stone fall away. '*Bonjour!*' I call again but no one answers. There is a distant hum in the air, of tractors in the fields. Perhaps everyone is out there working. Apart from the hum, there's no other sign of life at all, nothing.

'Hello!' I try for a third time.

Suddenly I hear a deep, lazy 'woof' and then a huge, terracotta-red dog, with wrinkles around his face and with skin way too big for his body, like he's wearing a onesie two sizes too big, lumbers to his feet and throws himself towards me. I stand still and put out a hand. He holds his head up and lets out a long, low howl, and long strings of drool start to slide from his mouth. Realising the dog is far more effective as a front doorbell than an actual threat, I hold out my hand again, inviting him to sniff it.

'Hey there, *bonjour*,' I say, letting him sniff my hand and then rubbing his red and greying head. He stops barking and sniffs some more. Then, without warning, he shakes his massive head and before I can back away, the strings of drool fly up into the air and off his jowls, like rubber bands from a band gun, released into the air and landing right on target, right down my trouser leg.

'Ew!' I look at the streak of slime. Holding out my hands, I have no idea how to get it off but I can't help but laugh and I rub the dog's head again. Then I walk, stiff legged, hoping the slime won't seep through the fabric, looking for a leaf or something to wipe it with and hoping the dog will lead me to his owner. The dog, however, just flops back down to where he was in the middle of the yard. I walk across the yard, behind the farmhouse, and there in front of me, dropping away down a steep slope, are rows and rows of vines. The wind blows and strands of my hair blow across my face. I wish I hadn't had it cut short now. At least if it was longer I'd be able to tie it back. I hold it away from my face. In the distance on the other side of the valley, towards Saint Enrique, is a large imposing château with a tractor and sprayer working just below it. Here, however, there are no tractors working the fields, spraying the vines either side with long arms stretched out. There is no sound nearby at all other than the occasional baa from the sheep in amongst the vines, obviously escaped from somewhere, the rush of wind in the leaves.

'Hello, *bonjour*?' I call again.

Suddenly I hear a clanking noise coming from the one of the barns. I turn away from the escaped sheep and retrace my steps towards the barn on the far side of the house. The big faded red dog lets out a gravelly bark once more but this time I manage to swerve him with a skip and laugh to avoid being slimed on again.

The black wooden barn door is ajar. I can definitely hear

clanking. Inside the long barn, to the left, are rows and rows of dark, aged barrels. In front of me are what look like concrete tanks. I push the door open and creep into the cool shadows, and then I see her – Madame Beaumont, the woman from the square – sitting on a small three-legged stool, cloth in one hand, large bowl of soapy water at her feet. She appears to be washing a huge quantity of green bottles. She lifts one from a bowl of soapy water and puts it next to some others. There are rows of them, set up like a ten-pin bowling alley. I step forward, and she looks up at me startled. I try to smile.

'Madame Beaumont?'

She frowns, deeply. '*Oui?*' she says gruffly. 'I am Adele Beaumont.' I think she's about to throw me off her land, recognising me as the hooligan who insulted her in the town square earlier.

In the distance I hear the church bell strike. It's a different bell from the one in Petit Frère. It must be Saint Enrique's. Then it rings again and I'm not sure whether that means it's one o'clock or two. But I know I have to get back. I can't be late. I think about Charlie and those sparkling green eyes and my tummy gives another little squeeze of excitement even though I tell it to stop being silly. But I have to get back and cleaned up. I look down at the drool smeared across my trouser leg. I have bits of the hedgerow in my hair and my blouse is sticking to my back. I tuck another loose strand of hair back behind my ear. I can't turn up for my first meeting looking like this!

Madame Beaumont is still frowning and I need to make this as simple as possible. She is now more suspicious than ever. I grapple for the purse in my pocket and pull it out. Recognising it, she looks up at me in horror. Oh God! Now she thinks I've stolen it from her.

'*Votre . . .*' I can't think of the word for purse. 'Um, oh, what's the word?' I hold it out.

'My purse,' she finally says in clear English.

'Yes. Thank you.' Thank God she speaks English, I think, relieved I'm not about to insult her again with my bad French. But she's still not looking very pleased that I've cycled all this way to bring it back to her.

'How did you come to have it?' She gives me a sideways suspicious stare.

'You left it behind, in the square. I tried to call to you, but you . . .' How do I tell her she looked at me as if I was a yob, shouting and insulting her.

'You?' Realisation is slowly seeping over her face. 'It was you calling me?' She rummages in the pocket of her blue and white overall, over her black dress and cardigan, despite the heat outside. Here in the barn it's very cool but I'm still very warm and feeling slightly light-headed. She pulls out some small wire specs and rests them on her nose; they settle at an angle.

She looks at the purse and then back at me. I shift awkwardly from foot to foot, hoping to shake the dots that keep popping up in front of my eyes.

'I couldn't catch up with you, so I cycled here.'

She slowly stands stiffly from her low milking stool. She pulls herself to her full height and still only reaches my chest. She has a slight stoop. Her long grey hair is pulled back in a bun. She puts out her thin, knobbly arthritic hand slowly towards the purse. She has dark brown eyes, bright like a vole's, and actually quite a whiskery chin, too. She is small, neat but plain.

'*Merci*,' she says with a nod and a look of disbelief and, frankly, mistrust.

'It's fine,' I hurry. 'Like I say, you left it when you were sorting out your bags and I ran after you but couldn't catch you. I asked in the shop where you lived.'

She looks down at the purse as if only believing it's hers now it's in her hand.

'You are . . .' still with some hesitation, '*très gentile*. Very kind. I'm sorry, I must have seemed very rude.' But she doesn't explain any further. Then she opens the purse up, checking I haven't robbed her, I suppose. My shoulders droop. I'm suddenly exhausted from the ride. I turn to leave. I need to get back. Hopefully the wind outside will help this blurriness I'm feeling.

'Please,' Madame Beaumont says suddenly, and I turn back to her. She's holding out a worn note. 'Take this, for your kindness.'

'Oh, no.' I hold up a hand. 'I don't want your money. I just wanted you to have your purse back.' Oh Lor', now I've probably offended her. She stares at me, still holding out the note. I back off, my hands up.

'Really, it's not necessary.' I wave my hands some more, backing away. 'I just came with the purse.' I suddenly feel even more light-headed, my head starting to spin, but carry on still backing away. 'I have to get back.' My head then dips and spins so much that I throw my hand out to steady myself, and my head does cartwheels and I feel hot, then cold and very sick. I back into whatever's behind me, grabbing for something to steady me.

'Oh shit!' Dark spots dance before my eyes. Suddenly bottles are crashing around my feet as I back into them and I try to turn in the right direction to stop myself, but end up knocking over more. Madame Beaumont is still staring at me as I spin this way and that, trying to right the fallen bottles. Then everything goes black and I tumble to the floor, barely noticing the rest of the bottles as they fall like skittles around me.

Chapter Four

I come round to the sound of church bells ringing in the distance. I look down at my watch and try to focus on the hands, try to remember if it was an hour ahead or an hour slow.

'I'm going to be late.' I panic and try to stand, but the spots are there like space invaders descending before my eyes again and I sit down heavily.

'Take your time. Nothing is so important it can't wait a little.' Madame Beaumont is handing me a glass of water in a small worn blue glass.

Then she leads me across the courtyard and into her kitchen. At least I think it's her kitchen. It seems to be her kitchen, sitting room and, if I'm not mistaken, bedroom as well. It's dark. The shutters on one wall aren't open. But it's also very cool, which is such a relief.

There is a large wood burner on one side and a selection of Formica units on the other. There are hanging wires down the wall and in the middle is a blue 1950s Formica table. Madame Beaumont gestures for me to sit and I sip a cup of cold water on a small Formica-covered chair. The room is disorganised, to say the least. There are piles of papers everywhere and she had to move a pile just to let me sit down. She puts down a little plate with a worn, gold edge with a cut-up orange on it.

'It is very hot. You have heat exhaustion. You must stay out of the sun in the midday and take plenty of liquids. Try to eat something.'

I nod. Heat exhaustion – of course – I think, feeling foolish, and tentatively suck on the orange, though I really need to get on my way. Its juice suddenly squirts into every corner of my mouth, taking me by surprise, filling my taste buds with flavour. Wow! It's amazing. Strangely, I'm starting to feel a lot better. The spots begin to fade and I help myself to another piece of orange and it does the same thing again. I finish the water and Madame Beaumont refills the glass.

An elderly black and white cat sits on a pile of unsteady newspapers, eyeing me suspiciously, much like Madame Beaumont did when I first arrived. But this woman seems very different from the one the shopkeepers and the mayor were talking about. They said she had a reputation for being stand-offish and unfriendly. Admittedly she was fairly stand-offish when I first arrived but once she realised I was just doing something kind, she seemed surprised and now she couldn't be more helpful and welcoming. I can't help but wonder what's happened to make her that suspicious to start with.

'Thank you so much, I'm feeling much better now,' I say, trying to stand again. 'I really must get back. I have to be at Featherstone's by two.'

'Ah, Monsieur Featherstone. How is he?'

For a moment I think she's talking about Charlie and then I realise she must mean Charlie's father, *the* Mr Featherstone.

'Um, I'm not sure. I haven't met him.'

She nods. 'He was a businessman in the UK. An accountant, I believe. But then he had a health scare and he decided to follow his true passion in life: wine. So he started to buy wine from small buyers out here and import it to the UK in his van. He worked hard and now . . . well, he has a big business. But I understand he's been unwell.'

'I had no idea,' I say truthfully, but I'm pleased to hear that the company sounds like a caring, family-run one. 'It's his son I'm working for. I have a meeting at two.' I must get back.

'Can I get you something else to eat?' Madame Beaumont turns stiffly, pulls opens a small fridge and peers inside. The light is on, but it seems to be empty. I'm guessing she probably doesn't eat that much herself, judging by her birdlike frame.

'Really, I'm fine.' I stand and push the chair under the table. A pile of papers wobbles but doesn't fall. Madame Beaumont looks around for something. I follow her eyes.

'Are you sure I can't give you something for your trouble? Where did I put my purse?' She looks around and I point to it in the nearly empty fruit bowl.

'Ah.'

'And, no. I really don't want anything.'

Her eyes narrow again and there's a hint of suspicion still there.

'It's me that's caused you trouble. Let me return later to help put right the mess I made of the bottles in your barn.'

'*Le chai?*'

'*Le . . . ?*'

'Shay,' she says slowly.

'Shay,' I repeat.

'Good,' she smiles. 'It means a wine-making barn, or cellar.'

'I'll come and help put right the mess,' I tell her again.

'Puh . . .' She waves a hand. 'It's no problem. I'll get it sorted. Don't worry.'

'No, please, I'd like to.' I can't bear the thought of giving this old lady extra work though I can't imagine she's running this place on her own; there's no way she could.

'Don't you have a machine to do the bottling?' I ask politely as she walks me to my bike. I bend and pat the fading red dog as we pass, moving on quickly before he swings his head again.

'A machine? Pah! Machines are only as good as the men who work them,' she says. 'Tell Mr Featherstone I'll have my wine ready to collect in a few weeks.'

'Of course,' I reply.

All the more reason to help put right the mess I've caused, I think. This lady is clearly one of Featherstone's suppliers and I don't want her talking badly about the new staff, saying we turned up and created a riot and left her to clean up the mess. That won't help my time here, or ensure I keep my job with Trevor. She walks with me to the road, where she sticks a hand straight out and I look down at it and realise I'm to shake it.

'*Au revoir*,' she says, encouraging me with a smile to reply in French.

'*Au revoir*,' I say, shaking her hand, up and down twice. She nods again. 'But I insist on coming back to help.' And with that I swing my leg over the bike saddle, and my thigh and buttock muscles cry out in pain. I'm going to be stiff later. I turn the bike down the hill and, with a wave to Madame Beaumont, I pedal off, hoping my journey back will be a lot quicker.

It is. And a lot less controlled. I zip past the busy vineyards, the nodding sunflowers, my loose curls flying across my face and the smell of wild thyme and lavender all around me. I shut my eyes and hug the hedgerow when a tractor passes and, with the stone bridge now in sight, head back towards the Featherstone's Wines headquarters. I am hot, sweating and my bum and thighs ache so much I may never be able to sit down again. I should just have enough time to wash my face in the toilets and try to tidy my hair as best I can. I dump the bike against the *gîte* wall and limp past the wisteria tree towards the big glass double doors where Candy, Nick and Gloria are standing together with a familiar figure in the cool shadows. My heart stops. It's Charlie.

'Ah, I thought we'd lost one already,' he says, smiling good-naturedly, and I blush and breathe a sigh of relief he's not cross. Then I try to sidle in behind the others so as to cover up my messy appearance. My heart is racing and I'm slightly out of breath. Nick gives me a raised eyebrow and Candy is practically repulsed.

'Sorry, I got lost . . . and hot. Hot and lost, sorry.'

'Easily done on a first day,' he says quickly, and then pulls back a big, friendly smile. 'But let's try and be on time from now on.' Charlie's obviously keen on punctuality, which usually I would be too. 'Well, if we're all here now, we'll make a start.' I take a deep breath, relieved I'm not getting a bollocking on my first day. That really would prove Trevor right. I put my hands together and listen, ignoring the looks up and down from Candy, the little snigger from Nick and the tiny sidestep away from Gloria. Charlie Featherstone is a very nice man, I decide, a very nice one indeed, and I allow myself a tiny smile.

Just then my phone rings.

'Sorry,' I mouth, and glance at the screen. Charlie, who is about to start his welcome speech, raises an eyebrow and is obviously expecting me to ignore it. But I can't. I put up a hand by way of apology.

'Hello, Dad?' I answer, and turn away from the others while I tell him where to find the tin opener and listen to him telling me how much colder it's getting.

'I'm in a meeting, Dad. With my new boss, Charlie Featherstone.'

'Oh! Right. Are they OK, the new people?' Dad asks.

'Lovely, Dad, really great, but I have to go.' I quickly press the off button and finish my call, my heart racing. I don't want to push my luck. 'Oh, by the way,' I tell Charlie as I'm putting my phone into my pocket and tucking another loose strand of hair behind my ear, 'I nearly forgot. I have a message for you. The Clos Beaumont wine will be ready for collection in a few weeks.' Then I catch sight of the slime stain on my thigh and a small twig falls from my hair on to the floor, and I hope with all my heart he hasn't noticed. But as I look up slowly, Charlie is no longer smiling. In fact, his face has very much darkened and I have no idea why.

Chapter Five

'So this is the main winery. In here we store wine made by vintners, who have made the wine on their own land. We store it here either in barrels or bottles.'

I am even hotter than before. We've traipsed round what feels like every part of Featherstone's winery. We've been through a myriad of rooms and had the wine-making process explained to us in mind-boggling detail.

Charlie leads us into a room with desks and a long work bench, like a sort of laboratory setup. 'This is where the backroom work is done, where the wine-makers work their magic, testing, checking and blending. It's the nerve centre.'

Then on into a huge modern barn at the back of the converted stables. There are palates of boxes, and a forklift truck is motoring noisily up and down across the concrete floor between the huge steel tanks and big yellow hosepipes snaking across the floor. There's a smell in the air, mostly cleaning fluids, making my head ache again. I can't remember anything of what Charlie's told us and I feel like I've stepped into some futuristic city of scientific experiments and chrome.

Despite Charlie's smart good looks and confident delivery, nothing he says is going in. I'm hot and I have a thumping headache. Jeff, who drove us from the airport, pulls up on the forklift truck, pulls out the cigarette from his mouth, smiles, waves, calls, '*Salut, tout le monde!*' and then drives off singing and calling out the odd joke that none of us understands. We smile and nod. My head bangs some more. Charlie leads us back towards the converted barns and offices and we stand outside in the sunshine.

'My father set up this business. He fell in love with wine and this part of France. Since those early days it's grown and grown. Now he's taking a back seat and I am taking Featherstone's to a whole new level. Up until now we've dealt directly with individual customers, shipping their orders from here to their door. I want to expand and put Featherstone's name in every restaurant but, more importantly, the shops and supermarkets in the UK. That's what you'll be doing. Hunting out the customers and getting the orders in.' His green eyes dance with excitement. It's certainly a long way from selling toilet cleaner and loo rolls. I know I should be excited and I'm trying my hardest to look as if I'm concentrating, trying to make up for my earlier shabbiness.

'In here . . .' Charlie leads us through to the first room by the door of the barn. As he passes I get a hit of his aftershave, powerful, punchy and spicy. I feel myself dip again and remind myself it's the heat and perhaps tiredness too. Charlie Featherstone is a very attractive man and it looks like I'm not the only one who thinks so as Candy smiles, runs her finger along her very white teeth to check for lipstick stains and pushes up her bra when she thinks no one's looking. She knows how to do it, I think. There's no way someone like Charlie would look twice at someone like me. I'm just another sales agent, I tell myself firmly, and concentrate! I turn away from Charlie and see Jeff climbing down from his forklift. He gives me another wave and I give an embarrassed, shy wave back with a sinking heart. I must not start fancying Charlie, I tell myself. Despite him being the type of guy that would tick all the right boxes I really don't need to be setting myself up for any more falls right now. I'm the one with slime on my trousers and twigs in my hair, for goodness' sake!

We move into the shop next.

'This is where we sell direct to the customers who have found us. They come here for tastings and to buy. Colette runs this area, but hopefully some of you will help out here and get to know our wines better. The better you know our wines, the better you'll be able to sell them over the phone when you get back to the UK.' Charlie looks around the shop, into the office and outside into the forecourt as if looking for something or someone, and frowns. Then with a flick of his head he leads us to a wooden staircase and upstairs. It smells of newly cut wood and varnish, as if this room has only just been finished. It's all a far cry from Madame Beaumont's *chai*, I think to myself. Hers is a crumbling barn with old black wooden doors that barely met the stone door frame. I'm the last to make it upstairs.

There, in front of us, is a big picture window, looking out over the Dordogne river. There are boats, with two and four rowers in them, followed by a little motor boat and a man with a loud-hailer. There are fishermen on three-legged stools, sipping from flasks on the banks of the fast-flowing river. In the middle of the room are four desks with phones, two of the desks already occupied. Behind us is another big window, this time looking out over fields of vines behind Featherstone's: row upon row, lining up like soldiers in dark green uniforms, protecting bunches of green grapes, standing proudly with their feet in light brown, sun-kissed soil. The vineyard rolls up and down towards the back of the big church, guarding the smart, well-kept cemetery, and beyond that, to the left, is the town with its colourful red, green and white awnings.

'This,' Charlie announces proudly, 'is where you will work.' He holds out a hand to let us take in our new surroundings and I stare practically open-mouthed at the views. 'You'll be expected to help out in all areas of the winery. You'll be learning about the wines and then you'll be putting your knowledge into practice and selling it here. Do you think you can sell our wines from here?' He turns to look out of the window at the stunning view and smiles widely. We all nod silently. It's a long way from our city-centre offices, overlooking the car park and rubbish bins and the tiny piece of green space I could see between two tall buildings if I craned my neck. We all mutter our approval to each other and look around, delighted with our new surroundings.

'This is Hannah and Ben,' Charlie introduces an older couple, maybe in their early sixties, on the phones, who each wave a free hand cheerfully at us. 'Hannah and Ben took early retirement, moved here from England and have been the permanent selling staff on site for a couple of years now, selling directly to our regular customers. However, they are moving on. Greece, isn't it, guys?'

They nod and Ben gives a thumbs up.

'They're buying a B&B out there. You'll be taking over

their regular contacts as well as making new contacts with bigger buyers.'

The couple look tanned, relaxed and happy as they chat to customers on the phones. Hannah is wearing khaki shorts and a white vest top, showing off her tanned, toned legs, and Ben is in calf-length combats, stroking his long beard as he talks. I look out of the window towards the vines. If I can't become a top-selling agent here, then I don't know where I will ever do it.

'You'll work here on the phones, take it in turns in the shop downstairs, help out in the winery if needs be and get a feel for what we sell here. You'll have wine lessons with our new wine-maker . . . when he gets here.' Charlie looks at his watch, large and quite possibly very expensive, and a flash of irritation crosses his face. Then he looks back at us and switches on his smile, which once again lights up the room.

'And here's the thing.' He pauses and then looks at each of us. When he looks at me I get a fluttery feeling in my stomach and blush. 'Of the four of you, the person that proves themselves to have understood our wines and sells the most will return to the UK as a team leader. That, of course, will include an attractive salary and a bonus at the end of these twelve weeks as well.'

Suddenly the chatter and appreciation for the room stops and a cloak of seriousness descends. Candy actually licks her bottom lip, as though she's ready to be let out of the starter's blocks. An attractive salary! No more basic wage and commission. And a bonus. So this is what Trevor meant when he said that there was a pot of gold riding on it. My heart quickens and my spirits suddenly lift. That would certainly help sort out the mortgage arrears. Gloria looks down at her feet and Nick looks at Candy, then at me and then back at Candy. I think about my bag stuffed with bills – particularly the red one that I still haven't opened that was on the mat before I left this morning. And then of course there's the office collection. I really need this promotion. Maybe, finally, a bit of luck is going to come my way. I need to be more like Candy if I'm to be in with any chance here. I must try for an air of professionalism. No more slime on trousers or twigs in hair.

'Here are your sales details.' Charlie turns to the table he's leaning against and picks up the pile of huge bound and printed books.

'You mean our scripts,' Nick corrects him in a know-all way, and I'm not sure Charlie's impressed by his comment.

'I love learning scripts,' Candy simpers, to which Charlie looks much more impressed and gives her a special smile all of her own as he hands out the weighty documents.

Gloria says nothing, just takes hers as it's handed to her, pulls out her glasses from her bag, slides them on and begins reading. In her other hand she has her hand-held battery-operated fan held to her face. She must have brought a case full of batteries to keep that fan running. I can practically see her mind whirring, already taking in and digesting the information.

My heart sinks as I take my script and open it. Thousands and thousands of words dance across the page in front of my eyes. At Cadwallader's call centre it's all about consistency and I'm guessing it's going to be the same here. You have to answer the phone exactly the same way.

'Hello, Cadwallader's here. Emmy calling. I'm ringing today for your weekly advertising/insurance/pet food supplies /wine (interchange for which department you work in) weekly health check.' Candy is great at the script, by all accounts. Me? I keep forgetting what I'm supposed to be saying and end up asking my customers how they are, and talking them out of spending any money. From now on, though, I need to stick to the script.

'OK, so you have your homework. But as it's Saturday,' Charlie claps his hands, jolting us out of our individual thoughts, 'I suggest you go back to the *gîte* and get yourselves settled in. Then meet us back here at six for aperitifs and then I'll be taking you to Le Tire-bouchon. For those of you without French . . . yet,' he throws out another killer smile, 'Le Tire-bouchon means The Corkscrew. It's the restaurant just down the river here. We'll be going there for a welcome meal.' He smiles and claps his hands together again and glances at his watch. We all turn to go, taking our 'bibles' with us.

'And, Emma, is it?' he calls after us, and I turn back, my heart giving a silly skip and I smile, delighted to have caught his attention.

'Emmy,' I correct him. 'Everyone calls me Emmy.'

'Well, Emmy,' he gives me a half-smile, 'you seem to still have half a bush in your hair and some sort of slime down your trousers. You might want to take a look at it before dinner.'

Great! If he didn't know my name and who I was before, he does now! My heart plummets. As first impressions go, I think we can agree I could have done better. I'll have to work really hard if I'm going to be anywhere in the running for the team leader's job. I dread to think what the alternative is if I don't.

Chapter Six

Back at the *gîte*, I run up the stairs and throw myself into my little shower room. Finally pulling off my hot and sweaty clothes, I drop them on the floor, turn on the tap to the shower under the eaves and then throw myself into the warm water and let the gentle trickle wash over me. Not a power shower, but just as welcome, none the less. I let the water run over my face and over my short, curly bob, wondering what to wear tonight. Trevor's words are still ringing in my ears. I need to be more like Candy, I think, if I'm going to get this team leader's job and finally be able to crawl my way out the pit of debt I'm in. I am determined to do better than I did today, that's for sure.

I pull a towel from the towel rail and wrap it round me, stretching it over my pear-shaped bottom, and step out into my little back bedroom. I look in the mirror on the wall, just inside the door, and stare. My fair skin is pink and tingling from the midday sun. I hold my hair back with one hand whilst the other is holding my towel. Then I turn slightly, look in the mirror and see if I can attempt a Candy pout, first left and then right. How does she keep her lips like that all the time?

'Very nice. But I don't think I ordered room service,' says a sleepy American voice.

'Shit!' I spin round to what I thought was my pile of luggage that I'd left on my bed ready to unpack but it isn't a pile of luggage at all. My luggage is now on the floor. My heart starts thundering like a young horse in its first Grand National. My eyes open wider and I clutch the towel more firmly.

It's a person, a body, a man . . . in my bed! I must be in the wrong room. Then I look at the pile of luggage again. The old holdall from the attic with my worn and faded Stereophonics sticker on the side is definitely my luggage. Yes, lying in my bed is a man, propping himself up on one arm. About thirty-five, he has dark hair, and he pushes the unruly mop of loose curls back off his long tanned face. He has dark stubble around his jawline, his chin and his top lip. He rubs his eyes with his forefinger and thumb. He has a long straight nose and, when he opens them again, I see very, very brown eyes, like dark chocolate, framed by thick eyebrows, and dark smudges under them. There's a brightness in those eyes that makes them look as if they're laughing, presumably at me, despite his having obviously just woken up. He runs his hand up his high forehead, showing off his high cheekbones to match. He's wearing a white vest T-shirt showing off his rounded shoulders and on one of them, a small tattoo that I can't quite make out. Round his neck are two or maybe three short necklaces, one of beads and one leather with a small silver charm on it. He doesn't say anything, just grins at me.

'What the . . . ? Shit . . . excuse me . . . what the . . . ?' I splutter, wondering if Candy and Nick are going to appear, laughing at their joke at any minute. But they don't.

The man sits up and grins again, a very white bright smile, and pulls a shirt on that he's picked up from the floor beside him, where he had clearly just discarded it. Then, clearly having discarded his manners somewhere too, goes to pull back the covers.

'Excuse me,' I say loudly, putting up a hand in disbelief, feeling outraged and flustered all at the same time.

He stops and lets the cover drop back down.

'Oh, sorry, of course.' He smiles lazily again, as if teasing me.

We look at each other, me waiting for an explanation or an apology for him being in my room, in my bed. And he . . . well, waiting for me to leave, by the looks of it. He tugs at the corner of the cover impatiently and raises an eyebrow. The leather bracelets on his wrist jostle with each other.

'Bathroom,' he says by way of an explanation, nodding towards the small en suite to which I'm standing in the doorway. I'm tempted to stand my ground but he waggles the corner of the thin cover again and sticks a foot out. Oh God, who knows what he's wearing under there, if anything? I lurch forward, grab my holdall and the towel tightly, and run out of the room to the sound of his laughter.

Isaac rubbed both his hands over his face. He was tired. It had been quite a journey to get here, and quite a party before he left, too. But, like a swallow who knows when the seasons are about to change, Isaac could feel it had been time to leave. Any longer and he'd have felt he was living back in California, and that would never have done.

He felt better already, knowing there were new wines to discover, new territories to explore. He could feel his interest reignite. A fire starting in his belly. He loved the feeling he got arriving somewhere new. And, let's be honest, he'd clearly set the cat amongst the pigeons with his arrival already. He hadn't meant to scare the poor woman. He'd just been in such a deep sleep, he'd almost forgotten where he was. Last time he was in a bed, he'd been slipping out of it before its other occupant awoke and had been on the plane before he could even text her goodbye. It was better that way. He didn't do long goodbyes. They hurt too much. Anyway, he'd be back at the end of the season, maybe. But he needed to focus on being in France for the next few months. This was a big opportunity for him and if he played his cards right, it could take him on to bigger, greener pastures, and California would be just another chapter in life, just the way he liked it. He smiled and finally slipped out of bed to the bathroom.

'A man! In your bed!' Candy shrieks.

'Ssh,' I tell her. He'd probably love the fact we're talking about him, I think. He is that sort: cocky and confident. I sling my case down on what I think is the spare bed in her room, although, judging by the amount of clothes, shoes and hair apparatus on each bed, I'm not entirely sure. I pick up a pile of assorted outfits and look this way and that for somewhere to put them.

'What are you doing?' Candy stops tonging her hair. She's

wrapped in a small towel, with two large rollers on top of her head. Her body is an all-over unnatural orange colour.

'Looking for somewhere to put this,' I say, stating the obvious. Candy may be one of the call centre's best-selling agents, but common sense isn't something she rates highly in.

'If someone is in my bed then I'm going to need somewhere to sleep,' I tell her, still rattled and irritated, balancing her clothes between the bedside table and a corner of bed space by her pillow.

'You can't stay here. There's nowhere near enough room,' she wails, going back to tonging her white-blond hair.

'This is the biggest room,' I point out patiently. It's twice the size of my room back home, maybe more. But then, I am still staying in the room I had when I was growing up, the one that looks over the back garden. Dad has the middle room, which used to be my sister's. Now she has a suite of rooms for her bedroom, en suite and dressing room, his and hers. She emailed me pictures not long after she married. She used to send pictures of my nephews too, to show them to Dad. That was before all the trouble. She doesn't now. I'd have liked to have sent some photos of here, I think sadly, looking out of the window to the fast-flowing river, and tell her what I'm up to, but there's been too much hurt for a catch-up email now.

'So? Who is he?' Candy cuts across my thoughts, looking hugely inconvenienced.

'Who?'

'The man in your bed!' She tuts with irritation.

'I've no idea,' I shrug, trying to push out of my mind the

picture of him in my bed and the annoyance that comes with it. 'Maybe a holidaymaker they forgot was booked in,' I try to dismiss him. 'Look, I know you're not keen on having me in here –' I'm not that thrilled myself either. Sharing with the women whose engagement collection I borrowed is frankly making me squirm with embarrassment – 'but it's the only bed left in the house, so we're just going to have to lump it.' I swallow hard. She falls silent for a while, turning back to the dressing-table mirror and tonging her hair again. I pull my belongings out from my suitcase and find an empty drawer to put them in, each of us ignoring the other. Then suddenly Candy turns back to me.

'You don't think . . . ?' she says mischievously.

'What?'

'You don't think he's joining our team, do you? Like, another sales agent?'

We both stop to think about this.

'Shit!' I say under my breath. She might be right. The competition is hard enough without there being any more contenders, especially not really annoying, cocky ones. Candy, on the other hand, practically blossoms at the prospect.

I go back to my holdall, pulling out my best and only dress, which I bought for my sister's wedding six years ago now, just after her first baby was born.

I can hear my best friend, Layla's, voice telling me I should've treated myself to something new, that I deserve something. But I'm skint. Layla used to work with us. We've sat opposite each other for years. Now she's left I feel, well, bereft, in a funny sort of way. Layla has finally found true love and is trying to convince me it's not too late for me either. But frankly, as the only prospective partners I ever meet are Cadwallader's sales agents, I'm not convinced she's right. I wish Layla was here now, I really do. I shake out the dress and find my thoughts flicking back to Charlie and wonder what Layla would make of him. Attractive, smart, in his own business – frankly, he has everything going for him. I look at the dress, wondering whether to put it on. Well, there's no harm in trying to make a better impression than the one I left him with. I start getting changed.

'Fancy yourself for this job then, do you?' Candy's smiling at me, like a teasing hyena.

'Well . . .' I clear my throat and try to smile confidently. I can't, my jaws lock up.

'You'll need to toughen up if you're going to be in the running. Especially if we've got a new, good-looking fella on the block. Mind you, don't tell my Dean. He gets really jealous.' Candy laughs and looks back into the mirror. 'And maybe lose the nanny look.' She nods at my reflection.

An hour later and I've changed four times but am back in my dress. I've added a bit more lipstick to brighten myself up, and a scarf, but I'm not sure about it. I know I shouldn't be worried what Candy thinks of me, but she must be doing something right. She's probably hot favourite for the job and is certainly looking pleased with herself. I need to be more like it. As Trevor always says before one of his Monday morning sing-alongs, 'A happy agent is a high-selling agent.'

I change my mind about the scarf . . . and the lipstick. And then I run a hairbrush through my curls and try to pin them back off my face, without success.

Downstairs, we gather in the living room. Nick is dressed in another pair of chinos, a light blue and pink shirt with a purple jumper over his shoulders, and Gloria is wearing a cotton button-up dress that is straining at the bust, a cardigan, presumably in case it's cold, and a scarf draped haphazardly but not seeming to care.

'Right, ready to go?' Nick rubs his hands together.

'Hey,' the man who was in my bed sticks his head out of the kitchen and waves a hand.

'Oh, no,' I mutter, and try and hide behind Nick, hoping he doesn't see me. Everything about him just seems to make my hackles rise. He had the cheek not only to be in my bed, but not even to apologise. He pulls a headphone out of one ear and lets it dangle.

'I'm Isaac. Anyone fancy a beer?' He's holding one in his hand and dropping crumbs of bread from the care basket that was left for us, in the other. 'Sorry, it's been a long day, long flight and all that. Hey, you look great,' he gestures to me behind Nick, dropping more crumbs. I try to smile a thank you. 'I didn't recognise you . . . with your clothes on,' he delivers, and laughs, getting the right reaction from the others. Gloria's mouth opens, Candy hoots with laughter and Nick pulls an 'awkward' face. I grit my teeth with irritation.

'Sorry, we have to be somewhere,' I say, far more haughtily than I mean to, and I turn towards the glass-panelled front door.

'Oh, me, too!' He looks at his watch and tosses the last of the bread into his mouth. 'Dinner at the Tire-bouchon, by any chance?'

My heart hits the worn, terracotta-tiled floor; so he *is* another agent.

'You're coming with us?' Candy sways towards him, smiling like a praying mantis.

'U-huh,' he nods. 'I'm Isaac. Charlie's new travelling wine man. Just in from California. I guess I'm the one who's going to be teaching you everything you need to know about wine.'

Candy suddenly switches from combative colleague to simpering student, slips her arm through his and leads him to the door, her big round full bottom swaying from side to side, followed by Nick, who has suddenly got a serious face on, and Gloria, who, typically, says nothing.

'I'm dying to know everything you can teach me,' Candy oozes as we step out into the warm, sunny evening. Over the river the sun is dipping in the sky, just like my spirits, as the prospect of the new job falls just a little further out of reach. If I'm going to have any chance of keeping the bailiffs from taking my and Dad's home I need to start making a seriously good impression. But how?

Chapter Seven

The walk along the riverbank is a quiet affair. Even the glass or two of crémant, a sparkling wine, in the tasting room with Colette hasn't loosened us up. Well, maybe Candy. Nick, Gloria and I follow behind Candy, who is walking with Isaac. There is an uncomfortable silence between us. We're all of us strangers, none of us has worked in the same department at Cadwallader's, but I can't help wondering if they've worked out about me, wondering what on earth I'm doing here. I need to keep my distance.

Knowing we are going to be housemates, even roommates, for the next twelve weeks and all of us hoping for the same prize at the end of that time, is playing heavily on our minds, by the looks of it.

The restaurant is a short walk back to the town and just the other side of the square. We pass the boules court where men are still playing as the sun dips over the Dordogne, and pass the *mairie* along the road that hugs the riverbank. The lights strung around the outside decking area as we approach Le Tire-bouchon look like fireflies, lighting up the front of restaurant. The smell of searing, seasoned steak over hot flames reaches out to greet us. It's a single-storey building with a decking area as big as the restaurant itself. There are two large red and white wind-out awnings, and patio heaters dotted around, although not on in this warm and balmy evening. There are tables full of diners spread out over the decking and young waitresses with dark hair piled on top of their heads, skinny black jeans and wraparound black pinnies, moving between them, taking orders, bringing bottles of wine and collecting plates. There is a convivial hum of conversation in the air and gentle jazz playing in the background, and suddenly the tension we were feeling seems to seep away as we step on to the decking. It's not a big place, but appears to be popular, with a traditional, relaxed feel to it. The river brings its own gentle chatter to the party, bumbling and tumbling past. A splash from the riverbank – a fish maybe – and another, and the quack of ducks pootling around, like they're having an evening stroll out. As earlier, rowers glide past, two and four in the boats, and behind them the whizz of the small motor boat with the man in it still shouting instructions into a loud-hailer, cutting through the chatter of the ducks and scattering them on their evening stroll. But even so, his French instructions seem to add a charm to the lovely atmosphere.

I breathe in the evening air. I won't be getting to eat out like this again while I'm here. Thank goodness the company are paying for this. I really haven't got any spare cash for meals out, especially in places as smart at this. My friend Layla and I used to go to a local pizzeria every so often: I'd usually have a starter and say I was on a diet. She always ordered chips and two forks, knowing I wasn't. I must text her later, I think to myself.

'*Bonsoir, Messieurs, Mesdames*,' says a smiling, friendly

woman, with short hair, glasses, clutching a big pile of menus to her chest, and she holds out an arm to show us to our table. I follow our party as we're guided through the large glass fold-back doors that lead from the decking into the restaurant. Inside, the hubbub of happy diners is even louder. Such a warm, welcoming sound. A smell of warm cream and zesty lemon wraps around me like a hug. There is a long table right in front of the doors. Sitting at the head of this is a man holding a walking stick. He looks up at me and smiles broadly. This must be old Mr Featherstone, Charlie's dad. Beside him is a woman, and Charlie is there, too. Right, I think, and swallow down my shyness, smoothing my dress. This is my chance. It's time to do some networking of my own.

'Mr Featherstone?' I smile, and hold out a hand, despite my nerves.

'Good evening.' He speaks slowly, and with effort. He doesn't put out his hand and I realise he might be not be able to. It looks like one side of his mouth and body are drooped. But he attempts a smile none the less and his eyes light up, just as his son's do.

'I'm Lena Featherstone,' says the small, smart lady next to him, and shakes my hand. Charlie stands up and greets us all.

'I'm Emmy Bridges from Cadwallader's call centre,' I try to say confidently to Lena Featherstone.

'Well, pull up a seat, dear, and sit down. The food here is excellent and it's so lovely to look out at the river.'

A waitress passes by with a plate of fillet steak, little neat stacks of creamy sliced potatoes and firm green beans, and I nearly pass out from hunger with the smells from the garlicky glossy red wine sauce.

'*À la bordelaise*,' Lena Featherstone tells me, and points to the passing plate as if helping me to choose what to have already. 'A Bordeaux speciality.'

In her other hand, as the waitress passes between the tables and seated diners, is a plate of white filleted fish covered in a light yellow cream sauce, a sprinkling of bright green parsley and a slice of lemon on the side, and my mouth waters like it's sprung a leak.

Candy grabs a seat next to Charlie and pulls Isaac with her. Gloria is busy looking around at the lovely surroundings of the restaurant, seemingly drinking it in and smiling softly to herself. From the open kitchen a big smiling chef in glasses, his whites stretched over his belly, waves a hand while standing over a hot, fiery grill, hissing and spitting out red and orange flames. The friendly woman in glasses, who I'm thinking might be his wife, is handing us menus. Gloria looks like she's in another world, looking everywhere and finally accepts the menu with a '*Merci, Madame*'.

'Charlie,' says Isaac, 'how's it going?' He sticks out a hand.

'Isaac?' Charlie looks Isaac up and down, taking in his leather necklaces and casual attire with a slight frown of disapproval. Then says, 'You made it,' and smiles.

'Yeah, man. Sorry I didn't catch up earlier,' Isaac says in his easy-going Californian accent, and puts a hand on his hip and runs his other over his hair. So that's who Charlie was waiting for when he showed us round Featherstone's earlier. And suddenly I remember, it was Isaac I saw in the restaurant, before I went to Madame Beaumont's. He'd obviously had lunch and gone for an afternoon nap – in my bed. Charlie looks as if he's awaiting a little more of an explanation or apology, but when it doesn't come he steps out from the table and puts out a hand to shake Isaac's. Isaac, however, grabs hold of Charlie's hand and pulls him towards him, bumping shoulders and slapping him on the back. Charlie is only slightly caught off guard before giving himself to the embrace and slapping Isaac on the back too.

'Here, sit down. How was your flight? Delayed?' I get the impression Charlie's taking that as the reason for Isaac's casual look. 'Did you find the *gîte* OK? Settled in?'

Isaac gives me a sideways lazy grin that make my hackles rise again.

'Oh, yeah, made myself at home, no problem. I just think my room may have been someone else's before I got there,' he jokes, then laughs and I cringe. 'Ah, come on, Goldilocks, it was a genuine mistake.' He opens out his palms and shrugs, still laughing. 'I just took the first room that I saw, like Charlie said, to make myself at home when I arrived. I had no idea you were going to come in and go straight . . .'

My toes curl, my neck burns hot. *Stop now*, I will him.

'I just needed to get some shut-eye. No sleep, see. It was some leaving party.'

'Ah,' Charlie says, flicking out his napkin, and I swear I see another slight frown. He's obviously a man who takes business very seriously. And why not? I think. That's obviously why he's doing so well.

'So it's bye-bye California, hello France for the next couple of months. Let's hope the welcome back party is just as good!' Isaac laughs again. Clearly he is a man who doesn't take anything seriously. Candy joins in the laughter. 'Ah, come on, Goldy,' he says to me. 'I haven't scared you off already, have I?' He stares at me teasingly, grinning, and I hold his stare, feeling just like I did at school when the boys teased me about my hair, pulling the ends of it and getting me into trouble for fighting back. I want to tell him a simple sorry for the misunderstanding earlier would've worked fine, but bite my tongue really hard. I can't let him get to me. 'It'll take a lot more than the sight of you in your boxers to scare me off,' I answer back with a plastered-on smile and a raised eyebrow, and then turn away, my neck and cheeks and even the tips of my ears burning with embarrassment.

I turn back to Mrs Featherstone. 'How long have you been in the area?' I ask, clearing my tight throat, hoping the blush in my cheeks will die down, just as I'm offered white or red wine and point to the white, which is poured into my glass over my shoulder. I catch a glimpse of Charlie, who is giving Isaac a sideways look as if trying to weigh him up. Isaac is leaning back in his chair, Candy hanging on his every word as he describes the Californian wine house he's just come from, where he's been working for the last few months. I can't help but find myself looking just a little longer than I should at Charlie's profile. He really is a very attractive man.

Mr Featherstone leans forward to me, jolting me from my thoughts and speaks slowly and deliberately. 'Since 1982. Charlie was a boy,' he says with effort.

'We've always loved it here,' says Mrs Featherstone. 'But we divide our time now between here and the UK.' She looks at her husband brightly and puts her hand on his. 'We have summers in the UK, especially with the grandchildren being there,' she tells me.

'Oh, yes, of course.' I look at Charlie, who is now deep in conversation with Isaac, as he asks about the wine made at his last place, their practices and production levels. He's married, of course he is! I tell myself off again for even letting myself find him attractive.

'And since his divorce we make a special effort to stay close to them.'

Oh, divorced! I quickly look at the menu to hide that I've probably been staring at Charlie and then realise I can't understand a word of it. I try to pull up my schoolgirl French again, but instead decide to order exactly what Mrs Featherstone is having.

'Soup and steak *à la bordelaise*.'

'It's wonderful.' Mrs Featherstone leans into me. 'Rich red wine sauce. And the steaks are cooked over vine cuttings.'

The friendly waitress smiles and takes my menu from me. Nick is loudly translating the menu for Candy's benefit. Candy tells Nick to order for her, but nothing with a head on it.

Gloria quietly but confidently slips effortlessly into French with a soft, gentle accent and says, '*Bonsoir, Madame. Je voudrais le confit de canard, au miel et au romarin, avec frites et haricots verts. Merci, Madame.*' Then, for the first time since we've been here, breaks out a big smile. The waitress smiles back.

'*Bien sûr, Madame.*'

So, Gloria speaks French, of course! That's why she's here.

'Lucky you, speaking French; wish I could,' I say,

forgetting I was going to keep my distance but I can't help but be impressed.

'Duck confit,' she tells me. 'In honey and rosemary. I've . . . I've holidayed here a lot,' she says by way of explanation, spreading her napkin over her thighs, surprising me. 'Not recently, though,' she adds thoughtfully.

So that's why she's up for the job and, as impressed as I am and pleased for Gloria, inside I wilt a little bit more. Looks like everyone has their secret weapon. Gloria has French, Candy is a top-selling agent and will use all her charms to get what she wants, and Nick, well, by the way Nick's studying the menu and referring to his translation app on his phone, Nick is a bit of geek and likes to know the details.

'Charlie is taking over the running of the business so we can take it a bit easier,' Mrs Featherstone continues as she hands her menu back to the waitress. I'm sure I hear Mr Featherstone harrumph. I catch his eye just briefly and then think maybe I imagined it.

'Don't mind him. He's just taking a little time adjusting to the idea that Charlie wants to take things in a new direction. Out with the old, in with the new.' She gives a light-hearted laugh, like a school teacher calming a playground spat. Mr Featherstone harrumphs again.

'Do you have family of your own?' Lena Featherstone smiles and asks.

'No,' I say, 'just my dad. Well, and my sister. But we don't see her much. She has a family of her own. Two boys. She's very busy. But Dad, well, he needs . . . looking after . . .' I can't really say anything else. I can't tell this lady we don't see my sister because she's the reason we're in this mess. And I can't tell her I care for my dad because he's ill. He's not ill like Mr Featherstone – there's nothing physically wrong with him – he just doesn't cope. He hasn't coped for years now. I check my phone and notice three missed calls from him.

'You live with your dad?'

'Yup,' I try to nod enthusiastically.

'Not married or engaged then?'

'Nope.' I still try to keep it light, wishing I could add something more interesting other than I have a serious charity shop habit, an addiction to *Location, Location, Location*, and my regular Saturday night date on the sofa is with *Strictly Come Dancing* and a packet of HobNobs.

Across the table Candy is describing the new car she's just bought and the apartment she lives in that she's going to rent out when she moves in with her fiancé, Dean.

At our side of the table conversation has run dry. I don't have a new car or place of my own or fiancé or family to talk about. The truth is, I have a rubbish job that barely covers the bills because I never make my bonuses, I've had a string of unsuccessful boyfriends. A small string. But then it's not easy bringing a new boyfriend home when your sixty-five-year-old father is waiting up with Horlicks and garibaldis.

I see Mr Featherstone looking at Charlie and Isaac, heads together talking intently. Mrs Featherstone is breaking up some bread for him. He seems to be able to use his left hand. In the corner of the restaurant, before a doorway to the toilets, I see a wheelchair and realise it's his. Thank goodness he has Mrs Featherstone by his side, and again I feel for my dad, who has no one. That's why I have to stay at home. There are candles along the table that light up Charlie's tanned face. Isaac picks up a glass of wine by the stem and swirls it round, sniffing before taking a sip.

Our starters arrive. The woman I think is the proprietress and two waitresses appear with plates and bowls. Mine is French onion soup, dark brown, with little clear glossy pools dotted across the surface from the melting cheese, on a round of toasted French bread sitting like an island in the middle of the deep white bowl. I breathe in and get a hit of garlic and brandy, if I'm not mistaken. Candy's is crevettes – prawns – orange and pink in yellow melted garlic butter, sprinkled with garlic. But I'm guessing it's not quite what Candy was expecting or what Nick had described.

'I thought you said it was like a prawn cocktail!'

'Oh, give it here.' Nick leans over and cracks off the crevette heads and peels off the shells and legs for her, rinsing his hands in the finger bowl with a slice of lemon in it. But Candy just grimaces and eats bread laden with white butter.

'Urgh! I think they forget to put the salt in this butter,' she moans, whilst trying to listen in on Isaac and Charlie's conversation, ignoring Nick's efforts.

With Candy's starter untouched – and I can't help thinking what a waste – the starters are cleared from behind us. I hear Mr Featherstone harrumph again in Charlie's direction. Charlie, realising what his father is expecting of him, drags himself from his conversation with Isaac and raises his glass.

'I'd like to take this opportunity to welcome you all on behalf of the Featherstone family,' he lifts his glass to his father and mother, 'to our town of Petit Frère and to Featherstone's Wines. Perhaps we could take a moment to introduce ourselves. I'm Charlie Featherstone. I have a track record in sales, mostly food and drink, and I'm happy to now be joining the family business. My father,' he indicates Mr Featherstone, 'and my mother, Lena,' he nods again at her and smiles ensuring he hadn't forgotten her part in things, 'set up this business together. Petit Frère has long been seen as the town living in the shadows of the well-known wine destination of Saint Enrique next door, on the hill. But it is my aim to take the Featherstone's business forward and with it give Petit Frère the reputation it deserves in its own right. We will be one of the biggest wine distributors around, a household name. Now then, who's next?'

We go around the table introducing ourselves and raise our glasses to 'the Featherstone team'.

'So, single, you say?' Lena turns and asks me.

'Oh, er, yes.'

'No, I can't think we've ever had an office collection for you, have we, Emmy?' Candy pulls down her mouth and cocks her head on one side. 'Best sales agent of the week? Engagement? House warming? Can't think I've seen you get anything.' She shakes her head, teasing me, and I want to say, 'That's because you had my share!' but I can't. I still have to find a way of getting her latest collection back to her.

'Of course, as I've said, Charlie is single,' Lena says with a twinkle in her eye.

'Mother!' Charlie warns, and Lena shrugs apologetically

and laughs, and I squirm a little. Is it that obvious I find him attractive?

'Just saying,' Lean teases with a pink flush in her cheeks, which could be the white wine. But Candy narrows her eyes as if new possibilities and horizons are opening up in front of her eyes.

'He's always telling me off for trying to find him a –' Lena looks at Candy and then back at me – 'suitable girl.'

'If someone calls you "suitable", it means you're sensible and boring,' Candy says behind her hand, and I smart as if she's slapped me. 'I told you to ditch the nanny look.' And of course, she's right. I know full well I'd never be in the running with someone like Charlie. Although, I think 'suitable' is a good thing. It means you're dependable, constant. I know my dad would think Charlie very 'suitable' and frankly, so would I. Candy, on the other hand, would never be described as that.

'Of course, we want an even playing field for this job, Mrs Featherstone. No favouritism!' Candy jokes with what feels like an iron fist in her velvet glove. She looks at Charlie and then back at me, then takes another swig of white wine from her glass before helping herself to the bottle on the table and topping it up.

'Not that you're really in the running, are you, Emmy?' Candy continues, and I feel like the stooge on stage beside her. 'I mean, the nearest you get to salesperson of the month is handing round the cakes and cava! Our own little Mrs Overall, like in *Acorn Antiques*!'

She squawks with laughter and Isaac throws his head back and laughs too, and asks, 'Who's Mrs Overall? Sounds dreadful!' The only one who isn't smiling is Gloria, but she looks sorry for me, which is even worse. I want to throttle them both, Candy and Isaac. Candy juts out her chin at me, like she's already grabbed the trophy. 'In fact, if you get that job I'll run naked down the street throwing toffees to children, and whistling the National Anthem.'

I pick up my glass and sip at my wine, and suddenly something inside me snaps. I may not be the obvious choice for this job. I may not speak much French or be a top sales person, or a bookworm, but I do want this job more than anything. I'm fed up with being Emmy from cleaning products, who does the collections. I want to be something more. I'd give anything to take that job from underneath Candy's nose, I really would.

'Really?' I say calmly. 'I'd like to see that.'

'So would I!' pipes up Isaac flirtatiously, and Candy shrieks with laughter all over again.

'OK, how about a bet?' shrieks Candy with delight. 'Winner takes all.'

'Now hang on . . .' Nick tries to step in.

'Tell you what. Seeing as you've never had a collection before, how about I bet you my engagement collection. Trevor's bound to have found out where it's gone by the time we get back. You win, I'll give you the collection. You lose, you pay me the same amount again.'

So, that will be double or quits then, I think, and swallow hard.

'Really, you don't have to,' Nick tries again. Charlie is sitting back, mildly impressed.

Candy is staring at me, challenging me. She licks her lips

and her eyes dance with excitement. She looks like a cat toying with a mouse. Emmy Bridges from cleaning products, world's worst sales agent. I look at Isaac. He's smiling lazily. I know I shouldn't be bothered but something in me wants to show him what Goldilocks can do.

'You're on!' I say to the sound of little gasps, in particular from Gloria.

Candy shrieks with delight and sticks out a hand and, as I shake it, I know I've just got myself into a whole lot more bother. So much for keeping my head down.

Chapter Eight

The next morning is Sunday and I feel like I've been hit by a bus. I don't think I've had a wink of sleep. Nick, Candy and Isaac stayed up late last night drinking in the kitchen. At one point I'm sure Candy was singing Meghan Trainor's 'All About That Base' at the top of her voice. I'm pretty sure I heard Nick joining in, too, or maybe it was Isaac. Beside that, the bells from the church rang every hour throughout the night, twice. Just to be sure you knew what the time was. And then, of course, there was Candy. I look over at her now, still sleeping. Her bed has actually moved from the wall, she is lying face down and one leg is hanging out, still with a high-heeled slingback shoe hanging off the big toe.

The noise she's made all night! It was like something in between snoring and a squealing piglet. I listen again now.

'Snurrrrr, weeeeee, snurrrrr, weeeeee . . .'

The church bell strikes seven but it's not just seven chimes this time. It rings like billyo, a peel of bells, no doubt letting us all know it's time we were up and going to church. The light is streaming in through the shutters in front of the big long windows, which open with a twist of the handle and a clunk. New windows made to look like the old ones, I suspect. It's warm already outside.

'Snurrrrr, weeeeee, snurrrrr, weeeeee . . .'

I throw back the sheet that covered me and pick up my clothes from on top of my case – so old and faded in comparison to Candy's bright new one taking up most of the floor space. I pad over the wooden floor boards to the en suite, wash, then get dressed silently and slip out into the morning. I breathe in the fresh, warm air. A cycle into town and a little exploring will clear my head, I think. I pick up the bike and head for the town square and Monsieur and Madame Obels' *épicerie* for a banana and maybe one of the peaches. The hot sun is pushing its way up into the sky. I can smell the comforting, heady aroma of baking bread. A young boy runs out of the *boulangerie*, holding a long French stick in one hand and a half-moon croissant in the other. He smiles, holds his face to the sun, and then bites into the croissant, crumbs tumbling to the ground from his mouth and hand, before running home with the rest.

I can't resist any longer. I rest the bike outside, nodding my good mornings to Monsieur and Madame Obels, outside their shop, as I do so. The smells and sight of all the different pastries behind the glass at the back of the *boulangerie* make me feel like a child in a sweet shop. But eventually I settle on a croissant, like the boy; big, fat, layered and flaky. I point to a bottle of water, too, pay and manage a '*merci*'. As I come out of the shop, the bells ring from church and older men, and women dressed smartly in dark dresses and low heels, begin to make their way across the square and up the church steps.

It's a far cry from Sunday mornings back home, where the streets are mostly full of debris and detritus from the Saturday night before. There is a flower stall beside the church. I decide to buy a bunch of gerberas, bright and cheerful daisy-like flowers in purples, yellows and oranges. I can see down the bend in the river, pass *la mairie*, the town hall, to Le Tire-bouchon – the restaurant from last night – closed now, chairs resting against tables – and think about what a lovely place it is. I pull out my phone, photograph it and text it to Layla.

Hi Layla. You'll never believe it. I'm in France! Trevor's sent me on a training course with a new client. Weather is hot, hot, hot. My French is dreadful and my roommate a nightmare! Still, it's only twelve weeks. That's 84 sleeps, right?! Miss you! X

Actually, I miss everything about home, I think, as I press send. Eighty-four sleeps, I tell myself, just like when we were kids, and my heart dips. Eighty-four sleeps seems like for ever.

OMG! She texts back, almost immediately. *Wish I was there with you!*

I wish she was here too. That way I may not have got myself into such a stupid bet with Candy last night. If I lose, which I'm likely to, I'm now going to have to pay back twice the collection money I borrowed. What on earth was going through my mind? I just wanted to wipe the smile off her and that Isaac's faces and now I've gone and got myself into even deeper debt than before.

I look back at the *gîte*. I'm not going back there yet, I think. There's somewhere else I should be. I cycle on, wobbling and swerving, and I don't think my flip-flops are helping. I try to avoid a battered old Renault coming towards me in the middle of the road and find myself veering to the left instead of the right, and getting a blast on the horn from the passing car, driven by a man in blue overalls, cigarette in mouth, flat cap. My nerves take time to settle again but by the time I get to the stone bridge I'm feeling a little more in control, other than when cars overtake me and I still wobble, hold my breath and screw up my eyes.

I make my way out of town and back up the hill, the same as yesterday, on the road to Saint Enrique. This time I'm more prepared, with the large bottle of water I bought in the *boulangerie*, the bunch of gerberas balanced across the handle bars.

By the time I reach the crumbling gateposts of Clos Beaumont, though, I'm hot, really hot. My thighs are screaming in pain. I put the bike against the post and little bits of mortar and stone fall away as I finish off the water. Swinging the empty bottle by my side and holding the bunch of gerberas in the other, I walk down the lane that opens up on to the yard, taking in the smell of thyme and lavender.

The big, reddish dog lets out a bark and slowly staggers to his feet, as if it's all too much effort, and I don't blame him. I bend to pat his head and as the slithers of slime start to form, sidestep him and he takes that as a sign that his work is done and lies back down with a *phump*.

'Hello? *Madame? Bonjour!*' I call, just like yesterday. I stick my head into the barn where there are big concrete vats at either side, and another long barn with rows of old wooden barrels along one very long wall.

The bottles I knocked over yesterday are all washed and stacked neatly once more and I want to kick myself for not getting back to help sooner.

'*Allo*,' I say, trying it out with a little bit of a French accent. I turn out of the barn and walk towards the opening to the vineyard that drops away from behind the house. There is a tiny little haze of mist lifting off the vines that spread down the hillside and, beyond, up towards the château on the hill opposite. There is an orange and yellow hue across the skyline. At the end of every third or so line of vines is a beautiful yellow rose bush with bees contentedly buzzing around it, just like I've seen on the vines on my ride up here.

There is no sign of Madame Beaumont. Maybe she isn't up. I go to the French doors at the back of the house. I knock and try the handle. It's open. I stick my head in tentatively and call, '*Allo*' again. The dark room is as chock-a-block as yesterday: piles of papers, washing hanging across the room, a pile of muddy vegetables on the table waiting for attention. Again, I can't help but wonder why everything happens in this room, despite it being quite a large house from the outside.

'*Allo?*' I call, this time more confidently. There's no reply. I turn away and look back at the sloping hillside. Then I see the small, bent figure walking up between the vines. It's Madame Beaumont. She's smartly dressed in a black dress and cardigan, despite the increasing heat of the day, and carrying a basket. Her grey hair is scraped back into a bun and she has a hairband across the middle of her head. As she walks she is talking, softly and constantly, running her hand through the leaves of the vines. She hasn't seen me and I don't want to spook her. So I move away from the house and stand in an obvious place and just watch. She's still talking, stopping every now and again to touch a bunch of grapes, inspect it, or study a large leaf and maybe break it off. If I'm not very much mistaken, she talking to the vines, like she's catching up with old friends, smiling fondly like she's praising a small child, and I find myself smiling back.

I'm so lost in the scene in front of me I'm suddenly shocked when she sees me. She looks up and I suddenly remember I'm standing in her back garden, staring.

'Oh, *excusez-moi*,' I say as she approaches. She looks at me with narrowing eyes and a slight tilt of the head that says she's not that pleased to see me. 'I was here yesterday,' I remind her.

'Yes, you brought me my purse. Have you come back for the reward?' she asks me directly, and I'm a little taken aback.

'No. Not at all.' My tongue ties itself in knots. 'I, er, I knocked over the bottles. I said I'd return to help out, put right the mess. Typical me. Clumsy.' My tongue is still not working with my brain.

Madame Beaumont says nothing and I get the impression she doesn't believe me.

'Really, I just wanted to put right the mess I made.'

Finally she says, 'There's no need. It's done.'

'Do you have someone who works the winery for you? I'd like to apologise.'

'No, it's just me.' She looks guarded again.

'Oh, I'm so sorry,' I say, mortified to have left this lady with the mess.

'It's no problem. I'm nearly done.'

'I'd like to help.'

'There's no need.'

Then she looks at me.

'So, how are you finding working at Featherstone's? Have you been here long?'

'About twenty-four hours,' I say, and I think that may have been a tiny smile at the corner of her mouth.

'And you are working in his wine business?' she asks, putting down her basket on the small table by the back door and removing the scarf from around her neck.

'I will be.' I nod, trying to look more confident than I feel.

'So, he has brought you here because you know all about wine?'

I bite my bottom lip and shake my head. Madame Beaumont raises her eyebrow but says nothing.

'I don't know anything about wine,' I say flatly. 'We're here to learn, so we can sell it back in the UK. You see, his son, Charlie, has taken over and wants to expand and sell more in the UK. But he needs a team leader . . .' All of a sudden I realise quite how ridiculous I am, thinking I could take on Candy for the job. My shoulders drop and I sigh and then explain, 'He has to pick a team leader. It's a good job. A good salary and a starting bonus . . .' I trail off. Madame Beaumont doesn't need to know all this.

Now I feel very silly standing there in my holiday shorts and Nelson Mandela T-shirt, telling this lady I've come to work in the wine business and I want a job I have no hope of getting. I look down at the dusty floor and wonder how to just excuse myself and leave.

Then, as if reading my mind she says, 'You cannot sell what you don't understand.'

I look up at her slowly.

'Exactly,' I shrug, and I can feel a wave of despair starting to wash over me, thinking about the tome we have to learn. 'We have to learn about each of the wines and how to answer questions,' I reply. 'We've got this book, we're supposed to memorise it . . .'

'Do you know what these are?' She points to the vines.

'Grapes?' I say, stating the obvious.

She laughs, a deep, throaty laugh.

'I like your honesty,' she says. 'I wish more people said what they meant,' and I'm not sure what she means.

'Your mother brought you up well. She would be proud of you.'

I move my head from side to side. My mouth seems to be running away with me when my brain is shouting, *Shut up, time to go!*

'It's just my father . . . and me. He . . . I look after him. And my sister, I have a sister, too.' I swallow, not sure why I'm telling a stranger about my home life. 'She's doing well. Her husband, he was a footballer. He's, um, in business now. Something to do with investments . . .' I trail off.

Madame Beaumont looks at me and tilts her head again. 'You brought up your sister?'

I bite my top lip and then nod and shrug. Maybe it's homesickness that's making me talk. 'It's just how it was . . .' I feel the familiar lump in my throat start to rise and I'm sure it's just homesickness.

Neither of us says anything for a moment. A cockerel shouts loudly from the field next door. A flock of birds noisily circles overhead. Madame Beaumont looks up as they start to land on the telephone wire.

'Cecil,' she calls, and the big old dog lumbers up and

begins barking and howling at the gathering birds, who fly away at his noise. He chases up and down, lifting his front feet off the ground.

I smile.

'What is Cecil? I mean, what breed?'

'He's a mix, like me.'

I'm not sure what she means again.

'He is half Dogue de Bordeaux, a mastiff, and half . . .' she shrugs, '. . . something else. His mother was a proud Dogue de Bordeaux, from this region. His father belonged to a traveller passing through. He is just Cecil.'

The tears that threatened to spill a moment ago as I nearly let my concerns about being here get the better of me, abate. I must be tired. Tiredness always makes things worse. But I feel a long way from home and wonder what on earth I'm doing here. Of course I'm not going to get the team leader's job. I don't know anything about wine. The closest I've come to buying wine recently was the Lambrini on offer for Layla's leaving do, and I'm not even sure that's wine at all. Not like the glorious wine we were drinking last night. That was soft and fruity and smooth, and didn't even give me a hint of headache this morning.

My phone rings. I quickly mumble, 'Excuse me,' and answer it.

'Hi, Dad, yes, I'm fine. You? Yes, yes. It's all going really well. Yes, I had a lovely meal last night.'

He wants to know everything, how it's all going. Madame Beaumont has turned to inspect her roses.

Then he says, 'The thing is, love, there's been another letter. We've missed another mortgage payment.'

'Don't worry, Dad,' I sigh, and my shoulders slump, despite me trying to sound upbeat. 'The boss, Charlie, has said the best-selling agent out here will be made team leader.' Why am I telling him this? I have no hope of getting it. Still my mouth motors on. 'Yes, that means we could sort out the arrears, no problem. It could sort it all out.'

'You'll do it, I know it. I'm so proud of you, Emmy,' Dad says, and then I really do want to cry. I tell him I love him and we end the call.

Madame Beaumont looks at me. I rub my itching nose.

'Your *papa*?' she asks, and I nod. She studies me, tilting her head to one side. 'He has great faith in you, *non*?'

'He just doesn't cope well on his own. He doesn't work any more. He got . . . ill.' The truth is, he gave up. He couldn't go on after Mum . . . after the accident. He just sat down in his chair in shock and has been there ever since. Work kept him on for a while. He was a salesman for a confectionary company. He loved his job. But all the joy went after Mum went. He couldn't look after himself, let alone me or my younger sister . . . So I did.

'He thinks I can do anything.' I give a little hiccup. 'I wish he was right. Me getting this team leader's job would sort out, well, all our problems.' I sigh. 'I don't know how to tell him I don't have a chance of getting it.' I realise I've said this out loud. 'I'm so sorry. Look, once again I'm sorry about the mess I caused yesterday.' I hand over the bunch of flowers I'm clutching. They're wilting a bit. I try to hold them straight as I hand them over. 'I should go now. *Merci*.'

'*Merci*,' says Madame Beaumont as the flowers bend over in her hands.

I turn and walk quickly away, down the drive. I'm just about out of the gate.

'*Attendez!* Wait!' Her sharp voice stops me as I reach out for the old bike. I turn back at her. The heat is starting to make my pale skin prickle and my flushing cheeks burn even more.

'How can you sell what you do not know?' she lifts her head, juts out her chin and asks again sternly.

I shake my head and shrug. 'I'll just need to learn the script . . .' I trail off.

She looks at me and then turns. '*Viens.* Come,' she beckons for me to follow her. At first I'm not sure I've heard her right. Leaving the bike, I start to walk back towards her. She stands and waits until I'm beside her. Then she calls to someone and to my surprise a large, heavy feathered-hoofed horse comes to the gate of the adjoining field.

'*Viens.*' She beckons with her head again and I follow her to the gate. There are still sheep wandering around in the vines and I wonder if she wants help to round them up.

'The sheep, Madame? Would you like help catching them?' I have no idea how to catch a sheep but I'd be willing to give it a try.

'No,' she shakes her head again. 'They are my gardeners.'

'Huh?'

'Keeping down the weeds,' she tells me as she opens the gate and pats the horse's huge neck. I stand back. I'm not used to such big animals. Apart from dogs I'm not used to animals at all really.

'*Voilà Henri,*' she introduces me to the horse, although I have no idea why. 'My assistant,' she tells me, and takes hold of my wrist with her bony hand and holds out my hand for him to sniff, which he does, a lot. His whiskers tickle my palm and make me smile, but she holds my hand firmly in place. I look up at his long face.

'He can't see so well. He is blind in one eye and the other is fading,' she tells me, and I look up at his milky blue eye.

'*Viens*,' she instructs Henri, and with that he walks out of the gate and into the yard. I step back very quickly. I wouldn't like to get my foot trodden on by one of those massive feathered hoofs.

Then I stand aside and watch as the horse, with a little help from Madame Beaumont, backs himself with precision in between the two side runners of an old wooden cart that's standing there.

'How does he know where to go?' I ask, watching in wonder.

'Instinct,' she tells me simply. 'Now, in the barn you will find a big white drum and a sprayer. Fetch it, please.'

I'm happy to do as I'm told. The black and white cat is there, narrowing its eyes at me.

By the time I come out of the barn, the horse is harnessed up. I watch in awe as Madame Beaumont leads him towards the vines.

'Walk with me,' she calls to me, directing me to put the plastic barrel on the trailer. Then she looks down at my feet and tuts.

'You cannot work the fields like . . . that.'

I look down at her feet. She's wearing clogs. I, on the other hand, am in flip-flops and I wobble and flip and flap over the uneven land behind her.

'Bring boots next time.'

She instructs the horse on slowly in between the first two rows of vines.

'So, these are my "grapes".'

I can tell she's teasing me and I find myself smiling. I mean, she's right. I know nothing about them.

'This is my Cabernet Sauvignon *parcelle* – a type of grape that grows well in these parts. Over there is my Merlot, and down the lane back towards the town I have a *parcelle* of Cabernet Franc.'

'And what about there?' I point to the vines running up towards the château. 'That's Saint Enrique over there, isn't it?'

Madame Beaumont looks at me sideways again, owl-like, quickly moving her head and then staying very still. She gives a slight nod.

'Those are mine,' she confirms, and carries on walking, inspecting the grapes on one row of vines, occasionally stopping and lifting the leaves. Then she stops, pulls out a small pair of secateurs from her pocket and snips off a large leaf, tossing it on the back of the trailer. And I feel as if our tentative new friendship has taken a step back and she, for some reason, still mistrusts me.

'The grapes must have sunlight or they will not ripen.' She says nothing more about the other *parcelle* of grapes I've pointed out on the other side of the hill. She walks slowly on, as does the horse, stopping occasionally. She inspects each bunch, or so it seems. 'Right now, these grapes need to fatten and fill out. We get rid of leaves that will shield them from the sun.' She cuts off another leaf and tosses it on the back of the trailer. 'You must nurture them if they are to grow up and do well. Even the naughtiest ones eventually learn what they must do,' she chuckles, and then says, 'So, you know nothing of wine and grapes?'

'No,' I confirm.

'Then, why do you want to sell it?'

We walk slowly on between the vines as I tell her about the call centre, life there, with 150 agents. I tell her how I came to be here, not by merit, but frankly luck, and about the team leader's job, and how mine and Dad's home now rests on my success, but that I have really no chance at all of getting it. I tell her about Candy, Cadwallader's best-selling agent and her fiancé, Dean; Nick, in advertising, and Gloria, on catalogue knitwear. And me, on toilet rolls and cleaning fluids for restaurants, bars, care homes.

'So, this could change your life, being here,' Madame Beaumont says, walking behind the trailer as the horse moves slowly forwards.

'It could,' I sigh resignedly, 'if I could prove myself.'

'And Candy?'

'Oh, she wants it. She wants a new car and the wedding of the century. She has a picture of it by her desk. We all have to put a picture of what we want most as our screen saver . . . a photo, on our computers,' I explain when I realise she doesn't understand screen savers.

'And you? What is your . . . screen saver?'

I swallow.

'It's a house . . . my house, with my own front door.' Actually, it's the cottage from *The Holiday*, you know, the one where Cameron Diaz moves to Kate Winslet's gorgeous little cottage in Surrey. I just want to own my own home, put down my own roots. Have a family of my own. I love my dad and I'd always want to be close to him, but when I moved back in after Mum died, I didn't realise I'd still be there now. Of course, he'd never sell the house. It's where his memories are. His roots . . . and mine, too. Mum's favourite mug is still on the rack in the kitchen, her dressing gown still hangs behind the door and there's still a bald patch in the lawn where she burned the gravy one Sunday and threw the pan out of the window. But I would love to buy a small house nearby, just feel I was on life's ladder, moving up like all the other agents in the office. I don't tell her the ridiculous screen saver shots I have in my head at night. I want that big happy family, round the table at Christmas. Instead, these days, it's just me and Dad.

Life seems to have stood still for me and unless I can get this job, it will never move on.

'And the job?'

'I'd like this job, make Dad proud and be able to afford to get the bailiffs off my back. But I'm not the one who'll get it. In fact, I'd say there are three other very suitable candidates before they'd look at me.'

'Sometimes a vintage that we were least expecting to do well turns out to be very exciting indeed,' Madame Beaumont says. She's silent for a moment and I try to take in what she's saying.

Then she starts to talk me through her daily routine of checking on the vineyard.

'Have you always been a wine-maker?' I ask.

'A vintner? Yes,' she replies simply. 'And my family before

me grew vines here. Some of these vines are eighty years old, some maybe older.'

We walk back up the next row of vines. She's talking to the vines as if greeting a classroom full of children.

She stops, tuts, takes the long spray attached to the barrel of liquid and sprays at a bunch of grapes.

'Do you spray all the grapes?' I remember the tractors with the long spraying arms in the fields coming up here. She tuts again.

'I believe in as little intervention as possible. Let Mother Nature do her thing. These vines know what they have to do. All that spraying, it's like giving morphine for a headache. We help, we don't interfere.' She bends and pulls out a weed. 'Soon all spraying must stop, two weeks before we harvest. And then I will bottle last year's vintage. It must be finished and the barrels cleaned ready for the new vintage to come. I think it will be an interesting one.' Her eyes sparkle.

As the sun sets that evening, she brings out a bottle of wine. Putting in the corkscrew she wrestles with it and I'm about to offer to do it, when, *pop*, out it comes, followed by a very welcome *glug* as she pours us each a glass of wine and we sit by her back door on an old veranda and watch the sun start to set over the vines.

'Thank you for showing me around today,' I tell her, sipping the wine.

'Thank you for bringing me back my purse yesterday and for helping me today.' She sips the wine. I cannot understand why this lady has the reputation she does in the town. They clearly haven't seen the Madame Beaumont that I have.

'There is a lot to learn about wine,' she tells me. 'Not all the stuff in books but understanding the vines, the *terroir*.'

I just know I'll never learn enough.

Then, to my surprise, she says, 'There is much I could teach you.'

She's looking at me, studying my face. I shake my head. I'd never be able to learn enough. I mean, Nick seems to know about wine already, Candy is a top-selling agent, and Gloria . . . Gloria seems to speak French like a native. 'I just don't think I could ever be in the running.'

'Lesson one. Know your enemy. See that château over there. It's owned by a local man who has bought up vineyards all over the world. It's what he does. He sees it and buys it. He has been trying to buy up my land for years.' She gives a shrug. 'They try every method but I won't sell. While I'm alive, I will make my wine my way.'

'That's terrible.'

'Keep your friends close, your enemies closer. There is so much more to learning about wine than what you'll learn from your guidebooks. I can help teach you about wine, but you have to want to learn. If you want the job badly enough, you'll make it happen.'

I look at her sceptically. Trevor only sent me to make up the numbers and, in his words, to stop me causing chaos with the cleaning fluid orders. I would give anything to be like the others, like Candy, working towards their goals. Instead I just seem to be treading water, and only just stopping myself from sinking. But a little bit of me would still love to try to go for it.

'Over there in Château Lavigne. They make a sparkling

wine. It is said to be hand turned thousands of times, and that the men have arthritic hands from the work.' She raises a sceptical eyebrow. 'It's good wine . . . if overpriced.'

We sip our wine and I wonder how you know when a wine is overpriced. When a good wine becomes an excellent one.

'Think about it. I'll be here if you want to learn. First of all, you need to learn to trust yourself.'

I mentally count up how many more weeks I have left here. A lot! I finish my wine, thank Madame Beaumont and stand up to go.

On my way home I think about what Madame Beaumont has said. Could I really do it? If I learned to trust my instincts? The image of Isaac and Candy laughing at me in the restaurant the night before plays over and over in my head. Her challenging eyes. His lazy smile. The bet. I have a tiny fantasy of winning the bet, where I'm in charge of Team Featherstone's and Candy is doing the office collection and the cake and cava run. Oh . . . that's after she's run through the town naked, throwing toffees and whistling the National Anthem!

Just for the hell of it, I decide to test Madame Beaumont's theory and trust my instincts by lifting my feet off the pedals and freewheeling down the hill, but the bike weaves and wobbles and I shove my feet back, realising my instincts are still way off the mark . . . way off.

Chapter Nine

I'm up early again. There's only so much of Candy's strange night-time noises I can stand. It's going to be another glorious day. I get up and walk to the traditional long windows and pull them open, the thin net curtains flapping in the light breeze. The pigeons are chatting away to their neighbours along the terracotta roof tiles over the office and tasting room, billing and cooing. But there's more noise, clattering and clanging, and I look up towards the town and realise it wasn't just Candy's nocturnal mutterings that woke me. It's Monday morning and there's a market setting up in the street.

I get dressed quickly in the bathroom and look round at Candy, who spent yesterday evening getting to know some of the local wines, and may, this morning, be regretting it. I look at my watch. It's seven thirty and we're not due to start work until nine. I have time to get out there and see the market. I pull Candy's covers, which are spilling over the floor, back over her and leave. I creep down the wooden steps, just in case Isaac is still asleep. I don't want to wake him and have to get into conversation with him. I creep out through the front door and up the road towards the fountain in the square, turn the corner, and am met by a sea of nylon knickers and bras, red and gold, turquoise and leopard print. Embarrassed, I try to skirt the hanging neon basques, flapping and wrapping themselves around my face, batting them away as I pass, eventually emerging out into the square opposite the fountain, to the amusement of the heavily made-up stallholder at the second-hand clothes stall opposite. The square is now full of stalls with red and white awnings. Along the road past the little restaurant where I saw Isaac on that first day there are rows of fruit and veg stalls. Sellers are putting tomatoes, oranges, strawberries and green beans into paper bags for shoppers. Women with bulging baskets are greeting each other with kisses and smiles. The bars are open for business and there's a smell of hot coffee and baking bread in the air. Rotisserie chickens, turning and gleaming under the heat in their hot ovens, are tempting me further into the town.

I wander round the clothes stalls and suddenly come across one with clothes piled high in the middle of a table, wrapped around each other like a tumbling toddlers. A big cardboard sign says '1 euro'. I watch a couple of women riffling through them, looking for the pick of the bunch. My charity-shop habit bubbles up. I step forward and start to pick up pieces of clothing. With Candy's words – 'Ditch the nanny look' – ringing in my ears, I finally find two summer dresses that I have no idea if I'll ever wear, and another T-shirt, all for three euro. I'm buzzing from my bargain buys. Swinging my blue plastic bag beside me I walk on, past Le Tire-bouchon restaurant, the road leading to more fruit stalls, Arcachon oyster sellers, stalls of *saucissons*, then wriggling eels being prepared by a young woman with corn plaits and a pierced nose. I push on quickly past the big pans of paella to the flower and plant stalls, and do a full circuit of the town, arriving back where I started in the town square by the church and fountain.

My stomach rumbles. I just have time to get something for breakfast. I look towards the *boulangerie*. There is a stall outside and I go over and point towards a *pain aux raisins*. The owner picks it up with her tongs, puts it in a bag and holds it out to me. I hold the warm, fresh pastry to my chest, pay and then, on a crest of confidence, go to the bar opposite, Le Papillon, to order a *café crème* to go with it. I still have half an hour before I'm due in work. What a way to start the day, I think, looking down towards the river and at the hustle and bustle as shoppers begin to fill the market and the stall-holders have finally finished setting up ready for the morning's work. I'm just finishing my delicious pastry, warm and flaky with a bit of *crème pâtissière* in the middle. I go to stand up and brush off the crumbs, flicking them all over a man trying to negotiate the crowded café's tables and chairs.

'*Fini?*' he asks; then, 'You leaving?'

I look up, my heart stopping for just a split second. It's Charlie. He's been jogging, by the look of it. Hot, glistening in the morning sunlight, dressed in loose joggers and a white, crisp T-shirt. His dark hair is as neat as ever, despite his exertion, judging by the flush in his cheeks.

'Oh, sorry,' I say looking at the crumbs I've brushed off in his direction. 'Um, hi,' I manage.

'Hi. Emily, isn't it?' I obviously haven't made a big enough impression for him to remember my name yet. 'Everything all right in the *gîte*?'

'It's Emmy,' I correct. 'And yes, thank you.' I nod, putting my hand over my mouth as I quickly try to swallow the last mouthful of delicious *pain aux raisins*. He smiles politely, and me trying to smile back doesn't help me swallow what's left of my pastry, which is now sticking to the roof of my mouth..

'Take your time,' Charlie says, looking around for another seat, and when he doesn't see one he asks, 'May I?' and points to one of the empty chairs at my table. I nod. *Absolutely.* I glance quickly at his toned arms and glistening forearms, suddenly in very close proximity, as he sits and puts his newspaper on the table, a British paper, and I wonder if that means that this isn't home for him, just somewhere he visits for work. Not like his parents, who clearly love it here. He crosses his foot to rest on his knee.

'So . . .' He looks as if he feels he should make polite conversation when he'd rather be sitting quietly with his paper. Suddenly feeling nervous – after all, this man has my future in his hands, and anything else if he asked, I shock myself by thinking – I swallow and wash down the last of the pastry with the dregs of my coffee. 'Um, another?' he points and asks. I quickly put up my hand and refuse. He looks at his watch.

'You still have time,' he says. 'And the boss isn't there yet,' he adds in a friendly manner. I smile and he orders an espresso and a glass of water, points to my cup and the waitress understands that I'd like another *café crème* and I smile gratefully.

'So, everything's cool in the *gîte*, all happy?' he asks, looking round the square as it begins to fill.

'Yes. Lovely.' Then when he doesn't ask anything else I try to make conversation by asking, 'You like to keep fit then?' I nod towards his trainers and the little hand weights he's pulled from his pockets and put on the table. He nods.

'My father's stroke was quite a wake-up call for me. Good living is all very well, but well . . . seeing him like that . . . I don't want to be in the same boat. I'm determined to be fit enough to enjoy myself when I finally retire.'

'Yes, dads can be a worry,' I say, knowing exactly what he means and realising we have something in common. It's like he's letting me glimpse under the professional surface. A young man worried about his dad too. He's mature and, well, in control of his life. He's stepped in to help out his dad's business. I'm still trying really hard not to find the man incredibly attractive, and failing. He's my boss, after all, I keep reminding myself.

'Was it hard to drop everything and come out here?' I ask.

He gives a shrug. 'Dad needed me . . . and, frankly, the business did. It was the right time for me. My wife . . . ex-wife . . . and I had just split up. She found my long working hours too much to deal with. She liked the money, but not the hours I put in to make it.'

'Oh, that's terrible.'

He shrugs again.

'But the timing worked out. Dad had his stroke and, as I say, Featherstone's needed pulling out of the Dark Ages!' He gives little laugh as our coffees arrive.

'Your dad must have been really grateful for you coming over and taking it on.'

'Ha,' he laughs again. 'Let's just say Dad and I have

slightly different opinions on the direction the company should take.'

I take a sip of coffee and so does he.

'So . . .'

'Do you?' We both go to ask a question at the same time. He laughs and so do I. He holds out a hand for me to speak.

'So, you enjoy keeping fit then?' I say, kicking myself for asking the same question but not sure what else to talk about.

He nods. 'Helps me think. Works through business ideas and plans I have in my head.'

I nod as if trying to relate to it. But I can't.

'What about you, do you keep fit?'

'Well, um, no, not really, not unless you count running for the bus most mornings,' and then kick myself again, hoping he doesn't think I'm always late. Thankfully, he smiles at my joke. I find myself relaxing a little.

'But I have a dad, too, one that needs me. So . . . I know what it's like . . .' I start to tell him when his phone rings.

'Sorry,' he says and looks at his text, rolling his eyes. 'My ex. Seems she still can't understand that we're divorced and I can't just nip round whenever she needs me.'

'And your children?'

'Phoebe and Henry. Great kids. They love coming out here. I divide my time between here and the UK, so it works out.' He looks down at his watch and knocks back the last of his coffee. 'OK, best we get to the office.'

'Yes, of course.' We both go to stand. I gather my shoulder bag and blue shopping bag. He picks up his weights and papers, and holds his hand up when I offer some money for the bill. Then we walk into the square, past a Moroccan stall with wonderful long tops, trousers and scarves, the big orange sun warming our faces.

We pass a number of stalls with wine bottles, large vats and some with presentation boxes. Charlie greets them all, shaking hands and kissing the women on each cheek.

'Local wine-makers,' he explains to me. 'We work with some. Not all, but it's good to know them.' He grins, seemingly feeling he's teaching me about the business and I'm keen to show him I want to learn. So when I see a window of opportunity to make an impression on him, I swallow hard, deciding to take it, and point to one stall.

'Château Lavigne?' I ask with more confidence than I'm feeling.

Charlie raises an eyebrow and nods. 'Yes,' he confirms. 'You know it?'

I swallow again, hoping it'll help my dry mouth.

'In Saint Enrique,' I say. Then, 'One of the biggest châteaux in the area.' I check sideways and see Charlie looks suitably impressed. 'They have vineyards all over the world. They make a sparkling wine. It's said the wine is still hand-turned, thousands of times.' I give the same slightly doubtful grin that Madame Beaumont did and Charlie raises his eyebrows even further. 'That the men have arthritic fingers from the many times a day they have to turn the wine. But it's a good wine.' And then, taking a deep breath: 'If a little over-priced,' I say finally.

Charlie stops and turns to look straight at me with those green lagoon eyes and I feel a little buzz of excitement as he smiles, like he's seen me properly for the first time since I've arrived.

'You've been doing your homework.' He taps his newspaper against his thigh and nods his head in pleasant surprise. I feel a little skip of excitement in my tummy.

'Keep it up,' he smiles again, still looking straight at me and it feels like the hustle and the bustle of the market just fades away around me. 'We need someone who knows what they're talking about to lead this team.' The little skip of excitement in my tummy turns into a jump. 'I look forward to hearing more from you,' he adds.

Suddenly I'm tingling all over. What if . . . what if I could do this? What if, like he says, I really could do the team leader's job? What if I could win that bet? I'm so excited I could . . . kiss him! But I won't, obviously.

'I enjoyed our chat,' Charlie says.

'Me too.' I smile and hold my breath, hoping he'll suggest we meet for coffee again, waiting for him to speak, when my phone rings, making me jump, and I grapple for it in my bag amongst the brown envelopes, bringing me back to reality.

'Hello, Dad?'

Charlie smiles, gives me a knowing nod, and then holds up a hand, indicating he's going to jog on and leave me to my call. I nod and wave, and watch him turn away and break into a gentle jog, disappearing off, leaving me feeling like a deflating balloon.

Could I finally have met someone who understands what it's like to have a dad that needs looking after? Could he possibly be interested in me? I might just finally have met someone I'd like to get to know better and that hasn't happened in a long time. Just maybe there was a good reason for me coming out here.

'Yes, go on, Dad, I'm all ears . . .' And I wander back to Featherstone's, swinging my bag of bargain buys, past the fishermen, who look at me with interest, with a little spring in my step.

Chapter Ten

'Pick me, pick me!' Candy is waving her hand in the air. She's wearing a white low-cut summer dress with large brush strokes of colour all over it and I'm worried that her bosoms bobbing up and down may make a bid for escape at any minute. I turn away and catch Nick's eye, both of which appear to be standing out on stalks, as if he's mesmerised and terrified at the same time. He looks away quickly when he sees me, coughs into a cupped hand and suddenly furrows his brow and fiddles with his smart ink pen.

'We'll take it in turns,' Isaac says, laughing, obviously enjoying Candy's enthusiasm. They seem to have become quite friendly over the last two nights. Staying up late, drinking. Candy is being flirtatious, and Isaac, although he doesn't seem as flirtatious back, seems to be enjoying her attention. Nick, on the other hand, has suddenly become quite introverted, different from the confident Nick who arrived here organising us all on Saturday morning.

'So tell me what you know about wine, what you like, what you don't like, what you know about French wine in particular. It'll give me an idea of where the gaps in your knowledge are, what we need to work on,' Isaac says, suddenly quite serious.

We're sitting around in a circle of office chairs up in the new call centre room. We're by the window looking out over the vines and up towards the cemetery with the market square beyond, to the left. Hannah and Ben are taking occasional calls whilst packing up their desks, smiling kindly like old sheepdogs watching the new pups, cluelessly enthusiastic.

Isaac is standing, wearing below-the-knee khaki shorts, a loose shirt over a white tight-fitting T-shirt. His long dark wavy hair, still damp from the shower, is pushed back off his face by his blue, mirrored wraparound sunglasses. He's holding a coffee in one hand and a pile of papers in the other.

'Candy, tell us about your experience of wine. You work in magazine advertising, is that right?'

'Yes. I work on trade magazines. One of them is *Pick 'n' Mix Monthly*. I know how to sell food and drink to customers. I know what people want.'

'And what about wine, Candy, any experience there?' Isaac is reading the papers in his hand and sipping from the white mug he's cradling in the other.

I'm feeling nervous, very nervous. I really don't want to make a fool of myself but frankly the closest I've got to any wine knowledge is that is comes in bottles with either a cork or screw top. I try to recall what I learned during my day with Madame Beaumont.

'I don't drink wine. I'm more a vodka-and-Coke girl, but I know that red wine gives me a banging headache, white wine tastes better after an hour in the freezer and rosé can be made if you mix red and white. My Dean taught me that.'

Isaac shakes his head, then throws back his head and

laughs. 'Holy shit!' When he stops laughing he asks, 'Do you think you can make enough sales to get the team leader's job, Candy?'

Candy lifts her chest and I swear, runs her tongue quickly across her top lip. 'I know I can. I can sell sand to the Eskimos, so my Dean says,' she says without missing a beat or realising her mistake. I'm dumbfounded. How does she do it? She has such high sales figures. She drives a car I can't even dream about owning the wheels on.

'Thank you, Candy. I'm liking your chutzpah.' Isaac raises his cup to her.

'Thank you.' She smiles. 'What's one of them?' she turns and asks Nick. Isaac smiles into his coffee and reads his list again. I take a deep breath in and hold it, waiting for my cue.

'Nick?'

I breathe out.

Nick cuts off his explanation about chutzpah, much to Candy's chagrin.

'Yes, hi,' Nick adjusts his glasses and clears his throat, sits up straight and with a quick sideways look at Candy, clearly intends to impress. 'I like wine. I drink red mostly, Jacob's Creek, Hardys and Penfolds.' Nick finally smiles and adjusts his glasses again.

'All Australian then, great!' Isaac raises his eyebrows and gives his head a shake. Nick blushes uncomfortably.

'Gloria, what about you? What's your knowledge of France and its wines?'

We all turn to look at Gloria, who straightens the edge of her light green blouse, switches off her fan, puts it in her lap, clears her throat and, without looking up, starts.

'Well, when I was married, we drank wine, of course, but my husband always chose it.'

'What?' Isaac flashes his lazy smile. 'He never said, "Do you want red or white, darling?"' Gloria looks up at Isaac and swallows and I suddenly feel we've touched a nerve. She picks up her hand-held battery-operated fan and holds it to her reddening face.

'No,' she replies flatly. There's a moment's silence.

'Emmy,' Isaac moves on quickly, turning and staring at me with his dark eyes, and my tongue suddenly feels like it's been tied in a bow again.

'Oh,' Gloria raises her hand as if in a classroom, suddenly remembering something she wanted to say and saving me from the humiliation that's inevitably about to follow.

'Yes, Gloria?' Isaac asks without a hint of his usual banter or so-called humour, and I'm not sure if he's dismissing her as useless or actually being kind, sensing her discomfort. I can't work him out. I hope it's the latter.

'I do speak French,' she says. 'Part of my college course. Always came in useful when we holidayed, down South,' she adds with a painted smile.

'Did you both speak French?' Isaac asks encouragingly, and Gloria's smile slips again.

'No, Paul didn't see any point, seeing as I could speak it.' She swallows hard again. I suddenly feel uncomfortable for Gloria. There's a sadness there. Despite being painfully shy, Gloria stands out. She's one of the few people in their fifties at the call centre, apart from Trevor. I wonder what's brought Gloria's to the call centre working alongside agents half her age. For a moment, I wonder if that will be me in another twenty years. The only one who didn't move on, get promoted, head hunted, married or have a family. Will I still be sitting in the same chair, clinging on to my job and never making my targets and bonuses? Maybe Trevor will get me to lead the Monday morning sing-along. Somehow, I can't see that ever happening. But is that it? My future? Sing-alongs and a collection for long service to bleach and disinfectant to look forward to . . . if I can keep my job, that is.

I glance at Gloria; she has a look in her eye that seems to be replaying an unwanted memory and I want to ask if she's OK.

'OK, thanks, Gloria.' Isaac turns back to me with a deep breath. 'Emmy!'

I feel myself jump and my cheeks blush, remembering that I'm supposed to be coming up with something informative. I see Gloria out the corner of my eye, discreetly dabbing the corner of her own with her chubby finger. I'm suddenly keen to move the attention away from her.

'Well, I know wine comes in bottles with screw caps and corks,' I suddenly find myself rambling and nervously laughing. I'm keen to keep the group looking at me but am not able to think of anything useful to say about wine at all. Suddenly I have on-the-spot stage fright, and an image of my dad in his Christmas cracker crown suddenly flashes into my mind: him, Mum, me and Jody, all sitting round, hats at jaunty angles, reading our Christmas jokes out. 'What did the grape say when it got stepped on?' I remember Dad saying and laughing, and hear myself saying it now whilst a voice in my head is shouting, *No! don't do it!* But I'm determined to brighten things and keep attention from Gloria so my runaway mouth carries on. 'Nothing!' I pause for dramatic effect, just like Dad did. Even Gloria seems to have brightened. 'But it did let out a little whine,' I finish. There's stunned silence and I look at Nick, then Candy and Gloria and, finally, Isaac.

'I don't get it,' says Candy with a down-turned mouth. A smile is creeping across Gloria's face and Isaac is clutching his head in his hands in despair before announcing it's time for a coffee break.

I shoot off my chair and rush to the loos, where I throw cold water on my burning cheeks. Gloria slips into the cubicle where I hear her sniff and blow.

'Gloria, you all right?' I tap on the door gently.

'Yes, fine,' I hear her say, though clearly she's not. She clears her throat.

'Anything I can do?' I ask.

'Um, you couldn't get my handbag, could you? From the office? I could do with some new batteries for my fan.'

'Of course,' I say, happy to help.

I pull back the door to outside. Candy and Nick are in the kitchen, just by the toilets, making coffee. Well, Candy's asking about teabags and complaining about 'the funny-tasting milk'.

'My Dean is a coffee drinker – likes it really strong. I prefer tea.'

I take the wooden steps quickly up to the call centre room where we've been sitting. Isaac is standing by the window with Charlie, both drinking coffee.

'Jeez! Charlie! I don't know where you got such a bunch

of losers from. There's not a bit of wine knowledge between them.'

I stop and stand stock-still, realising I'm now walking in on the middle of a private conversation – very private, it would seem.

'You'd be better off ditching them and starting again. They're like a pack of seagulls standing round looking at a cigarette butt, wondering how to eat it!'

My hackles shoot up, my cheeks flare with fury. How dare he? I stand rooted to the spot, not sure whether to make my presence known or to leave as quickly as possible without being seen and wondering whether the floorboards under my feet will squeak and give me away.

'Let's just say the deal with Cadwallader's was the best around. So, it's down to you to train them up. That's what you're hired for. It's in the contract. To make wine and train up the seagulls!' And Charlie slaps him on the back and they both laugh. 'You do a good job and I'll see you're well rewarded.' I make a sudden lunge forward, grab Gloria's bag, and then turn, but the floorboards give me away. I stop and face them as both Isaac and Charlie turn to stare at me. Neither says a thing. So I slowly lift my chin and walk out of the office and down the stairs to Gloria, who is waiting by the loo door for me.

'Thank you,' she says with a sniff, taking the bag and pulling out her powder compact. 'By the way,' she says with a watery smile, whilst I'm deciding whether to tell her about Isaac's comments. He clearly doesn't want us here. 'I liked your joke,' she smiles at me for what feels like the first time since we've been here.

'Thank you,' I say, and touch her elbow and decide to say nothing more. Isaac may not want us here, but suddenly I want to prove him wrong, very wrong indeed. I want to wipe that lazy Californian smile right off his face and I may just have an idea of how.

Chapter Eleven

'So, let's start by talking about where we are, in south-west France. I'm going to talk you through the wines of the region,' says Isaac after our coffee break.

Isaac occasionally catches my eye and then looks away, uncomfortably. He knows I heard him. He obviously doesn't want to be doing this. And neither do I. But the offer of a good bonus from Charlie was clearly enough incentive for him to keep ploughing on with us.

My mind begins to wander and I stare out of the window, much like I used to do in school. Only today I'm looking out on vines and towards the cemetery, not the school car park, when I see a small figure dressed in black that I recognise. It's Madame Beaumont. She's working her way through the cemetery, slowly and surefootedly, just like when she walks through the vineyard, with slow, purposeful determination. She has a basket with her, over her arm, the other hand touching it.

Try as I might I can't keep what Isaac is saying in my head. It's all just gobbledegook to me. Nick is taking notes and Candy is staring at him, swirling her chewing gum from her mouth round her finger; it's apparently the only thing she's discovered in France that she prefers the taste of to the

British. Gloria is holding her pencil in one hand, her fan in the other is buzzing and she's concentrating very hard. I turn back to the window and watch Madame Beaumont. She stops by a gravestone. It's big, black and shiny. She places her hand on it and bows her head. Then she drops to her knees, slowly but confidently. She pulls back the cover over her basket. First she takes out a duster and polishes the headstone, all over, as if it's a big window. Then she takes out the flowers from the vase at the base and goes off to refill the vase with water from a nearby standpipe and then rearranges the flowers. When she's done she pulls out some fruit from her basket – a peach, I think – and with a small knife sits and cuts it into pieces and eats it in silence and solitude. Having finished the peach she folds up the tea towel and repacks her basket. Then she drops her head again, touches the headstone, and prays. Prayers said, she gets to her feet without looking round, turns and makes her way back out of the cemetery and through the vineyard in the direction of Clos Beaumont.

'Emmy? Emmy?' I suddenly realise someone's saying my name. Isaac is looking at me like a disappointed teacher, head tilted, arms folded.

'Sorry, what was that you said?' I say, trying to look interested, picking up my pen and poising it.

'I said, lunchtime, but I see you've already decided to excuse yourself from this session.' He raises an eyebrow.

Candy sniggers and the others stand and make their way out. My phone rings. It's Dad, explaining the boiler won't work. I finish my call and Gloria is waiting to walk into town with me to get a 'sandwich' from the *boulangerie*.

After lunch Charlie comes into the office with Isaac and my heart gives a sudden lurch. He smiles and hands us a contact list each. 'Contact each name and number, tell them who we are, what we're doing. Learn the scripts I gave you, or rather the information booklets. And send out brochures or direct them to the website.'

Candy leans over to look at my sheet. 'Just making sure we've all got the same amount of contacts,' she says, eyeing me carefully.

'Yes, Candy, they're all the same length,' Charlie smiles, and I shove my head lower to study them. 'Contact them. Then make follow-up calls and secure an order. If they introduce you to a friend, there's a discount, so hopefully you can generate some more business that way. Remember,' he waves a copy of the heavy document we're supposed to be learning, 'this is your bible. It contains descriptions of all the wines, tasting notes, what they should be paired with, what the vineyard and wine-makers are like.' He waves the document. 'Learn it, inside out. You'll be tested.'

And I intend to, I do. But, my thoughts turn back to Madame Beaumont earlier, in the graveyard. I can't help but wonder whose grave she was visiting and why she's all alone.

Later that afternoon we spend some time helping out in the shop, well, lingering by the till, and the same in *la cave* itself, where the wine is made, watching Jeff at work and handing him the watering can as he syphons off and tastes the wine from the barrels and then tops them up, telling us what he's doing and laughing at his own jokes. At five, we finish. I could go with the others for dinner, but instead I decide to run back to the *gîte* and grab the bike. If I'm going to prove Isaac wrong – and I'd very much like to – I'm going to need Madame Beaumont's help. Hoping her offer is still open, I set out for Clos Beaumont, a tiny bit less wobbly than before.

'Madame Beaumont!' I call, and wave, stooping to pat Cecil on the head as I pass, and he lifts his weary head and gives a lazy, welcome bark. I look first in the barn where all the vats and barrels are and where I knocked over all the bottles. She's not there. So I run round to the back of the farmhouse and look. It's Henri, the horse, I see first, standing in between the vines waiting for his instruction. The sun is like a huge orange ball on the horizon, slowly starting to set. The breeze up here is cool and refreshing after a hot day inside.

'*En avant,*' I hear, and then I see Madame Beaumont, standing up from where she's been using the handspray. Across the way, at Château Lavigne, a tractor is going up and down with its two big scarecrow-like arms spraying the vines, thoroughly and completely.

'Madame Beaumont!' I call again.

'*Arrête,*' she calls to Henri and stands to watch as I make my way through the vines towards her.

'*Bon . . . soir, Madame Beaumont,*' I plump for, looking at the setting sun again.

'*Bonsoir,*' she smiles and nods her head confirming my use of words and puts out her bony, gnarled hand to shake mine. I smile as I stand in front of her and shake her hand.

'You came back.'

I nod. 'Yes, please, you said you could help me, show me

about the vines and wine,' I say, hoping she meant what she said.

She looks at me and then nods gently and I breathe a sigh of relief.

'What can I do? Do you want me to start bottling in the barn or shall I spray?' I'm eager to get stuck in.

'*Le chai*,' she says.

'Sorry?'

'*Le chai*, where I make the wine. You will need to start using the French words,' she says as if starting her teaching.

'*Le chai*,' I repeat. 'So, what would you like me to do?'

'Walk with me. Come and introduce yourself to the vines. Make friends, get to know them.'

I laugh.

'Only when you know them will you know if they are sick or need help. These are the Cabernet Sauvignon, a common grape, hardy, thick-skinned. Gives full body to wine. It ages well,' she smiles, and holds out a hand and raises an eyebrow and I realise she's serious. I have to get to know the vines.

And I do, each evening after work, as the others head for the bar at Le Papillon, led by Isaac. He is now being welcomed there like a local, shaking hands and greeting regulars, joking with them, Gloria tells me. She tries to tempt me to join them, but I always turn her down.

'Learning her bible,' I overheard Nick telling the others. 'I swear she's suddenly full of wine knowledge. Cramming, that's what she's doing.'

'I bet she's seeing Charlie. I swear she fancies him,' I heard Candy saying, and I blushed, not wanting to hear any more. She's right, of course. I do fancy Charlie, not that there's been a repeat of our early morning coffee.

'Avoiding me,' Isaac said. And he's not wrong. The less time I have to spend with Isaac, the better. Instead I head out on the rusting bike to Madame Beaumont, Henri, Cecil and the vines, where we are getting to know each other very well indeed. A little haven far away from the stresses of daily life at Featherstone's. I do the same thing every evening for the next two weeks. There, I find myself bringing them up to date with my dad, the difficult situation with my sister; with Candy and the missing collection money, her Dean, Gloria and Nick, life at the *gîte* and about the bet. As the weeks go on I tell them something of what I remember about life in my house, the house I'm about to lose, with my mum, Christmases growing up, birthdays . . . but not that Christmas. We don't know each other well enough for me to talk about that Christmas. I tell them about the good times we spent together, the smell of shepherd's pie cooking when I walked in the front door from school, the Saturday nights together in the front room watching TV, the three-tiered birthday cakes she'd make. As I talk, Madame Beaumont points out the grapes that are doing well, shows me where to trim leaves, pick out weeds, pick off bugs, and where to spray if needed. Every now and again, the tractor next door drives close along the boundary and Madame Beaumont shouts and shakes her fist as it sprays everything in its path regardless.

'Sometimes it is better to let the vines find their own way. Otherwise, they will all end up the same . . . and taste the same,' she tells me crossly, watching the tractor and the vineyard worker, Bernard, pass. Neither acknowledges the other.

Each night after being at Clos Beaumont I go home to the *gîte*, exhausted, get into bed, pick up the Featherstone's bible . . . and wake up with it on my face, not having made it past page two.

Chapter Twelve

Just as next door's vineyard owner and Madame Beaumont have skilfully spent the years ignoring each other, despite working beside each other every day, so Isaac and I have managed to ignore each other pretty successfully for the last fortnight in the *gîte* – ever since I walked in on his conversation with Charlie.

It's Saturday morning, two weeks on from when we first arrived here in Petit Frère, and September is now making way for October. The bells ring out with gusto at seven to tell us to get up. What I really want to do is roll over and go back to sleep but instead, as the second lot of bells ring out, I throw back the covers with effort. Candy grunts and I make my way to the bathroom to wash and dress, quietly leave the *gîte*, stopping off in the square for my *pain aux raisins* with a nod and a '*bonjour*', and then on to Monsieur and Madame Obels to buy some strawberries and peaches to share with Madame Beaumont.

Then I cycle to Clos Beaumont. I even manage to cycle with the *pain aux raisins* in my hand, taking mouthfuls as I go, and hardly a wobble as cars pass me.

I stop halfway up the hill and text Layla, sending her a picture of the rows of vines.

Two weeks in and I'm learning to talk to the vines! The harvest is about to begin and soon these babies will be turned into wine! À bientôt (as they say in France!).

I sign off with a kiss and get another quick *OMG!* in reply. I smile, put my phone away, and cycle on.

'So where do we start this morning? Shall I go and talk to the vines or get Henri out?' I ask Madame Beaumont, keen to show her I'm learning.

'*Non*,' she says, holding up a hand and then presents her cheek for me to kiss, and then the other one.

'*Bonjour, Emmy*,' she insists.

'Oh, sorry, I mean, *pardon. Bonjour, Madame Beaumont*,' I say, and kiss her on each cheek. '*Comment allez-vous ce matin?*' Slowly but surely my school French is returning to me.

'You must make time to greet people, show them respect, so they in turn respect you,' she scolds. 'Plus it uses your French.' Then with formalities over she allows me to start the conversation over again.

'*Non.* Today we stop spraying. We'll pick after the full moon, so now there must be no more spraying. Now we wait and we must let the vines do their thing on their own. We must let them find their own way and hope we have brought them up to be strong enough to do that. In two weeks we pick. Now we wait.'

'Really?' I look out at the vines. 'Is that it? We just wait?'

'We do. We still talk to the vines, let them know we are here for them, but they are on their own now.' She nods firmly, like a head teacher watching her pupils go to their exams.

'Gosh, like letting them go to their first nightclub . . .' I joke but trail off.

'Yes, I will feel happier when they are safely in,' Madame Beaumont nods towards *le chai* and breaks into a smile.

'Do you have any children, Madame Beaumont?' I ask as we walk towards *le chai* companionably.

'No, I don't,' she tells me. 'It was just me here. My mother and grandparents lived here too. But no, I never met anyone. It wasn't really possible. We didn't mix with the town people. These are my family now.' She waves towards the vines before pulling back the door of *le chai*. I wonder if that's who she visits in the graveyard every day. But I don't ask.

'So, if we're not spraying this week, what are we doing?'

'We must bottle last year's vintage.' Her eyes sparkle with excitement. 'And when we have bottled the wine, we must clean *le chai*, ready for the new arrival, God willing.'

I ache from head to toe from sitting on the floor of *le chai*, filling each bottle by hand and then putting in corks. It's a tiring week, spending my days in Featherstone's and each evening bottling at Clos Beaumont. As the weekend comes round, I'm exhausted. But Madame Beaumont and I will be labelling all the bottles and it wouldn't surprise me if we were doing that with a quill and ink!

Regardless of this, tonight is Friday evening and I'm going to try to relax. Clutching two bottles of the wine we've bottled earlier today, which I've carried home in a basket balanced on the handle bars, I rest the bike against the wall of the *gîte* and plan to run straight in and up to the bathroom and grab a hot bath whilst the others are at Le Papillon and pour myself a glass of wine. Isaac and I have managed to avoid each other for another week – other than his lessons, of course – and I plan to keep it that way.

But as I push open the front door I can hear a strange noise, like something's in pain. I tuck the bottles under my arm and run straight to the kitchen where Candy is hunched over the table, head in hands, occasionally throwing back her head and wailing. Her face is red and blotchy from her tears. There are balls of screwed-up toilet paper all around her. Nick has an arm around her, comforting her. Gloria is making tea.

'It's Dean,' Gloria mouths to me.

'Oh,' I say.

Candy does the low moaning followed by the wail again. 'Of all the people! Harmony!' she wails.

'Dean has decided that he couldn't wait for Candy to get back from France and has . . .' Nick clears his throat, '. . . moved on to pastures new,' he finishes diplomatically.

'He didn't even like Harmony! Said her teeth needed sorting out,' Candy wails.

'Well, they say love is blind,' I say helpfully, but Candy just scowls at me and then blows her nose loudly. Nick peels off more toilet roll and hands it to her, reaching out and holding her spare hand as she blows.

'Um, wine, anyone?' I hold up the bottles and, taking in the general agreement, look around for a corkscrew. Gloria hands one to me and I get to work opening the bottles that I've only just sealed. I pour the wine into short, stubby tumblers. Just as I'm handing them out Isaac arrives back at the *gîte*, obviously having stopped off for a few beers at Le Papillon, and my heart sinks. It's amazing how some people can just fit in anywhere they go. I'd never be able to just arrive somewhere, start drinking in a bar and get talking to people. But in the short time we've been here Isaac seems to know everyone and everyone knows Isaac. He's carrying two bottles of wine, as he is most evenings; apparently they are samples from the vineyard owners. I suspect they are to try to get him to buy bottles for himself from the back door.

'Hey, great. Wine!' He is full of bonhomie and then he spots Candy. 'Candy, what's up?'

'It's Dean, her fiancé,' Nick fills in the gaps while Candy sobs. 'It's over. Harmony moved in on him,' he mouths, handing her more loo roll and keeping a firm hold on her hand.

'Ah, Candy. Well, he obviously wasn't good enough for you,' Isaac says, spinning round a chair and sitting back to front on it.

'Really, you think?' she sniffs and brightens, and Nick holds her hand even more firmly.

'I know so. There'll be someone much more suited to you out there.' He takes a glass I've poured and sniffs it.

Candy looks considerably brighter and pulls her hand away from Nick's and he suddenly stiffens.

'I think you might be right.' She rubs her nose and picks up a glass and copies what Isaac does. He sniffs again, then swirls it, sniffs again and then he sips.

'Hey, this is . . . good,' he says, surprised. 'Where's it from?'

'Clos Beaumont,' I reply.

'Where's that?'

'Towards Saint Enrique,' I say matter-of-factly, but silently notching up a point to me. 'It's practically organic.'

'How come you have it?' he says, sniffing it again, tipping it to one side to see if it has 'legs'. Nick and then Gloria copy him. Candy just takes a huge gulp. 'You buying from the back door too, then?' he grins, confirming what I thought about his bottles of fine wine he's collecting in his room.

'I've, erm,' I wonder how to tell them all what I've been up to. 'I've been helping her get this year's vintage bottled. She was . . . she's quite old, I was just helping her.'

'Who?' Isaac asks.

'Madame Beaumont.'

'What? The old lady with the purse?' Nick screws up his nose. 'That's where you've been going all this time? Like when we ask you to come to the bar and you turn us down and we all thought you were learning your bible and being a right swot?'

Candy stops sniffing. 'You haven't been with Charlie then?' she asks directly.

'No!' I half laugh at the ridiculousness of it despite my cheeks burning.

'I thought you two—' she carries on.

'No!' I cut her off.

'I thought you were just avoiding me,' Isaac says as he leans over the glass, not looking at me, and puts his long nose into it and breathes in. Then he stands up, turns his chair round as if suddenly taking things seriously, looks at the wine again and then leans back in his chair, rests one foot on his knee and sips at the wine, making a kissing noise as he draws in air and swirls the wine round the glass, still studying it.

'And you know nothing about wine?' Isaac asks, finally looking at me and frowning. 'Apart from bad wine jokes?'

My throat closes. I don't know what it is about this man that just infuriates me and makes me tongue-tied.

'No, well, that's the thing, when Trevor sent me out here. I hadn't even put in for the job,' my mouth starts running away with itself.

'What? You didn't even want to come? Why did he send you?' Isaac asks.

'Harmony was having her teeth done.' I suddenly realise what I've said and look apologetically at Candy. 'I was a last minute . . . stand-in. A sort of sideways shift.' I take a big gulp of wine. 'I'd done something . . . got into some bother . . . I'm trying to sort it out . . .' I mumble, thinking about the bet, the wine slipping down quickly.

'So who keeps ringing you? Is it Charlie?' Candy asks in her direct way again, eyes narrowing, her nose red like Rudolf's, and still slurping at the wine.

'My dad,' I say quietly, wishing I wasn't here and trying to convince people that I deserve to be, when I really don't. I sigh, exhausted; tired of trying to hide what I've done.

'Why did you get to come then?' Nick looks at me. 'You don't strike me as being one of Trevor's top sales team. I mean no offence.'

I bite my lip and look down. There is an inevitability to this conversation, like a concrete wrecking ball careering towards me, about to blow apart my life, again.

'You're right, I am a fraud. I shouldn't be here. I can't

even sell disinfectant to a boarding kennels.' I take another big swig of wine, followed by another. Suddenly I feel far more relaxed, almost a little light-headed.

'Actually . . .' I hear myself saying. They're all looking at me. I should probably stop, say nothing. But I'm not sure I can keep up this charade any longer and the wine is making me feel like throwing caution to the wind. Getting it all out in the open.

'Actually,' I repeat, and I look round at them all staring at me. *Don't do it!* a voice in my head says. *You still have a chance to say, 'Oh, nothing'!* I take a deep breath and blow out. 'It was me. I borrowed the office collection. Dean and Candy's collection!' There, I've said it. For a moment no one says anything. They all just stare at me, stunned.

'Oh. My. God!' Candy says as realisation starts to dawn on her face. 'That was you!' she shrieks. 'You stole mine and Dean's engagement collection?'

'Borrowed. And yes, that was me,' I say, pouring myself another glass. 'And, Candy, I'm truly sorry. It's just . . . I was desperate. And I know it's no excuse, but I am sorry.' Isaac is listening and sniffing his wine but saying nothing. 'But just think, if I lose the bet, you'll get twice the amount back!' I take another slug of wine and suddenly my glass is empty.

The others say nothing. I recklessly top up my empty glass. Well, why not? Looks like the shit has well and truly hit the fan. These guys aren't going to want to work with me now they know who I am.

'I'm in last-chance saloon here. If I don't manage to make my targets, I'm out on my ear anyway.'

'Well . . . looks like you knew it wasn't going to work out

with Dean, then.' Candy sniffs and then adds with narrowing eyes, 'I had you all wrong. I thought you were a right Goody Two-shoes. And you did, too, Nick, a right teacher's pet. You said you thought she'd get the team leader's job because she was having it away with Charlie and I said that would've been cheating, especially as we had a bet on it.'

Nick squirms and so do I.

'This wine is surprisingly good,' Isaac suddenly cuts across the conversation and everyone turns from me, to him. 'I mean, rustic, very rustic, real rough edges, but you could do something with this.' He's almost talking to himself, but everyone is listening to him now, relieved to have a distraction. He holds up the glass and tilts it. 'It's got legs. And a real punch. The tannins are great too. And it's practically organic, you say?'

Isaac raises an impressed eyebrow at me and suddenly I want to throw myself on him and hug him for taking the sting out of the situation. Isaac, who I can't usually stand, has just saved me from more humiliation.

'She does it all herself, with sheep to keep the weeds down, a horse and cart . . .' I say quietly, realising my time here still is probably done. 'There's a big château next door, desperate to buy her land, but she won't sell to them.'

'Wooh, really rustic.' Isaac sips again. 'In a good way.'

'So, looks like the field's wide open, then. And I've still got a bet to win!' Candy suddenly brightens, pulling my attention back to her. 'Good job I'm not the one who's going to pay me back the office collection, twice!' She tilts her head at me and looks like she's sucking a lemon. 'And Charlie's single too, then?'

Isaac splutters a laugh.

'What about Dean?' Isaac asks.

'Looks like it was never meant to be.' She wipes around the edges of her eyes, removing the smudged eyeliner and mascara.

'Um, yes, he is single,' I reply. Much as I wish he wasn't, and that I'd been spending lots of time with him on secret dates, I haven't. I've hardly seen him since that day in the market. In work he's in the office or out on meetings with vineyard owners, and in the evenings I'm at Clos Beaumont. I'd love to have had more time to talk to him and tell him I understand how hard it is when your father needs your support.

'I can see the signs. No wedding ring, but an indentation where one used to be. That car he drives. I'm very good a spotting the signs. I mean, take Nick, I knew you were gay from the day I saw you in that pink jumper,' she says, stopping us in our tracks. Nick opens his mouth to speak. 'Which is a shame because you'd make a fabulous boyfriend.' He shuts his mouth, looks at me briefly and looks down. 'And Charlie, well, he's living out here, isn't he? He's got to be single. Let's be honest, if any of us had family ties we wouldn't be doing this would we?'

Gloria takes a sip of her wine and swallows, hard. A stab of guilt twists through me as I think about my dad, on his own all day.

'We all have a good chance of getting that job,' says Gloria, patting my hand kindly as I catch a waft from her fan and I know if I look at her I might cry. 'Don't you think, Isaac?'

'Don't look at me. I'm just here to make the wine and then I'm off.' He holds up his hand, returning to his irritating self, and I realise what I thought was an act of chivalry was probably just a fluke.

'Where to?' Nick asks.

'Not sure yet. Depends. If I can get into one of the big wine houses as their chief wine-maker that would be good. There's a couple of big ones I'm in contact with, so fingers crossed.'

'Don't you ever want to just stay put?' Candy asks, wrinkling her nose at the wine.

He throws his head back and laughs, his hair shaking. 'Never!'

Candy looks around the kitchen, narrowing her eyes at me, and why wouldn't she? She didn't like me before she knew I'd borrowed the office collection. She must hate me now.

'So come on, who do you think is going to get the job? Would you say we all have a good chance?' Candy asks.

But I know exactly what Isaac thinks of the chances of one of us pulling off the team leader's job and frankly, he's probably right. After this couple of weeks with Madame Beaumont I realise how much there is to learn about wine, and I am no nearer knowing about it or learning my script. Cleaning barrels, filling bottles and telling the vines my worries I seem to be brilliant at, but learning about wine? Nothing! And time is running out.

Chapter Thirteen

It's Saturday morning and whilst Candy works hard topping up her tan on a towel on the tiny piece of lawn outside the *gîte*, only moving to turn in the direction of the sun, Nick devours *A Year in Provence* and Gloria has walked across the bridge towards the little abandoned café on the other side of the river. I, on the other hand, am spending the day bent over the old Formica table in Madame Beaumont's cool kitchen. I'm using a stamp and ink pad, making hundreds of labels to go on the bottles. They simply say 'Clos Beaumont 2015. Vin de France', which means it's a basic, table wine.

Then we move into *le chai* to stick a label on each of the bottles. It's back-breaking work, but it keeps me busy and stops me from worrying about Dad, who is still ringing at least six times a day.

After lunch Madame Beaumont picks up her basket, puts on her headscarf and makes her daily visit to the cemetery whilst I carry on with the labels. I don't ask who she visits or why. But every day it's the same. She looks up at the huge blue sky with its white cotton-wool clouds and checks for rain. She calls for Cecil and he comes out, whooping and woofing, slobber flying, seeing off the birds and anyone who comes within swinging distance of his drooling jowls.

In another week Madame Beaumont will start her new harvest and the grapes are swelling beautifully. I, on the other hand, having helped get last year's vintage in, will be back in the sales room at Featherstone's and listening to more of Isaac's talks about changing tastes and modern techniques. I put the last label on the last bottle with a flourish and then stand up and stretch out my aching back like the old cat, who eyes me from afar but is never out of sight. Now the bottles are finally finished I can't help but feel, well, actually very proud. I hold a bottle at arm's length. I helped make this – bottle it, anyway. But it feels really good to have actually made something that people will buy and enjoy. I read the label, trying to remember what Isaac has told us about the information on them.

'The label should tell you everything you need to know about the wine,' I can hear him saying. The only thing I can actually remember is that most wines have an appellation, identifying the area, village or vineyard where the wine comes from. It guarantees the wine comes from a specific grape and region, even specifying the quantities of grapes used too.

'Why don't you have the appellation on these?' I ask Madame Beaumont on her return, studying one of the bottles again as we put them into cardboard boxes.

'Pah!' Madame Beaumont replies in what has become her customary way when she disapproves of something, usually something I've told her that I've learned in our wine classes with Isaac at Featherstone's. 'Rules and regulations. Telling people how their wine should taste. They want you to use this amount of that grape, that amount of that grape,' she's making pouring actions, her mouth downcast, and I laugh.

'Pah! I use the grapes I have from each harvest, see what mix tastes the best. Who wants to be like everyone else anyway?' She looks sideways at me and I wonder if she's talking about the wine or, in fact, me.

I take a picture of the bottle on my phone and text it to Layla.

Embouteillage! I type with a flourish, meaning 'bottling', which I've learned from Madame Beaumont, and send.

First thing Monday morning I cross the white stone courtyard at Featherstone's to find Charlie in his office. He's looking out the window, his back to me, and is on the phone. He's in shirtsleeves, but not casually dressed, despite the hot day. I look at his muscular shoulders under his sharply pressed shirt as he looks out of the window, one hand in his pocket, holding the phone in the other, and my stomach flips over and back again with a flick-flack of excitement.

'Great, look forward to seeing you then.' He finishes the call.

He suddenly turns and sees me, beaming, those mesmerising green eyes fixing on me.

'Oh, Emma,' he carries on beaming, which is a good sign I think, even if he still hasn't quite got my name right yet.

'Emmy,' I correct him, and smile back widely.

'Of course, yes.' He gives a little cough to clear his throat.

'How's your dad?' I ask brightly.

'Oh, you know, good days, bad days.' His smile drops a little. 'Yours?'

'So-so . . .' I reply.

'Good, good. So, what can I do for you?' His eyes have me in their sights, like a snipper focusing on its target – or should that be prey? I feel another flick-flack of excitement in my tummy. And he's going to be even happier when he hears what I have to tell him.

'Madame Beaumont's wine, the one I was telling you about, it's ready for collection.' I deliver the news with an imaginary drum roll.

'Whose?' His smile drops for a moment.

'Madame Beaumont's. Clos Beaumont? You're expecting it, remember?' Suddenly my heart quickens to the beat of a minor panic.

'Ah, yes, Clos Beaumont, one of my father's small artisan producers,' he says as if indulging his father in a hobby like record collecting or train sets. I feel a tiny surge of irritation, but maybe he's just joking, I think, and I chastise myself for being so scratchy. I'm just tired after all the hard work at Madame Beaumont's and I guess I just wanted him to be as excited as I am about it.

'Great. Well, it's ready to pick up from her *chai* whenever you're free,' I tell him with a smile, and turn to leave and join the others in the salesroom where I have some catching up to do on the phones.

'Actually, Emma – Emmy,' he corrects himself quickly, frowning at his computer screen. 'Is that the old lady who lives up the lane, Clos . . .' he peers at the screen, '. . . Beaumont? Last house before Saint Enrique?'

'Yes.' I nod enthusiastically and breathe a sigh of relief. Thank God, he's realised who I'm talking about. 'Her wine is great. A real—' I'm about to tell him it's a rustic gem but he cuts me off.

'Very small producer,' he says, looking from a log book

laid out on his desk, back to the computer screen; obviously referring to his father's original books and his own updated records. 'Dad had a habit of picking up . . . lame ducks.' He glances up at me and his eyes have gone darker, like the sun has gone in over the lagoon. 'Had a thing about sourcing small producers, cutting out the middle man and selling direct to the customers. I'm changing all that, of course. I want to get into the supermarkets, the restaurants, the big suppliers. Fewer small labels and more well-known affordable ones we can roll out.' He pulls back into his wide smile again and my stomach does that flick-flacking thing, despite my head wanting to disagree.

'Oh, but—' I start to tell him that every vintage should be different and individual.

'We'll take this vintage. You obviously feel strongly about it.' He gives me an encouraging smile. 'But I'm not sure there'll be a place for her wine in the shop next year. I'm looking for people who can produce consistent quality wines in quantity. I don't think Madame Beaumont really fits into what we're looking for now.' He shrugs apologetically.

'What? But you can't do that!' The panic flies back into my heart. 'If Madame Beaumont doesn't have Featherstone's she won't have any customers at all. She'll have no choice but to sell to Château Lavigne.'

Charlie's eyes suddenly become very steely indeed.

'Maybe it's a good thing, if she's on her own and getting older, and we know how age can suddenly catch up with us, don't we?' I think about Dad. 'She can't make wine for ever. This way she'll sell and I'll have more room for the stock we do want. It's probably in her best interests,' he says, suddenly pulling back one of his cheeky grins, and for a moment I wonder if he might be right. 'Now, as I've said, we'll take this vintage. I'll send someone up for it when we've got a minute. This evening, OK?' He raises he shoulders by way of apology. I can see the conversation is over. 'I'm not a monster, Em-m . . .'

'E,' I finish for him.

'I'm just trying to take Featherstone's to the next level and hopefully you'll be there with me. The fewer small wines we have, the more orders we can get for the bigger labels.'

I understand his logic. If he expands like he says, the more work we'll get, the more my money problems will be solved. And I do need to solve our problems: the mortgage arrears, the collection money.

But where does that leave Madame Beaumont?

'Actually, could you do it? Do you drive? You could take the van? You seem to have got some kind of rapport going on with this woman. From what I remember my dad saying, she's a bit of a tricky one. Hard to get along with. Dad liked her, though. Liked her spirit.'

'Yes, she's very . . . independent. Fantastic spirit,' I say, still hoping to win him round. 'But no, I don't drive.'

'Sadly spirit alone isn't going to take this business where I want it to go. Colette?' he calls out, looking for her. 'Oh, well, don't worry, I'll send someone up there,' he says, but I have a weird feeling that I should worry. I should drive again, too. He gives me another killer smile but this time I can't return it. 'And leave it to me, I'll make sure she knows that we won't be taking her next vintage. She needs to look for a new market.'

'But there aren't any other buyers, not like Featherstone's,' I try once more.

'No, and that's exactly why we need to change.'

'But her wine is individual, just as she is.'

'It's a good sales pitch, but it's just a Vin de France. If she applied for the appellation at least we could ask a higher price.'

'She won't,' I say quietly.

'Then there's nothing we can do. Now, we have a big buyer coming by tomorrow. I've just got off the phone to her. A supermarket buyer. She's just made an appointment.' His eyes are suddenly wide with excitement again and back to being speckled green. 'She's on a buying trip and we need to do everything we can to impress her. You couldn't give Colette a hand getting the tasting room ready, could you? Organise some nibbles, that kind of thing, yes? I can see you're quite resourceful.'

'Of course,' I sigh. Looks like I'm back on cake and cava duty all over again.

'It was good to catch up. Give my best to your dad,' and my spirits lift just a little from the floor though my head is in turmoil. On the one hand, I can't help but find this man very attractive and what he's saying makes a lot of sense, for all of us. But I'm just not sure Madame Beaumont would see it that way and I wouldn't blame her.

That afternoon Colette leaves me to set up the tasting room whilst she shows some passing tourists around the shop. Colette is wearing bright red lipstick and her scarf slung around her shoulders. She looks very efficient, in a Dolly Parton way, with pen in hand and leopard-print glasses firmly fixed on the end of her nose. I get the feeling that, like Isaac, she really can't see the point of the trainees; that she thinks we're all after her job, which, of course, we're not.

I lay out the glasses on a white, pressed tablecloth, having rinsed them in hot water, but no washing-up liquid, just like Madame Beaumont told me. Hot water only. Washing-up liquid affects the taste of the wine. When the British buyers have left Colette comes in to check the room, with a critical eye. She walks over to the glasses, lifts one and holds it to the light. Then she smells it and runs a finger along the inside. She turns to me and lifts a pencilled eyebrow.

'No washing-up liquid,' I confirm, wagging a finger at the bottle.

She nods slowly in agreement. After a final look around the tasting room she can't find any reason to keep me so I'm free to go. I have a little glow of satisfaction as I get straight on the bike and ride up to Clos Beaumont. Because, if Madame Beaumont is going to have a future at all I need to make sure her wine gets to Featherstone's, quickly.

Chapter Fourteen

I can hear the commotion before I see it. There are raised voices, Madame Beaumont's and a man's. Cecil is barking. I can even hear Henri snorting. Hot and puffing, I push on to the top of the hill, the front wheel of the bike twisting this way and that as my legs run out of steam. I jump off, catching the leg of my cut-off jeans on the cracking saddle, nearly tumbling over but recovering and pushing the bike the last bit towards Clos Beaumont as fast as my aching thighs will let me.

'*Non! Allez! Allez-vous-en!* Go away!' I hear Madame Beaumont shout. My heart jumps into my mouth. What on earth is going on? I'm running as fast as I can as I reach the top of the plateau and see a little burgundy 2CV van parked on the roadside by the gateposts. Madame Beaumont is still shouting. I dump the bike somewhere in the direction of the posts and run round the van, spotting the Featherstone's sign on the side. What on earth can the problem be?

'*Allo! Allo!*' I shout, running into the yard. The big orange ball of sun is setting on the other side of the valley, over Château Lavigne, momentarily blinding me. I get a hit of wild herbs and lavender as I always do when I arrive here and, holding my hand up to shield my eyes, I finally see her.

Madame Beaumont is standing in front of the *chai*, frowning and waving her arms at the man in front of her, shaking at him the thumbstick she uses when she walks through the vines. I finally coming to a stop and let out a sigh of relief.

'Madame Beaumont!' I call, trying to catch my breath in my burning lungs.

'Just put down the weapon, for God's sake, you mad woman!'

She jabs in his direction again and he lifts his arms and jumps back, like the thumbstick is a fully loaded rifle.

'Issac?'

'Ah, jeez! Thank God,' he says, throwing his hands up in the air as he turns towards me, then putting his hands on his hips, just above his low-slung combats.

'Isaac?' I hold my chest. 'What on earth is going on?'

'I was told to come and find Madame Beaumont.' Isaac rolls his eyes at me in despair, his back to her.

Cecil is barking for all he's worth, and drooling lots of drool, and I'm keeping my distance just in case he flicks his head.

'You know this man?' Madame Beaumont scowls, jabbing the thumbstick towards him.

'She's mad! See?'

She narrows her eyes at me. Back to the mistrust of our first meeting.

'No, no . . .' I shake my head and hands, trying to telling her there's nothing to worry about.

Her grey eyes narrow further. 'See, I knew it! He's from the château. I came back from the cemetery to find him here, snooping around in my *chai*. Trying to see if I have made my vintage this year, no doubt; trying to find out what makes my vintage different from theirs.'

'No.' Isaac walks towards her, extending a hand. She lifts up the thumbstick and waves it at him again like a gun.

'Whoa.' He steps back quickly, holding up his hands, ducking behind me and I get a sudden urge to giggle. I cover my mouth. 'Sort this out, will you?' he says in my ear. 'Please.' Suddenly he is completely unarmed. Without his jokes, flirtation and bonhomie that have worked their charm on so many people he hasn't a clue what to do and it's like I'm finally meeting the real Isaac.

'You two do know each other?' Madame Beaumont waves the thumbstick between us.

'Yes,' I say firmly, stepping forwards, reaching out and taking hold of the end of the thumbstick. 'He is a—'

'Close personal friend!' Isaac cuts across me loudly, and pointing between the two of us, still looking unsure of Madame Beaumont even though she's been disarmed.

I swing round and give him a hard stare, telling him to leave this to me. He's done enough damage, by the looks of it. Close personal friend indeed! I need to calm everything down. If Madame Beaumont blows this with Featherstone's, she'll have to sell up and I can't let her shoot herself in the foot like that.

Isaac, on the other hand, steps forward and slings an arm around my shoulder, making me feel like I've stuck a fork into an electric toaster, sending a thousand volts round me. I freeze.

'What are you doing?' I hiss into his ear, smelling his pine-scented hair.

'Trying to get on her good side. She'll like me more if she thinks I'm with you. I need to get her to trust me so I can pick up the wine.' He pulls me closer and I feel his breath on my neck, making me quiver in spite of myself, and I hold my breath. 'I mean, it's not like we haven't shared a bed, now is it, Goldy?' he whispers in my ear and grins. Infuriatingly, I shiver all over again.

I move my foot over his toe and gently press on it to get him to move away. But nothing. I move my weight over his toes some more, then risk a glance down and see he's wearing Caterpillar boots. He grins some more. I turn back to Madame Beaumont and attempt a calming smile.

'Close friend? *C'est vrai?* I've never heard about a close friend,' she says quizzically.

That's because I haven't got one, I think, infuriated. If I didn't need to calm this down I'd turn round and kick the idiot right in the shins and suggest another type of word beginning with F.

'I—'

'Great friends,' he says, laughing now. Thankfully, Cecil muscles his way in between us and sniffs at Isaac's leg.

'He's from Featherstone's,' I finally manage to offer sensibly. 'He's the Featherstone's wine-maker.'

'That's what I've been trying to say. I'm here for the wine.'

'You're here from Featherstone's? To pick up the wine?'

'Yes,' Isaac and I say simultaneously, and I almost laugh with him. Slowly Madame Beaumont lowers her thumbstick.

'Are you Monsieur Featherstone's son?' she asks. He gives another laugh and shakes his head. 'No, I'm just the hired hand,' he says, finally taking his arm from my shoulder, and

I breathe a sigh of relief. Madame Beaumont starts to nod.

'He's their travelling wine man. He's Californian,' I say, as if this explains everything, but of course it means nothing.

'And you and he . . . he's . . . you are . . . ?' She points to me. I take a deep breath to explain he has a funny sense of humour, but before I can, he jumps in.

'Yes,' he beams. 'Good friends, very good friends indeed.' He's wearing a white and blue bandana round his head. His small diamond earring flashes in the sunlight. 'Now, where are these crates I've been sent to pick up?' he says, rubbing his hands, seemingly happy that the misunderstanding is sorted, just as Cecil shakes his head and a large strip of drool lands across his thigh. This time it's my turn to laugh, covering my mouth with my hand. But to my surprise and slight annoyance, he throws his head back and laughs too. Even Madame Beaumont seems to have thawed a little with that.

He reverses the van down the lane, backing it up to the *chai*, neither of us saying much to each other, and then we all help to load the boxes of wine. Despite our protestations, Madame Beaumont helps, moving slowly but steadily, lifting boxes and carrying them to the van. One box to every three or four of ours. I, of course, am determined not to be outdone by Isaac and make sure I'm carrying them as quickly as he is, and I'm sure he's trying to push me, that lazy smile never far from his lips.

He slams the van doors shut finally, pulls up the back of his slipping combats, dusts off his hands and looks around.

'It's an interesting place you have here, Madame Beaumont. Is that Saint Enrique over there?' He points and

I realise he's probably hasn't actually seen the area he's been living in for the last few weeks. Too busy tucked away in his laboratory with books and test tubes or in Le Papillon with his new local friends.

'Perhaps Emmy would like to show you,' Madame Beaumont nods, showing she's happy for him to come on to her land and I feel very privileged she's taken that step because of me. I realise not many people get past Madame Beaumont and her ring of mistrust.

I'd much rather Isaac just got on his way but I really don't feel I can turn down Madame Beaumont's offer. I don't think it happens very often. 'And please, accept my apology . . . for earlier. I didn't realise you were . . . a friend of Emmy's.'

'Oh, forget it, no worries. Emmy's explained about Château Lavigne. Been hassling you about selling your land. I don't blame you for keep up your guard.' He waves a hand.

'I didn't put it quite like that.' I try to remember what I did say in the kitchen the other night. But Madame Beaumont nods again and turns back down the steps into her big kitchen.

I now have to show Isaac the vineyard.

'So this is Henri. He does all the heavy work,' I walk over and rub his nose and he snuffles and snorts, clearly recognising my voice.

'Where's the machinery kept?' Isaac looks around.

'No machinery, just Henri,' I say and smile, scratching Henri's chin and watching his top lip curl up in pleasure.

'You're kidding, right?'

'No, not kidding.'

'Can he see?' Isaac peers at the horse.

'A bit,' I smile, and rub Henri's nose.

'How does he work?'

'By instinct and trust,' I say, smiling and relaxing, enjoying the warm evening sun on my skin and the familiarity of the vineyard I have walked up and down for the past few of weeks, and strangely, feeling happier and more content than I have in a while.

I point out the Merlot and the Cabernet Franc, and where the vines run up the other side of the bowl towards the château, bathed in evening sunlight, streaks of blue sky and red sunlight creating a lavender hue across the sky to match the scent filling the warm evening air.

When we walk back towards the house I'm keen to get back with the wine as quickly as possible, but Madame Beaumont has a bottle on the table.

'Please, join me, by way of an apology.' She gestures to the rusting wrought-iron table and chairs.

'Maybe we should get the wine back,' I say quietly.

'No way. That would be very rude,' Isaac says under his breath and then smiles at me. 'We'd love to,' he says loudly, and strides towards Madame Beaumont, taking the bottle that she's opening with her knobbly hands and expertly opening it for her.

'*Merci*,' she nods.

'My pleasure,' Isaac says, and I can see he's working his charm already.

Isaac sits down and then back on the old iron chair, taking in his surroundings whilst Madame Beaumont goes inside, presumably for glasses. It seems strange seeing him out of the office. He's unusually quiet and seems to be studying the skyline, across the little valley to the château, taking pictures on his phone as Madame Beaumont returns with three mismatched glasses. Then she returns to the kitchen and seems to be gone ages before bringing out little toasted bits of baguette, with something like duck rillettes on them, on a small round plate, which I suspect may have been her supper. Then finally she picks up the bottle and pours. I'm beginning to love the sound of the glug, glug. Not like back home when you open a screw top or pull out a plastic plug. This wine has been made with love and pouring it seems to be part of the pleasure.

Isaac suddenly sits up as she pours the wine into the first glass, his interest spiked too. He's watching the ruby-red wine from the unlabelled bottle as it tumbles into the glass. She passes him a glass, watching him. He lifts it, looking at it. Then he tips the glass on the side.

'Checking the legs?' I say, showing I have been paying some attention and wasn't a total waste of space.

He smiles and nods. It appears the one thing Isaac does take seriously in life is wine. He puts his nose into the glass and breathes in deeply. Then finally, after he's swilled it round the glass, he sniffs again and then sips and draws in air as he does. Madame Beaumont is standing beside me, holding the back of my chair. She is in a fresh overall, I notice, one of the many that usually hang in a row on the line to the side of the house, next to the ancient peach and fruit-laden plum tree.

Madame Beaumont and I watch him as, finally, his Adam's apple bobs up and down in his long neck as he swallows. Then he looks at us, his face breaks into that wide, slightly lazy smile and he nods appreciatively.

'This is good, man,' he says, swirling, sniffing, sipping and drawing in air again.

Madame Beaumont then replies, '*Oui. Je sais*,' and smiles, and just for a moment I forget all my frustrations with Isaac and feel a surge of gratitude to him.

Suddenly an idea comes to me. If Isaac appreciates Madame Beaumont's wine, so will others with a good palate. If I'm going to stop Madame Beaumont having to sell out to the château, I'm going to have to make sure that her wine is in that tasting room with the supermarket buyer tomorrow, whatever it takes.

We bid goodbye to Madame Beaumont, and Isaac reverses down the lane in the van full of wine. I feel excited, nervous, buzzing with adrenalin. Maybe, just maybe, everything is going to turn out right. Isaac speeds up as we reach the gates and then I hear the crunch of my pushbike under the wheels of the van and I put my head in my hands and do actually let out a little scream of frustration.

Chapter Fifteen

This is madness. Only four weeks into my time here at Featherstone's and I'm risking everything. But I have to try. The supermarket buyer will be here this afternoon. I have to get this bottle of Clos Beaumont into that tasting room. I swallow and look both ways. It's quiet. After a morning in the salesroom, everyone's at lunch and if I don't do this now I'll miss my chance. I know exactly where Madame Beaumont's wine is because Isaac and I stacked it here in the storeroom last night. I can see it. I rip open a box and stuff a bottle down the front of my shorts. I'm wearing a hoodie to cover it, despite the hot midday sun. My heart is beating so hard, it's deafening. I go to walk as quietly as I can across the gravel courtyard. I've taken the first few steps on tiptoes when Colette pokes her head out of the shop door. I freeze, heart thumping even more. I raise a hand and the bottle slips scarily down inside my waistband. I slam a hand against it, hoping and praying it doesn't slip out of my trouser leg, and stand still, knees pressed together. She briefly nods back and looks to the road for her lunchtime lift. Another day, another suitor, no doubt. As she turns away, I do lots of very quick steps across the gravel and into the glass-fronted tasting room. The video is playing in there, as it always is, giving guests a chance to get an understanding of the region and the wine-making process here at Featherstone's. I open the door and shut it quickly behind me, hoping Colette hasn't seen me. This could be a one-way ticket back to the UK and the dole queue if I get caught, but I have to try to repay Madame Beaumont for her kindness towards me. I can't just let her just go under. I look round and realise my hoodie has caught in the door and the wine nearly slips down my trouser leg again. I pull forward, the door opens and then slams shut behind me and I want to say 'Ssh!'

Unhooking myself, I go over to where the other bottles have been lined up and shuffle them around. All of them have Featherstone's wine sleeves on them and I quickly put my bottle into a wine sleeve and add it to the others. My wildly beating heart starts to slow down to a steady canter. I check and double-check that it doesn't look as if the bottles have been tampered with. But what if Charlie notices there's an extra bottle? There's only one thing I can do. I slip a bottle of their best seller back into my baggy shorts and wrap the hoodie around me again. I have to get out of here, quickly. Clutching the bottle, I turn, just as I hear a voice on a phone coming this way.

'That's great. We'll see you then. Yes, just turn left after the fountain in the square. You can't miss us.' Charlie is walking across the forecourt with the phone to his ear and stops, just outside the glass door, facing out towards the river. I snatch a breath and hold it. I'll just wait until he's gone. As ever, he looks smart and confident. I imagine taking Charlie home and introducing him to Dad. He'd be so happy. Just the sort of boyfriend he'd want me to have, I find myself thinking, and then give myself a little shake, remembering that I've only had one coffee with him and I am trying to sneak in a bottle of wine he has specifically said he doesn't want to stock any more.

'See you then,' he says, finishing the call, puts the phone in his pocket and walks towards the office. I start to breathe again, just little shallow, life-saving breathes. Then suddenly a phone rings again. He stops, pulls his out of his pocket and looks at it. Only this time it's not his, it's mine! I screw up my face and hope it'll stop. I think I might die. He looks around as my phone still rings . . . and its vibration in my pocket is making the hidden wine bottle jiggle. Charlie turns round and looks straight at me through the glass doors. I smile tightly. There's only one thing I can do . . . answer the phone.

'Hello, Dad,' I say tightly, still trying to hide the bottle under my hoodie as the temperature in my world suddenly soars and I'm boiling, desperate to take the hoodie off, but I can't. Charlie sees me and starts to walk towards the tasting room.

'What do you mean, the water tank's burst?'

I listen to Dad's painfully detailed explanation as Charlie opens the tasting-room door, gives me a smile and a nod and starts to double-check that everything is ready for his buyer. I'm a bundle of nerves.

'Dad, I can't talk. You'll have to phone a plumber.' I hate to cut him off again but I just can't risk getting caught.

'I'm a bit tied up, Dad. I'll ring you back later to get all the details. I promise.'

Charlie is looking at the bottles and glasses but giving me

sideways glances as he walks around the table. My heart is thundering. 'Dad, really, I have to go.' I get more high-pitched. 'Phone a plumber!' I grip the cold bottle neck against my thigh and start to limp towards the door, pushing the off button on my phone, guilt twisting in my guts. My poor, gentle Dad. I'll phone him back in a bit. Once I've got rid of this bottle. I'll explain everything. A little surge of annoyance rises in me. If only my sister was there to help him out. I hold the phone and stare at it.

'Everything all right, erm . . . Elle?' I sigh. Not much chance of Charlie ever being boyfriend material; he can't even remember my name. I just don't feature in his world.

'Emmy,' I tell him, not turning round, fighting back the stinging in my eyes. 'Yes, fine. Just checking the glasses were clean in here,' I lie, not looking.

'All OK at home?' he asks, and still I can't turn round. The bottle will definitely slip if I do.

'Just, y'know . . . dads!' I say, screwing up my eyes, worrying just how much damage the burst water tank has done. From the sounds of it, it burst and was leaking all through the ceiling and into Dad's bedroom.

'Right, well, get yourself some lunch. The buyer will be here just after two.'

I throw open the double doors, not bothering to shut them behind me as I go as fast as I can to the *gîte* and shove the bottle into the bottom of my holdall and under my bed. Letting out a huge sigh of relief I fling the hoodie off and gasp for air, sitting on the floor against my bed. I can't actually believe I've just done that. I'm going to have to get a story straight for when Charlie finds out. Say it was a mistake when I was setting up the tasting room – that I mixed up the bottles. He'll think I can't tell one bottle of wine from the other. My heart is still racing.

I try to ring Dad back but it's permanently engaged. I give up for the time being and head off into town. I need a new wheel for that bike if I'm to get back to Madame Beaumont's this evening.

I rub my oily hands down my shorts as I try to fix a new wheel to the bike I bought from the supermarket heading out of town on the other side from Featherstone's. I'm exhausted and frankly my nerves are in shreds.

'Let me do that,' Isaac offers when he sees me arriving back.

'No, I'm fine,' I say, propping the bike up against the *gîte* wall and starting work, determined to keep busy.

'Well, let me help, at least,' he says, standing from the outdoor table and chairs, his hands held out after dusting off the crumbs from a final piece of bread, and finishing what looks to be a large salad niçoise.

The others have gone into the town for the twelve-euro lunch at Le Papillon, including wine. I passed them all sitting outside. Jeff was there, looking jollier than usual, chatting away, telling his jokes. And tonight, he told us in his 'franglais', he would be dancing down by the river, he pointed further along.

'*Dansant!*' he proclaimed, holding an imaginary woman in his arms and swaying, puckering up his lips. He pointed again, past the abandoned café by the river, towards the campsite on the outskirts of town, at the bar there. It's the end of the season and they're having a disco, Gloria translated. They are also doing a tea dance on a Sunday. Jeff looks at Gloria, asking if she'd like to join him, but she shakes her head shyly and puts her fan on to full speed, holding it close to her flushing face.

'Are you sure you won't join us?' Gloria asked me as I passed them having lunch. But I shook my head, still not sure that Candy or Nick would want me there, and went in search of a new bicycle wheel instead.

As I walked back with my wheel over my shoulder I could hear Candy hooting with laughter, and I'm guessing that was at my expense.

'Shit!' I say as the bike slips as I try to unscrew the nut on the front wheel, remembering that Dad would give me that look for bad language. Just thinking of Dad gives me a pang.

Isaac doesn't take telling twice and steps in, swinging his leg over the front wheel. I briefly look up and see his thighs either side of the wheel, at eye level, as I try to unscrew the nut on the front axis. For a moment the strength leaves my hands and I wonder if he's going to just step in there too, but he doesn't. I turn the nut harder and watch his smooth tanned thighs flex, taking the strain beneath knee-length patterned shorts. I look away from his muscular limbs and up at him. His dark neck-length hair is hanging down round his olive-skinned face and he smiles at me, and suddenly my insides jolt, leaving me feeling flustered. This is ridiculous. This man makes me tongue-tied. Why on earth would the sight of his shining, flexing thighs make me react like that? There is no way I could find this man attractive. Must be the sun.

I ignore my spinning insides and give the spanner and nut an extra hard twist.

'Ooff,' he says, and his smile drops as the wheel spins violently to one side.

'Oh, sorry,' I say, not knowing my own strength but realising that all my frustrations and worries about the burst water tank and my dad, and worries over my job, and, if I'm honest, a flash of annoyance at the effect Isaac's suddenly had on me, were all behind that thrust, as the rusty nut spins off and across the gravel, losing itself amongst the little stones.

The crunching on gravel makes us both turn. Charlie is marching towards us.

'Have you seen Colette?' he asks.

'Colette's gone to lunch. The others are in Le Papillon,' I tell him.

Charlie lets out an exasperated sigh. 'The buyer's on her way. She'll be here any minute.' He bites his bottom lip. I look for the rusty nut.

'Actually, you couldn't come and give me a hand, could you . . . ?'

'Emmy,' I help him out.

'Emmy, of course. I need someone to help out at the tasting. Perhaps you'd like to?' He smiles straight at me with those damn eyes.

'Really?' I put my hand up against my eyes as if shielding them from the sun.

'Yes, please. Come and join me,' he says, and my heart quickens with panic. I'll just have to remember to say it's a genuine mistake.

'Yes, um, of course.'

I wipe an oily hand across my forehead as I straighten up, put down the spanner, Isaac swings his leg off the bike wheel and it slowly falls out if its axis.

I quickly lift up the bike and lean it against the wall, happy to be away from Isaac and his flexing tanned thighs.

'Where do you want me?' I stand next to him, and push my hair behind my ear. It's got longer since I've been here, a little more free-spirited. I stand as far away from Isaac as possible, his arms folded lazily across him, and close to Charlie. My nerves are jangling.

'Actually,' says Charlie with a slightly apologetic pull of his mouth, 'could you erm . . . clean yourself up?' He flashes me a big smile.

'Of course!' I say quickly. I'm all over the place, nerves getting the better of me, making me behave like a silly schoolgirl. 'Big buyer and all that.'

Charlie turns to Isaac. 'And you, perhaps you could put a shirt on and join us?'

'Sure, man.' Isaac picks up the runaway wheel and props it against the wall with the bike. Charlie marches off to the office, my eyes following him. Now what? What will he think of me when he discovers I've switched the bottles? I do know I've blown any chance I might have had of ever having that second cup of coffee with him, that's for sure.

'I'll put a shirt on,' Isaac breaks my thoughts and I turn to see him grinning and following my gaze with interest with his head on one side, 'but he didn't say anything about me changing out of my shorts.'

I reappear wearing one of the dresses I bought in the market, still trying to wipe the last traces of oil from my hands. I make my way to the tasting room where Isaac is standing, holding a glass of red up and looking at the 'legs' on it. He's wearing a fitted shirt, no tie and the same Caribbean-patterned surf shorts he had on earlier. He gives me a tiny sideways glance and a smile tugs at the corner of his mouth, and I give a little nervous laugh. Charlie, on the other hand, is looking smart, expensive and in control. He even smells expensive. But all my thoughts are on that bottle and I eye it nervously. Maybe I shouldn't have done it. I'm going to be found out. I'll get sacked. But it's too late now with both Isaac and Charlie here.

A smart Renault pulls into the courtyard and Charlie marches over to meet it.

'Selina,' I hear him greet an attractive dark-haired woman, in a fitted red dress, with high heels. She smiles, picks up her briefcase from the passenger seat and gets out. Charlie kisses her on both cheeks and I wonder if she's British or French. I have no idea. I try to keep my nerves at bay, wishing I had never started this. Had I known I would be standing here serving the wine there's no way I would have done.

'This is Isaac, our wine-maker.' Charlie holds out a hand to Isaac as he shows the buyer in.

'Hi,' Isaac says, not bothering with the French way of saying hello, and the buyer looks a little disappointed; her red lips, the exact colour of her dress, pout just a little.

'Hi,' she says in a crisp Home Counties accent, making a note on her tablet.

'And this is . . .'

'Emmy.' I stick out a hand and step forward.

'Right.' Charlie rubs his hands together. This is a very big deal for him. 'Let's try some wines.'

It's a quiet affair, apart from the slurping and the spitting. I attempt to slurp and end up coughing and choking so I stick to clearing glasses and pouring wine instead. They have done four wines. Selina nods but says very little. Charlie has hardly touched a drop, saying he knows the wines and putting his abstinence down to his fitness regime. Isaac, on the other hand, isn't spitting. One more wine and then it's Madame Beaumont's. I pour, they taste and then I collect the glasses, which clink together in my shaking hands as I go to put them in the sink.

'So, just this last one. Our biggest and best seller,' Charlie tells her. One of the glasses slips from my hands and clatters into the sink. They all turn to look at me.

'Sorry,' I say, heart doing its bass beat again, deafening me.

Charlie pours the wine. Isaac lifts a glass. Charlie pours me one and hands it to me. I take it with shaking hands and he smiles encouragingly. Isaac sniffs the wine and then swiftly looks at me, quizzically, frowning and then takes a big draw through his nose on the wine again. I follow and sniff, the familiarity of the wine's bouquet comforting me a little. Charlie doesn't seem to have noticed anything is amiss. He's watching Selina, sniffing, swilling it round the glass and looking at it. Charlie doesn't sniff it, just holds it.

'Interesting,' she says, looking slightly confused. Isaac throws me another look. He knows . . . oh God, he knows. A hot flush creeps up my chest and into my cheeks, making them burn.

Finally, after they have swilled, studied and sniffed, Selina and Isaac sip, as do I. The taste reminds me of Madame Beaumont's vineyard. It tastes of the sunny hillside, the wild herbs that grow there, rosemary and thyme. It's rich and thick. I can picture the light brown stony soil that the vines have worked hard to draw moisture from and I imagine the breeze that is always there. There's a hint of something I can't quite put my finger on but reminds me of the sunny evenings I have spent there.

No one says anything. Isaac is now giving me a raised eyebrow. Charlie is watching Selina. Selina is still moving the wine around her mouth and finally she swallows.

She gives a slow nod and then looks at me and says, 'What do you think, Emmy?'

For a moment I'm stunned and can't say a word. I look at Isaac. He nods at me. Charlie turns to me a little surprised and slightly nervous.

'I, er, I believe it's . . .' I clear my throat, 'an interesting take on the standard claret. Grown on south-facing slopes and really fabulous *terroir*. Practically organic, the grapes are left to grow and develop without too much intervention. Well-established vines, giving a high-quality yield.' I omit that the vines are ancient and have a very low yield. 'It has the traditional blend of the three grapes of the region, and then . . .' I wonder if I've said too much but can't stop now, 'a little something extra.'

Isaac gives an approving smile, holding the glass by the stem, swirling as he always does, before tipping the glass back and drinking.

'It is easy drinking, appealing to wine lovers and the

uninitiated alike. It tastes of wild thyme, rosemary, and is grown right here in Petit Frère. It has all the quality of a Saint Enrique wine without the price tag. This is a wine that's made with love, passion and patience, and I believe it shows,' I finally finish, and wonder whether I should have told her about Henri and Cecil and Madame Beaumont.

Isaac slides off the work surface he's been sitting on, puts down his glass and claps. 'Well done, Emmy, great notes.'

Suddenly I replay everything I've just said about the wine, surprising myself and actually feeling a surge of pride. I blush all over again, but turn back to Charlie, who still doesn't seem to have realised, and my mouth goes dry.

'May I see the bottle?' Selina holds out a manicured hand.

'Sure,' Charlie lifts the bottle from its sleeve and I know I'm about to be found out. I go hot and then cold.

'Sorry, there seems to be—' he starts to say, and turns to look at me, but Selina cuts him off.

'If you can guarantee a high-quality, consistent blend that matches this, and that you can provide a constant supply, I'm interested. Let me know. I have a few more places to visit but this is definitely one of my favourites on this trip so far. We're looking for a wine that we can roll out to all our stores, a good solid claret with just a hint of something remarkable is what I'm looking for. This could be it. I'll be in touch.' She puts down the glass and scoops up her car keys from the table.

Charlie is stunned, still holding Madame Beaumont's bottle. I want to squeal with excitement. Isaac is grinning broadly.

'Well, that's fantastic.' Charlie spins to me on his heel and then back to Selina.

'I have another meeting to make, a wine-maker in the next town,' Selina says. 'Nice to meet you, Emmy,' she smiles, 'Isaac.' She lingers on Isaac's name a little longer and gives him a nod of the head goodbye. Charlie seems a little flustered, dumbfounded. He opens the door for her.

'Thank you. Great. We'll be in touch soon,' he says as she steps out.

'Emmy, we'll talk,' he turns back to me and suddenly my little happy bubble is burst and I'm gripped by dread. *Shit!*

'I can explain!'

'You know,' he says, putting his head back in through the tasting-room door. 'You've obviously learned enough about wine to know it was no mistake that bottle was there instead of the other one.'

I cringe.

'But luckily for you, it looks like things might just have worked out for the best, so like I say, we'll talk.' Then Charlie breaks into a massive smile. 'Over dinner. My treat,' he beams, and I smile widely back as he goes to wave goodbye to Selina.

Suddenly there is silence in the tasting room and a great big elephant is standing in the middle of it between me and Isaac.

'Well,' Isaac says, and then tips back his head and drinks the last of Madame Beaumont's wine. He smacks his lips. 'This will be a great wine to work with.' He looks as if someone's just dared him and he's well up for it.

'Pull this deal off and you could get your job and your

man,' he says, for once without smiling, and lollops out of the tasting room, back towards the lab.

I pull out my phone and try to ring home. I need to take my mind off Isaac's words running through in my head, ruining what just happened, and I need to put things right with Dad. But this time his phone just rings and rings.

Chapter Sixteen

The bubbles tickle my nose like a feather duster as I take a sip of the amber liquid.

'Crickey,' I say, holding the back of my hand to my mouth and hoping the bubbles don't make me hiccup.

'Everything all right?' asks Charlie, putting the bottle back in the wine cooler and covering it with a thick, white serviette.

I nod and take away my hand.

'It's not like the Jolly Sava Cava I buy for the call centre.' I look at the glass. I'm twittering, I know. Charlie holds his glass up and then meets my gaze with his sparkling green eyes, burning a hole in my soul, and I'm suddenly silenced. His silver wine bottle cufflinks catch the light. He gives me one of his wide, cheeky smiles.

'It's Château Lavigne. Only the best. Here's to you, Emmy. You did a great job today.'

'I really am sorry I swapped the wines.'

'Like I say, it could have been a very different story. You could have totally stuffed things up, but I like your balls. You showed a lot of passion for the product in there today. You killed it! I didn't know we had such a star player in our midst.'

I feel the bubbles of excitement fizz up inside me.

Holding the glass by the stem, Charlie takes a tiny sip.

'The crémant – the sparkling wine,' I say, just in case my accent has let me down. 'It's delicious.' As he sips he holds my gaze. I copy him and I think the bubbles of excitement might just explode in me. I take away the glass from my lips and this time I do hiccup and then blush.

'Shit,' I say under my breath.

He laughs, looking straight at me, those eyes gleaming. He looks different, interested, attentive. His face more relaxed away from the office. He holds my gaze once again, making me feel like I'm the only person there in the busy hilltop town, in the bustling restaurant. My insides melt and I don't want the evening to end.

The table for two is on a terrace under a patio heater, looking out over the town of Saint Enrique. The early October evenings are beginning to lose their heat and I'm glad I've brought a jacket. Brass lanterns light the way down the steep cobbled streets like molten lava rolling through the tiny, tight alleys, passing the low-ceilinged, busy shops cut into the steep hillside. I can see why this is seen as Petit Frère's better-known neighbour.

I pull the pashmina I've borrowed from Gloria around me. It's getting cooler. There are big cream candles burning all over the terrace, creating a golden glow off the cream stone-work. There are huge cream cushions with twisted cord edges on the black wrought-iron chairs. There are black settees under an arbour, draped with cream awnings where people are enjoying aperitifs and coffees. This must be the most expensive restaurant in the town. Its location is amazing. Over the stone wall surrounding the terrace, as far as I can see, are neat rows of vines, and big cream châteaux dotted across the patchwork quilt of vineyards. It's like looking at a painting. I find it hard to drag my eyes away to the menu. There are no prices on mine.

Tourists are walking past, stopping to read the framed menu outside and looking in enviously at the busy yet serene ambiance on the restaurant terrace. I'm feeling very lucky – I look at Charlie in the golden candlelight – very lucky indeed.

I've covered myself in the insect repellent Gloria offered me, just to be on the safe side. I look down from the beautiful view to the menu, and it's still all gobbledygook to me.

'So, what do you fancy?' Charlie is reading the menu and I find myself having a really naughty thought that says, *You!* Then I quickly tell myself that the champagne may taste nice but it's clearly having a rather loosening effect and I take a sip of water instead.

The waitress is beside us. I don't want to look stupid, not now. And I don't want to say, 'I'll have what you're having.'

'*Madame?*'

'I'll have what the chef recommends,' I say with a smile I hope looks confident, handing back the menu.

'Of course, *très bien*,' the efficient but not smiling waitress replies.

Charlie raises an impressed eyebrow. 'I'll do the same. *Moi aussi. Merci*,' he says, handing back the menu.

'*Bien sûr, monsieur*,' smiles the stick-thin, olive-skinned beauty, taking away the menus and making a jotting on her electronic notepad.

'So, you know about wine? I didn't realise.' Charlie leans forward, twisting his glass of sparkling water next to his practically untouched crémant. 'Isaac never said.' At the mention of his name I feel a strange shifting inside me again. Not so much irritation any more. I can't help but think fondly about the smile he put on Madame Beaumont's face when he told her he liked her wine. I take another swig of the glorious fizz and wonder whether to lie to Charlie and tell him I've learned all about wine, but I've diced with danger once already today when I hid that bottle. I won't risk it again.

'Actually, no, I don't know about wine,' I say honestly. 'Just that wine.'

'Ah yes, Madame Beaumont's wine, not our best seller, which I thought Selina was trying.'

I feel like a naughty schoolgirl in the headmaster's office. I chew my bottom lip. It was always the same at school: I'd get into trouble for not doing my school work, or getting it wrong. Or standing up to the boys who pulled my thick curly hair in class, or for defending my sister when she started school and the same gang would tease her because of her pigtails and glasses. They should see her now – stunning! And then of course, after Mum died, well, I had to be there for Jody. I didn't mind if I got into trouble. Nothing the teachers could say to me could be worse than what had already happened.

When Mum went out that night, Dad kept telling me she'd be back soon. I wanted to run after her, tell her not to go, but he told me not to, she'd be fine. They'd had a silly row. Mum had been working a double shift, Dad was supposed to be doing the tea. He'd put the sausages on the side and next door's cat stole them. I think it was just the last straw. Money was tight; they were working all they could. Dad was being forced off his patch by another sweet sales rep. They were stressed. It was just a stupid packet of sausages. But it was all they had for tea. Mum went out to buy some more.

It was wet and miserable. A huge thunderstorm. Dad said she'd be back soon. And maybe she would've been if the driver coming towards her hadn't been driving too fast in the rain. It was just after my A levels retakes. I was due to start a nursing course. Mum and Dad were so proud of me. I started, but Dad wasn't coping and I hated seeing him that way. The school were worried about Jody, so I came home. Just until things settled down and then I'd go back. It was never meant to be for ever.

'So how do you know Madame Beaumont and her wine?' Charlie interrupts my thoughts and is topping up my glass, and I push them to the back of my mind, letting myself enjoy feeling deliciously light-headed. 'Dad says she doesn't like to deal with anyone but him usually.'

'She's been helping me . . .'

The waitress arrives with our starters. '*Et voilà. Fois gras avec truffes.*'

It looks wonderful. A small square of pink pâté, with shavings of black-edged truffle on a bed of curly, green salad leaves. She places a basket of sliced French bread in between us, soft and fluffy inside, and glossy and crunchy on the outside.

'*Merci*,' I smile at the non-smiling waitress. 'She's been

showing me about the vines and the wines. Helping me learn.'

'Hasn't Isaac been doing that?'

'Oh, no, it's not that . . . it's . . .' Oh shit! I can't tell him I find learning from the page hard – that I'm dyslexic – it would be professional suicide. Exams were always particularly hard. I used to learn stuff by sticking it on Post-its all around the kitchen. Dad would sit with me when I was writing out homework late into the night, even if there was nothing he could do to help. And Mum would try to get me to make up songs to remember stuff. Maybe I should try that with the Featherstone's bible now! But instead I tell him what the voice in my head is saying.

'How can you sell what you have not experienced?' I say with a rather exaggerated Gallic shrug, and I realise I am completely channelling Madame Beaumont now. Definitely the champagne talking.

Charlie lifts his eyebrow again and nods in agreement. In the background there is a pianist inside playing soft and gentle jazz music.

'So you've become good friends?'

I don't know about friends but I tell him the story of the purse and then me knocking over the bottles and going back to help put them back. But it had already been done and I wanted to help out.

'She's an old lady. I thought she might find it hard to cope alone. I wanted to help.' How little I knew, I think.

'This is excellent.' I'm not sure if he's talking about Madame Beaumont or the *fois gras*. 'And I understand the *terroir* is pretty amazing up there,' Charlie says.

'How do you know that? Sorry, I'm even sounding like Madame Beaumont now,' I say, and he laughs.

'Isaac,' he answers.

Oh, Isaac, of course.

'He says you gave him a tour. Perhaps I should come and talk to Madame Beaumont, tell her what's on offer. If she lets us take over the care of the vines, the harvest, produce the wine, we can make it consistent and quicker.' Charlie suddenly sounds much more business-like.

I find myself laughing.

'I don't think she'd take kindly to that. I mean, I'm sure she'll be really appreciative that you still want to take her wine, but, well . . . she's not too keen on strangers. Ask Isaac.' I smile at the image of Madame Beaumont holding him hostage with her thumbstick, his hands in the air, and jumping this way and that as she swipes at his ankles with it.

The starters finished and cleared, glasses now topped up with a thick, gutsy red, Charlie nods, listening.

'So how should we handle this?' he asks.

'*Voilà!*' says the very skinny waitress, seamlessly putting down large white plates in front of us.

'For Madame, wild seabass,' she announces with a flourish. The smell hits my senses before she's even taken her hand away. 'With fresh herbs, caviar from Arcachon, wild rice risotto and leeks. For Monsieur, *magret de canard*, a local speciality. With mushroom from the region, prunes, *frites* and *petits pois*. *Bon appétit*,' she says, refilling our bread basket and checking we have everything before turning away.

'Wow, this looks amazing,' I sniff it in and then look at Charlie's.

'*C'est bon?*' the maître d', in short-sleeved white shirt and waistcoat, stops and asks us.

'*Bon*,' I agree, and smile.

'So she's not going to jump for joy at this proposition.' Charlie frowns, knife and fork poised, bringing us back to Madame Beaumont despite the seducing smells from my plate.

'She just needs careful handling,' I tell him. 'She's very suspicious.' The wine is loosening my tongue. 'Oh, don't get me wrong,' I say quickly, 'she needs the business.' I cut into the fish and take a mouthful. It's wonderful, filling my mouth with buttery fish flavour and herbs. I finish my glass and then carry on. 'She'd go out of business without Featherstone's. And then the château would want to take over.' I stop.

'So Château Lavigne want the land?' Charlie tops up my glass.

'It adjoins theirs. They've been trying to buy it for years. Apparently they have vineyards all over the world.'

'Yes. Well, we must look after Madame Beaumont and make sure she understands that we're here to help.'

I feel so much better. I haven't messed things up then. Charlie cuts into his duck, pushing some of the straw-like French fries on to his fork, and begins to eat.

'You're in a perfect position. We know Madame Beaumont has been a small producer until now and we need to help her realise how good this could be for all of us. We use her grapes and others we can source,' he says quickly, and I'm not really taking it all in but it sounds great. 'Blend them to her recipe and we all get what we need. Madame Beaumont sells to us at a good price, better than before, and we're all happy.'

'Sounds great,' I agree, savouring the flaking fish.

'Isaac will be working on the blend, refining it, smoothing out the edges so it would be useful if you and he could work closely on this.'

I swallow. Isaac and I have spent so much time avoiding each other, I wonder how we will get on working closely.

'Perhaps you could assist him . . . let him know what he needs to make this work. I'm sure Madame Beaumont will be delighted not to have to work so hard. Tell her we could bring in any staff she wanted.'

'Oh, I'm not sure she'd agree to that, not straight away. She doesn't like change. We'd need to suggest it . . . gradually.'

'Fine, well, you keep working with her. If you need to take time to be up there, just go ahead. The others can cover for you in the office.'

'Really?'

'Sure.'

'But my targets?'

'If you manage to pull this agreement off with Madame Beaumont, you'll blow the others targets out of the water. There will definitely be a place for you on Team Featherstone's. I'd say that team leader job'll be in the bag.' He raises his eyebrows and flashes his wide smile, and I feel my stomach take ten floors up and down again in a lift.

I find myself staring wide-eyed. Me? Emmy Bridges. Team leader? Team Featherstone's! I get a feeling now that it's my time – that finally I'm going to fit in and start rising up life's ladder – and I feel myself start to swell with pride.

My shoulders drop and I find myself holding my head a little higher and smiling to myself.

'I'd love that,' I smile.

'Here, try some duck.' Charlie leans forward over the candlelit table and feeds me a forkful of the duck and prune marmalade. I close my eyes and open my mouth – just delicious – and my stomach zips up and down in the lift again.

I ask, 'So, what about you, Charlie, what does Charlie Featherstone want from life?' buoyed up by crémant and a little wave of confidence.

'Well,' he puts down his knife and fork and looks straight at me. 'For me it's easy. I want to work hard now. Make this company as profitable as I can, sell up and retire early. Enjoy the good life.' He smiles, takes up his cutlery again and cuts some more of his food. 'I love to keep fit and I want to be young enough to enjoy my life. Snowboarding in the winter, windsurfing in the summer. Sadly, my wife – my ex-wife – didn't see it like that. She couldn't cope with the hours I worked, became suspicious when I was with work colleagues and, well . . .' he shrugs, 'let's just say we weren't working towards the same goals. She wanted me to take time off, take more time with the family. I felt it was settling for second best. I want to work hard now and then retire in style. I'm working to give my family the best I can, the best schools, the best of everything.' He takes a sip of water.

'Of course, that's not to say I want to do it on my own. Obviously I hope to find someone to share it all with, someone who understands what it takes to get a business like this to be the best. Understand the work involved.' He sips his water again, not letting up on his eye contact. I feel a little skip of excitement and I look down at my food to hide my blushes.

After our main courses we share a plate of cheeses and then each have a delicious trio of desserts: a tiny *tarte tatin* made with pears, a small but perfect *crème brûlée*, and home-made ice cream with tiny black flecks of vanilla running through it.

Charlie excuses himself to use the bathroom and I'm staring out into the dark night, no longer able to see the vineyards, just a deep inky blue sky over the surrounding countryside. No light pollution at all, just bright diamond-like stars and the orange glow of the street lanterns pouring their light down the hillside. The bells from the church next door ring out and I'm just thinking they have a lovely sound when I realise my phone is ringing.

'Hello, Dad?' I suddenly panic. 'Everything all right? Look I'm really sorry about earlier.'

'No, love, it's fine. As it happens, the plumber's an old school friend of mine. Still doing a bit to keep him going in his retirement. The only thing . . . it's the bill.'

'Don't worry, Dad. Tell him I'll sort it. I'll get the money. I think I've got this sorted.'

'You're such a good girl, Emmy. I wish I could do more.'

'Don't worry, Dad, it's all in hand. I love you,' I say, before putting down the phone.

'Boyfriend?' Charlie asks, returning and sitting down again.

'No, no boyfriend, my dad, again,' I say, smiling.

'Oh? Well, that is good news. Coffee?'

Did he mean what I think he meant then? I get a ripple of excitement running through me. Maybe, just maybe, everything was going to go my way for once after all.

'Coffee would be lovely,' I reply.

'Of course, we could always stay if you wanted.' He nods towards the hotel and, slightly taken aback by his forwardness I find myself blushing. Then he smiles widely. 'Perhaps another time? Or maybe I should take you away for a weekend, down south maybe, or Paris?' He grins again and I realise he's joking. At least, I think he is.

We walk back through the town after the coffees, which were delivered with a plate of pink and green macaroons, in the orange glow of the brass lanterns, under the stars like diamonds on a black blanket. People are still walking in and out of the cloisters, drinking in the coolness of the evening air. As we make our way down the steep cobbled hill, Charlie offers his arm to steady me and I take it. Then I look up and in the direction of Clos Beaumont, just visible across the valley, and feel a warm glow of contentment. The steep hill flattens out, but he keeps my arm tucked in his, pulling me closer. As we head back through the vine-lined backroads to the *gîte*, I have a nervous feeling of expectation in my tummy.

'Well, good night, Emmy,' Charlie says quietly as we stand in the stone shadows of the *gîte*. 'Well done again today.'

'Thank you,' I say, 'for this evening.' I'm just about to turn and go inside when suddenly he leans forward and kisses me, first on one cheek and then the other. Then, without any forewarning, he quickly moves on to my lips, kissing me more and more hungrily. He'd taken me so by surprise I wonder whether to pull away. He'd seemed interested, yes, for a man who couldn't remember my name until today. This has come as a bit of a shock. Maybe it's the wine, the setting or the fact that this gorgeous man wants me, but I find myself letting myself be kissed, kissing him back. Why not? I think, buoyed up by crémant and red wine, the warm evening air and smell of the wisteria tree. It's a fabulous end to a fabulous night. Charlie fancies me as much as I fancy him. His hands start to run over my body and he moves me back further into the shadows and against the rough stone wall of the *gîte*, his body pushed up against mine. Then suddenly he stops, and takes hold of my hand, looking this way and that in the shadows.

'Come on, come back to the house. We can make a night of it.' He gives a tug at my hand. I'm all out of breath and find myself half wanting to carry on this moment of madness and half thinking that I should probably stop, right now.

'I . . .'

'Come on, it'll be fun.' His eyes are dancing, inviting me to dive in. He runs his hand over my back, then lower.

And I know I shouldn't but I can't help but think how very nice it would be. A carefree night with a gorgeous man. It's not like I'm a teenager. I'm a mature woman. I'm thirty-five! And it has been a very long time since I've spent any time with a gorgeous man, alone, without my father asking if they're staying for supper. Except it wouldn't be carefree. He's my boss. And I don't want to this to be just one night.

'Come on.' He tugs again.

'Hello?' Suddenly Candy's voice comes from the upstairs window. 'Emmy, is that you?' she asks suspiciously.

Suddenly I can't help myself: I giggle nervously.

'Ssh,' says Charlie, pushing me up against the wall again and putting a finger to my lips.

Then the window shuts with a bang.

'I'd better go in,' I say, feeling like a bucket of cold water has been thrown over us, cooling things down, which probably isn't a bad thing. 'Don't want them to think that I'm trying to get off with the boss and that there's any favouritism going on,' I add sensibly.

'No, you're right.' Charlie runs his hand through his now dishevelled hair. 'Best to keep this between ourselves.'

'Yes, I think that's best.' I step away from the wall, my raging wantonness quickly subsiding. 'We have plenty of time to get to know each other.'

'Look, take down my number, call me when you can get away again.' Charlie pulls out his phone and I do the same, saving his number.

'Let's do it again, soon,' he says, putting away his phone and stepping out of the shadows. 'Catch up with all the news from Clos Beaumont. Take up where we left off. I'd like that.'

'Yes, I'd like that too,' I say with a shiver of excitement.

He gives me another killer smile. 'Why not take tomorrow to go and see Madame Beaumont, get things moving?'

'Sure,' I reply through numb lips, sore lips.

'Promise?'

'Promise,' I assure him.

And then he disappears round the corner to the Featherstones' house. I stand for a moment and touch my swollen lips. I can't believe that just happened. One minute

I'm hiding bottles down my trousers, thinking I'm going to get the sack, the next I'm having dinner with the boss and practically crawling into his bed. Charlie Featherstone is drop-dead gorgeous with those amazing eyes, he's successful and, what's more, he fancies me. Yay! Slowly and slightly stunned at the turnaround in events, I let myself into the *gîte*.

Inside, Isaac is in the kitchen, feet up on the table, playing guitar.

'I understand we're going to be working closely together from now on,' he says without looking at me and I wait for one of his jokes. But nothing comes. Instead I blush and turn and make my way up to bed where I know Candy will be waiting to interrogate me, wanting a full report on my evening. A report she'll get, but it won't be full one.

Chapter Seventeen

'*Bonjour, Madame Beaumont*,' I try to say breezily as I step in through the French doors the next morning, and down the three steps into the living-cum-kitchen-cum-bedroom, feeling like I have a guilty secret, wishing I could tell her outright about the supermarket buyer, but I know that I need to put this idea to her gently.

Then I realise that's not the only reason I'm feeling a little guilty this morning. That kiss. It was *just* a kiss, I remind myself, but a very passionate one, and I can't help feeling it was all a bit quick. I had no idea he even liked me!

The door to the rest of the house is firmly shut as it always is, and the big wood-burning stove with its silver snakelike flue going up the wall to the outside is flickering pathetically. Despite the days still being warm, the nights and early mornings are cold.

'*Bonjour, Emmy.*' Madame Beaumont kisses me, looking surprised. 'You're not usually here in the morning. No work today?' she asks.

'Just . . . a day off,' I tell her. I don't tell her Charlie told me to come. 'You don't mind, do you?' I suddenly worry.

'Of course not.'

'Shall we walk the vines?' I ask brightly, and she nods, pleased.

'*Bien sûr.* Actually, I would like to walk to the graveyard, through the vines,' she says, standing stiffly. Then she looks at me. 'Perhaps you would like to join me?'

'*Oui. Absolument*. That would be lovely.' I know Charlie's keen to tell Madame Beaumont about the buyer and to get working on this year's vintage. I have to speak to her today and this is the perfect time. I promised. The memory of Charlie's kiss comes back to me but instead of making me feel excited, I feel a little embarrassed about that too. Snogging outside the front door like a teenager. And to think what might have happened if Candy hadn't interrupted us.

Madame Beaumont and I walk through the vines, in more silence than usual, both of us thoughtful. The ever-present breeze up here runs through my hair. There is a hint of autumn in the air, a feeling of change, letting us know September is over. We walk all the way through the vines, across roads and between vineyards on the well-worn track to town and the graveyard. Passing through the big wrought-iron gates, which squeak on their hinges, we reach the black shiny headstone and stop and stand beside it, taking in the peace and quiet.

'Is it someone in your family?' I look at the gold writing on it. She nods and then, as I've seen her do from Featherstone's window, pulls out her duster from her basket to polish it. I look up at Featherstone's building and swear I can practically feel Candy glaring back at me from indoors as she works on the phones. I look back at the headstone.

'My mother was cremated,' I say suddenly.

Madame Beaumont looks up. 'Tell me,' she says.

'I think I told you it was when I was much younger. She died when I was nineteen, going on twenty. Sixteen years ago now. I'd just retaken my A levels. I got just enough to get to study nursing. It was hard. I'm dyslexic, which is why I'm not great at books and all of that. But I did love the idea of nursing.'

She says nothing and I find myself just talking.

'I think money was tight and with a family to feed . . .' I still find it hard to talk about. 'My sister wanted to go on a school trip and my mum was working extra hours to pay for that and extra tutoring for me. It was hard. There was a silly row, but it was over nothing. They were great parents to both of us.'

'It's sad you don't see your sister these days. Is there no way of putting things right?'

'She married young,' I raise my eyebrows, 'got pregnant at twenty-one. She had hoped to go to college, but well . . . that didn't happen. But she was happy.' I find myself smiling at the memory. 'He was a promising footballer. She got pregnant and they decided to marry.' And that's when she left us, I think.

'Go on,' Madame Beaumont encourages and I sit on the grass just beside her and sigh.

'They were girlfriend and boyfriend at school. But then her husband, Dion, had an injury, on a skiing holiday. It finished his career. He couldn't play any more without the injury recurring. It was really sad. But they stayed together even when he was finding life tough. And then he went into business. Property development. He needed some money to invest and, well, Jody asked Dad. He gave her the insurance money, Mum's insurance money. It was meant to pay off the mortgage after her death, but he lent it to Jody. She promised to pay it back almost straight away. Dion was investing with some other guys who'd done this kind of thing before. Buying at auction, doing up the houses, selling them straight on.'

'And did she? Pay your father back?' Madame Beaumont brings out a peach from her basket and a small knife and cuts it, offering me half.

'Well . . . that was four years ago. And no, they didn't pay it back. Now we're about to lose the house because we're behind on the mortgage payments.'

I bite into the juicy, sweet peach, sucking up the juice from my fingers, letting some slide to the ground over my hand.

'I have a nephew; two, actually, but one I've barely seen. One's six and the other must be four now.'

'And your mother? How did she die?' Madame Beaumont asks. We might as well get it all out in the open.

'A car crash. It was wet. A terrible night. My dad . . . well, he's never got over it. Actually, none of us has. He told me not to go after her. That she'd come back. And he believed she would. I still think he does.' I give a half laugh, half hiccup.

'And so you look after him?'

I nod.

Madame Beaumont rearranges the flowers on the gravestone.

'Don't you want to leave, make a life for yourself?'

'One day. But right now, he needs me.' I shrug. 'Without Mum and Jody, he has no one.'

She finishes the flowers and goes to stand. I put out my hand to help her up, but she ignores it and pulls herself up. She looks up at the sky and then out at the busy road, tractors laden with grapes from all the vineyards and châteaux pass by at speed. The harvest has begun in earnest.

'Shouldn't you be starting too?' I ask, looking at the tractor passing along the road, bouncing this way and that with a trailer of green grapes.

'It's nearly time,' she says. 'We will harvest soon.' And I breathe a sigh of relief. I was worried she was going to leave it too late. I'd hate for her grapes to spoil. 'But not yet,' she adds, 'not until after the full moon,' and gives me a little grin.

We walk back through the vines, she leaning heavily on her stick.

'And what of your father now?' she continues.

'Actually, I'm a bit worried,' I find myself telling her. 'He rang me yesterday to say there was a problem in the house. But I couldn't talk. Now I can't get hold of him.'

'Perhaps he's out?' she shrugs.

'Dad never goes out. Not since Mum died. He took early retirement after gardening leave at fifty-two and, well, he's never done anything since.' I think about the difference in my dad and Madame Beaumont, who must be seventy, if not more. 'He used to be a really gregarious man. And great at DIY – he'd take on anything.'

'It must be where you get it from,' she smiles, and I feel a little surge of pride.

'He was so proud of me when I got just enough GCSEs to go to college and do A levels. He knew how hard I found it.'

'Some people are just more practical, others think they can learn all they need from books . . . like that friend of yours.' For a moment I think she means Charlie and then realise she actually means Isaac. 'You have to feel and understand your vines to make good wine,' she grins.

'Actually . . .' I go to say. I have to tell her that Isaac's not really my friend, close or otherwise.

'I didn't know my father.' She looks straight ahead as we head up to the farmhouse and I stop what I was about to say. I get the feeling it has been a very long time since Madame Beaumont has talked about this, to anyone.

'He planted these vines.' She is running her hands over their big green leaves as if rubbing the heads of children and in some way connecting her to her father. The wind is lifting the corners of their leaves. Where leaves have fallen she picks them up. The bunches of grapes are hanging low, now full and fat. We look back at the farmhouse on the other side of the bowl. 'He loved it here.'

'Was he a wine-maker too?'

She shakes her head. 'He was a young German soldier, stationed here in the war.'

It takes a moment or two for it to sink in.

'That's why your first name is German – Adele?'

She gives a gentle nod and a smile.

'But why Beaumont?'

She takes a deep breath and I realise this Pandora's Box has been tightly shut for some time.

'They weren't married. After the war my father returned

to Germany, before I was born, vowing to return. In neighbouring villages, women who had become close with the German soldiers, collaborated,' she looks at me, 'were lined up and had their heads shaved, shaming them. In other towns, they were shot. Here, we were just shunned.'

I think about the townspeople: Monsieur and Madame Obels, the mayor. Looks like she's been an outsider for a very long time.

'But my grandparents and my mother brought me up to be proud of who I am. Hence my German name.'

I feel a tennis ball in my throat and my eyes prickle.

'My mother and father loved each other very much.'

A single tear slides down my cheek and I brush it away quickly.

Slowly, we walk back towards Clos Beaumont turning our attention back to the vines.

'See here, just about ready.' She points to the big fat bunches of grapes as we reach her land. We both wave away the gathering birds on the telephone wire, Madame Beaumont with her thumbstick – '*Allez, allez, allez* . . .' – and me swinging my arms around like great big windmills, as if I was six again, and feeling the same sense of freedom and joy. Out of breath and both of us laughing at our exertions, we walk back towards the farmhouse. As we get closer I can see a dark silver Audi and the familiar figure of Charlie standing by the door looking like Simon Cowell in his aviator sunglasses. Instead of my heart lifting at the sight of him, it dips. I know exactly why he's here.

'Who's that?' Madame Beaumont returns to the scowl. 'Not another visitor from the château?'

'No, it's Charlie Featherstone. Mr Featherstone's son,' I explain.

She seems to relax a little, but I don't. Why is he here? Does he want to just take over, like the château, without thinking about Madame Beaumont? He said he'd leave it to me. Forgetting our kiss and how attractive I found him last night, I start to march towards him. This is not what we agreed. I need him to let me do this my own way.

'Why is he here? We have delivered all last year's vintage, *non*?' she asks.

'*Non*, I mean, *oui*. We have. He probably just wants a word with me.'

As we reach the top of the hill and the end of the vines, Charlie steps out to walk towards us, but Cecil has other ideas.

'Woooo, woooo, woooooooo.' He stands up, front feet first, pulling himself to all four as if his old joints really are finding it all too much like hard work these days. But his efforts are enough to stop Charlie from getting any closer. He stops and Cecil's jowls wobble, a long slick of drool starts to grow and Charlie backs away.

'Hi, Charlie,' I say as brightly as I can, patting Cecil and expertly swerving his drool.

'Great, you're here! So how are things going?' he says charmingly but also briskly, flashing one of his big white smiles, fixing me with his eyes. 'It's harvest time.' He looks around, frowning. 'It would be great to know that we're in here, y'know, bringing in some of the Featherstone's team to oversee things,' he says pointedly to me.

Madame Beaumont joins me by my side.

'Ah, Madame Beaumont, I was just saying to Emmy—' But he's stopped in his tracks by Madame Beaumont.

'*Monsieur.*' She nods and puts out her hand to shake. '*Enchanté.*'

'*S'cuse em moi,*' he nods his apology and acknowledges his schoolboy error. '*Madame Beaumont. Je suis Charlie Featherstone, fils Eric Featherstone, mon père,*' he says by way of introduction, slowing the whole conversation down, which quite possibly was Madame Beaumont's intention as she sizes him up and I seize the opportunity to take control of the situation.

'Charlie is just here to see how your harvest is coming along, isn't that right, Charlie?'

Madame Beaumont gives a little laugh. 'The harvest will happen when it's ready to happen. These things mustn't be rushed. Mother Nature knows what she's doing.' She smiles, and so do I, feeling I've held him off.

'I'm just about to make my way back to the office,' I say trying to push things along and get him to leave.

'The thing is . . .' he starts again, and I suddenly feel a little flare of anger. Just like when my sister was bullied at school, when Trevor wanted me to sell to older clients who didn't need or could afford any more stock, when the bailiffs were in our house, looking through our belongings. I can't bear seeing people railroaded. It really would be better if I told her about the supermarket buyer and Charlie wanting to bring in his own wine-maker, Isaac.

'The thing is!' I say loudly to stop Charlie in his tracks. He looks at me in surprise. 'Charlie is really pleased with this year's vintage, aren't you?' I'm nodding at him slowly, eyes narrowed and glaring, in order to get him to leave me to this.

He promised! Pushing her like this is not the way.

'Yes, I am. Delighted in fact . . .'

'*Bon. Maintenant, du café?*' Madame Beaumont says, turning towards the French doors.

'No, no, we must be going.' I go to stand in front of Charlie, blocking his way, but before I know it, he's side-stepped me.

'Actually, Madame Beaumont—' he carries on.

'No, Charlie!' I blurt out and grab his wrist. He will totally blow this if he goes in like this. She'll never agree to having Isaac here or selling to the supermarkets like this. Especially after what she's just told me about her parents and how much the vines mean to her. They're . . . well, they're more than just grapes to her. She'll need time to come round to the idea of having strangers here.

'Excuse us,' he says to Madame Beaumont, who is looking at us in bewilderment, and steers me towards his car, talking quietly to me.

'Leave this to me, Emmy. Really, I know what I'm doing.'

'Charlie, I hate to disagree, but you really don't . . .'

'Emmy, I'm still your boss,' he reminds me, silencing me as I smart. 'Now, we need to get organised. It works for everyone. Madame Beaumont has a good but rustic wine. I have an interested buyer and a wine-maker who can smooth it out.'

Strip it of its character, I think. 'Leave it to me. Let me make her understand how we'll work with her. She won't want you to take over. This is her family's vineyard, it's as precious to her as her actual family.' I try to persuade him, but he's not listening.

'With the harvest upon us –' he looks around, noting that nothing is happening in Clos Beaumont – 'I need to have our team in here, getting the grapes in. I'm helping. Leave this to me now, Emmy.'

'Leave what?' We turn. Madame Beaumont is frowning and she looks at Charlie, then at me and back again, raising a grey eyebrow.

'The thing is, Madame Beaumont . . .' Charlie's voice drops as he starts to deliver his pitch.

Don't do it, Charlie! a voice is shouting in my head. It's like I'm listening to the sat-nav going down the wrong route and heading for disaster.

'. . . Your wine is good, but you don't make enough of it for me to continue selling it next year.'

Madame Beaumont's face doesn't move. I'm frozen to the spot; there's nothing I can do. He's going to completely ruin everything.

'But,' he says, as if delivering her a golden ticket, 'there is a buyer, from the UK, a supermarket buyer . . .'

'Nooo,' I try but know my words are now falling on deaf ears.

'. . . who loves your wine. She wants to take it and turn it into a blend, a "good, basic claret", and roll it out to all her stores. So, what we want is to work out your blend. We'll bring in pickers and a wine-maker, get it all done for you, and blend your grapes with other grapes from the area.' He smiles.

She still says nothing, just stares at him. In the distance is the hum of tractors in the neighbouring fields, harvesting.

'Oh, and one last thing, we need to make your vines as

high-yielding as possible. Obviously your *terroir* is fantastic. That's what makes this wine so special. But I understand they're quite old. So I suggest ripping out the vines you have here and we'll replant them up with new high-yielding ones. We'll do it in stages, *parcelle* by *parcelle*.' He's beaming now, like he's delivered the winning lottery cheque right to her front door and waved away all her worries with his magic wand. My hands fly up to clutch my head.

My toes curl and I'm praying for the dusty ground to open up and swallow me. Standing here, watching him come in here like a wrecking ball, I'm actually beginning to wonder what exactly it was that I found so attractive about Charlie last night. Thank God I didn't go to bed with him. A flush rushes up my chest and into the tips of my ears, making them feel like they're on fire as I wait for Madame Beaumont's response. The silence is deafening.

Still she says nothing. Slowly I raise my eyes from where I've been staring at my toe making circles in the dusty ground. Her face is set.

'I . . . I . . .' The right words won't come. I want to tell her it's not as drastic as it sounds, he's just trying to help, that without this lifeline she'll have no income at all next year and I didn't want her to have to sell out to the château.

'You knew about this . . . this plan?' she says slowly, and despite us being outside on a glorious autumn day, with the birds singing and the hum of tractors, you could hear a pin drop. My throat goes dry, my eyes prickle and sting, my ears still burn.

'Yes,' I croak.

'Well, we just thought that with Emmy here helping you,

she'd be the best one to tell you the good news.' Charlie's smile slips slightly, letting on that this hasn't quite gone according to plan. Uncertainty is circling us like the Mistral wind.

Madame Beaumont's eyes dim, the sparkle gone. Her nostrils flare a little, her back stiffens. Her eyes darken further. Where there was friendship and an understanding, now there is hurt. I feel terrible. I can feel her hurt. She thinks I've betrayed her. The bond we've built over the past few weeks, and the closeness we experienced in the graveyard has been well and truly broken.

'I think you'd better leave,' she says to me finally, and turns towards the French doors.

'Madame Beaumont, please.' I put out a hand and run to follow her.

She turns back and says sharply, 'And this supermarket buyer, how did she come to learn of my wine? How did she get the idea I would like it turned into a supermarket blend to sit on the shelves and be like all those other wines that have no character or soul?'

'I only had your best interests at heart, you have to believe me.' There is a crack in my voice.

She nods stiffly, slowly meeting my eyes. 'Then you obviously have no understanding about me or my wine.' I can feel the anger in her measured words. 'You would have me be like everyone else, pretending that each vintage is the same.' She raises an eyebrow. 'I find myself feeling very disappointed.' And I swear there's a crack in her voice, too.

'Madame Beaumont!' I go to run after her again. I just can't bear the thought of her believing I was here to deceive her. 'Please, I just wanted to give you time to come round to the idea.'

'I will never come round to that idea. I trusted you. Now, please, leave,' she says sharply. 'Just go.'

She turns and steps into the house, slamming the door firmly behind her and swishing the curtain across.

I hiccup, trying to stifle a sob, biting my top lip, trying not to let the tears fall. Cecil barks and looks at me, making me need to fight back the tears even more. I run past Charlie, out of the gates and as I do, I swear I hear a raised voice and a clatter of pans from Madame Beaumont's front room. I have to get out of here as quickly as I can. I pick up my bike from the wall, barely able to see through the tears swimming in my eyes now. I swing my leg over and mount, but wobble this way and that down the hill, sniffing and trying to wipe my nose with my sleeve, and every time I take my hand off one of the handle bars, the bike wobbles violently across the road, just as it had when I first arrived. It takes a while for me to realise Charlie is following behind me. When the road widens, he draws up beside me.

'Would you like a lift? You don't look very safe,' he asks out the window. I see my reflection in his aviator sunglasses.

'I'm fine!' I snap back, nearly going head first into a ditch to my right as a tractor comes up the hill towards Saint Enrique. My heart squeezes thinking of Madame Beaumont living in the shadow of that château and having fought for so long not to be swallowed up by it. And now, here am I suggesting exactly the same thing! I don't think I could ever feel much worse than I do right now.

Chapter Eighteen

The phone at the other end rings and rings and I'm about to give up when it rattles out of its cradle as it's finally picked up.

'Dad?' I say, unable to stop the catch in my throat.

'Emmy?' I'm stopped in my tracks when I hear the familiar voice, as familiar as if we've spoken only yesterday. Only we haven't, it's been years. My beating heart suddenly goes from walk to gallop.

'It's me, Jody,' she says tentatively. Why on earth is Jody in our house? I pull the phone away from my ear and double-check I've dialled home. I have. What on earth can have happened? Something dreadful, if Jody's been called to there.

'Jody? Where's Dad? Is everything OK?' My mouth is dry, my head banging and I look down and try to focus on the uneaten salad niçoise next to the small glass of rosé that's now only half full. I seem to be taking little sips, little and often. Charlie told me to go straight to lunch when we got back to Featherstone's and he marched off to see Isaac about 'the Madame B problem'. So I'm sitting at a small round table outside Le Papillon. The owner is kind and polite, and realises I'd like to be left alone. But still I turn my back on the other lunchtime diners coming in from the vines for their two-hour break.

'Yes, there's no problem. Dad's fine,' Jody says quickly to reassure me. Is she lying, trying to ease my guilt about leaving him? But then why would Jody do that? I can't find any words. Where do you start with someone you've loved your whole life who ripped out your heart and stamped all over it?

'Just thought I'd visit. See how things are.' I hear her try to clear her tight throat. I can hear her two boys arguing in the background.

'When did you get there?' I finally manage, wondering what it is she wants and wishing I was there to find out. There's no more money, that's for sure. She's had everything. Not that she'd need money, what with her husband being a big property investor these days.

'Last night,' she replies, and then with forced cheerfulness: 'Dad made us macaroni cheese and bacon, just like when we were kids . . .' She trails off.

'Dad made macaroni cheese?' I say, astounded. 'With bacon?' He struggles to boil an egg on his own! Which is why I spent all my time filling the freezer with ready meals for one before I left.

The noise from the children is getting louder and I'm not sure if they're playing or starting a war.

'Is Dad there? Can I speak to him?' I ask, my heart twisting, wanting to ask how she is, how the boys are, but something's stopping me.

'Dad's gone to the pub, The Castle, with his mate,' Jody says, almost matter-of-factly.

'Sorry? Did you say . . . Dad's gone to the pub? What

mate?' Now I'm really worried. What is going on? I push the tuna around my plate and Jeff passes, waving a cheery greeting on his way for his lunchtime aperitif. I wave back and call '*Salut*' without thinking.

'Gosh, you really are getting to grips with the lingo, aren't you? Dad says you're doing really well out there. You always were the clever one,' I hear my sister say, and there's a slight shake in her voice.

This is all a bit surreal. My sister, whom I haven't seen for four years, is in my house, visiting. And my dad is in the pub, somewhere he hasn't been in fifteen years. And he certainly hasn't got any mates.

'Jody? What's up?' I say, taking a firm hold of the situation. 'Did Dad phone you about the water tank?'

And she suddenly breaks down in tears.

'I've left him, Emmy . . . Dion. I've left him.' Her voice is thin and she's taking big gulps through the strangled sobs.

'Dion! What, husband Dion?' I say loudly. Heads at the bar turn to look at me and I quickly lower my voice. 'Jody?'

She sniffs some more.

'The two-timing shit!' she spits out.

'Oh, Jody . . .' And no matter what's happened, the years seem to melt away and I just want to be there and wrap my arms around her.

'It's been going on for ages. I just didn't have the guts to leave. When he was still playing, there were always girls around, wanting to bag a footballer of their own, but I thought we were different.'

'Why didn't you say something?' I ask, but I know why.

'He'd pushed me away from you and Dad. Said it was him and the kids or you and Dad. Said he'd fight for custody. So I stayed. It felt like I didn't have a family any more . . . and after what he'd done, I didn't feel I could just pick up the phone.'

There is a silence. I know we still have so much to talk about, but right now none of it seems to matter.

'Well,' I say, a crack in my voice, 'I'm here now, whenever you need me.'

'Thank you,' she practically whispers through the tears that I know are falling, and I want nothing more than to pull her to me and tell her everything will be OK.

'Ssh, ssh,' I tell her, just like I used to when she'd cry herself to sleep after Mum died. I'd crawl into bed with her, wrap my arms around her and rock slowly back and forth, just as I'm doing to the phone right now.

'Oh, and Emmy?' Jody says through the sniffs, just before I hang up. 'It's great to see Dad sleeping back in his and Mum's old bedroom, really great.'

'He isn't,' I reply, confused.

'He is,' she says more brightly. 'Apparently after the tank burst and water came through the ceiling in his room, he moved back in there.'

Dad's been sleeping in Jody's old room for several years. I'm stunned. 'Oh, and he's cooking toad-in-the-hole tonight, too. My favourite. Love you loads, sis,' says Jody, sounding even brighter, finally hanging up.

Words fail me. Toad-in-the-hole? I wrap my arms around myself and let the tears flow. I'd give anything to be at home with Dad and Jody having toad-in-the-hole. I want to go home, I realise with absolute certainty. I just want to go home.

'Hello, my name's Emmy, I'm calling from Featherstone's Wines. I just wondered if you'd had a chance to look at our brochure or website and whether you'd like to order anything this afternoon . . .'

'My name's Candy from Featherstone's Wines . . .'

'Nick . . .wondered if you'd had a chance . . .'

'I'm Gloria . . . anything you'd like to order this afternoon?'

The same repetitive script is bouncing off the walls of the office as we sit, phones glued to our ears. I try to concentrate really hard on what I'm supposed to say, but my eyes are constantly drawn to the vineyard behind and the graveyard beyond it. But Madame Beaumont doesn't make her trip to the graveyard all afternoon and I know I've hurt her very badly indeed.

'One case of mixed red and white?' Candy's saying to her customer loudly for his benefit and ours. 'Is there anything else I can help you with today?' She trots out her word-perfect, well-practised script, giving me a smug sideways glance.

I refocus on my call.

'Sorry, would you say that again, a case of which?' I ask my caller to repeat. 'Oh, six cases? A fine, full bodied . . . red wine.' I try to remember the description but fail. 'A very good choice,' I say instead and I can feel Candy glare at me as my customer orders six cases of one of our most expensive red wines.

'For your daughter's wedding? Oh, congratulations. What are you having to eat?'

'Well, she keeps changing her mind, but I think she's gone for the chicken now.'

'Chicken, oh . . . well, in that case, you might want to go for . . . hang on . . .' I look up on the website. I'm sure there was a white on offer. 'Yes, have a look at this one. And if you buy six cases, you get an extra discount. It'll make it much cheaper for you.'

I can see Candy's face out of the corner of my eye turning from a scowl to a smirk as she thinks I'm doing myself out of sales again. I can't help it. And there's no point in me trying to match her sales figures; I'll never be able to.

'Hello, my name's Candy from Featherstone's Wines. I was wondering if you'd had a chance . . .'

She's like a mighty machine. I'll never catch her. I'll never win the bet. I can't do it. No matter how hard I try I can't be one of them. And after this morning's débâcle there's no way Charlie will keep me on now. We've lost Madame Beaumont's wine and I've probably lost my job too. I have no idea how I'm going to get Dad and me, and now Jody and her boys, out of our mess. No idea at all.

'Well, that does look like a good buy,' my customer is saying. 'Tell you what, how about I take the red and the white, just in case she changes her mind, and what about sparkling wines too?'

I talk him through the sparkling wines on offer and work out a brilliant saving for my customer.

'Are you sure it's not too much?' I double-check with him.

'My dear, I own a small estate in the Scottish borders. I

can definitely afford my wine bill. But you've been excellent help. I'll be sure to come back to you, thank you.'

We finish the conversation with me wishing him well and then realising I've barely looked at my script. As I look up Charlie is standing by my desk making my heart clatter and jump all at the same time. He's not looking happy.

'Emmy, can I have a word?'

Candy flashes me another smug smile and lifts her chest.

'Hello, my name is Candy . . .' She shows off loudly.

Both Nick and Gloria stop making calls for a moment as I follow Charlie out to his office. Then, as I go down the wooden steps I hear them pick up their phones and start working through their spiel.

'So, things didn't go quite to plan this morning,' he says, one thigh on the desk, but I don't find my insides shifting like they did when Isaac helped me with the bike. I make myself cross by thinking it, and shove the memory away.

'Actually, Charlie, you're right,' I take a big breath. 'I've completely messed things up. I'm not cut out for this.' I'm never going to make my targets. I'll never be in line for the team leader's job or to win the bet and pay back Candy. I need to get home and find another job – fast! I'll apply to the new superstore and every store in Cardiff. I must be able to find something. I have to be with my family right now, they need me far more than Featherstone's does.

'Well, I agree things haven't gone according to plan.' He adjusts the line of pens on his desk to make them perfectly straight.

'I've made a decision.' I look up from my hands in my lap.

'I think I'm the one who should be saying that,' he interrupts me, half joking. I ignore him.

'I'm going home,' I tell him, looking him straight in the eye and he looks visibly shocked. 'I have to. My family need me.' I feel just like I did when the school rang me to say they were worried about Jody; that Dad wasn't coping after Mum died. I just dropped everything and went. I'm shaking. My only concern is getting back to them as quickly as possible, just as I did then. We'll find a way to cope, we always have. I could work double shifts in the superstore if needs be. Again I'm catapulted right back to the night of my Mum returning home from a double shift. Her tired, worn-out face that was once so full of fun and life. Before the worries of keeping up with school trips and extra tuition fees, trying to be like everyone else.

'But I thought . . . you can't just leave. I mean, there's Madame Beaumont. The wine. The buyer. You're our only hope.' He sounds momentarily flustered and on the back foot.

'I think we can agree I've well and truly messed that up.' I go to stand, looking at the wide floorboards.

'And then, of course . . . there's you and me,' he says clumsily, suddenly pulling back one of his smiles and cocking his head to one side. He puts his finger under my chin, lifting my face to his, catching me in his gaze. I wish he didn't have this effect on me, where I feel like I've been metaphorically pinned against the wall and undressed with his eyes. I wish there could have been a 'you and me', but I'm still not convinced he is really interested. Lovely as it would be, I have to go. My sister and my dad need me, just as they did when Mum died. And right now, I need them too. Madame Beaumont certainly doesn't need my interference any more.

'Look, take your time. Why not sleep on it? You and I could take some time out at the weekend. Maybe have that weekend away we talked about yesterday,' he smiles. 'Separate rooms, of course. If that's what you wanted. I could show you a bit more of the country. Show you what you'd be missing. I really want to persuade you to stay.' And again my silly head and heart clash, wondering whether it's me he wants to stay or whether he merely thinks I can still work on Madame Beaumont, which I definitely can't. I excuse myself quickly, before I get taken in by the daft idea. I mustn't be foolish and rash. I need to work out what Dad, Jody and I are going to do now.

I break into a run as I head back to the *gîte* and bump straight into Isaac. He pulls out one of his headphones he's permanently attached to.

'Hey, you OK?' He holds my arms, the bud earphone swinging across his chest. 'Don't tell me you let Candy finally get your goat?'

'No, no, sorry, um, I have to be somewhere.' I sidestep him and head for the bike leaning against the log store. Isaac is the very last person I want to see. If it hadn't been for Isaac telling me I could have my job and my man, maybe I wouldn't have made such a mess of things. But I know really I have only myself to blame. As usual I'm too busy trying to sort out other people's lives and making a complete pig's ear of my own and theirs along the way.

Isaac follows me, then catches my elbow.

'Look, I overheard you and Charlie talking. I was in the

shop. For what it's worth, I don't think you should go, Emmy.'

'And why would I care what you think?' I cling to the bike handle bars. 'You think we're all useless anyway! What was it you said? "Like seagulls round a cigarette butt, wondering how to eat it."' I wish I could suck the words back in as soon as I've said them.

He doesn't respond but looks embarrassed.

'It's my family,' I tell him quickly, so as not to cause any more trouble than I already have. 'They need me.'

He nods. 'OK. I understand.' But I don't think he does really.

He shrugs, turns away and walks back to his work room, and I leave the bike and run into the *gîte* to splash cold water on my face at the kitchen sink.

'So is it true? Is she really going?' I can hear Candy saying to the others as they file out of the office, coffees in hand.

'That's what Colette told Gloria,' Nick is telling them.

'Apparently her family needs her,' Gloria is telling Candy. I watch through the window as they head towards a table and chairs in the early autumn sunshine.

'Shame. She was really getting to know about this wine game. Did you hear her on the phone this morning?' Nick says, surprising me.

Candy harrumphs, not surprising me.

'Least that means I get a room to myself now,' she says like a true prima donna.

'I'll share with you,' Nick offers, and my eyebrows shoot up.

'Oh, Nick,' I hear Candy laugh, 'everyone should have a

gay best friend like you.' I walk back towards the bike, and I don't hear Nick laugh in return.

I set off one last time on the bike. I cycle as hard as I can and the bike doesn't wobble. I don't even stop when cars pass me on the other side of the road. I look over to the abandoned café where there seems to be work going on; workmen in overalls. I put my head down and ride confidently and quickly, like I've been doing this route all of my life, over the stone bridge with ease and powering up the hill. I have to tell Madame Beaumont that I'm sorry and that I've decided to leave. I can't stay here now. I hope she'll forgive me. But I need to warn her that she has to find another way of selling her wine next year. Maybe I could talk to some of the other wine merchants in the town when I get back. Oh, there I go again, always thinking I can fix other people's lives. When am I going to realise that I should just leave people alone. I need to sort my own life out first. And right now, seeing as I'm about to throw in the towel here, I need to get home and find a new job to support my family, which has grown since I've been away. I'm not sure that Jody has ever worked, and Dad certainly doesn't have a job or any likelihood of getting one. I push on, up the hill, standing on the pedals, and realise I would never have been able to do this when I first got here. But I should never have come in the first place. The sooner I get this over and done with, the sooner I can get home and find out what on earth's going on with my family.

Chapter Nineteen

I'm hot when I arrive, though the breeze has really picked up here.

I'm as nervous as I was the time I had to stand up and give a recital in the school assembly. I was ten years old, but it still feels like yesterday. It was harvest time, just like now, and I was supposed to be reading a poem about autumn. But the words all blurred on the page and I knew I'd be the laughing stock of the school.

'*Allo? Allo? Madame Beaumont?*' I call, walking round the yard. The wind catches my hair as I turn this way and that in the ever-increasing gusts. I find an elastic band in my pocket and manage to tie up the sides in a little bunch on top of my head. I run round all the usual places where Madame Beaumont might be but there's no one around. Even Cecil isn't lying in his usual place in the middle of the yard. I put my head into the *chai*, but she's not there. I go to the vines to see if she and Cecil are seeing off the birds. She's not there either, but the birds are, back in the trees and on the overhead wire, gathering in numbers, eyeing the ever-ripening grapes. I run at them, shouting and waving my arms, expecting Cecil to join me at any moment, but he doesn't. All of a sudden, Henri lifts his head, his mane flying in the wind and lets out a high-pitched whinny. Nostrils flaring, he dips and bucks and then canters towards the gate as if trying to join me. The wind is blowing up through the vines, lifting Henri's tail high as he canters up and down, whinnying. It's so humid now. I look out across the vines to see if Madame Beaumont might be on her way back from the graveyard but there's no sign of the small black-clothed figure, just more gathering black clouds. I turn towards the farmhouse. It's a far cry from the smart farmhouse and *gîte* at Featherstone's, but somehow I fitted in far better here than I ever have there.

The warm wind blows my hair over my face as I turn and I peel it back, fighting it with both hands. As I do, I see Cecil lying, stretched out across the French doors at the back of the farmhouse, his head between his paws. He must have seen me when I arrived but he didn't make a sound. My heart lurches. Oh God, what if he's . . . what if he's ill? I run towards him.

'Cecil? Cecil?'

He lifts his head slowly and I let out a sigh of relief.

'Hey, Cecil.' I bend down and rub his head, he looks up at me, his eyes even sadder than usual, then flops his head back down and lets out a whimper. I don't know what's wrong, but something is. Henri is still thundering up and down the field and I doubt he's moved that much in years; he'll ache later.

I rub Cecil's head and look around.

'Where's your mistress, then?'

I stand up, swallow, roll my shoulders back and hear the click of tension in them. Then I clear my throat again before knocking on the French doors. The curtains are firmly closed just like when I left, when Madame Beaumont banged the door shut and swished the curtain across. There's no reply. If she is in there she clearly doesn't want visitors . . . and in particular, this one.

I feel wretched. I turn round and look at the scruffy farmyard that has become so familiar. I look at the *chai* where we have scrubbed the equipment, where I have hosed down concrete vats, inside and out, so you could eat your dinner off them. Clean and ready for the new vintage. I look out at the heavily laden vines, with big fat bunches of dark, marble-like grapes ready to start their new beginning too. I feel strangely sad I won't get to see them on the next leg of their journey. I knock again, but again, nothing. Cecil lets out another low sigh, repositioning his head between his feet.

'Come on, Cecil.' I try to get him to his feet, calling him to me. But he won't budge. I drop my hands to my side in frustration. Even Cecil won't acknowledge me. There's nothing here for me. I'm not wanted. It's time to go. I walk towards the lane and my bike.

Suddenly Cecil lifts his head and gives a bark. I turn back.

'I have to go, Cec.'

And just then I swear I hear a noise, a strangled shout.

'Madame Beaumont! Is that you?'

I can't leave if she'll speak to me.

'Adele? Where are you?' I'm looking around and suddenly my heart is beating faster and faster. I run round the *chai* and the other barns, calling her name, searching. Suddenly Cecil is up on his feet, barking.

'Madame Beaumont?' I shout, and run to the French doors. I try the handle. It's locked. But I'm sure I hear her again. Cecil is now barking for all he is worth. Big, fat rain drops begin to fall and I try to brush them from my face and eyes. I start to sweat as I jiggle the door handle again but it doesn't move.

'Shit!'

I look this way and that. She's not going to thank me for this if she's shouting at me to go away, but I can't leave not knowing. I pick up a rock by the door and, taking off my denim jacket, wrap it over my hand, then aim it at the pane of glass by the handle . . . I pull back my hand.

'Cecil?' I turn to check he's standing back. He is, barking like a metronome, evenly and steadily. I turn my attention back to the window pane, lick my lips and then chew on the bottom one. Just do it, I tell myself. And I do. I smash the rock at the glass. It cracks, shatters and breaks into tiny pieces, and I jump back as the glass falls at my feet.

I punch out the rest of the glass with my hand inside my jacket and then carefully put my hand through, unlock the door and pull down the handle.

'It's OK, Cecil, we're in,' I say, and he suddenly stops barking and lies down.

I open the door and pull back the heavy curtains with a whoosh along the iron curtain rail, but the rings get caught and I find myself fighting my way through them. My eyes adjust to the dark as I emerge from the curtains' clutches and then my heart lurches and the heat drains out of my body, and I suddenly feel very cold. I have found Madame Beaumont.

Chapter Twenty

'*Je savais que tu reviendras.*' Though her voice is thin and weak, she tries a smile, but her face contorts with pain.

'Of course I came back,' I say, the words catching in my throat.

'You're stubborn . . . like me.' I'm not sure if that's an insult or compliment, but either way she's probably right.

She isn't moving. She is lying just at the bottom of the three stone steps. She is grey she's so white, lying on the floor in front of me.

'Don't move, don't try and speak.' I run down the steps and straight to the settee, picking up a thin cushion, and then a blanket off the little bed in the corner.

'Just get me up and I'll be fine. Just a silly fall,' she says, but her face contorts as the pain drives through her and she slumps, slipping into unconsciousness. The old black and white cat is curled up in the small of her back.

'Oh God!' I pull out my phone and hold it high, swinging it around for a signal. I go back to the top of the three steps, looking down at Madame Beaumont. She looks tiny and frail, not like the small yet strong woman I have come to know.

I don't even know what the number is for the emergency

services. I bet it was written in my Featherstone's handbook. I should've read it.

I press Charlie's number. He'll know what to do.

The wind is howling now and the sky has darkened.

'Hi, this is Charlie Featherstone,' says the business-like voicemail message. I click it off.

'Stay awake, Madame Beaumont. Don't fall asleep.' *Oh God, Charlie, where are you?*

I ring the Featherstone's office number. It's the only other number I've got for anyone. I haven't become firm enough friends with anyone at the *gîte* for us to swap numbers. Far from it. I've been keeping my distance more than usual today, since the dinner with Charlie in Saint Enrique. I don't want them thinking – or should that be knowing – that there's something going on between us. Candy's office-romance radar is on permanent alert. She even thinks Nick has got a thing for Isaac because he keeps asking questions in class.

The phone is suddenly picked up and I'm waiting for the 'Featherstone's Wines, my name is . . . how can I help you?' But it doesn't come.

'Charlie?'

'Er, no, it's Isaac here. Look, Emmy,' he dives straight in before I can speak. 'About you leaving. I, um, if it's anything I said, I'm sorry, I know I can be a bit of a joker . . . the first night . . . the Goldilocks thing, and that other thing I said, about the seagulls—'

'No, no, it's nothing, really,' I cut him off. 'Um, but do you know where Charlie is?'

'Are you OK?'

'No, actually, it's Madame Beaumont. She's fallen. I need an ambulance. Can you ring one?'

'Sure, straight away. You stay with her, I'll sort it,' he says, and I thank him and hang up. It must be the most civilised conversation we've had, ever. Who knew Isaac could be so . . . well, grown up?

I shove the phone into my back pocket and run down the three steps. I kneel down on the cold stone floor by her head. Her usual pinned-back hair and bun are now strewn in wispy strands around her head, grey and thinning. I stand up and grab another cushion to sit on, my bare legs turning to goose-bumps. She's cold and I put another thin, threadbare blanket from her bed over her. She murmurs her thanks and I know she is just conscious. I have to keep her that way, by any means.

'I rang home . . .' I start to tell her about Dad going to the pub, moving back into the front bedroom and then my sister arriving and that I'm worried. But then I tell her Dad's made macaroni cheese, like he used to make. Dad was always the cook in our house. I can hear heavy rain continuing to beat down on the roof, there's a flash of lightning and I listen and count from the moment I see the flash to see how many miles away the storm is. Dad taught me how to do that when I was scared of the storms. My fear of storms has never gone away, not after Mum died that night. My nerves are jangling and I wish the ambulance would hurry up and get here.

'One, two, three, four . . .'

Bang! The thunder clap is huge, making me jump, but I look down at Madame Beaumont, who is getting colder and slipping into unconsciousness. Cecil lets out a low howl and even the cat looks at me and meows pitifully.

'How about a song?' My voice is high-pitched and shaky, but I'm determined not to let her slip from me.

'*Alouette*' is the only song that comes into my head, from my schooldays.

The lightning comes again.

'One, two, three . . .'

Bang!

'Arrr!' I shriek. '*Alouette, gentille alouette. Alouette, je te plumerai.*'

I keep singing and shrieking with every flash and bang.

'One, two . . .'

Bang!

'Arrrr!'

And then, the French doors fly open.

'Arrrr!' I shriek again, heart racing. The lights flicker off and back on again. That was a close one. I close my eyes tight and hold Madame Beaumont's hand even tighter.

'*Alouette, gentille alouette*,' I keep going.

Suddenly there's a male voice singing with me. Very close. '*Alouette, gentille alouette*,' and my heart jumps into my mouth, stopping me singing.

I open one of my eyes, just a tiny bit. There's that dark hair, the bandana, the hanging earring and an American twang to his '*Alouette*'.

'Thought you might have been the ambulance,' I say quietly, not wanting to alarm Madame Beaumont.

'On its way.' Isaac goes round the other side of Madame Beaumont's head, sits down on the floor and crosses his legs. 'How's she doing?'

'We're doing fine, aren't we, Madame Beaumont?' I say loudly. There's another flash and I count. The lights go out. I pull out my phone and use it as a torch.

' Two, three, four . . .'

Rumble.

'It's moving away, Madame Beaumont.' I sigh with relief.

Madame Beaumont mumbles and I bend down to hear her.

'Sorry, what's that?'

'I said, *Bon*. Now, can you stop singing that song?'

And I give a little laugh, delighted she's still with us and at the same time a tear rolls down my cheeks and I brush it away.

'Can I get you anything?' Isaac looks around.

I shake my head, knowing there won't be anything in. I don't think Madame Beaumont lives this frugally out of choice. I move my sitting position and lift Madame Beaumont's head into my lap. She doesn't seem to mind. I'm sure I'd know if she did. The cat stands up, turns round and lies back down again in the small of her back and I'm sure, in some way, he's doing his part too. I tuck the stray strands of hair behind her ears and redo the clips that have fallen.

'When's it going to be here?'

Isaac shrugs and looks unusually worried.

'It's coming from Bordeaux. I guess the weather isn't helping and sat-nav's not really going to help them out here. It's not like this in California,' he smiles, and for once I'm grateful for his jokes. He looks as worried as I feel and I want to take his mind off things.

'I'll light the fire.' He busies himself chopping up the wood in the basket into kindling.

'What is it like? Where's home for you?'

He shrugs, gathering the little wood splinters from the fire to put on top of scrunched-up paper.

'Nowhere permanent. I move around, working from winery to winery.'

'But you must have a home somewhere, family? Girlfriend? Where your parents live or something?'

He shakes his head. It's wet and the usually wavy hair has turned curly at the ends. I bet he had a full head of curls when he was a little boy.

'Both my parents are dead.' He lights a match and puts it to the paper.

'Oh, I'm sorry.'

'Don't be. They were wonderful. Just old. I was in care for part of my life. But my parents adopted me when I was twelve. I was a bit of a hell raiser at school. They straightened me out. My dad gave me two things in life: a love of wine and a love of travel . . . oh, and surfing. Growing up in California, how could I not?' The fire flickers into life after lots of encouragement from Isaac.

'So you always been afraid of storms?' he asks, sitting with his back to the fire as it gradually takes hold, and somehow, with the darkness and the worry, I let my guard down with him.

'I lost my mum. She died in a storm. Car accident. I just have my dad,' I find myself telling him as the storm rumbles away in the distance.

'Jeez, that's rough.'

'He hasn't ever really got over it.'

'That's why he rings you?'

I nod, look down at the phone in my hand and rub my thumb over the screen as if it helps me to stay close to him. I've lost one person I cared about to a storm, I'm not about to lose another.

'So, how does your girlfriend cope with you being away so much?' I change the subject quickly and keep the conversation flowing to keep Madame Beaumont with me.

Isaac puts his knees up and rests his elbows on them, hands held together. His leather wristbands, his friendship bracelets slide up his arm. His headphones hang round his neck. He looks towards the door. He's smiling.

'Let's just say, there's no one special in my life.'

'I'd say there's lots of special people in your life, just all in different countries and no one knows about the others.' I manage a little laugh.

'You got me.' He looks back at me and suddenly my insides jolt, like they've been stopped and suddenly restarted. 'Just waiting to meet the right one.' My heart beats absurdly at double speed.

'What about you and Charlie? You two have got something going on there, haven't you?'

My heart slows again and I blush. 'Oh, I don't know, especially with me going back to the UK now. Actually, have you any idea where he is?'

'Gone off to visit a château with Selina. Man, these wine sellers are all over the buyers like a rash,' he says matter-of-factly, and for a moment I get a tiny pang of jealously but it passes the moment I look down at Madame Beaumont's grey face.

Isaac stands up and I suddenly realise I don't want him to go.

'I'll get some logs in,' he tells me.

Any other time I'd be dying to get away from him, but I have to say, he's been brilliant here. Suddenly, I prick up my ears. I hear something. My hopes start rise.

'That could be them,' he says, going to the doors. He steps out into the rain and I can hear a siren getting closer.

'I'll go and hail them,' he says, giving me a reassuring smile, making my insides jolt again. It must be the stress of it all. I stroke Madame Beaumont's head and breathe a sigh of relief that the ambulance men can take over from here.

'Thank you,' I say looking up at Isaac, not so much the joker and fool any more. I don't know how I'd've got through that without him. Any man who can join in with my '*Allouette*' has got to be worth my respect.

Chapter Twenty-one

Outside the rain has finally stopped as they bring out Madame Beaumont on the stretcher and place it on to a trolley on wheels. Big drops of rainwater hang like crystals on a chandelier from the vine leaves. The ambulance is in the middle of the yard with the back doors open: a white van with light blue writing and a star symbol on it. Very different from the British yellow and green boxlike ones. I'm shivering. Isaac puts a sweatshirt round my shoulders and I thank him.

Madame Beaumont is wrapped in warm blankets but she still looks so frail and grey. The cry of pain she gave out as they moved her on to the stretcher keeps playing over and over in my head.

'Where are you taking her? *Où?*' I ask the two smiling paramedics. One is a fat man with a balding head and a moustache, called Laurence, the other a slight woman, carrying the drip.

'*Oh là!*' says a voice, and I turn round to see a man getting out of his car, which he's parked in front of the ambulance.

'It's Monsieur Lavigne, from Château Lavigne,' Isaac whispers.

'How do you know?'

'Trade magazines. He has vineyards all over the world. He's a very big name in the wine world.'

He heads straight for the stretcher.

'*Monsieur, Dame,*' he nods to us. 'I saw the lights.' He nods towards the ambulance and shakes the paramedics' hands. '*Qu'est-ce qui se passe?* What happened? Madame Beaumont . . . ?'

'Madame Beaumont, *elle est tombée.* She has had a fall,' I tell him.

'*Mon dieu, Madame Beaumont.*' He places a hand on the stretcher and she makes a tiny move to snatch her hand away.

'Madame Beaumont, we may not have seen eye to eye on many things, but I am your neighbour. Whatever I can do to help,' he says to her in French, 'just say.'

'I have known you all my life, Monsieur,' she says in a thin, croaking voice. 'You have never done anything to help.'

Monsieur Lavigne takes a step back, as if he's touched an electric fence.

'Where are you taking her? *Où?*' I ask Laurence.

'Bordeaux Hospital,' the paramedics both tell me.

'Would you like to travel with us?' Laurence asks.

'Yes, of course, *bien sûr.*' I nod.

Suddenly Madame Beaumont grabs hold of my hand tightly. I move quickly, closer to her, taken aback by the strength of her grip.

'Please,' I lean in to hear her, 'stay here,' she says hoarsely.

'Oh, but I can come with you. It's fine,' I tell her.

'No, stay here! Please! You're the only one. I need you to stay.'

'I . . .' I hesitate, not quite understanding what she means.

'I can stay,' Isaac pipes up, but she barely looks at him. She pulls me closer so I am leaning over the stretcher.

'Look after my vines. You are the only one. Please. I beg you. You know them. Don't let them fall into anyone else's hands.' She looks pointedly at Monsieur Lavigne, who is glancing around the yard, but he snaps back to give us his attention.

'I am happy to help out with the harvest if needs be,' he says, pulling out his phone and beginning to text.

'Please,' Madame Beaumont begs of me again. 'Bring in my harvest.'

'How? How will I know what to do?' I feel completely useless.

She smiles a wry smile through the pain. 'Instinct, of course, trust your instincts.'

I look at Monsieur Lavigne and then, digging very deep into my bravery bucket, I lift my head.

'It's OK, *monsieur*. There's no need for you to help. We're fine,' I say far more confidently than I feel. I swallow the big ball of panic in my throat 'I'll be looking after the harvest.' I look back at Madame Beaumont; she has tiny sparkles of tears in her eyes. Then I look up at Isaac, feeling terrified and helpless, both about Madame Beaumont and the vines.

I swallow. 'But what about going with you to hospital?' I ask her.

'You must stay here. Keep my vines safe, and look after Cecil and Henri.' Her voice is a mere whisper now and I lean closer to hear her. She harrumphs at Monsieur Lavigne.

'Like I say, you have never supported my family, Monsieur Lavigne – why start now?'

I love it. Even in her ailing state she is still as feisty as ever, fighting her corner. How can I not follow her lead?

'Perhaps your friend can accompany me?' she says, meaning Isaac.

'Happy to.' Isaac steps up to the stretcher and smiles, and suddenly I'm quite proud to call him my friend. He's been fantastic. She looks him up and down as much as she can and gives him a slightly disparaging look, which I love about her as well, as if he has yet to prove himself to her. Cecil is standing right beside the stretcher, panting heavily.

'*OK, allez,*' Laurence says, starting to move the trolley forward.

Henri wickers from his gate. He is snorting and stamping, plumes of steam curling out of his flaring nostrils as he nods his head over the wet gate, up and down.

'*Arrêtez,*' Madame Beaumont commands Laurence, putting up a weak hand. She is barely able to keep her eyes open now with the pain she's in on her left side.

'Henri,' she whispers.

'He'll be fine, I'll look after him,' I say again, a lot more confidently than I feel. I've never looked after a horse in my life. Never even had a riding lesson. I'm a city girl, not a country one. 'Madame Beaumont, I am so sorry for all of this. I will make it up to you, I promise.'

'I must see him.'

'You'll be back in no time, you'll see.'

'But in case I'm not . . .' she struggles for breath, 'I need to say goodbye.' She looks at me with shiny, crystal-like tears in her eyes to match the raindrops on the vine leaves. For a moment I want to hug her and tell her it will all be fine. But I know if I do that, I will sob and she wouldn't want that. What she wants is for me to be strong and to help her see Henri. I can only nod.

'*S'il vous plaît, Laurence?*' I ask, and Laurence nods. If they are on some kind of time schedule to meet target waiting times, no one is saying so. They stand away from the stretcher respectfully and hold their hands in front of themselves. Even Monsieur Lavigne does the same.

'Do you want me to?' Isaac points towards Henri. I shake my head. I need to do this. I made this mess, I have to try my very hardest to make up for it. I walk towards the field, hot tears blurring my vision. I stumble on the uneven ground, as if I'm wearing somebody else's glasses. Henri is whickering and lifting his front legs. He's agitated, a white lather over the front of his chest and the tops of his legs.

He's rearing and then dipping his head and I'm worried he's going to hurt himself or run at us and hurt someone else if I open the gate.

'There, boy,' I try to soothe him, but he won't be placated. I try to grab his head collar but he tosses his head, pulling me this way and that, and I can't hold on to him.

'Trust your instincts,' I hear Madame Beaumont saying, and I know what I have to do, as mad as it sounds, but it just feels like the only thing to do. My hands are shaking as the horse becomes more and more frustrated, weaving his head back and forth. I know I have to act quickly or he'll hurt himself. Pulling up my chest, deep breath, brushing away the hot, angry tears, I lift the rope from the post and push the gate back as hard as I can, stepping away and closing my eyes tightly as Henri lets out a whinny and my eyes ping open again. He pushes through the opening with his big solid shoulders, brushing past me, hot and sweating, making me stumble backwards on to the brambles there, which snag at my calves.

I hold my breath and watch everyone take a step or two back as the horse dips its head and canters towards the waiting ambulance, and for a moment I wonder if it was madness to do this, as he's actually going to canter out of the main gates and down the road. Losing him right now would be unbearable. He canters towards the stretcher and I see the concern on Laurence's face as he puts a hand out. Isaac also tries to catch the horse, but he swerves and arrives at a sudden halt just by the stretcher where he whinnies again, and drops his head over Madame Beaumont's. She reaches up with her hand, paper-thin skin over dark veins, and touches his soft pink nose, soothing him, reassuring him. The little crystal tears that were in her eyes earlier are now rolling down the sides of her face as the horse's hot breath rises as steam from his nostrils and his body glistens in sweat. No one moves, not the horse, not Madame Beaumont, and not the onlookers.

After a while Isaac comes to stand by me. We don't look at each other. A tear slides down my cheek and I brush it away with my sleeve, only for it to be quickly followed by another.

'*Au revoir, mon ami, mon cher ami. À la prochaine.*'

Henri puts his soft nose into her hand.

'What am I going to do?' I say quietly to Isaac.

'How do you mean?'

'I was going to go home. My family need me,' I tell him.

'Looks like Madame Beaumont needs you more right now. You'll be fine, Goldy.' He gives my hand a little squeeze.

He's right, of course. Dad and Jody will manage. They have each other. Madame Beaumont has no one. I have to stay.

Laurence looks up at me and I step forward and slide my hand into Henri's head collar. This time he doesn't fight me.

'*Merci,*' Madame Beaumont says, her face wet with tears. I lean forward and brush some away.

'Of course I'll stay. I promise I'll make sure no harm comes to anything or anyone here. I'll do my best.'

'I know you will,' she says, and she slumps down. I watch as she is loaded into the back of the ambulance. Isaac touches my elbow and then gets in behind the stretcher. He looks up at me, his dark hair curlier than ever with the damp, and gives me a little wave.

'Thank you,' I mouth again.

'No worries.' He shrugs and smiles again as the door shuts and the lights start to flash on the ambulance, and they suddenly drive off at speed down the lane.

Monsieur Lavigne watches the ambulance go and then turns to me. 'Let me know when you need my help. Because you will need my help,' he says with a tug at the corner of his mouth. Then he gets in his car and leaves.

'Over my dead body,' I say out loud, and I pat Henri on the neck before leading him back to his field.

'Over my dead body,' I say again, watching Monsieur Lavigne go and feeling my backbone stiffen.

Chapter Twenty-two

'Excellent, this is excellent,' I can hear Charlie saying as I arrive back at the *gîte* and stand in the doorway to the kitchen.

'I beg your pardon?' I frown deeply at Charlie's back, suddenly outraged that he may be talking about Madame Beaumont and Clos Beaumont.

Charlie spins round to face me and pulls back his face into a big beaming smile, making my traitorous stomach flip over.

'Ah, you're here. Great. I was just coming to look for you.' He beams some more. 'I hear you're going to be staying on with us.'

He's holding a nearly empty glass of red wine. Candy and Nick are at the table, an open bottle of wine in the middle, and Gloria is standing at the cooker stirring a big pot. Her face is red and shiny and relaxed. Her little fan, nowhere to be seen. The smell in here is fantastic, something with wine, with herbs, but despite the welcoming aromas, I feel distinctly nauseous. I'm tired and scratchy. Having watched the blue lights disappear in the direction of Bordeaux, I fed Cecil and Henri, who turned his back on his feed bucket, then I cycled back here. My knees are shaking like jelly and I have a crushing headache.

'How's Madame Beaumont? Terrible about her fall.'

Charlie follows this up with quickly sliding an arm around my shoulders by way of comforting me, but it doesn't.

'The paramedics think she's broken her hip. She looked really unwell. I thought she was going to . . . How do you know? About me staying on?' I ask, confused. I barely know myself. My knees wobble some more and I grab the back of one the chairs as I feel myself dip.

'Here, sit down,' Gloria insists, pulling out a chair, but I don't move. I'm not sure I can. 'Isaac rang the offices, Candy spoke to him,' she tells me, turning back to the cooker and stirring the pot with a wooden spoon, 'to let us all know what had happened.'

'I've got his number, just in case,' Candy practically simpers, waggling her phone.

Of course, Isaac and Candy, that would make sense. Candy gives a little wriggle in her chair and fans her face as if to ward off a kind of exaggerated blush.

'Looks like you're not the only one to have an admirer around here,' she whispers to me, flashing a knowing look and a nod at Charlie, who's finishing his wine and looking like he's about to leave. My cheeks burn with embarrassment at the memory of that kiss.

'Isaac told us what you did,' Nick butts in, deflecting my attention from Candy.

'What I did?' My cheeks are still burning.

'How you went back to the vineyard, broke in and found Madame Beaumont,' he says.

'Oh . . .' Realisation slips slowly across my face and through my shoulders and chest. God! What if I hadn't gone back? I can't bear to think about it.

'Yeah,' says Candy, suddenly straight-faced, and I wonder if she's going to make a sarcastic comment. 'Respect,' she nods. 'Wouldn't catch me smashing a window and breaking in somewhere on the word of a deaf dog and a blind horse.' She looks at her nails and I guess that's as big a compliment as I'm going to get from Candy.

'Sit yourself down, love, go on,' says Gloria, sliding a light throw from the living-room sofa around my shoulders. I'm cold and shivering. My chest tightens and I feel like crying, great big gulps. The *gîte* has a whole different feel to it: welcoming and warm. Up until now everyone has come and gone in the evenings, eating at the cheap and cheerful Le Papillon. But tonight it feels like a home.

'Come on, there's coq au vin here. Haven't cooked for people in ages.' Gloria has a wide smile and her rosy cheeks are like little red shiny apples. I don't know if it's from the cooking or the glass of red wine by the cooker, but she looks really happy. 'Thought you might like something when you got in.' She lays a place in front of me.

'I can't stay,' Charlie looks at his phone. 'But I do have some other good news. Selina from Morgan's Supermarkets has persuaded her company to hold a medal competition, for local wine-makers. Whoever wins the gold is the one she'll roll out into all the stores. It's to be held up at the château after the harvest. Local wine-makers will be invited to submit a sample of this year's vintage. Madame Beaumont's has been nominated, of course. If it wins, it'll be a great coup. It'll really put Featherstone's on the map. There'll be bonuses all round,' he beams. 'This could turn out to be our flagship wine if we can keep it up.'

'Yay,' Nick and Candy both say and clap a little. Gloria beams too.

Charlie puts his arm around me and says quietly, 'I'm delighted you're staying, Emmy. For lots of reasons.' But my stomach doesn't flip over any more, I realise. Where was he when I was trying to ring him? Why didn't he pick up? I'm beginning to think Charlie is only interested in Charlie. I realise, the more I think about it, that Charlie doesn't really talk about his dad, his illness. Charlie's only interest seems to me to be proving to his father he can turn Featherstone's into a bigger and better company.

'We'll catch up soon, yeah? Anything you need up there, just say, OK? Anything. And well done again, Emmy. We need team players like you. This is what I brought Isaac here for, to find me a blend that I could make our own and roll out. Looks like you've done that. So, Isaac and you will work closely on this.'

'Look after her, Gloria.' Charlie kisses me on both cheeks and leaves, saying, 'Don't forget, call if you need any help.'

I want to scream that of course I need help! I haven't a clue what I'm doing. But I'm too exhausted.

His kisses feel wet and cold, and I feel a shift take place in my body and in my head. A shift in loyalties that is leaving me feeling light-headed. I'm not doing this for Charlie or Featherstone's, or to be team leader. If the wine wins, that bonus could save our house, my family. I'm doing it for them and for Madame Beaumont, too. I have to put right the damage I've caused. I have to try to win.

I look at Gloria, who motions to the chair again, and Nick stands up to usher me to it, putting a glass in front of me and filling it up with red wine as Gloria puts down a steaming bowl of coq au vin in front of me.

'Thank you,' I say quietly. I'm so unused to letting others do things for me, but I'm too exhausted to argue.

'Talking of Isaac—'

'We weren't,' Nick cuts across Candy crossly. Candy tuts. That's not like Nick and Candy, and I suddenly wonder if Isaac's phone call has thrown a spanner in that friendship. If that's what it is. From where I'm sitting I think the scales of friendship may be a little uneven.

I pick up my fork and begin to eat.

'Thank you for everything.'

Before long, though, I go to stand up, picking up my plate, apologising for not eating it all.

'Here, love, let me. Why not get an early night?' Gloria says.

'I'm going to wait up to hear from Isaac,' I say, and Candy bristles. 'I need to know how Madame Beaumont is.'

Candy's phone trills into life with a text message.

'It's him. He says Madame Beaumont is OK, feisty as ever. *Paramedics were right. Looks like she broke her hip when she tripped*,' she reads, and a pang of guilt cuts through me. She only fell because she was slamming the door and pulling over the curtains because she was so cross with me. 'But apparently, she's not too well. *They're monitoring her*,' Candy reads.

My whole body droops with worry and guilt. 'It was all my fault.' Suddenly my tears start to fall.

After tissues are produced by Gloria, and another glass of wine is poured by Nick, followed by hugs from Nick and Gloria, I feel a little revived.

'Now how about a hot bath and that early night?' Gloria puts a hand on my shoulder.

'Actually, I'm going to grab some things and head back to Clos Beaumont. I don't want to be away for too long,' I tell them.

'Does that mean I get my room back?'

'Candy!' Gloria and Nick pipe up together.

'What?' She lifts her shoulders. 'I was just saying.' But actually, she's not the only one who's relieved we won't be sharing any more.

'At least we'll know who the snorer is,' Nick attempts to lighten the mood, and laughs. Candy looks horrified.

However tempting it is not to be sharing with Candy any more, I have no idea what my sleeping arrangements will be at Clos Beaumont, but I do have to get back there, for Cecil, Henry, and to make sure no one comes near the vines. I get up stiffly from my chair in the warm, cosy kitchen and go up to pack some clothes, as many as I can carry on the bike, and then come down ready to say goodbye, leaving behind my suits and court shoes. I don't think I'll be needing them in the vineyard.

'Are you sure you'll be OK?' Gloria asks, concerned.

'You could wait for Isaac to run you up there later,' Nick suggests.

I shake my head. 'He's done enough to help me already.' And I'm sure he has things he'd much rather be doing. I look at Candy and take a deep breath.

'Candy, just so you know, I am staying on with Featherstone's for now, but just until Madame Beaumont is well enough to come home, to help her get her harvest in.

I'm not after the team leader's job. You'll be great at it . . . honest.'

For a moment Candy says nothing and then as I turn to go she says, 'Sorry for being a bitch. I don't know why I do it, I don't. And as for the collection, forget it, eh? Dean and I aren't even together any more. I'll say I blew the money on a night in a hotel, if anyone asks. Male escorts, the lot! And the bet? Forget that too. It was a stupid idea. Yeah?'

That makes me cry a little more. 'Thank you, Candy,' I sniff, shredding a tissue.

'Shame,' says Nick. 'I was looking forward to seeing you running naked round the town throwing toffees to the kids!'

'I wished I could've been more like you, Candy, but I guess I never will. You are a top-selling agent. I am, well, not. And never will be. I just want to try to hang on to my old job, that's all. Win that wine award for Madame Beaumont.'

Suddenly she throws her arms around me and hugs me very tight. 'You're a lovely person.' I look in amazement at Nick and Gloria. Gloria is smiling. Nick seems to have a tiny tear in his eye and looks away quickly.

'We'll help you with your stuff,' Nick says, picking up my bag.

And they do, and wave me off up the lane as I wobble and weave, bags swinging on the handle bars and banging the wheel, back to Clos Beaumont in the fading light, the big orange sun low in the sky.

Once at Clos Beaumont I text Layla: *Am now in charge of six sheep, a dog, a cat, a horse and a vineyard!* Then I ring Dad to tell him I'm staying on. But Jody answers. He's out, again.

'We'll be fine. Don't worry,' Jody says. 'You just go for it. I know you can!'

I tell her what's happened and then switch off the phone. Holding it to my lips, I look out at the vines. Suddenly I feel overwhelmingly protective towards the vines, Clos Beaumont and Madame Beaumont. That shift in loyalties seems to have rearranged all my organs inside, which are now trying to settle again as if finally finding their right place. I have to do this. I have to get the wine made and try to win the award. 'There's no one else' – her words keep coming back to me. There's no going back.

'I won't let anything happen to them, I promise,' I say, thinking of Madame Beaumont but talking to the sky, and I swear I hear her sigh with relief, like the wind in the trees.

Chapter Twenty-three

It's late now, and dark, but I need to sweep up the glass from the step and find something to cover the broken window pane. I end up using a plastic bag that I nail across the frame with some kindling wood to keep it in place.

I try the lights, which thankfully have returned after the power cut in the storm. They crackle and fizz before throwing a dim yellow glow over the kitchen-cum-living-cum-bedroom. It feels cold and dark, a long way from the warmth of the kitchen at the *gîte*, and part of me wants to run back there now and settle in for the night with another glass of wine and chat with the others. But I know I can't. I have to stay here.

I look around. One day, I will live somewhere where everything works. A new flat, small and perfectly formed, just for me, with no draughts and creaking floorboards. Hot water on tap and central heating.

But, first things first, I open up the fire and scrunch up paper. Then I go back outside to the wood pile. The wood is as disorganised as the house, large logs abandoned all over the place.

Henri is still facing away from the gate, his back to his feed bucket. I go over and pat him on his hind quarters.

He jumps, making me jump in turn.

'We'll be OK, Henri, she'll be home soon,' I try to reassure him, but he's not listening. '*Ne vous inquiétez pas*,' I tell him, realising he probably doesn't even understand English, and I make a vow to speak more French.

Inside, I light the fire and get it roaring, and this makes me feel a little better. I make a note to get the firewood cut and stacked before Madame Beaumont comes home. I drag up a chair in front of the fire and roll up my hoodie, by way of a cushion. It's dark now. I look at the closed door leading to the rest of the house. I have no idea what's behind it. I stand up and go to it, slowly turning the handle. It creaks open and, as it does, cobwebs stretch and fall. It's way too dark to see in. I shut the door again quickly.

Maybe I should just go straight to bed. I lie down on Madame Beaumont's thin, hard bed. Despite its hardness, the mattress is moulded to the shape of her small frame and I just don't feel right here. If I turn too suddenly I may just fall out. I'm wondering if the floor would be more comfortable.

I shut my eyes but, despite my fatigue, sleep isn't going to find me any time soon tonight. I open my eyes again, sigh, get up and go to find a bottle of wine, which I do in the cupboards under the kitchen sink. I open it. Smell the cork like Madame Beaumont has shown me to do and then pour some into a short stubby tumbler. I sniff it and then I hold it up to the poor light and look at it. Even though I'm here on my own, these traditions seem important to uphold. And then I sip. It's good, really good. But Isaac's right: there's a taste to this that's different from the other clarets he's got us trying. I try letting the wine sit on my tongue before slowly swallowing. What is it? What does it remind me of? As I do this I walk round the big room. There is a breeze blowing under the French doors and the plastic bag is rustling in the window frame, making me think there's someone there.

I look at the bare Formica cupboards, the meagre store cupboard. There are plates on the wall and a small wooden box of keys. There are piles of newspapers by the fire and ceramic bowls on the side full of clutter. For a woman so proud, she has a lot of clutter to sort out. Madame Beaumont doesn't seem to have thrown anything away, ever.

I sit back down on the bed and turn on the little lamp. It crackles and fizzes as well. I wish I'd brought my Featherstone's script to learn. That always seems to send me to sleep. This is going to be a long night. Now I know how my father feels, up most of the night, napping in his chair by day. I look at the bedside table.

There are some photographs by the bed and I feel like I'm invading Madame Beaumont's privacy but I can't help but look at them. They're black and white and I'm assuming they're of her parents.

I pick up a tiny silver frame off the crowded table. It's a picture of a man in a uniform. As I pick it up, something falls to the floor. I bend to pick it up. It's silver, oval shaped, with five oak leaves round the outside like a wreath, a pair of acorns at the base and, inside it, an eagle with folded wings. I take a sharp intake of breath, realising it must be her father's, and I put the picture and the badge back on the little table where they were, feeling like I've burned my fingers. I adjust the frame so it's back just where she left it, hoping

Madame doesn't realise I've touched it at all.

I pick up another chair and take it in front of the fire. I take the threadbare quilted eiderdown off Madame Beaumont's bed and, pushing another chair in place for under my feet, climb into my makeshift bed and pull the eiderdown up round me. I sip the wine. Tomorrow I definitely need to find somewhere else to sleep.

I leave the light on by the bed just for comfort. I think about Madame Beaumont, safe in her hospital bed. I think about my dad, and then about my sister, whom I haven't seen in so long but who is there now with Dad, and I feel slightly comforted by that. And then, smiling, I think about Isaac. He completely came up trumps for me today. Then I think about Isaac and Candy, and I find myself sighing. It was inevitable. I can't help suspecting that Candy had had her eye on him since day one. And what Candy wants, Candy usually gets. As her Dean said, she can sell sand to Eskimos!

The door rustles again and this time I'm just going to ignore it.

'*Psst, psst*,' the wind hisses through the plastic.

'Psst, psst.'

It's not the wind! My eyes ping open. My scream catches in my throat as I realise the door is wide open and there's someone standing there.

'I thought you'd like to know how she is,' says Isaac, standing in the doorway, and my stomach does a little dip and rise, like a rollercoaster ride. I nod, lots, mouth still open, eiderdown pulled up round my chin. 'And I came to sort out the door.' He brandishes a hammer and a small piece of wood at me. 'But I see you've done it.'

'It'll need mending better tomorrow,' I say, my throat dry.

Isaac drops the hammer by his side. 'Were you asleep? Did I startle you?' He looks concerned.

'No,' I answer, shaking my head and smiling warmly. 'Would you like a drink?' I feel it's the very least I can do to say thank you. I jump up and find him a glass.

I fill up my own glass too, and take the bottle over and join him by the fire. We sit in silence for a moment mulling over our thoughts in the low light of the flames.

'I thought she was going to die,' I finally whisper what I've been thinking all evening, my throat tight.

'Me too,' he shares back, his usual joking humour gone.

'How was she when you left?' I want to picture her.

'Well, she's not out of the woods. It may be pneumonia, from the time she was on the floor. She was pale, tired, but told me in no uncertain terms to do my shirt up and to tell you not to worry. She says to look after yourself and remember to believe in yourself. And to trust your instincts when it comes to people, too.'

A hot rash runs up my chest to the tips of my ears. I tuck my hair round them. If I didn't know better I'd say Isaac was a little pink, too.

'They've made her comfortable. They're keeping a close eye on her. The nurse I was talking to said that, what with her age, she may have to go to a rehabilitation unit once they've mended the hip, like a convalescent home, until she's really fit.' My mind wanders to Isaac and the nurse he was talking to and I wonder if he's worked his charms there too.

'Oh, and I left her my iPod, in case she wants to listen to music,' he shrugs.

'You did what? But you're always listening to music when you're in the lab,' I say. I've seen him, headphones in, holding up small sample bottles, tasting and writing notes. In fact, he has his headphones in most of time. 'I have my phone,' he says, waggling it at me. 'Don't need the iPod really,' and I stare at him, still surprised by his kind act. Although I'm not sure Madame Beaumont will really appreciate the sacrifice.

'I thought she might be bored,' he adds with a look that says he has no idea why he left her it. And we both laugh.

'She said, "Pah!"' He does an imitation of Madame Beaumont. 'I tuned it to a classical music radio station. But she said that if she wanted to listen to music she would go to church.' We laugh again and it feels really good. He shrugs, sipping his wine. 'I left it for her anyway.' He laughs and sips again. 'She says you have a good palate, you just have to believe it.'

I tut, embarrassed, and take a big gulp of wine.

'She's a wise woman.' Isaac gazes into the fire.

'Oh, really?' I raise an eyebrow and he knows what I'm referring to. This time he really does have the good grace to look embarrassed.

'Look, I'm sorry about that, I really am. I was just shooting my mouth off. By the looks of it you've been doing a good job up here, and at Featherstone's. You work harder than any of the others. You're great with the customers and you've got a really . . . unique way of describing the wine. But you're bang on. Not like Nick – he thinks he has to swallow a textbook – and Candy, who is great at learning the script but who doesn't have the palate. And Gloria . . . Gloria is just loving being here.'

'You should have seen her tonight, totally at home in the *gîte* kitchen, cooking and looking after us all. Like she was born here, a French *maman*,' I tell him. We both manage a little laugh and then look into our wine glasses.

'I mean it.' He looks up at me. 'I am sorry. You didn't deserve what I said.'

I nod, accepting his apology but still not quite believing what he's just been saying.

'So you and Candy?' I blurt out, wanting to shift the attention away from me.

'Sorry?'

'Oh, I mean, sorry, if it's a secret . . . I mean, if it's not . . . oh shit!'

He tosses his head forward, shakes it and, to my relief, laughs.

'Candy? Candy is a lovely girl and will make someone very happy one day.'

'Oh, sorry, I thought you and she . . .'

He shrugs and drinks his wine.

'She's fun. But I'm not looking for anything serious. Candy's looking for a great big engagement ring and a big family wedding, and that's not me. I don't do commitment in that way.' He looks straight at me. Something in his eyes tells me otherwise and I get the feeling my insides have shifted again. It must be the wine. I take another sip. Whatever it was, it felt weird . . . nice but weird.

'You? How are things with Charlie?'

'Great!' I say without thinking, and then suddenly wish I hadn't.

'So there's no one waiting for you back home then?' He stands up and my heart starts racing faster as he leans towards me and then tops up my glass, before sitting back down and topping up his own, putting the bottle on the hearth by the fire.

I should refuse, but it might be the only thing that gets me to sleep tonight if my stomach doesn't stop flipping over and over like a child on Christmas Eve. In an attempt to slow down my racing metabolism I go to the kitchen and pull out some cheese and pâté Gloria put in a basket for me as I was leaving, put them on a plate with some bread and place them between us in front of the fire.

'Ah, great. I'm starving,' Isaac says, cutting a corner of pâté, putting it on bread and taking a big satisfying mouthful. I can't help but smile. 'So?' He's not letting me off the hook.

'There was someone. We were at school together.' I laugh, the wine loosening my tongue. 'That was a long time ago now. But we had life mapped out. I was going to college to become a nurse and he went to work at the call centre. He had it all planned. The car he'd buy, the house we'd buy, the holidays we'd go on. Then, well, my mum died and after that nothing went according to plan.'

'Does it ever?'

'I moved back home to take care of my sister and my dad. Dad stopped working and so Kevin got me a job in the call centre with him. But as time went on and others there were either getting engaged or married or having children, he got more and more frustrated. He wanted me to move out, get a flat with him. But I couldn't leave Dad or Jody. And we couldn't really have much of a romantic life with Dad sitting there watching reruns of *Dad's Army* and my sister doing her GCSE homework at the dining table each night.'

'So?'

'So we split. He met another agent. They got engaged. I was asked to look after the collection and buy the cakes and cava. They married, bought the house, had kids. He got everything he wanted. He moved on to work at Danbrooks, a bigger call centre, and she followed.'

'And you, what did you want?'

'I just wanted . . . it sounds silly . . .'

'Go on.'

'I just wanted my sister to pass her GCSEs, for my dad to stop feeling so low. For us to start to move on. I just wanted to have a chance at a normal life – like everyone else.'

'Be yourself, everyone else is already taken.' Isaac gives me one of his lazy smiles, then pops a piece of bread into his mouth. 'Oscar Wilde,' he says, surprising me, and eats some more. This is a side to Isaac I haven't seen before. For a moment we say nothing and watch the flames lick up the side of the wood burner.

'Can't you sell the house?'

I shake my head, having taken a big sip of wine.

'Dad would never do that. All the time he's there, Mum's memory is still there with him. We're still there as a family.' I swallow hard and think of her mug in the kitchen, and her dressing gown on the bedroom door. 'It would kill him.' I pick at the cheese. 'What about you?'

He lifts the glass to his lips and I see the worn signet ring on his right forefinger.

'No wedding rings?'

He shakes his head.

'I came close once, back in California.' The wine is definitely having a truth-telling effect. 'But when I got the chance to start training as a wine-maker, I had to go away, get the experience under my belt. After that, I just kept moving and discovered I prefer it that way,' he smiles. 'New town, no commitments, and I can move on. With Mum and Dad gone, there's nothing holding me to one place any more.'

'Don't you want to have that again? I can't imagine ever leaving my home. It's who I am.'

'It's not where you've come from that makes you who you are, it's where you're going,' he says.

'What if you don't know where you're going?' I say quietly, and look at him. He holds my gaze as if understanding exactly what I mean and we fall back into thoughtful silence and finish our wine.

'Now,' he goes to stand up, 'you take the bed, I'll take the chair.'

'What?'

'I'm not leaving you here on your own tonight,' he says. 'Call me old-fashioned but my father would have had something to say about that.'

I can't help but smile, too tired and a little too light-headed to argue.

'Tell you what, you have the bed. I'm happy here.'

'You sure?'

'Sure.'

'Look, Emmy, I'm here to help, not to be your enemy. We'll work on this together.'

'Sure,' I say.

'Charlie wants this to work out. We have to try and get along.'

The very mention of Charlie and his plans sobers me straight away. We're not becoming friends because we want to, but because Charlie wants us to work together. But I am never going to let him or Charlie persuade me into ripping up Madame Beaumont's vines.

'Yes, of course, we must try,' and my happy, mellow bubble is burst. He's right. I do need him.

'Great. Let's make a promise to try and get along.'

'No more teasing?' I raise an eyebrow.

'I . . . will try and promise. No more teasing,' he laughs. 'No more schoolmarm?' he says.

'I am not a schoolmarm!'

He raises an eyebrow.

'OK, no more schoolmarm.'

'You'll be more relaxed,' he says, 'unless it's about the wine, of course. Then we need to play it by the book.'

'And you'll be less laid-back, unless it's about the wine, in which case . . . you need to let nature do her job.'

'And no more not believing in yourself.'

'No more insults, saying we can't do it?'

'Promise.' He crosses his heart and puts out a hand to shake. 'Honest, colleague.'

'Honestly.' Only I have my fingers crossed behind my back, because if I was honest right now, I would tell him I find him really quite attractive and that isn't something he needs to know. I am never going to be another one of his conquests.

He's here because Charlie wants us to get along. He's being paid to keep me happy, I keep reminding myself as I lie on my chairs, listening to the gentle snores coming from Madame Beaumont's bed behind me, and hoping to God he's kept his trousers on this time.

Chapter Twenty-four

My neck is agony. I try to straighten it as I open my heavy eyes.

Isaac is up making coffee, or trying to.

'There's nothing here. Nothing at all. Is this all the coffee there is?' He holds out a tin, showing me the scrapings at the bottom.

'Probably.' I grimace as a pain shoots right through my neck and shoulder. 'Madame Beaumont lives very frugally.'

'We'll pick up some more later,' he says bossily.

'Later?' I try to straighten my neck again and wince.

'On our way back from the hospital. I'm presuming you want to see her, and I don't think that bike is going to get you all the way to Bordeaux.'

'No. Thank you,' I say, rubbing my neck.

'You need to organise your harvest. Lots of the other *vignerons* have started and the rest will start in earnest today. Check your grapes, see where you're at. Organise pickers and decide when to start. I can check the sugar quality in them over at the lab at Featherstone's.' He's firing on all cylinders this morning.

I nod, not really taking anything in.

'Emmy? Are you listening?'

'What?'

'You have to bring in the harvest. Both our jobs depend on this. I'm not the only travelling wine man out there looking for his next gig. You're only as good as your last vintage, so a complete no-show wouldn't bode well for me.'

'Yes, of course.' I have to organise the harvest. I need pickers. Where do I find pickers?

Just then a small van pulls into the courtyard and a small man with a moustache and blue overalls stretched over his round belly gets out. He's holding a piece of paper and walking towards the farmhouse.

'*Bonjour*,' he smiles and nods.

'*Bonjour*,' I reply.

He's looking round like he's been allowed into Willy Wonka's chocolate factory, a place no one's seen inside for years.

'*La fenêtre?*' He points to the broken window pane in the door and explains he's been sent by a Monsieur Charlie Featherstone to repair it.

I thank him and let him get on with his work, flexing the hand that I put through the window last night.

'I'm going to check back at the winery and then pick up some things and come back.'

'What? You don't need to move in!' I don't want Isaac watching over my every move.

'We can't let this go wrong, Emmy.' He looks at me seriously and deeply, and I feel a crackle and fizz like the lights.

'And it won't. Really. There's no need for you to stay here. I can manage. Besides, you're needed at Featherstone's too.'

I run back inside and quickly change into shorts, a faded T-shirt, hoodie, socks and boots, and scrape my hair back into a scrunchie before the glass repairer returns from his van. I know where he is because he's whistling, tunelessly and constantly.

There is the clatter and rumble of traffic on the lane outside. I've never heard it so busy.

'I have to organise the harvest,' I repeat to myself, throwing open the shutters on the farmhouse kitchen-cum-living room. Bits of ivy, spider's web and snails fall as I push them back. Evidently they haven't been opened for a very long time. I throw open the windows, too, to air the room as the October sun starts to climb the sky. On the road there is the constant rumble of tractors pulling trailers full of grapes, heading for the château, no doubt, or back the other way, maybe to Isaac, to have their grapes turned into wine. I need some help here. I look around for a desk to find a list of pickers so I can tell him who to ring. Maybe there's an office.

Isaac has offered to take me to see Madame Beaumont later. I want to be able to tell her I'm organised, that I've got the harvest in hand.

The whistling glass repair man sets to work, with a smile and a wave of his hammer. I have to do the same. I push open the door into the room next door, hoping to find an office, somewhere I can start to organise things.

It's a big room with green embossed wallpaper on one wall. There are two mismatched wing-back chairs either side of a huge black fireplace. There are two big windows with wooden slatted shutters either side. Old sheets have been thrown over boxes. I go into the hall and discover a door with steps down to the cellar, but I'm not going to brave that today. The house feels like it's been preserved in aspic. Nothing seems to have been moved for years. I go upstairs and think that I may have at least found somewhere to sleep tonight. There is a smell in the air, musty. The whole place needs airing. I throw open the window of the front bedroom, which looks out on to the road. Another tractor trundles past. There's an eiderdown here, in much the same state as Madame Beaumont's downstairs. I gather it up and hang it over the windowsill to air, and look up and down the road. I have to get on. I go back downstairs. There's another room further on that is full of boxes but I don't think I'm going to find an up-to-date list of pickers there. I go back to the living room. It's actually very beautiful, if dated and stuck in time. I run my hand over the dusty wallpaper and fireplace. There's a square black clock with a gold face on the mantelpiece, but it's not working. But there's no desk anywhere with anything that might help me. No obvious piles of papers to help me. I need to find out where I get pickers from. There's nothing for it: I need to get some help from the horse's mouth.

That afternoon Isaac drives me to the hospital in Bordeaux. Madame Beaumont looks pale and grey, and she keeps coughing. She has an oxygen mask over her face. Pneumonia, the young nurse confirms. But at least she seems pleased to see me. She writes down the address of Alfonso, with a weak and shaking hand. He'll organise a gang of pickers, she tells me. Alfonso is a Spanish gypsy. They come every year to work the vineyards. He'll organise everything.

Madame Beaumont is tired now, drifting in and out of

sleep, and it's a shock to see her looking so frail. Isaac keeps a distance so as not to tire her even more.

'Don't forget,' Madame Beaumont instructs me with snatched breaths. 'You are running the harvest. Only intervene if Mother Nature needs your help.'

I nod and try to understand what she means. 'Can I ring you if I need you? What about a mobile – have you got one?'

Madame Beaumont looks at me and manages one raised eyebrow.

Of course not, I think. My heart sinks. The bell goes to signal the end of visiting. I stand to leave and she lifts her cheeks to me to kiss her goodbye. As I do, I see Isaac's iPod on the side table. A nurse is walking through the ward telling us all it's time to go.

'Wait!' I pick up the iPod and headphones. 'If you want me, iMessage me. You can message me on my phone.' I hold up the iPod to show her she has to talk into it. 'It's like a video message. You should be able to work it out. This way we can stay in touch.'

I hand it to her and Madame Beaumont takes it and looks at it like it's a banana after the war and has no idea whether to peel it, eat it or talk into it. But the nurse isn't going to let me have time to explain and it drops to Madame Beaumont's side as she slips into a drowsy sleep again.

On the drive back from the hospital, Isaac assures me she's in good hands, and I nod. I know that. It was just difficult to see her like that.

'So, what did she have to say about the harvest?' he says, distracting me from my worries about her health.

'To remember to take Mother Nature's lead and not to start until after the full moon.'

'What? She's farming biodynamically? Aw, man! I mean I've read about it, but I've never actually worked at a biodynamic vineyard. That's going really screw things around.'

'Madame Beaumont would call it "natural" farming. Working with the rhythm of nature.'

He lets out a loud laugh and his dark shiny, uncut hair shakes. 'Next you'll be planting a goat's horn full of manure and harvesting by moonlight or whatever strange rituals it is they do!'

I raise an eyebrow.

'You know, harvesting by moonlight can often help keep the temperature down on the grapes.' I'm repeating something he'd told us in one of his training sessions.

'*Touché!*'

I watch him, looking at the road straight ahead, as he laughs again and find myself smiling too. Somehow he's easier to talk to and get along with when he's not looking at me. Then I look out of the window again as we leave Bordeaux and head towards fields full of vines.

'And, sorry, no more teasing.'

'You promised.' I glance at him.

'I did, you're right,' he says playfully back.

We drive a little further in silence as green space between the buildings becomes larger and odd *parcelles* of vines are dotted between them.

I pull out the address Madame Beaumont has written down for me.

'Could we go to this address?' I read it out as slowly and carefully as I can. 'It's a camp, just out of town. Madame Beaumont says Alfonso will organise pickers for me. He's the man who can sort it all. Once we have pickers, we're ready to go.' Hopefully that's made him realise I've got things in hand and everything else should fall into place, I think, pleased to be finally feeling I'm on top of this.

'Great, let's go then.' He puts his foot down and, with the windows open, the warm wind blowing our hair around, he turns the radio up and my spirits lift. Just maybe this will be OK, just maybe . . . this might be fun. I can't remember the last time I had fun.

Isaac is waiting in the car, window open, elbow out, listening to the radio still. It's a rough-and-ready campsite. There are a pair of young girls whispering, giggling and waving at him. A boy with a stick is chasing a dog, or it may be the other way round.

'So, all set?' he says, putting the van into gear as I get back into the car, still holding the paper.

'No.'

'What? What's the problem?'

I can't believe it. I have no idea what to do now. I feel like I'm suddenly on a train that's come off its tracks and is careering down a hill, get faster and faster out of control.

'They're not coming,' I say with a hint of panic in my voice. Isaac takes the car out of gear but lets the engine chug away and turns to look at me. Suddenly I feel all tongue-tied again.

'What do you mean, "they're not coming"?'

All my feelings of fun and excitement have been chased away and replaced by a terror now gripping my throat and stomach.

I take a deep breath. 'It's Château Lavigne. They've offered more money. All the pickers have gone to work there.'

'What?' Isaac looks as infuriated as I feel.

'He's stolen Madame Beaumont's pickers!' I exclaim, suddenly furious. 'In fact, can we go there? I'm going to tell him he can't do that! It's terrible!'

Isaac puts the car into gear and gently pulls away.

'You can't do that,' he says, driving away from the campsite, Alfonso watching us as we go.

'I can. Watch me,' I say angrily.

'Look, it's exactly what he wants. Don't let him think he's won.' Isaac swings the car round the outskirts of the town and towards Clos Beaumont. 'Beat him at his own game.'

'What game?'

'The wine! Win the wine medal,' he tells me.

'Now what am I going to do? I have so much to do! I have to check the *chai* is ready, get the crates ready, get Henri to eat and, actually . . . I have no idea what else I need to do!' Suddenly the enormity of the situation hits me.

'Leave the pickers to me. I'll get you pickers,' says Isaac, and I'm not sure whether to feel reassured or even more terrified.

'Just don't turn up with picking machines and tractors. We're doing this the traditional way,' I tell him, and he raises what I think is an impressed eyebrow. Then tuts jokingly and drives the van up the lane towards Clos Beaumont.

* * *

The next morning Isaac arrives at the door with steaming cups of takeaway coffee and a bag of croissants. I take the coffee and a croissant from the bag and smile, thanking him, then slip on my boots and together we walk the vines in the early morning mist. I feel ridiculously nervous. He gives me a little reassuring smile. Eventually, when we've walked a little way, he stops and inspects a bunch. I hold my breath, trying to see what he's doing but not wanting to intrude, feeling like a new mother waiting for its baby to get the all clear at the doctor's. Cecil is by my side and I put a hand on his head for comfort. Finally Isaac turns to me and beams.

'They're ready.'

I take a deep breath and breathe out slowly.

'We can pick!' he announces.

I have to do this. Slowly I shake my head. 'Not yet.'

'What? But these are excellent. They're ready. We can start the harvest. The sugar levels are fine.'

'Not yet,' I say, digging my heels in. 'We must wait. She told me not to start until after the full moon. That's not for another two days.'

'Nonsense! We need to go now. Everyone else has started. Look, the grapes and grape juice are arriving thick and fast at Featherstone's.'

Still I shake my head but inside I haven't a clue. Should I go with Isaac, who says they're ready? I mean, he's the expert. Or do what Madame Beaumont says?

'We can't get this wrong, Emmy. If these grapes over-ripen it will ruin the wine,' he says, more serious than I've ever seen him.

Fear and terror grip me again.

'Jeez, now is not the time to be indecisive. If you're no good at decision-making, don't be a wine-maker!'

'I'm not a wine-maker! I'm a sales rep . . .' and a rubbish one at that, I want to add.

'Everything all right?'

I jump and turn to see Charlie, smiling his big confident smile, walking towards us.

'How's it all going up here?' It's like he's referring to a different planet, which, in many ways, it probably is.

'Fine!' Isaac and I say at the same time, and glare at each other. His nostrils flare and my eyes widen.

'Great.' Charlie doesn't walk any further in. I notice his polished brown brogues, and Isaac and I go to meet him by the rose bush at the end of row. 'So, we're on course to get the harvest in and this vintage under way, then we'll start looking at where we go from there. I'll keep Selina in the picture.'

Isaac's phone rings. It's a vintner on his way with his grapes.

'I'll meet you there. *Oui, dix minutes*,' he attempts in French, and I find it strangely endearing as he makes his arrangements and tells the vintner not to worry.

'All this fresh air suits you, you know,' Charlie says quietly in my ear, and I find myself doing that nervous laughter thing. 'Look, now you're not working with the others, maybe we could try and meet up.'

'Yes,' I say brightly, but not feeling it. I can't seem to think about anything else other than this harvest at the moment. I eat and sleep it. Or rather I don't eat and I don't sleep because of it. He looks straight at me, gives me a smile and fixes me with his green eyes, but I don't feel like diving into them any more. 'Need to keep my vintners happy!' he smiles again, then he leans in and kisses me on the cheek, taking me by surprise. I can smell his expensive, spicy aftershave, a complex blend of different smells. I blush as we clash noses as I go to kiss his other cheek and he ends up pecking me on the lips, reminding me of the kiss we shared outside the *gîte*, what seems like a lifetime ago. 'Ring me if you need me. You're doing great. And remember, play nicely, you two,' he jokes, pointing to Isaac and me, and then pulling out his mobile to answer a call. I hold the back of my hand to my lips.

'Yes. Oh, hi, Selina. I was just getting a lowdown on the Clos Beaumont harvest. Yes, all on track . . . We'll get this vintage in, then make plans for rolling out the blend. Yes, it'll be the same as the bottle you tasted. We've got a brilliant wine man here. He can make it just the same.'

When I finally meet Isaac's eyes, he raises an eyebrow at me as if asking what's going on. But I have no idea. Charlie waves a goodbye, jogs round Cecil and makes his way back to the car and out of the yard.

'I've checked the grapes. They're as good as they're going to get. We should just get started,' he repeats firmly.

'After the full moon, Isaac,' I say just as firmly, and we glare at each other. I'm not backing down.

'OK, OK.' He looks round to make sure Charlie is out of earshot. 'We'll wait. But just until after the full moon. Then we're picking.' And with that he marches off towards the Featherstone's van. Something in me skips a little beat in triumph.

Over the weekend, I am flat out getting everything ready in time for the harvest, stocking up food and cleaning everything and anything. I ring the hospital and speak to the nurse about Madame Beaumont's worsening condition.

'We need to get started,' Isaac keeps nagging me, but I remind him of our agreement. He tuts and mutters about 'utter mumbo jumbo' though he doesn't push it.

I walk the vineyard twice a day, and in between I visit the graveyard and polish the headstone for Madame Beaumont. I talk to the vines, and sometimes I even listen to see if they're talking back. I even film them on my phone and send images to Madame Beaumont. She doesn't reply and I don't expect her to but I hope she'll see them at some point. I may actually be going mad. Perhaps it's down to the full moon. In the valley below, tractors and picking machines are working up and down the straight lines of Château Lavigne vines. Everywhere is a hive of activity but here. Here, it is like the calm before the storm. Isaac and I are barely speaking at all now. The atmosphere is as frosty as it can get, considering the warm temperatures and gentle breeze outside.

'Perfect for picking!' Isaac keeps telling me.

What will happen if I get this wrong? I keep repeating in my head.

But then that night I look up at the dark sky and the full white moon. It's here. I hold up my phone, snap a picture and send it to Madame Beaumont. Then I text Isaac the same picture with the message: *I think it might be time.* The full moon is here and tomorrow we must start to pick. I only hope Isaac manages to bring me some pickers.

Chapter Twenty-five

There is a slow, low mist curling its way up through the low-hanging branches of the vineyard and a soft orange and yellow light is creeping in as the sun begins to rise. I stop for a moment and stand and stare, the ever-present breeze lifting the ends of my hair. I haven't really taken the time just to look at how beautiful this place is since I've been here. I've always been busy keeping up with Madame Beaumont. But the way the hills roll away, and then up again to the château on the other side of the valley, and then keep on rolling into the distance, is truly breathtaking. I feel actually quite privileged to be here all of a sudden, even if I am just the caretaker.

I hold up my phone, photograph the view and send it to Layla.

La vendange est arrivé! I text her, and receive a usual *OMG!* back.

I shake my bucket at Henri but still he doesn't turn round and look at me. Cecil, on the other hand, follows me and barks when I clap my hands at the birds on the wire.

I stand, and take in the view again, drawing courage from the beauty of the place, the peace, just as the Featherstone's van pulls into the yard. I watch, hoping this is Isaac arriving with the pickers. This is it. It's time to harvest. The passenger door opens, followed by the two at the back.

'You're joking!' I say as I watch the pickers pile out of the Citroën van. 'No way!'

'It's perfect!' Isaac beams as I watch Candy, Nick, Gloria and Jeff climb out and stretch.

'They've never done it before; I've never done it before!' I say through gritted teeth.

They all look at me.

'Candy? I didn't expect you,' I say with a smile.

'Hmm, me neither, but Nick told me it would be a kind thing to do, y'know helping out. Eww . . .' She backs away from Cecil, who is sniffing at her floral dress. But at least she's wearing a sunhat.

Jeff is here to help too, he tells me.

At least I think he does, as he waves his arms, a little stub of cigarette bobbing up and down in his mouth.

'*Jusqu'à midi*, the middle day,' he rattles off at speed.

'He says he has to go by lunchtime,' Gloria translates his 'franglais' with a smile to him and he back to her, which makes me think this was a private conversation between them. And it's a good job Gloria understands him when no one else can.

'Now let's see these grapes.' Isaac starts walking towards the vines and their bunches of fat, purple grapes. The others stay put, as if they've been dropped in the desert and are looking for a star to follow.

In the neighbouring field there is a big rumble and vehicle lights come on.

'What's that?' Candy shrieks.

'I'm not sure, but I'm guessing it's a mechanical picker,' I say, watching Isaac.

'Why can't you borrow that? The man from the château said he could help you with anything.' Nick recounts the story I told him about Monsieur Lavigne.

'Because here we're checking for quality as we pick,' I say, sounding like someone who knows what she's talking about, though my shaking knees say differently. My mouth is dry and I swig from a bottle of water. It's going to be a hot one, I think, looking out over the haze chasing in after the mist.

'Make sure you've got hats and suncream on,' I say nervously, worried they're going to change their minds at any minute. I run to catch up with Isaac. He's standing with his back to me by the vines. Then he turns slowly and stares straight at me. I'm shaking with nerves and fear. Then a slow, wide lopsided smile spreads across his face.

'These grapes are fantastic!' he says really slowly.

I can't help it, I squeal, do a happy little dance and grab him and hug him, and he hugs me back, lifting me off my feet and swinging me round.

'Well, I gotta say. I thought you'd really stuffed it up there. But you . . .'

'Go on, say it.' I'm grinning so broadly my cheeks hurt.

'You . . . were . . . right,' he says, smiling but rolling his eyes, and I can't help but think there's a hint of admiration there. 'I'd hate to play poker against you. You really took a chance.'

I smile even more, because I can't not!

'And just so you know, that wasn't flirting there.' He

points a finger between him and me, a faint smile in the corner of his mouth. 'Just so you know . . .'

'Oh, absolutely,' I agree with him, trying to sound serious, and hold back the smile still pulling at my cheeks.

'Now, I have to get back to Featherstone's. I have wine being delivered, but I'll come back later. Let's get this harvest in.' He claps his hands together and gives a little whoop, and again, I can't help but smile. But I still have to do this . . . on my own. The euphoria seeps away and, in its place, fear returns.

'So, what do we do first, Emmy, love?' asks Gloria, who has obviously spotted the terror in my eyes. For a moment, a thought flashes through my mind. I wish Isaac were staying. But I push the thought out as quickly as it arrived. He's busy at the winery and I certainly don't want to have to run to him at every turn.

Trust your instincts . . . I hear Madame Beaumont's voice inside my head.

A silver Audi pulls in behind them at speed, making Cecil jump and bark, and Charlie gets out of the car. He walks over and this time kisses me firmly on both cheeks. He does not look like he's ready for picking.

'This is an excellent idea,' Charlie nods, and Isaac beams behind him, arms folded lazily across his body, soaking up the praise.

'I mean, you're doing a great job.' He turns back to me. 'Getting Featherstone's into Clos Beaumont is exactly what's needed. First you, now the rest of the team. Brilliant!'

I feel my hackles rise. It's like he's suggesting this was all on purpose.

'I just didn't have any other pickers,' I tell him firmly.

'Now, dinner later at Le Tire-bouchon? You can tell me how the harvest is looking, whether we've got a winner on our hands.'

'I can't,' I say firmly. 'The grapes will need crushing as soon as they're picked. They can't stand around waiting. I can't leave the vineyard.'

'Of course, of course. Once it's in, I promise you, we'll celebrate,' he smiles. 'But you don't have to worry about the grapes. We can do it all back at the winery. I'll send the tractor.' He beams again.

I swallow hard. 'No,' I say.

'Pardon?'

'No, I'll crush the grapes.' I remember my promise to Madame B.

'But that's insane. We have all the equipment ready to go there.'

'I promised I'd do it at the vineyard. That's why she agreed.'

'Very well,' Charlie sighs, and both he and Isaac say their goodbyes and leave. I really am on my own with this, I think, as the car and van are driven off down the lane, Isaac giving a toot and a wave as he leaves. I raise my hand warily, wondering what on earth I've let myself in for.

'Can I drive the tractor?' I hear Candy ask. 'I mean, I'm a really good driver. I even did Silverstone once. It was a Valentine's present from . . . I can't quite remember. But you've seen the different cars I've had. I'm a brilliant driver, honest.'

'Um, we do things slightly differently here,' I say. Candy

tuts as I turn away. 'Nick, could you hand out the buckets and the secateurs?' They are long, thin blades, red-handled and held together when they're not open with a catch. I've washed them all and even sharpened some of the blades with a little stone.

'This is so exciting,' says Nick, handing out the buckets. 'Real wine-making.'

'Be careful,' I warn, 'they're very shar—'

'Ouch!' Candy shouts, and sucks her finger. The sooner we get on with this the better, otherwise I'll be pickers down before we've started.

Just then Charlie's mother, Lena, drives into the yard with Mr Featherstone, whom she helps out of the car and hands him his walking stick.

'I'm not sure how much use we'll be but he insisted on coming when he heard,' she smiles at me.

'Bloody right,' says Mr Featherstone in his slurred voice. 'Can't sit back and watch a vintner in trouble.' He's right. We have to get on and help. I direct them towards buckets and secateurs as he leans heavily on a stick, his left hand limp and useless. I leave Gloria in charge of making coffees and handing out croissants, which she seems delighted to do.

I smile and make my way to the gate of the field where Henri is still standing with his back to me.

I open the gate and push back a few of the sheep who are keen to get involved. But Henri doesn't move; his feed bucket is still full.

I walk up to his head but he turns away from me.

'I know. *Je sais.* I know how you're feeling,' I say quietly. How mad is this? Now I'm talking to a horse. In French! I catch hold of him and pat his thick neck and then, because I feel it would help, I slide my arm under his neck and pat him on the other side.

'I know you miss her and I do too. I'm just not sure I can do this without her. I've never even seen a harvest, let alone led one.' I am close to tears. I feel his head turn back to me and I lean my head against his thick neck, somehow taking comfort from his strong presence, running a hand over his soft, closed eyes.

'In fact, I'm not sure I can do this at all. *J'ai besoin de toi*,' I say, all my instincts picking up their baggage and heading towards the exit sign.

Suddenly Henri gives me a nudge, nearly lifting me off my feet and knocking some of the wind out of me. He nudges me again in the stomach and I let out an 'Oomph!' knocking back any self-indulgent tears that may have been welling up there. Then, his back legs moving first, he starts to turn round, his head still by me but his whole body slowly turning to face the gate. He takes a couple of steps forward with his big feathery hoofs and stands, his head hanging over the gate. Then his lifts his head, nostrils sucking in and out, as if sensing the gathering group of pickers for the first time, and gives a little whinny.

Suddenly I feel . . . could it be excited? A little shudder runs up and down my spine and there's a fizzing in my tummy I haven't felt since, well, I can't remember when. I try to think when I last felt excited about something. No, still can't remember.

'I will if you will,' I say with a growing smile and, with that, I lift off the rope that's holding the gate shut and watch as Henri moves forward with the movement of the gate. I shoo the sheep back into the field.

'Not your turn yet, oh woolly ones,' I say and watch as Henri walks towards the pickers, Candy shrieking and jumping behind Nick, clinging to him for dear life. Gloria and the Featherstones quieten and watch as the big horse, with one milky wall eye, comes to a standstill by the trailer. I run to the barn and gather up his heavy leather tack, holding it as I've been shown. My hands are a bit sweaty as I try to fit the tack on him, but he's patient and just stands still, even dropping his head for me to get the head collar over. Then when I think it looks right I step forward and turn the trailer towards his back end and then say, '*Allez*,' just as Madame Beaumont did. He begins to reverse in between the two shafts, to the delight of the little audience. I move round him, doing up the buckles and hoping I've done it all right.

'Hang on a minute, are you telling me there's really no tractor?' Candy pipes up from behind Nick, where she's still clinging to his shoulders, and Nick appears to be grinning from ear to ear.

Finally I smile too.

'No, like I say, here we do things a little differently. Think of it as organic, making the most of what nature has to offer,' I tell Candy, and Mr Featherstone shouts, 'Hear, hear,' or at least I think that's what he says.

'OK, so only pick the ripe-looking grapes. Take one row at a time and work either side in pairs.' I turn back to Henri.

'*En avant*,' I say, and he moves forward, the trailer behind him, the pickers behind that. They split into pairs: Mr and Mrs Featherstone, Nick and Candy, Gloria and Jeff. Me, I'll have to go up and down my row of vines twice, but I think I may just have begun this year's harvest.

By lunchtime the sun is high in the sky. The tractors all around us in the neighbouring vineyards have fallen silent and I call time on my workers, ushering them back to the house. There is large soft terrine I bought from the woman down the road and bread I went out and bought first thing that morning from the *boulangerie*, where the baker was fascinated I wanted so many loaves. Then it's ragu – beef stew that I also bought in the town. It's followed by a big round white creamy brie, and fruit salad.

Everyone makes their way to the back door, chatting about the grapes, their secateur technique and testing each other with the backs of their hands for sunburn.

The table from the kitchen is lifted outside by Nick and Jeff, and it's a hive of activity as everyone else helps with taking out chairs and laying the table with mismatched crockery and glasses.

Baskets of bread are cut and placed along the table and everyone grabs a seat and starts to pass round the crusty bread with its white fluffy middle, followed by the soft pâté and cornichons, little gherkins. As the table fills with food and chatter I dash into the kitchen to check the oven. The ragu's been in on a low temperature since I got back with it from town. It doesn't smell great, like it should. I sniff and curl up my nose. I pull out the casserole dish out and take off the lid. It's dry as a bone.

'Oh, no!' I wail, and Gloria is at my side in an instant.

'Don't worry, love. Leave this to me. You go and pour

some wine,' she says, picking up a wooden spoon and a bottle of red wine. And I do as I'm told.

'Candy, you really need suncream,' Gloria tells Candy as she brings out the bubbling stew. 'Emmy, pass down the plates. Keep your cutlery, everyone.'

'Oh, Gloria, that's fantastic!' I feel ridiculously grateful. I don't know how she's saved it, but she has.

I take the first of the plates and hand it to her as instructed.

'I can help put it on.' Nick jumps up to stand by Candy, armed with a bottle of suncream.

'No, I'm fine. I need some sunshine. Been stuck in that office for weeks! It'll brown up nicely now,' she says, lifting her head to the sun. Nick keeps looking at her, snatching glances, but he does that a lot, I've noticed.

'You OK, Gloria?' I ask as she holds her hands into her back and arches it.

'Yes, fine, dear. Just a bit stiff,' she smiles.

'If we keep on like this, we should get this *parcelle* done by today,' I say with a rush of optimism that I quickly put down to the wine and adrenalin.

'This means a lot to you, doesn't it?' Gloria says, passing round the plates, piled with the ragu, jacket potatoes I put in the oven earlier, and *petits pois* from the freezer. The smell of the beef, carrots and tomatoes is heavenly. Appreciative sounds from around the table agree, and after a round of '*bon appétit*', the sound of cutlery on china begins to fill the air.

'I made a promise. It's essential Madame Beaumont has her harvest in. She needs the money from the vintage.' I hand the bread to Candy, thinking and worrying about Madame Beaumont.

Gloria smiles at me. 'She's lucky she has you.'

And I wonder for a moment who Gloria has.

Just as we're finishing lunch, bread is being wiped around plates soaking up the last of the juices and wine is washing it down, the Featherstone's van pulls into the yard at speed. It's Isaac.

'Had a window. Thought I could help,' he grins, and my heart does that stupid skipping thing again. It's probably because an extra pair of hands means we'll definitely get the *parcelle* in.

'OK, where do you want me?' he asks, rubbing his hands. Gloria makes him up a plate of food and explains the pairs. 'So you're with Emmy.'

'Perfect!' he says. 'You're the boss.'

And I feel my spirits lift. I raise my head and smile. 'OK, everyone, let's pick!'

That afternoon it's hot. I've knotted my T-shirt under my bust to try to cool down, and my hair is just about tied back from my neck. I run the back of my arm across my forehead as we reach the final row of vines on this *parcelle* and drop my secateurs into my bucket, then look up and breathe a huge sigh of relief. I turn round, put my hands on my hips and beam at the pickers, dotted up the hillside. They're looking hot and tired. I can't believe how much we've achieved today. I feel ridiculously proud.

With the final bucket tipped on to the trailer we make our way back to the sheds. Everyone is chatting happily, hot, tired and aching, and we traipse out of the vineyard behind Henri and the trailer, the grapes tossing this way and that as the wheels bump off the divots. Nick is still glancing every now and again at Candy. Cecil stands and barks to herald our return from the vines, seeing off any birds in the process. Day one and I think I may have done it!

We head up to the *chai* where Henri stands and I unbuckle his harness. He has walked up and down the vines in the heat all day, moving on when I've asked, stopping still when I've asked. And then taking the grapes up to the *chai* when the trailer has been full. He hasn't put a foot out of place. I rub his nose in thanks and although he doesn't need me to show him, I lead him back to his field where I fill his water bucket and give him an extra scoop of feed. Finally he sticks his head in his bucket and eats and I breathe a sigh of relief, patting his neck.

Now, all I have to do is get this *parcelle* of grapes from these crates on their way to the barrels. That means crushing them and getting them into the concrete vats to settle, I tell myself, as if going over Madame Beaumont's notes in my head.

'Come on, slow coach,' shouts Isaac, and for once I'm grateful for his silly banter spurring me on. I smile and take a deep breath. Every bone in my body aches, but I have to keep going.

Chapter Twenty-six

Isaac is standing by the doors of the *chai*, his arms folded, watching me. The sun is starting to dip and back at Featherstone's it would be the end of the working day and everyone would be heading for Le Papillon's bar. But here there is still a little more work to do until I can call it a day.

'So, what we need to do, is um . . . get the grapes into the destemmer crusher,' I tell the team.

Mr Featherstone is beaming as he sits back in his wheelchair, looking tired and hot but very happy. He has walked slowly, with Mrs Featherstone's aid, up and down the vines, and between them they have picked many bunches of grapes. It was true team work and really heart-warming to watch. Mrs Featherstone takes a seat now in the shade, wiping her brow.

'This will take off the stems and break the skins, allowing the juices to start flowing.' I'm saying it out loud as much for my benefit as everyone else's, pointing to the old piece of metal equipment in the doorway to the *chai*.

'That thing's not just vintage, it looks as though it's come off the Ark!' Isaac looks on in disbelief.

'It's in good working order,' I tell him. I know it is because

I washed and cleaned and checked it with Madame Beaumont, before her fall. It has a wide bucket at the top, like a big hungry mouth, a series of large cogs on the side, and a huge drum under it, with a barrel beside it to collect the pulp and juice. The juice will then be pumped into the vats. 'Nick, how about you turn the handle?' If I heard myself, I'd think I know what I was talking about; it's just the shake in my voice that gives me away.

'It's not even motorised,' Isaac says as we stand beside the buckets and crates of grapes, ready to sort and tip the first batch in.

As we set to work the group gets a second wind, excited, chatting, joking and I can't help but think how much I would love Dad to be here with us now, doing this. He used to love gardening when I was young. Now, of course, the garden is overgrown. Maybe I'll even tackle it when I get back.

With any luck we'll be through these fairly quickly. I start to relax, even smile. While Nick is winding the handle on the crusher, Gloria, Candy, Isaac and Mr Featherstone are checking over the grapes on a sorting table and things are going at a great pace.

'Let's go! If we work quickly, there may even be time for a drink in Le Papillon,' I call, and everyone cheers. I tip up another crate and we all quickly run our hands over the piles of grapes within, checking for any rotten ones, and push the rest into the crusher. We're on a roll and I don't know why I was worried.

Then I hear *Clunk, clunk whirr, clang, judder, judder . . .* the destemmer crusher judders and shakes, and then there's the sound of metal pieces falling off. And then silence.

'Shit!' I finally say as we stand looking at the crusher. 'What on earth just happened there?'

Isaac peers into the crusher and then tries the handle again. He bites his top lip and then shakes his head. He steps away from the machine and turns to the pickers, resting his hands on his hips.

'Anyone lost anything?'

'No.' They all look at each other, shaking their heads.

'Well, someone's lost their secateurs and I think we've just found them,' he says. looking round again, and I suddenly feel a rush of boiling blood burning my cheeks. Mortified, my hand flies to my mouth.

'I left them in my last bucket,' I wail.

'And now they're in the crusher and I think we can safely say that's not coming back to life without the help of the local farm machinery repair man.'

'Can we phone him?'

'He'll be up to his neck in it at this time of year.' Isaac shakes his head. Then he takes me by the elbow and leads me away from the others. 'Look, you're tried. You did a great job today but you can't do any more. Madame Beaumont will understand.'

'But I messed up!'

'Let me get Jeff to bring the tractor. We'll get the grapes down to Featherstone's and get the juice extracted there. You can't just leave them, and who knows when this crusher will be fixed?'

I let out a huge sigh. He's right, of course. I can't believe it: I've bloody well gone and fallen at the first hurdle! I walk out of the *chai*, kicking at the loose earth under my feet.

What else can I do? I'll have to agree. Time is of the essence. We have to get these grapes crushed. But if they go to Featherstone's, will I ever see them again, or will they just get stacked up ready for the Featherstone's blend?'

Isaac pulls out his mobile and I can hear him giving Colette instructions in his pidgin French.

Frustrated, I wipe my hands over my face and pull them back to look at the slowly setting sun in the sky over the valley, turning it from red and blue to the lavender hue I've come to love, which joins the smell of lavender in the evening air, and think that I have never been anywhere more beautiful. I can see why this place is so important to Madame Beaumont. This wine has been made here for decades. Am I really going to be the one to break that tradition? Or am I going to get stuck in?

'Do it your way,' I hear Madame Beaumont.

'This is no place for indecision,' Isaac's words interrupt my thoughts too. 'We need to get these grapes into their vats. Come on!' he shouts.

'No, wait!' Isaac pulls his phone away from his ear, looks at me and frowns.

'I have an idea.' I turn back to the *chai*.

Isaac looks at me half intrigued, half as if I'm mad, and he's probably right.

'You know me, I'm just the hired hand. I just need to get the job done, one way or another,' he reminds me. 'But that is madness. No way!'

'Yes way!' I say, and smile at him. For once he's speechless.

Chapter Twenty-seven

'You have got to be kidding me!' Candy wails.

Nick looks thrilled at the prospect and Mr Featherstone actually claps his good hand against his weak one with glee. Isaac, on the other hand, is frowning, arms crossed, shaking his head. He turns away as if wanting no part of it.

'We have to try.' I plonk down a bucket of soapy water and the armful of towels I've brought from the house.

'But we have a fully equipped winery a couple of miles down the road!' He holds out his hand, exasperated. 'This will take for ever! It's a complete waste of time!'

'I don't think so,' I say quietly, wishing I felt as confident. 'Socks and shoes off, then wash your feet in this bowl and then take it in turns in twos. Carry on with the destalking by hand in the meantime.'

'Huh! You are too stubborn for your own good! We need that juice in. Now will you let me take it to the winery?'

'No!' I say firmly. 'You're too set in your textbook ways to see it can be done differently.'

'Huh! I need to check the wine back at the winery. At least there is proper wine-making going on there,' Isaac says, storming off to the van.

Bugger! What if he's right? What if this is the stupidest

thing I've done and I'm ruining the wine? Oh, Madame Beaumont! I think in frustration. I could stop it all now, but Nick is already in the barrel, his trousers pushed up over his knees and trying to guide Candy in, with her dress tucked into her knickers.

Candy is squealing like a piglet and Nick is laughing as he holds hands with her and they start to stand on the grapes, letting the fruits break and ooze through the gaps in their toes whilst holding each other's gaze like a rite of passage tribal dance. I realise now exactly how Nick feels about Candy and I can't help thinking things may never be the same for these two.

When Nick and Candy step out of the barrel, Nick goes to stand at the outside tap to rinse off his feet. Maybe it's the air, the wine-making, I don't know, but I feel I have to say something. Nick looks up from washing his feet.

'So, are you . . . going to tell her?' I whisper to him as I'm hosing down his feet and handing him a worn, holey towel.

'What?' He suddenly looks anxious.

'That you're not gay,' I tell him kindly.

He swallows. 'I can't! She's assumed I'm gay from our first day here. If I tell her I'm not gay, everything will change. I know I should have corrected her at the time, but she trusts me because she thinks I'm not interested in her . . . in that way. How can I tell her I've been in love with her from the moment we arrived?' He shakes his head. 'I just can't. She can't find out.'

Back in the *chai*, even Mr Featherstone is having a go at crushing.

'This is the best physio I've ever had,' he says slowly with a wide smile. Mrs Featherstone's cheeks are pink with happiness as she holds her husband's hands and they walk up and down in the vats. When they're all out of breath, Candy and Nick take another turn.

'Get away.' Candy is flicking at a wasp. Word is obviously spreading amongst the bee and wasp community and they're beginning to arrive in their numbers to sample the deep red grape juice.

'Just leave them and they won't bother you,' I say as if talking to Jody when she was little. I know I sound like a mum a lot of the time, but maybe that's because I was one to her for so long. I have missed having my sister around. I would have loved to have seen more of her and her boys. I'm worried for her now she's separated. What's life going to be like for her? My heart twists a little at the fun we might have had here all together, but I know that that will never be. I smile as we seem to be nearing the last of the grapes, everyone checking carefully for secateurs. At least Isaac can't complain I didn't get the grapes in and crushed.

'Aowwwwww!' Candy's face is suddenly puce, the colour of the juice and contorted. 'I stepped on a bee! I stepped on a bee!'

Nick is out of the barrel in an instant, scooping her up in his arms and she clings instinctively to him still screaming, flapping her purple-stained feet around. Nick carries her to the water butt and drops her in it, from where she fumes at him even more. But he doesn't say anything and I wonder if he ever will.

* * *

By the time the grapes are crushed, everyone is exhausted, hungry and has purple feet. The moon is out, though it isn't yet dark.

'You get off, I'll be fine,' I tell them all. 'I just have to pump it up into the vats now. Shouldn't be too hard.' I've seen Jeff and Isaac doing it in Featherstone's. I scratch my arm; something must have bitten me. It's red and sore, but I try to ignore it.

Isaac is back to pick up the Featherstone's pickers and doing his best not to look impressed at our crushed juice.

'I'll run everyone back. Don't do anything until I return,' he instructs, and the pickers climb stiffly into the little van, Candy, with her foot bandaged in a towel, leaning heavily on Nick as he helps her into the front seat.

I busy myself tidying up the crates and washing them for tomorrow's picking. I do the same with the secateurs, giving them each a little sharpen with the stone and line them up with the buckets and crates. I straighten out Henri's tack so I'll be able to put it straight back on him tomorrow.

I feel so stupid about the secateurs. I've phoned the farm repair shop and tried to explain in my pidgin French, but he can't do anything for a couple of weeks . . . after the harvest. It's going to take us much longer at this rate. I have to crack on. I look at the pump that's going to take the juice and skins from the barrels to the big concrete tank at the back of the *chai*. It can't be that hard. The quicker I get on, the sooner we can finish for the day. Although my body thinks this day is a week all rolled into one.

The wasps and bees still think they're in Ayia Napa, and the party goes on. I need to get these grapes away from them.

And Isaac did say we needed to work quickly. We'll be here all night if I wait for him.

I put the ladder against the big concrete tank that Madame Beaumont and I spent ages cleaning out. I put the end of the big hose over my shoulder and begin to climb. It's after about four rungs of the ladder that I wonder what on earth I'm doing and that I should probably wait for Isaac. It's getting dark here at the back of the *chai*. Suddenly something flies at me and I shriek and wobble. I turn round to look.

The small black flying bombers are swooping in and out of the open door at the back of the *chai*. Bats! I need to do this really, really quickly now. Outside, an owl hoots very close by. My heart is thundering. Back home I'd simply be hearing the noise from the road, the occasional bus, or neighbours rowing and banging car doors.

I cling to the wobbling ladder, not daring to look down, trying to keep my head as low as possible to prevent bats getting caught in my hair, as fear flickers up and down my spine.

I flip the end of the hose into the top of the tank and then quickly climb down the ladder.

'OK.' I breathe a sigh of relief that I'm down, not ducking and swerving little black bats. I give another little shudder. I take a look out of the *chai* for Isaac: no sign. I can't wait. I just want to prove to him this was the right decision and I'm not a total idiot, looking to the moon for my answers or any other 'mumbo jumbo'. I know what needs to be done and I'm doing it. I look at the pump, check the connector to make sure it's in securely, and then turn it on. There's a loud whirring and gurgling and then a rumble, and the pipe starts to judder as the grapes move up it. I run forward and grab hold of the pipe, lifting it to help the grapes on their way up the tube. I'm holding the pipe above my head just as the grapes explode out the other end.

'Yes!' I could burst with pride. It's doing it! As I raise my head to watch the juice pump into the tank, the end of the pipe flips out like a snake, spewing up its last supper. Red, lumpy liquid roars forth from its jowls.

'Shit!' I drop the pipe and rush forward into the fast flow of juice as it pumps all over the floor, up the outside walls of the tank, over the clean crates and buckets and the stacked barrels against the long wall. I grab the end of it to stop it flying around. There's a really strong smell of fruit filling the *chai*. The end of the pump is still spewing crushed grapes and juice. I drop it on the floor and it swishes and snakes to and fro. I run to the pump and turn the circular red tap until finally the pipe coughs and splutters and then falls silent, as if the snake has been slayed. I stand stock-still, shivering and soaking. There is grape juice dripping from every part of me, running down my face, dripping off the end of my tied-back hair, my fingertips, and even my trainers are soaking.

'Jeezuss! What the hell happened here?' I hear the familiar Californian drawl.

Oh great, that's all I need. Isaac the Doubter is back. I lean my back against the concrete tank wall and slide down it, my T-shirt snagging all the way down and sit on the wet floor. The smell of summer fruits fills the air as I look up at bats dipping in and out of the barn overhead.

'I told you to wait for me. Goddam it, you've lost loads. Every glassful is money, y'know!'

'I know,' I sigh, so tired and feeling so stupid I can barely get up off the wet floor, the grape juice sinking into my behind, making me feel cold, wet and miserable.

He stands over me and I can't look up.

'I don't need you to make me feel any more useless than I already do. So far today I've managed to break the destemmer machine, get one of my pickers stung and now lose half the day's harvest!'

'Hey!' he says sharply, making me jump. I look up at him, his brown eyes staring down at me, hands on hips. His checked shirt is open as usual with a vest top underneath hugging his torso, the necklaces around his neck entwined with each other, and his bandana holding his untamed hair off his tanned face. His friendship bracelets dangle on his wrists resting on the waistband of his low-slung shorts, barely hanging on to his hips as he slouches slightly, tapping one foot.

'That kind of talk is for quitters and what I'm beginning to learn about you, Emmy Bridges,' he pauses, 'is that you're no quitter.' Then, unbelievably, he taps my behind with his toe.

I glare up at him, furious with him now as well as with myself.

He does it again.

'Hey!' I push at his leg.

'Come on. Get up, we've got work to do.' He looks around. 'Cleaning up the mess you've made, for starters.'

I purse my lips crossly.

'If you hadn't been running around after Candy then—'

'OK, OK, I was a bit longer than I expected.' He holds

his hands up and laughs, and this time I can't help it, the corners of my mouth smile with him, much as I try not to.

He nudges me again, this time with his knee. 'Come on, get up.'

Grape juice drips down the sides of my face and slides down my neck. I brush it away, along with the tears that had threatened to spill but thankfully didn't. I run both my hands over my face, take a deep breath and with it comes a sniff, and I can't help but let out a laugh this time. I must look hideous.

'These grapes can't wait,' he says with a slightly more serious tone in his voice. Isaac may be a joker, but he takes wine-making very seriously indeed. 'Look, Goldy, look at what you've done so far. You've taken on the harvest, smashed it, got the grapes crushed. You can't give up now. This is wine-making! You're doing great,' he says seriously. 'This is just what you promised you'd do.'

And he's right. This is what I said I'd do and I am doing it. I'm not going to be beaten now. I'm certainly not going to lose the vineyard to the château over some spilled grape juice. No way! I just have to stop feeling sorry for myself and get this juice sorted.

'OK, OK,' I say, pulling back one leg and putting my hand out to steady myself on the concrete tank wall to pull myself up.

'Here.' I feel him go to take my hand.

'No, I'm fine really.' I start to stand soggily.

'No, let me help.' He takes hold of my hand and it's like I've grabbed hold of electric fencing by mistake . . . whilst wet! A thousand volts whoosh through me, nearly knocking me off my feet. I stagger to get my footing.

'I'm fine,' I say belligerently, shaking him off, no idea what on earth happened there. I shake my head and then he takes hold of both my hands and pulls me to my feet, his brown eyes staring straight in mine. He's holding my wrists, firmly as if he's about to say something.

My insides just seem to turn to mush, the same as the grapes I've just sprayed around the walls here.

'You go and get dried off and changed. I'll make a start here,' he says, looking straight at me as if trying to read my soul. I can see why so many women fall for his charms; no wonder Candy is besotted. Poor Nick doesn't stand a chance if he's as in love as I think he is. Thank God I'm immune to Isaac's charms, I tell myself very firmly. I still have Charlie to think about. He seems to think we might have something going on. Do I still fancy him, in spite of how he dealt with Madame Beaumont? I try to force an image of him up in my head but all I can see are Isaac's dark eyes, like pools of liquid chocolate, looking at me, interested, as if just for that moment I'm the only person in the world who matters. And I think that's probably right. But I also think that may be Isaac's problem: he only lives in the moment, wherever that might be. I blush under the grape juice and drag my eyes away from his.

'Yup, I'll go and get changed,' I say, my mouth suddenly very dry. 'I'll find us some leftovers from lunch too. Sandwich OK?' I'm twittering, I always do when I'm nervous. But I have no idea why I should be nervous right now. It's just Isaac, me and a bunch of bats, and a load of grape juice. At least the wasps have gone to bed. I try not to look at him. He lets go of my wrists as I turn to go, feeling the drips of juice running down my fingertips as I drop my hands to my side.

'Wait.' He grabs hold of my wrist once more and, surprised, I turn back to him.

He holds up my dripping wrist, and then, my mouth falls slightly open as I watch him dip his head and then put his lips on the inside of my wrist and suck. My mouth falls open, I feel my eyes widen like saucers, and this time the voltage going through my body is off the scale. It's like I've been properly shocked and I'm rooted to the spot.

Then Isaac lifts his head, grins his lazy smile and says, 'Good grape juice. Fantastic sugar levels.' His smile broadens and I manage to snatch my hand away and march as fast as my wobbling knees will take me back to the farmhouse, where I wash and change, put on shorts, a sweatshirt and some wellies I bought in the Intermarché. But still the inside of my wrist tingles.

Back in the *chai* Isaac has made huge headway mopping up the grape juice. We work late, filling up the concrete tanks. Climbing the ladder, this time I put the hose in further and Isaac starts the pump. We take it in turns.

The grape juice is sucked up into the tank but by the third barrel, what with pulling the hose up the ladder, I'm so tired I think I may fall asleep there and then.

We bicker late into the night.

'Look, why don't you do the pump and I'll do the ladder . . . ?'

'No, it's my turn up the ladder . . .'

By one o'clock in the morning we're washing down the

barrels and crates for the next day. At two a.m. I bid Isaac good night and finally fall into bed, tired, hungry and aching in every bone in my body. Isaac was right, maybe I am too stubborn for my own good. But he's just as bad.

I am desperate for sleep to come and claim me, but every time I shut my eyes his lips are on my wrist again and again and again.

Chapter Twenty-eight

'I look like the elephant man!'

The next morning Candy's foot is swollen to the size of a football. She can't even get her beaded flip-flops on, and not for want of trying.

'I think you look lovely,' says Nick, but she doesn't hear him.

'What am I going to do? Quick, don't let Isaac see.' She dodges behind Nick as Isaac gets out of the van and explains he's got to get back to Featherstone's to see in another batch of wine and barrel it. He's brought a couple of Moroccan ladies with him to pick. They smile and shake my hand.

'*Enchanté*,' I say, and smile.

'They can stay just until lunchtime. Then they have to get back for their children. I'll be back with the yeast for the grape juice.'

'Yeast?'

'Yes, we'll add it when I get back. What we want now is a nice balanced, controlled fermentation for the next ten to fourteen days. The more stable I can get it at this stage, the more uniform it will taste when we come to blend it. Getting the mix right now is essential.' His brows furrow as they always do when he's being serious, usually about wine.

'And what's in this mix you're working out?' I frown back.

He taps his nose and suddenly breaks into a smile. 'That's where a wine-maker plays his cards close to his chest. This is why they pay us big bucks!'

'Really?'

'Or, will do, one day.' He throws his head back and laughs, tossing the van keys up in the air and catching them again. 'I have to get on. Have a good day's picking, everyone. Candy, take care of that foot.' He winks at her and heads to the van.

Candy groans. She comes out from behind Nick. She is bright red with sunburn from yesterday, exactly the colour of a cooked lobster, and her foot looks like a balloon with five little baby balloons sticking out of the top.

'Candy, you'd better stay inside today. Everyone else OK to keep going?' They nod. 'Grab a coffee and I'll go and sort out Henri. Today we start on the next *parcelle* over.'

A hare shoots through the vineyard, followed by another, darting in and out of the mist, surprising me and making me smile, reminding me why it's a privilege to be here.

'Henri!' I call, holding his harness in one hand and a bucket of pony nuts in the other. The horse lifts his head and without hesitation marches purposefully towards the gate and waits for me to get there.

'*Bonjour,*' I say to him, rubbing his nose. '*Prêt pour un autre jour?*' Then I open up the gate and he walks out and stops just by the trailer. The sheep try to make a run for it at the same time but I herd them back in, catching one between my knees and walking him backwards into the field before shutting the gate.

'OK.' I shout to the pickers. 'I want you to remember, no rotten ones, don't forget, hang on to your secateurs and treat the grapes gently! We're making wine with love and care here.'

Gloria and I are picking together. She's got Madame Beaumont's little three-legged stool that she moves with her down the vines.

'How's your dad?' she asks once we get into our picking routine, her breath rising like smoke from the other side of the vine. Although it's going to be hot, there is the hint of an autumnal chill in this early morning air, making us move quickly.

'Actually,' I find myself frowning, 'I'm not sure.'

'You're not sure? I thought he was always ringing you.' *Snip, Snip.*

'No, well, he was but now he's . . . well, he's always out!'

'That's good isn't it?' *Snip, snip.*

'I'm not sure. He has barely been out since . . . well, since my mum died.'

'Oh, I'm sorry.' She shuffles the little stool forward.

I never know how to answer that, so I don't.

'And now, every time I ring, according to my sister, he's out. At the pub or helping out his mate, the plumber. He came to fix our water tank a couple of weeks ago. Turned out they were at school together.'

'Oh, well, that's a good thing. Sometimes in life it helps to go back to your past in order to move on to your future. And it's good your sister's there,' she says, moving her stool down to the next vine, and I'm with her.

'Well, that's the other thing. I haven't seen my sister in

years. We fell out. But she's recently separated from her husband. I'm worried. I wonder how she's managing on her own with the boys. I just hope that she's going to be OK.'

'It's good you're worried about your sister, no matter what's happened. That's family.'

'Well, I brought her up. She was only twelve when Mum . . . She married young, to a promising footballer. They were childhood sweethearts. He was a few years older than her. I never really liked him. He didn't like her spending time with her family, was very possessive. He borrowed our family savings, never repaid them, and after that we never really saw her again, until now, now that she's separated from him.'

'I'm sure she's enjoying spending time with your dad,' Gloria says reassuringly.

I look around. Picking's going well, but slowly. We still have so much more to do.

'What about you, Gloria? Do you have family?'

Snip, snip. The sound of the secateurs is all I can hear for a moment and I'm about to apologise if I've upset her in any way, then she says, 'I was married . . . for a long time. To Paul.' I actually hear her swallow and I feel like I'm in a confessional box, listening from behind the big green vine leaves.

'He left me just over a year ago. Huh,' she gives a hollow laugh, 'for his secretary. How predictable can you get?'

'Oh, Gloria!'

To my surprise she carries on, talking as she's cutting as if she's telling the vines, not me. I almost feel like I'm eavesdropping.

'The thing is, Paul was a company man. An engineer. We moved a lot with his work, lived abroad, all over. I never really felt like I had a home. We'd stay somewhere for a couple of years then have to relocate. I couldn't wait for him to retire, so we could finally settle down and start living, maybe even come to France.' She stops cutting just for a moment, lifting her face to the warming sun, and it seems to help push away the pain.

'Do you have children?' I ask gently.

'No, no children. We were never in one place long enough to have a family. I didn't want to have them to send them to boarding school. We couldn't even have pets. I always swore I'd have a cat when he retired.'

I can't believe it: kind, motherly Gloria, dropped like a second-hand Jaguar whilst her husband updates to a newer, younger model.

'But why the call centre, Gloria? Was it your way of reclaiming your independence?' I suddenly love the thought of this.

'No,' she says flatly. 'I'm broke.'

'What?'

'I've only ever paid married person's National Insurance, so I won't even have a pension. He managed to cut me out of everything.'

'But that's not right. You were his wife. You're entitled to half of everything.'

'Not if he cleverly manages to convince the judge he hasn't got anything. Lost his job and says he isn't earning. I've no idea where it's all gone. But his new wife will be well set up.'

'But what about the house?'

'Rental proprieties. We'd planned to buy a flat in London and a holiday house out here in France, once he retired.'

'Oh, Gloria.' I want to run round the vine to hug her, but we're halfway down it and actually I don't think it's what she would have wanted.

'So, I couldn't have been more chuffed when this opportunity came up,' she says, reverting back to her usual optimistic self.

'You're a fantastic cook, Gloria.' I think back to the night of the coq au vin when Madame Beaumont fell. 'You should do that for a living.' There I go again, trying to fix other people's lives.

'Thank you. I used to cook for my husband's work colleagues, the whole corporate wife thing.'

'Harrumph!' I say.

'Actually, I loved that bit of it. I love to cook and feed people.'

'Well, I can't tell you how much you've helped me.'

'I've loved it. It's made me feel like we're the family I always wanted.'

Tears suddenly prick my eyes and there's a ball in my throat that I swallow down.

'It was the fact he stopped me feeling like a woman I resent. At a time when . . . well, I just felt invisible. I wasn't the young, pretty executive's wife any more, who listened to his work plans and helped him with his presentations. I had no children to be proud of. No career of mine own. And then finally, I didn't even feel like a woman any more, just someone existing . . . with hot flushes!' And she manages a little laugh.

'Did you ever want a career, Gloria?' I keep cutting and dropping the grapes into the bucket.

'Oh, I started out as a bookkeeper – that's how we met – but once we started travelling it was much harder. I always thought our time would come, but it never did. You can't wait for your life to start, I've realised; you may just run out of time.'

We carry on snipping until the end of the row.

'Tell you what, why don't I do the lunches for the rest of pick?' says Gloria brightly.

'Really?' I ask with a mix of amazement and relief.

'Yes, I'd like to.'

'Well, that would be fantastic. Agreed!'

The sun is starting to get hotter. I make sure everyone stops for water and puts on hats and suncream. I can't afford to lose any more workers.

By lunchtime, Nick has fallen by the wayside with an old back injury from his rugby playing days.

'Ooh, rugby!' Candy coos as he lies on the cold kitchen floor. 'There was that Welsh rugby player who came out as gay. So brave,' she sighs, looking at him in total admiration.

Gloria is back in the kitchen and I'm leaving her to it. She puts more ice on Candy's foot, instructs Nick to rub after-sun balm on her and finds him paracetamol from her bag, which seems to contain a potion for everything.

'Paul was such a hypochondriac,' she tells us, suddenly talking freely about him, like a tap that's been switched on and is now flowing again.

She then serves eggs with thick, creamy, yellow homemade

mayonnaise, my favourite, followed by wild boar casserole with lentils, garlic, thyme and a red wine. And *tarte au chocolat* for dessert.

The pickers move on to the cheese: a big round brie, white on the outside and its soft, yellow inside oozing across the worn wooden board, to everyone's delight. The bread basket is topped up by Gloria as the long creamy strings of cheese are negotiated and guided on to plates.

I'm smiling with the others when suddenly my phone rings in my shorts pocket and I move away from the table, pulling it out and looking at the screen. I go over to where Henri hangs his head over the field gate while I hold the phone out in front of me to see who's FaceTiming me. The image is blurred and I can't tell who it is.

There is a rustle and some talking that sounds a lot like Madame Beaumont giving a nurse short shrift.

'Madame Beaumont?' I stare at the screen.

'*Oui? Allo?*' she says, but all I can see is her ear.

'It's Emmy!' I find myself shouting. 'Look at the screen. Don't hold it to your ear.'

'Emmy? Is that you? Are you harvesting?' Suddenly she looks at the screen and I can see her face, close and peering into the iPod. A nurse seems to be close by, trying to give a helping hand, but Madame Beaumont seems determined to master this on her own, making me smile.

'How are you?'

'Not dead!' she says flatly in a rasping, husky voice, giving the nurse a sideways look. 'But out of the woods, they say,' and she coughs. 'Now, *écoute*, listen. Have you begun the harvest?' she says in a stilted way as if she's sending a coded message.

'Um, well, we're getting there. The grapes are coming in and I've made juice.' I tell her the edited highlights.

'*Bravo!*' I hear her in the distance, as if she's moved the phone back to her ear. I drop my voice.

'But, um, what about yeast?' I ask her. I need to know what she thinks. 'Should I add yeast?'

'What's that?' she shouts back.

'Yeast? Do I add it?' I shout back and turn round to the lunch table, but thankfully no one appears to have heard.

'*Mon Dieu! Non!* Whatever you do, don't let him put yeast in the wine. It must stay wild. The wild yeasts from the hillside, naturally there, will do the job.'

'But what if . . . ?' But the screen goes black. I run my thumb over the screen and try and call her back, but she doesn't reply. I try again, still nothing. It's hot. I turn back to look out over the vines and I wish Dad could see this, but as he has only just rediscovered the pub after fifteen years, he's hardly likely to come here. I wish my nephews were here, running in and out of the vines, laughing.

I know it can't happen, but I want to tell them about the harvest anyway. I take a picture of the vines and then the pickers. *La vendange!* I type, and then send it to Layla. I get her usual reply followed by lots of yellow happy faces. Then I press the button to ring home.

'There's no one here right now, please leave a message after the tone.'

I sigh. I won't leave another message. They'll probably think I've been drinking, leaving mad rambling messages about Clos Beaumont and the harvest. I move away from the vines. The sun is hot on my shoulders as I walk back to the lunch table and put my phone down on it. I sit at the end of the bench and a hand reaches from behind me with a bottle, pouring wine into my glass. I turn.

'Oh, no, it's fine, I won't, Nick,' I say, putting up a hand, thinking I still have so much work to do.

'Wasn't it you who said you can't make what you don't know about?' It's Isaac, not Nick. He's back and topping up my glass.

I can't help but laugh.

'Actually, I think you'll find it was Madame Beaumont who said that. She's out of the woods. On the mend,' I smile at him.

'Well, here's to Madame Beaumont then.' He raises a glass, as do I, and my homesickness seems to dissolve for the time being, replaced by the excitement I feel when Isaac is around these days and we're talking about the harvest.

Chapter Twenty-nine

'Ouch,' I say, itching again.

Gloria takes a sharp intake of breath. Gloria and I are working a *parcelle* of Merlot grapevines together. One each side of the vine. Mr and Mrs Featherstone have had to bow out today but are vowing to return, but right now it's just me and Gloria.

'Same here,' she says. Every few steps one or other of us stops to itch. It's slowing us down.

By the time we have trodden the juice in the barrels and pumped it into the vats I'm itching all over, on my stomach, my arms, even under my breasts.

'Jesus!' Isaac takes a couple of steps back as he arrives from Featherstone's to drive Gloria, Nick and Candy home. Nick is still laid up with his back but is keeping Candy company in Clos Beaumont's kitchen. She's been working on a laptop.

'What the hell?' Isaac is still recoiling.

'What?' I panic. Have I messed up the wine? I turn this way and that to see what's happened. 'What have I done?'

'What happened to you?' His face screws up like he's sucking a sour sweet. I stop and look down at the bites.

'Oh, that, erm, I'm not sure. Gloria has it, too. She needs

to go back to the *gîte* and then get to the pharmacy.'

'If it's what I think it is, you both need the pharmacy.'

'What do you think it is?' I ask.

'Harvest bugs. Mites that lay eggs in warm places. There's no avoiding them. Finish up in here and get yourself in the bath. I'll take the others back and go to the pharmacy for you. And that's an order,' he says firmly, and I find myself shivering all over.

The big iron bath takes for ever to fill, and when I get in I keep slipping down under the water because my feet won't touch the end of it. But still, it's bliss. I eventually heave myself out, once the water goes cold. Standing on the wooden floor, I look down at my bites.

Ewww.

I dry and dress quickly, slipping on some shorts and a hoodie and some flip-flops, which seems to have become my uniform since I moved in here, and make my way outside to start washing down the *chai* for tomorrow's picking. Madame Beaumont says the *chai* has to be spotless if you're to make good wine. In no time at all I'm soaking all over again and cold, now the sun has gone down, and I start to scratch at the bites on my arms just as I hear a car pull up in the yard.

'Hey!'

I turn to see Isaac standing in the doorway.

'Come on into the house! This place is so clean you could carry out open-heart surgery in it.'

Wearily I do as I'm told. I switch off the buzzing overhead light with a clunk of the big old light switch and follow him to the house.

'OK, now then, take off your top.' he says, dropping an overnight bag on the floor.

'I beg your pardon!' I'm standing in front of the wood burner, shivering. 'Look, I'm really not interested in having a fling with you.'

'No,' he says flatly, 'and I don't want a fling with you either.' He opens the fire, throws in some paper and kindling and puts a match to it.

I'm not sure whether to be relieved or insulted that he doesn't want a fling with me. Relieved, I think. It's much easier for us to work together if there is absolutely no attraction between us, but still my cheeks burn as if I've been slapped across them.

'I can't imagine how you're such a hit with the ladies with those chat-up lines,' I try to joke.

'I meant,' he sighs, 'put on a vest top or whatever and then let me put something on your sores. It's the mites' eggs that are making you itch.'

'Oh, yes, of course,' I say, mortified, and quickly run upstairs to put on a dry T-shirt and shorts and then hang my other clothes out in front of the fire on the fragile old clothes horse.

'They'd run out of cream at the pharmacy.'

'Oh, no. Now what am I going to do?' I think the itching might actually drive me mad.

'Apparently aftershave is just as good,' Isaac tells me evenly.

'But I haven't got any . . .'

He pulls a small black bottle out from his bag. 'But I have. Right, where are they?'

I show him first the backs of my legs, red, blotchy with white marks bubbling up. The aftershave stings like hell and I cry out. He looks concerned and I bite my lip.

'OK?' he asks before carrying on.

I nod. When the stinging subsides, it seems to draw the heat and itching from the sores too.

Then I show him the crooks of my elbows. The scent is earthy, woody, with a hint of citrus wrapping round me like a cloak, making me feel quite light-headed. I pull off my sweatshirt and lift my T-shirt and he dabs gently at the bites around my middle, his head so close to mine I can feel his breath on my skin, while my lungs fill more and more with his smell and, despite me knowing how hideous I must look, a thousand volts of electricity are shooting through me again. Then he pushes up the edge of my T-shirt.

'Undo your bra,' he says quietly and the thousand volts just shoot off the scale. Every bit of me is shaking. My cheeks are on fire. Suddenly I ache and I think if he touches me under my breasts, where the mites itch the most, I might just explode.

'Here,' I say, and our fingers touch as I take the cotton wool from him, nearly making me drop it, dabbing where I can feel the worst offenders itching. It stings, makes my eyes water, and banishes the feelings that were building in the very pit of my stomach.

'And here,' he says, pointing, as I hold one hand over my breasts, lifting them. 'Sorry, would you rather I didn't,' he suddenly says, realising the intimacy of the situation.

I swallow, hard. 'No, no, of course not. Please . . .' I must try to be a grown-up here. I can't do this without him.

'OK,' he holds my gaze for just a minute with those dark eyes, the colour of chocolate hazelnut spread.

I can't understand why I'm shaking so much.

'And here,' he points. I lift my breasts higher. Don't touch me, I'm thinking as he points towards my breast. My lips are even starting to ache. Suddenly aching with a desire to be kissed. I have no idea what has come over me. It must be heat stroke.

'No, here,' he takes my hand and directs it towards another bite, and I'm grateful for the stinging, eye-watering smack back to reality.

I need to distract myself from these ridiculous feelings I'm having.

'So, erm . . . about the next stage,' I try to say casually, but my voice comes out as a weird kind of nervous squeak. 'What about using the wild yeast instead?'

He shakes his head and I swear his hair is going to tickle my tummy, making me feel ticklish and tingly at the thought.

'And by wild yeasts I presume you mean adding no artifical yeasts at all. Just what's found in the vineyard on the grapes?' He raises an eyebrow, then shakes his head again. 'Too risky. We need to get the yeast I've brought into the vats tomorrow. Those grapes have been sitting for a few days. They need to start their fermentation. Like I say, we want a nice controlled fermentation over the next ten days, two weeks. It'll make it a more controllable wine when we come to blend, and then next year when we roll it out and blend it with bought-in grapes.'

'But I thought that using just the wild yeasts makes a more complex wine, gives it better character?' I still try to sound casual. 'Ouch,' I wince as he dabs more aftershave on the cotton wool and hands it to me and I place it on a bite.

'Top marks, Miss Bridges,' he smiles, and I really hope I don't have to stand up because my legs are jelly and if he touches me again, I'm going to melt. I feel my arms and legs have become all disjointed and there is a fireball rolling round my stomach and up and down my thighs.

This time when he hands me a piece of cotton wool he doesn't let go and I don't pull away either. He looks at me and even if I wanted to I wouldn't be able to pull my eyes away. The wood burner suddenly bursts into life, throwing reflections of orange flames across his dark, shiny skin and his bright eyes. My head moves slightly closer to his and I'm sure his moves closer, too. I know I shouldn't but I just can't seem to stop myself edging a tiny bit closer and then looking at his lips, soft and glistening in the firelight. The pain from the bites has all but gone, but my breasts remain on high alert.

My head is swimming with excitement.

'Hey!' The French doors fly open. 'Not disturbing you, am I?' Charlie jokes as he breezes in, bringing in a blast of cold air. I yank my top back down and fall back in the chair.

'No, not all,' says Isaac coolly with just a hint of fluster, turning his head away quickly. 'Just giving Emmy something for her mite bites,' he adds, dropping the lid to the aftershave on the floor and looking down and around for it. I feel like the bubble we were in has burst and all that's left is its debris to clear up.

'Jesus! It smells like a brothel in here.' Charlie waves his hand around. 'Just thought you'd like some cheering up,' he says, and flourishes a bottle of wine and a small box of chocolates at me. Then he grimaces as he takes in the blotches covering my body. 'But I can see you're probably not feeling up to it.'

'I'll be off,' Isaac says, packing up his bag. 'I'll see ya in the morning. Good night,' he says to me, then: 'Charlie,' he says stiffly as he brushes past him to leave, and I suddenly feel hugely disappointed.

'Hang on,' says Charlie, and I'm hoping he's going to persuade him to stay. 'I'll come with you. Fancy one at Le Papillon?'

'Sure. But are you sure you should be leaving Emmy? Those bites are pretty bad.'

'You'll be OK, won't you, Emmy? I want to have a catch-up with Isaac, find out how it's all going here,' he beams, putting down the wine and chocolates. 'You're doing brilliantly, by all accounts. Apart from sending back my staff like the walking wounded.'

Isaac doesn't move.

'Sure you'll be OK?' He looks straight at me and asks gently. And right now I know that if he stays, I'll do something I'll regret.

'You will, won't you, Emmy?' says Charlie.

'Go!' I say jovially. 'I'll see you tomorrow. Have fun. I'll be fine!'

But I suddenly feel like I've been left standing on the dance floor on my own before the song has finished as I wave them off. I must think about Charlie. Why did he turn up here tonight with wine and chocolates? Is he interested in me, or is this just about the wine? My head is whirring. He's good-looking, after all, and he has dreams. Charlie's making a future for himself. And he's looking for someone to share it with. Isaac, on the other hand, is just living in the moment. And I certainly don't want to be a notch in Isaac's travelling bedstead. Charlie is clearly someone with prospects, family business, smart, ambitious. It's a no-brainer. He ticks all the boxes. He's clearly making an effort and I should too, a voice in my head says loudly. He turned up with here with chocolates and wine. I have all the answers I need. He likes me! But the question is, of course, would Charlie have spent the evening dabbing aftershave on my mite bites if I'd asked him? And I have a feeling I know the answer to that too.

That night in bed I am wrapped in a cloak of Isaac's aftershave. A wave of excitement takes me off to sleep, occasionally waking to thoughts of what it would have felt like if Isaac's lips had met mine. And for the first time in ages, I sleep. I sleep as if his arms are wrapped around me, telling me everything's going to be just fine.

Chapter Thirty

The next morning, every part of my body aches and itches, but the mite bites are looking a lot less angry and red. And a night's sleep has done me the world of good.

Isaac arrives in the van at speed. The doors open.

'Morning.' His usual cheeriness has all but disappeared. He's polite but distant.

Nick gets out stiffly and then straightens, putting his hands in the small of his back and wincing. Candy follows, limping, her foot still swollen. Gloria looks red and swollen all over too.

'I'm so sorry, Emmy, the doctor says I'm to stay out of the sun for a few days.' Gloria looks really sorry. 'But I can still cook.'

'Don't worry.' I try to smile but I am worried. *Really* worried. We're dropping like flies and I'm never going to get the grapes in at this rate.

'And maybe . . .' She hesitates.

'Yes?'

'Well, it's been a while, but maybe I could take a look over Madame Beaumont's books, straighten out the accounts,' she says shyly.

'That would be great, Gloria. I'm sure Madame Beaumont

won't want to have to come back to lots of paperwork. I think they're in a box in the living room.'

Gloria beams. 'I'll get on to it.'

'I can't pick, but I've been setting up a blog,' says Candy.

'Yes, and once the painkillers kick in, maybe I could get back to picking,' Nick says, holding his back.

'I think you'd better lie down. I'll take care of you,' Candy smiles like he's a cute puppy she's going to fuss over all day.

Isaac gets back in the van and starts the engine. I run round to the van window.

'Can't you stay?' I ask.

He shakes his head.

'What am I going to do?'

'Just make a start. I'll be back as soon as I can. I've left the yeast in the *chai* for you. It needs adding to each of the vats. There's a measure there. We may need to pump it over then. Get one of the walking wounded to help you.'

'Add the yeast, OK. Pump it over . . . right. How was Charlie last night?' I ask quickly, wondering whether he mentioned me.

Isaac chews his bottom lip. 'Seems to think you're doing this for the "Featherstone's team". Talked a lot about what a great girl you are and how he hadn't seen it straight away. Just talked about if we win the Morgan's Supermarkets wine medal. We'd get prime position on the shelves and loads of publicity. It could really put a little family-run company like Featherstone's on the map. Growers will be knocking at his door to get them to make their wine. He's in touch with a big wine company in Australia. Really big. If I can get in there, well, the world's my oyster!'

'That's great!' I say, but despite hearing everything I wanted to hear, for some reason I can't feel as happy as I want to.

'Yup! We'll all do well out of this,' he says without looking at me.

I can't help but think there's a bit of sting in what he's saying.

'What do you mean by that?'

'Just sayin', we all get what we want, that's all.' Isaac is staring straight ahead, holding the steering wheel. He's right, we do. So, why don't I feel more pleased?

'Where are you off to? I need help here. If we are all to get what we want.' And now there's a sting in my voice.

He looks at me, then suddenly the corner of his mouth pulls back into a smile. He puts the car into gear, drops off the handbrake and starts to drive off.

'Don't forget the yeast!' he calls out the window. 'I'll explain what else you need to do when I get back.'

'Isaac! Where are you going? How long will you be?'

'To find you more pickers.'

I watch as the little van disappears down the lane.

He's right, if I want this wine in, I'm going to have to do as he says. I'm going to have to add the yeast. And let's be honest, will Madame Beaumont really know?

It's not as hot in the vineyard today, which means I can work faster. But as it's just me, no matter how hard I pick, progress is slow – very slow. I am never going to get this done in time. There's just too much to do.

'I know it's not your fault, it's just there's so many of you and only one of me,' I tell the vines, wondering if they have become bilingual. 'If only Isaac was here. Then at least we'd get it done twice as fast. I just don't know how I'm going to do it all.' *Snip, snip. Snip, snip.*

I can't help but feel utterly beaten, and really cross. Isaac went off ages ago to find me pickers and hasn't come back. I can't believe he's let me down like this.

'*Allez, Henri*,' I call to the horse, and he slowly moves between the rows of vines.

'Woah!' I call again, and he does.

'I mean, it's complicated. On the one hand he frustrates me with his silly jokes and his laid-back attitude, but when it comes to the wine, everything has to be done just so. Charlie. Charlie doesn't infuriate me like Isaac does but he doesn't . . . well . . .' My mind flips back to Isaac dabbing the aftershave on me last night. I can still smell it now, making me feel like it's put a sway in my hips. 'Stupid, I know,' I tell the vines as I pick, drop the grapes into the bucket and then load them on to the crates on the trailer. I push the memory of last night out of mind, just as I promised myself I would, but somehow my hips keep swaying as I walk.

I'm just following Henri up the fourth row of vines when I hear a car pull up in the yard. Thank God! Isaac!

I put my secateurs in the pocket of my shorts, pull off my baseball cap I bought in the market, gather my now longer hair together and push the cap back on again, pulling my ponytail out through the gap at the back. Henri stands patiently and waits. I pat his big hind quarters.

'*Tu attends. Bon garçon.* I'll be back in a minute.' My trainers are dark and stained from the earth, and look worn and tired. A bit like me. But the sway in my hips and the smell of the earthy, woody aftershave, still lingering on my skin, keeps me moving on up the hill. I arrive at the top of the slope, slightly out of breath and stop and look at the yard. It's not Isaac. It's Charlie.

He's getting out of his car, pulling off his aviator sunglasses. Cecil pulls himself up on to his two big front legs, lifts his head and lets out a jowl-swinging round of barks. Charlie sidesteps him as he starts to get his back legs to join his front ones and stand. As usual there is a trail of drool hanging from Cecil's mouth.

'Hi,' I smile, and raise a hand, feeling a little disappointed. He doesn't look as if he's come dressed for picking either, I think, taking in his smart, sharply ironed pink shirt, open at the neck, the cuffs neatly folded back. And his dark suit trousers and chestnut-brown shiny shoes. Now the weather is cooling, Charlie looks much more in his comfort zone when it comes to his wardrobe.

'Hi,' he beams, and holds my shoulder, kissing me on both cheeks. His aftershave is tropical, floral and warm. He frowns. 'What's that smell?' He sniffs me again, wrinkling his nose, and I realise it's Isaac's aftershave he can smell.

'I thought you might be here to help me pick,' I say, realising he's just come to check on progress, which frankly right now is really slow. 'I know it looks like I'm only about halfway through, but I've got a lot of it already starting to ferment.' I quickly try to put his worries aside. 'Isaac's gone to find me some more pickers.'

'Ah, we had a delivery of juice, he's back at the winery putting it into vats,' Charlie tells me, and I could throttle Isaac.

'He could've called me!' I wail. 'Now I'll never get it all

done.' Suddenly I feel totally and utterly beaten. I bend over and hold my knees. I'm shattered, I ache, and even the smell of the woods and citrus aftershave doesn't lift my spirits now.

'In that case, this might help you out.' He opens the car door and I lift my head a little. 'Mind your feet on the seats . . .'

'Are you our auntie Emmy? We came on a plane and Granddad bought us Cokes and . . . Wow! Who's that?' The two smartly dressed boys stop and stare wide-eyed at Cecil.

Am I imagining it? I give a weak, incredulous laugh and stand up straight. Still my eyes won't focus properly, but those two fast-moving little people that have just tumbled out of the back of Charlie's car are the same ages as my nephews, about four and six. I do a double-take. It is! Luke and Arthur!

They run over to Cecil and rub his big head like it's a giant basketball. Cecil loves having his ears rubbed and in no time at all the long string of drool has stretched and he suddenly shakes his head, the drool flying.

'Whoa!' the boys laugh in utter respect at such a fantastic trick.

I turn back to the car, still not really understanding what's going on.

'Jody?' I stammer as my sister slides out of the car, tentatively at first. She stands in front of me, but then breaks into a huge grin, runs at me and hugs me tightly. I hug her tightly back and Charlie looks on appreciatively, I notice. But, God, I need this hug. I shut my eyes. I can't speak. There's no need for words. Finally I open them and Charlie opens the passenger door, and slowly and stiffly, putting his brown shoe and grey sock on the dusty ground and pulling himself out of the car . . . I can hardly believe it, I catch my breath, the tears well up in my eyes again so I can barely see him as his pulls himself out of the car.

'Dad!' And I fling myself at him, hugging him hard whilst Luke and Arthur are running round and round the yard.

'Hello, who's this?' Gloria and Candy have come out to see what's happening.

'This is my family,' I turn and announce with a huge tennis ball in my throat.

'Thought you could do with a hand, picking,' Dad says, sounding choked, too.

'I can't believe you're here.' I wipe away tears spilling down my cheeks.

'Neither can I, love, neither can I,' he laughs.

He hugs me again and, over his shoulder, standing by the driver's door, Charlie has the look of a man who knows how to make a big gesture. This is the most wonderful thing anyone could have done for me. My heart fills to bursting and it's all because of Charlie. He understands what it means to me. He understands how much I've needed to see my dad was OK. I suddenly feel that he and I might be back on track. He wouldn't have done this if he didn't care about me. He still wants us to try to get together. Maybe I am going to find love here after all. Only someone who *really* cares about me would do this.

'How long are you here for?' I ask, wanting to make the most of every minute.

'Just a few days, what with the kids and changing schools. But we thought it would help you out.'

'Oh, it does. Wait, changing schools?'

'I'll let Jody explain.' Dad smiles a slightly teary smile and I hug him tightly again.

'You smell nice,' he says, hugging me back.

'Thank you.'

I turn to Charlie. 'Thank you, Charlie, so much,' I mouth.

'You're welcome,' he mouths back and smiles, and I feel like I'm walking on air.

'Yes, thank you, Charlie, for organising all of this.' Dad turns and smiles his approval and my heart does a happy little dance again.

'Gloria, got room for some more for lunch?' I ask her.

'Of course!' She waves a tea towel at me.

'Come on, Dad, let's find you some suitable picking gear,' I say, my arm round him, leading him to the house, excitedly showing him around and feeling like all my Christmases have come at once.

Chapter Thirty-one

'OK, don't stand on any bees, take a break if you're aching. Dad, we'll get you a stool. Cut from here. Don't cut rotten ones, hang on to your secateurs and be gentle! We're making wine with love here.'

We work all morning and at lunch Gloria serves us the most glorious roasted wild boar made from meat Jeff brought to the house in the back of his car, a gift from a friend, he said, and Gloria happily cooked it and serves it with new potatoes glistening with butter and green beans. This is followed by big fat strawberries and crème fraîche from a local farmer Gloria met and got talking to when she was out walking over the other side of the river. And of course the big round of cheese comes out again. I'm amazed where Nick puts it all. He's as thin as a rake and eats twice as much as any of us.

'That was fabulous,' Dad says, rubbing his tummy and titling back his hat. The boys get down from the table and run around with Cecil, who barks and does his slobber flinging trick, much to their delight.

After lunch the pick is suddenly back on track. Dad is wearing long shorts, green socks and leather sandals, the same ones I think he had when we holidayed in West Wales when I was a child. That's where I first met my best friend, Layla. Years later we ended up both working at the call centre and realising we'd been childhood friends, camping by the beach on holiday. Dad must have kept his summer clothes in the attic. He looks just like he did back then, with his legs so white they're almost green poking out from the bottom of his shorts. He's wearing a short-sleeved shirt and I've insisted on the hat, despite it being more overcast today. Nick's lent him his panama and he looks very smart.

With lunch cleared away and the heat of the day passing, Gloria, with her arms and legs covered in long sleeves and trousers, decides to come back out to pick with Dad. Candy and Nick are helping each other, slowly making their way down a row of vines like two wounded soldiers. And Jody and the boys are picking too. I watch her with them, encouraging them, explaining what to do and laughing. She's wonderful with them, I think proudly.

The trailer is filling up way faster than it was this morning and my spirits begin to lift. I can't thank Charlie enough for organising this. I don't know why I was starting to doubt how I felt about him or how he felt about me. Clearly, getting Dad, Jody and the boys here, well, it must mean he cares about me. He understands me and my commitments. And Dad seemed very taken with him. He's just . . . well, just perfect. Finally, my life might be starting to take shape. Maybe I'm at last getting something right. I may even have a 'plus one' to take to the Cadwallader's Christmas party, instead of spending the evening dodging Lecherous Louis from car insurance, or avoiding skinhead Melody, who is always showing off her new tattoos and piercings, is first to photocopy her bum, and trying to get as many people under the mistletoe as possible. Her record is thirty-three. Suddenly I'm thinking about my desk back at the call centre. It's right by the window so I can look out at the tiny bit of green park between the two big buildings – like my vortex to the outside world. And at least by the window I get to see a bit of sky. I look up at the big sky above me now. I'll never have sky like this again. I look over the valley to the château and then to Saint Enrique and notice the clouds beginning to gather on the horizon.

'OK, everyone, we need to get moving,' I shout, and put my head down and pick furiously, as does everyone else.

We finish the *parcelle*. Only a couple left to do now: the big section down the lane and then the *parcelle* beneath the château.

We follow Henri and the trailer back to the *chai* where we start unloading the grapes, destalking them, and Luke and Arthur come into their own, treading the grapes. They can't believe they're allowed to get so mucky and not get told off! Even Dad has a go, smiling like I've never seen him. For someone who hasn't moved from his armchair for over ten years and never misses an episode of *Pointless*, he's a changed man. Mr and Mrs Featherstone come up to join in, although Mr Featherstone hasn't quite recovered from his exertions earlier in the week and so sits in his wheelchair and watches us as we work with a huge grin on his face.

That night my family return to the *gîte* with Gloria and the others. Gloria moves in with Candy, Jody and the boys take her room, and Dad has Nick's, who sleeps on the floor downstairs, saying he'd prefer it because of his back.

* * *

The next day I'm up and at it early. The sky is darkening even more and the breeze has really picked up. Everyone's here.

'Let's crack on. We have to get the *parcelle* in before the rain comes.'

Jody and I are picking together as Isaac is up to his neck in it at the winery. And once again I thank God that Charlie contacted my family and I think what a lucky person I am that he's come into my life. Because of him, we may actually get this vintage in, and my spirits have really lifted.

'Dad seems to be having a good time. Is he OK? I mean, he's been out more in the last ten weeks than he has in the last ten years. What's going on?'

Jody and I cut and move together down the vine, quickly and in unison.

'Honestly, Emmy, he's a changed man. Ever since Ralph the plumber came to fix the water tank, he's been to the pub, out to see the rugby with him, and he's even planning to go on a coach trip to Bath before Christmas with a couple of ladies they met in Doug's Diner whilst having the OAP's all-day breakfast. He's even talking about applying for a job at the local DIY superstore. They like older, more experienced people, apparently.'

'You're joking?' I say, astounded. *Snip, snip.*

'Whether he will or not, I don't know, but he's certainly got a spring in his step. He's been great with the boys too, cooking for us, taking them out. Even built them a camp in the garden.'

'What, our garden? But he hasn't been out in it in years. It's like a jungle out there.'

'Yes, that's what he told them, that it was just like *I'm a Celebrity Get Me Out of Here*. They loved it! Back home it's all computer games and play dates.'

There's a pause. We empty our buckets into the trailer with Henri, go back to our row and start cutting again. I take a deep breath.

'And how are things . . . with you . . . back home?' I ask tentatively.

Jody breaks her rhythm for the first time and I stop with her as we finally both stare at the elephant in the vineyard through the big leaves between us.

'I'm not going back, Emmy. I've left him for good.'

'Oh, Jody.' Frustratingly I can't get round the vine to hug her.

'Actually I think he left me a long time ago. He's had two lives with different women for some time, it turns out. He just forgot he was married to one of them.'

My heart squeezes and twists, and I hate the fact that I haven't been there for Jody because I've been so cross about what happened with them taking the money.

'It's all gone, Emmy,' she says quietly. 'Mum's insurance money. It's gone.' She swallows and I do too. 'He asked me to ask you and Dad for the money. It was a fantastic investment opportunity, he said. A hotel complex that was being built and he could get in there at the start. He'd bought into a few properties in this country with two guys who were supposed to know what they were doing.' She stops and takes a swig of water. 'He was in debt up to his eyeballs and he thought the way out was to invest more.'

'So where was this hotel complex?' I finally ask.

'Greece,' she replies. And for a moment neither of us says anything. Then she says, 'They lost the lot. I didn't know for ages. He kept telling me everything was fine. We had the house, smart cars. It was only when the kids' nursery and prep school fees bounced I realised something was wrong. He was robbing Peter to pay Paul all over the place. I have no idea how many credit cards he's run up debts on, or how many people he owes money to. I only know that as time went on, I barely saw anyone. He stopped me seeing people, ringing them . . . I'm so sorry. You must hate me . . .' Finally her voice cracks and she can't say any more. For a moment I see red, thinking about what he's done to Jody and my dad, taking his money and losing it. But then the mist disappears and I just see Jody, and it's the only thing that matters.

'The money doesn't matter, it really doesn't. We'll find a way of getting through this, I promise. You can even stay with me until I leave. If this wine does well, we'll be fine, Jody. We'll keep the house.'

She sniffs, runs her sleeve under her nose as if she's twelve again, and shakes her head.

'It's fine, really. I can stay with Dad, just till you're home. I'm going to get a job and find us somewhere to rent. Use those A levels you worked so hard for me to get!'

I push my way through the vines and hug her.

'I'm really proud of you. You're a great mum,' I tell her into her hair, unable to stop the tears, making her hair wet.

'I wish I was more like you,' she says, sniffing.

'Like me?' I pull back and hold her at arm's length.

'You never run away from your problems. Not like me. I had my head so buried in the sand I couldn't see or hear anyone or anything. You just stand and face them. I mean, look what you did at home. You could have gone back to college, but you didn't, you scooped up the problems and got on with it. And here . . . you could've run home, but you stayed, you didn't run away.'

'Maybe because this is the first time I've been anywhere in years . . . maybe ever!' I try to laugh.

'Since Mum died.' Jody looks straight at me.

'Yes,' I answer despite the waver in my voice, 'since Mum . . . since she died in the accident.' And I suddenly feel like I can breathe a little easier for the first time in a very long time.

At the end of the day, as the sun starts to set, we take in the last of the grapes and tread them. Jody and I hold hands and now I've got her back I don't want to let her go. Then I pump the juice into a concrete tank and, with lots of helping hands, I seem to manage it without spilling a drop. Then we scrub the table and barrels and hose down the floor of the *chai*.

Gloria comes outside with a tray of glasses and a bottle of Clos Beaumont, some homemade lemonade for the boys, and a bowl of salted nuts. The boys appear from the *chai* and Dad gets up from the deckchair he's been sitting in, looking out over the valley. Jody has been helping Nick straighten through the rest of the house, and, if I'm not mistaken, Candy's nose is ever so slightly out of joint by the looks she throwing the two of them.

Then Isaac turns up to see how things are going and Candy brightens up considerably.

'This is my family,' I introduce them to Isaac.

But when I introduce him to Dad, and Isaac says, 'Hi, how's things? Great to meet you,' Dad frowns and I feel slightly uncomfortable, like he's taken an instant dislike to him.

'Yes, fine. Just thought I recognised your accent,' he says.

Just as well it's Charlie, not Isaac, I'm hoping Dad will be seeing a lot more of when I get home. I allow myself to feel a little squeeze of excitement.

Candy raises her glass. 'Here's to team work!' she says over everyone.

'Team work!' I smile, and realise right now I couldn't feel happier. But I know it can't last. Dad, the boys and Jody will be leaving tomorrow, and then what? Can I really do the rest of this on my own?

And then I remember it . . . the yeast. In all the excitement, I've forgotten to add Isaac's yeast. But there are still some wild yeasts on the grapes already. I just have to hope they work like Madame Beaumont told me. I cross my fingers, willing the fermentation to start. What am I going to tell Isaac? Whatever happens, he mustn't find out.

Chapter Thirty-two

The next morning I hug Dad, and then Jody. Last night, I sat with Jody outside, under the plum tree in the garden, while she explained to the boys how they were going to go back to Granddad's house and then were going to look for a new house of their own, without Daddy. And how much they both still loved them.

Now, the boys are hugging Cecil round the head, asking about their new schools excitedly and whether their camp will still be in Granddad's garden. This trip seems to have done them the world of good, too, a chance to readjust to their new life. Cecil raises his head and lets out some impressive deep 'woofs' to the boys' delight as they bid him goodbye.

'You're doing a great job, Emmy,' Dad tells me. 'I'm so proud of you. You know we all make mistakes in life, but it's learning from them that counts,' and I'm not sure if he's talking about me feeling responsible for Madame Beaumont's fall or Jody and the insurance money, or he having lost so many years to daytime TV.

Jeff arrives in Charlie's car, which Jeff seems hugely excited about. He's come to take my family to the airport. Charlie's busy, Jeff explains with lots of hand signals. I wave them all off as Jeff disappears down the dusty track at speed, with a toot on the horn.

As the tail-lights disappear, I run over to see Henri, burying my head in his big neck and letting the tears flow. I still have grapes to get in and I really don't think I'm going to do it without my family. I feel like an emotional wreck, a wet rag that's been squeezed and wrung out. I miss Dad, Jody and the boys already, as if someone's kicked away the crutches I've been leaning on. Slowly I walk back to the *chai* and start loading up the trailer with crates. They're heavy and I'm working slowly, when I see two cars, very different from the Featherstone's little van, pull into the yard. One is long, low and shiny, the other an expensive four by four. I step back into the shadows, not wanting to face anyone right now. Hopefully they'll think no one's here and leave again.

'Oh, it's so rustic.' I hear a deep Home Counties woman's voice as car doors open and bang shut and Cecil starts up his war cry.

'I heard about this place from my wine merchant. He's on all sorts of wine forums,' I hear a loud man's voice say. They must be lost, looking for the château.

I stay where I am, hold my breath and listen.

'Whoa there, boy, good boy,' says the loud voice with a slight tremble.

'What is that dog?' another man, not as loud, but just as posh, asks.

'Ugly!' replies a woman with a shrill laugh. My hackles rises.

'Urgh, gross!' The laughter stops and I'm guessing Cecil is

showing them how long he can make the drool strings from his mouth.

I wait for it, knowing what's coming.

'Argh!' comes a unison cry.

Bingo! I give a little smile of satisfaction, knowing Cecil has shaken his head and released the slime strings. I decide that I'm going to have to go and redirect these people to the château or they'll be here for ages and I need to get on.

I go to step out of the *chai*, then stop when I hear the loud-voiced man saying, 'Apparently they do a Vin de France here and it's up for the wine medal at Château Lavigne later this year. It's really good. Heard that Morgan's Supermarkets are interested in taking it over. The couple in the grocery shop in the town gave me the directions.'

I hold my breath and listen.

'A supermarket slurper?' the other man says like he's stepped in poo.

'From what I hear,' the loud man lowers his voice only slightly, 'it's a bit of a find. Featherstone's have brought in their own team. There's a new woman in charge and a travelling wine man. Presumably to turn it into their own blend.'

'Where did you hear that from?' the shrill woman asks.

'I read it on a new blog. Candy's Comments, or something.' They all laugh.

'Well, let's see what it's like,' says the other man.

I can't believe they're talking about Clos Beaumont.

'Yes, once they roll it out to the supermarkets, it'll have all the character knocked out,' the loud man guffaws and the others follow. 'Or maybe he'll put a bit of class into it. Could become a keeper?' says the deeper-voiced woman.

'You're right. Could be worth getting some before it's some supermarket best buy and every bugger's heard of it,' says the not-so-loud man.

'And while it's still cheap, before they whack the price up. Apparently the owner's a bit of a tricky kettle of fish,' the loud man bellows. 'People at the grocery shop told me.'

I throw the crates I'm holding down on the floor. How dare they come here, criticising Madame B, assuming the wine is just a supermarket slurper, and calling Cecil ugly?

I step out of the *chai*, put my hands on my hips and lift my chin very slightly. I can see clearly now: there's a big dark Range Rover and a silver Mercedes there. The back of the Range Rover looks to be full of boxes of wine.

'Ah, *excuse em moi*,' booms the loud man, with a very large belly and not taking off his sunglasses. Next to him is a taller, thinner man and two women. Both blonde, one with an immaculate bob, the other curly shoulder-length hair, both in white jeans, floral short-sleeved tops and beaded mules. As I step forward, the toe of my Wellington boot catches on loose stones, throwing up a cloud of brown dust, which makes them step back and cough.

Cecil starts up his bark again and everyone steps back further.

'*Nous sommes voudraiz une degustation*,' says the man, grinning and doing a drinking action with his hand.

'Sorry, we're not actually open for tastings,' I say, folding my arms across my chest.

'Oh, good, you're English,' he says as if not having heard me.

My hackles go up even further.

'We were told the owner was French. A Madame Beaumont?'

'She's . . .' I don't want to tell these people too much. I don't want it getting back to Monsieur Lavigne at the château that Madame Beaumont is still in hospital, that she's recovering from pneumonia and a broken hip, and that I have no idea when she's coming home and what's going to happen when she does. All I know is, I need this year's vintage ready for blending in its barrels, safe and sound. Like children tucked up in bed at night.

'Actually, it's the harvest. We're up to our necks in it,' I say as politely as I can, hoping they'll take the hint and go.

'We'd really like a tasting and a look around,' says the woman with the short bob. 'We have a holiday house not far from here. We've heard some really good things about this place.' She looks around unsure.

'Sorry, it's just—'

'Hi, Candy from Featherstone's.'

I turn to see Candy marching out of the farmhouse with hardly a limp at all now. She's holding out her hand. 'Welcome to Clos Beaumont.' She's beaming, lipstick freshly applied.

'Hi,' they all say, shaking her hand warmly and turning away from me.

'I see you've met Emmy. Emmy runs the operation here. But if you'd like a tasting I'm happy to help.'

'Great.' They start to gather up their cameras and bags and lock up their cars. Why, I have no idea. It's not like Cecil is going to mug them for their sat-navs. Then I realise I would be the same if I'd just arrived.

'Candy, what are you doing?' I turn away from them and whisper crossly to her. 'I have a harvest to get in – what are you playing at?'

'About to make some sales. From what Gloria says about the state of Madame Beaumont's books, she could do with all the income she can get right now, for when she gets home. There's some of last year's vintage in the *chai*, right? And other years.'

I nod, swallow and then smile gratefully. She's right. Madame Beaumont is going to need all the help she can get.

Candy turns back to the group of four.

'Now, let me show you around. This vineyard is one of the oldest in the area.'

I'm not sure if Candy knows this or is just making up a spiel on the spot, and then I realise, it must be in the selling script I never finished. I'm watching her in awe as she talks about the location of the vineyard and gives a sprinkling of information about how the area was occupied during the war. Another script I never learned.

I fold my arms, stand back and watch the master at work.

'Emmy,' she suddenly calls, and I'm so busy listening to her informative tour that she takes me by surprise.

'Sorry, um, yes?' I run over to join the party.

'Perhaps you could talk us through the grape varieties, the *terroir*, that kind of thing. Oh, and how the harvest works . . .' Candy instructs, and despite feeling nervous I start.

'Oh, yes, of course. Well we have three main types of grapes here . . .' I tell them about the grapes, how the soil here is so good because of its position and how the breeze helps keep away disease. I introduce them to Henri and he lets them stroke his nose and nudges them for polos they've brought from home.

'The vines have very little intervention. Everything here is as Mother Nature intended it unless they really need help. The harder the roots have to work, the deeper they go and the better the wine. These grapes are cared for with love and words, not pesticides and sprays.' I look over to the château vines where the tractors are at work like bees, picking and gathering and delivering the harvest to the Queen Bee.

'Wow!' say the visitors together, filming it all on their iPads.

'So, we pick here and then . . .' I pull back the doors on the *chai* as far as they will go, 'this is where we make it.'

'You're kidding me?' The loud man looks amazed.

I shake my head and hold back a laugh.

'Honestly, you do it by foot?' says the other man.

'No way!' says the bob-haired woman.

'Yes, way.' And I can't help but laugh out loud and so do they, and I realise I'm loving telling them about the vines here at Clos Beaumont but happy that Candy steps in to help me out when they want to know about buying and pricing.

'OK, how about a tasting?' Candy says. 'Emmy, you grab the glasses.'

I run happily back to the farmhouse. I'm not sure we have five matching glasses.

'Gloria, do we have any matching wine glasses? There are some tourists here doing a wine tasting with Candy.'

Gloria pulls off her spectacles and jumps up from the Madame Beaumont's accounts and into action in the miraculously tidy yet full little kitchen. She pulls out glasses, rinses them under the tap and uses a clean, if threadbare tea towel to rub them, holding them up to the light, but working as quickly as she can.

Nick sticks his head out of the living room where he's been rearranging the furniture, by the looks of things.

'A lick of paint and this place would be gorgeous. There's some lovely pieces here. Not worth much, but lovely. Have you seen the sweet little French clock on the mantelpiece? And the wing-back chairs are fabulous. Very shabby chic. I mean, there are shops back home selling this stuff as French antiques, which really means they went to France, bought some stuff second-hand and fancied it up.' He smiles.

'Tourists here for a tasting,' Gloria explains quickly, and he dives in to help her with the glasses. Together we seem suddenly to be working as a very efficient team.

'Now, who fancies doing some picking?' Candy asks as the group drain their glasses and order crates of wine.

I look at Candy in complete shock. Her chutzpah is something else.

'Oh, yes, that would be lovely,' says the curly-haired blonde.

'Really, can we?' asks the thinner man.

'We happy to pay the going rate for a day's picking,' agrees the big-bellied one.

Candy looks at me for approval.

'Of course,' I finally manage to say, once I've closed my gaping mouth and smile. 'Gloria? Room for four more for lunch?'

* * *

As we near the end of the *parcelle* the rain starts to fall. I should stop. They have over at the château, but I need to get the *parcelle* finished. It might stop in a while, or it could get heavier.

'Keep going,' I call. 'As quick as you can.' Isaac would tell me to stop now but I won't have this kind of help again.

We're going to finish the *parcelle,* I decide.

The rain starts to fall gently and I wipe it from my face until the last grapes are in and Henri, wet but patient as ever, finally pulls the trailer up towards the *chai*. We follow, wet and tired.

After a day's picking with Henri doing his bit, and treading in the *chai*, money has changed hands and been passed over to Gloria. There's the sound of closing car boots and doors, goodbyes and *au revoirs*.

Finally, the cars drive off down the lane with tooting horns and Cecil barking to see them off.

I turn to look at Candy; she's beaming and so am I.

'You were brilliant!' I say, my cheeks hurting from smiling.

'No, you were,' she says, and we hug each other in delight.

Gloria brings out a tray with another bottle of Clos Beaumont on it, opens it and hands round glasses.

Just as we're taking our first sip, the Featherstone's van pulls into the drive. Isaac! Finally!

'Hey, how's it going?'

'Great,' Candy beams. 'We just did our first degustation and sold loads.'

'It was Candy that did it.' I nod to her.

'No, it was you,' she bats back.

'So, it went well then?' Isaac looks from me to Candy and back again.

Gloria hands him a glass of red.

'Very well. At least that's a bit of money for Madame B's coffers for when she gets out of hospital.'

'And only one more *parcelle* to pick!' I feel a thrill of excitement charge through my body. We're nearly there. Nearly done.

'Then the worry starts. You have to keep this grape juice safe so it turns to wine!' he grins.

Then the worry starts?

'Really?' I don't think I've ever known worry like it before!

'It was Emmy who nailed the sales,' Candy distracts me for a moment. We're all huddled outside under the old veranda, not caring about the spots of rain.

'It wasn't. My God, talk about master saleswoman. No wonder you have sales figures like you do.'

'Yes, but I just learned all that stuff. You actually knew what you were talking about. It was real.'

She's right. I'm not at a desk here, selling from pictures in a catalogue. This is real. We sip wine and banter away, enjoying each other's compliments. My hands are stained purple from the juice, I notice, as I lift my glass to my mouth. But I don't care. I feel alive, really alive.

'It was that line . . . how did you say it? No wait –' Candy puts up a hand up, not to be interrupted – 'about "everything here is done just the way Mother Nature intended". That's why they bought so much. Lapped it up,' she laughs, and takes a big gulp of wine.

'But it's true,' I say, the laughter seeping from me as I take another sip. But instead of it slipping down, the wine sticks in my throat. That's what makes it unique, I think, unable to look at Isaac.

Trust your inner voice. Madame Beaumont's words are playing round my head.

Suddenly I know exactly what my inner voice is telling me. Today proved it to me. If this wine is going to win an award, it needs to be itself, not the same as every other vintage out there. There's no way Isaac is ever going to agree about the yeast, but there's no way I can add it now.

'And no problems with the yeast at all?' Isaac asks.

I jump. 'No, none.' And I guiltily sip my wine to cover my burning cheeks and my crossed fingers in my pocket.

'I'll go and check,' he says.

'No, it's fine,' I say.

'Emmy's got it all in hand, don't worry, she's brilliant at this.' Candy tops up his glass. 'Trust her. She knows what she's doing. To Madame Beaumont and a great new vintage.' She raises her glass merrily.

Isaac raises an impressed eyebrow. 'Are you sure?' he asks me evenly.

'Yup. It's all fine,' I agree with Candy, who is still holding her glass up high.

'To Madame Beaumont and a great new vintage.' We all cheer, and I know I can't let her down, risky though it may be. I just have to make sure he never finds out.

The rain gets heavier and I breathe a sigh of relief I finished picking the *parcelle* when I did. Looks like I made the right decision after all. Let's hope I've made the right one about the yeast as well, because once everyone's gone I need to get rid of the evidence.

Chapter Thirty-three

The *chai* smells different the next morning. There's a strong smell of fruit as I pull back the big wooden doors. It's still raining outside and there are darker clouds rolling in.

I grab the ladder and the thermometer, shove it inside the front pocket of my hoodie, put the ladder against the concrete tank and climb up.

It's started! The fermentation has started! I can hear it. The wild yeasts are working their hardest to turn all the fruity sugar into alcohol.

The sound and smell of fruit gets stronger the further up I go. I can't help but smile. It's really happening. At the top of the ladder I look over the edge of the tank and can see there's a cap of fruit, covering the juice, starting to form. I'll need to mash that down now. And keep doing it. With the sugar turning to alcohol the juice is starting to give off carbon dioxide. It's doing just what it's supposed to do.

I know I have to take the temperature three times a day. Isaac told me that. I put the thermometer in the juice and watch the reading. It mustn't go above 29 degrees. Perfect, right where it should be, and I'm suddenly grinning like the Cheshire cat.

I climb quickly back down the ladder, and check the other

vats. Then I run back to the farmhouse. The rain is falling heavily now, creating big puddles across the uneven yard, which I dodge and sidestep. The sky is really dark, and suddenly there's a crack of lightning right across the sky, like it's splitting the dark blanket in two. I jump, give a little yelp and run even faster to the house.

'One elephant, two elephant, three elephant, four elephant,' I'm counting as I reach the back door.

Bang!

'Eek!' I throw myself in through the doors of the house where the smell of soup – onion, quite possibly – fills my nostrils. Gloria is stirring a big metal pot whilst staring at Madame Beaumont's accounts book, balanced on the side, as she does. The fire is blazing and there's a neat stack of wood either side of it.

'It's Saturday, what are you guys doing here?'

'Thought you'd like the company.' Gloria smiles, and I think I could burst with gratitude.

'It's started!' I say, dripping rainwater all over the floor, making puddles on the top step.

'It certainly has,' Gloria agrees, looking out of the window to the side of the French doors.

'Another storm,' Candy sighs, looking at the computer.

'No, the fermentation. It's started. The juice is starting to turn to alcohol.'

'Oh, that's fabulous, love,' says Gloria. 'Well done!'

'Yes, great. I'll put it on the blog. What d'you think?' Candy turns the screen to me and shows me what looks to be a blog about our harvest, including pictures of the pickers, the lunches, taken on her phone. 'I've been updating it bit by bit.'

'It's fabulous, Candy,' I say with real surprise. It's like a wonderful scrapbook of the harvest at Clos Beaumont. 'Madame Beaumont will love to see these pictures.'

The French doors open suddenly and Nick steps in, shaking his wet hair, his glasses splattered with raindrops.

'Woah! It's a biggie,' he says. He's holding a paintpot in each hand.

I pull the door to firmly behind him, hoping to shut out the storm. But as I do the next flash of lightning is bigger than the last and I jump again and count elephants in my head.

'And I found a load of paint out in the wood store. Thought maybe we could give some of the walls a quick lick, just to freshen things up before Madame Beaumont comes home,' Nick beams.

Another flash and bang follow quickly on the heels of the last, making my nerves jangle, and I start the count over again.

'Are you OK?' Nick asks, still standing next to me holding the paint.

'Yes, fine, um, just worried about the last *parcelle* of grapes, that's all.'

'What, worried the rain will damage them?'

I nod.

'Oh, don't let me give you anything else to think about then,' says Nick, stepping down into the room to put the paint on the table. 'Just me with silly makeover ideas again.'

'It's a lovely idea, Nick.' I follow him into the room, stripping off my coat, and suddenly I feel quite choked by his efforts. By the efforts of everyone. 'In fact, I could do with something to take my mind off things.' Not just the storm, but the fermenting wine in the *chai*, I think, but don't say. 'I can't do anything until this rain stops . . . except worry.'

'Well, in that case, if we all pitch in we could get it done over the weekend before we have to go back to the office on Monday morning.'

'Really? You'd give up your weekend to do this?'

Nick nods and smiles.

I suddenly get a pang of sadness. Our time here together at Clos Beaumont will all too soon be at an end.

'And I thought I could put some soups in the freezer,' says Gloria, 'and finish these books. It's been fascinating looking back over them. They're like a history lesson. Do you know, there's a whole year, just at the end of the Second World War, when there was absolutely no vintage at all? Nothing. I wonder what happened to stop the harvest here then. Look,' she points to the book and the worn, brown page dated 1945. 'There's just a line through it.'

There's another flash and I suddenly remember to count elephants in my head, but lose count and can't remember if I did five or did it twice or went straight to six.

Nick goes out and comes back in with paint, brushes and old sheets, and starts handing them round.

'Come on, Candy, bring your phone and you can add the finished pictures to your blog. Or have you got some poor unsuspecting punters to come for a day's painting party?' and we all laugh.

There's another flash of lightning, only now it doesn't feel nearly as frightening as the last storm here. As I pick up my paintbrush and take a tin of paint from Nick, I actually forget to count elephants at all as the thunderstorm rumbles off into the distance.

Chapter Thirty-four

It's Monday morning and the gang are back at Featherstone's. I'm here on my own. The rain has finally stopped and I walk through the vineyard to the graveyard to leave fresh flowers from the hedgerows at Clos Beaumont on the grave Madame Beaumont tends.

On my way back I still talk to the vines, even though, apart from in the last *parcelle*, the grapes are all gone. It'll be time for pruning next, but by that point I'll be back in the Cadwallader's office, looking out at the space of green between the two tall buildings. My mind flits back to the fermenting wine in the *chai*. It has been in the forefront of my mind all weekend. The temperature has been gently rising, in spite of all my efforts. I've been checking it three times a day, sometimes more, and at night too, tiptoeing across the yard in the pitch-black with just the hoot of the owl and the swooping of bats for company. But there's been no drop. It just keeps going up. This morning I've left all the barn doors open in the hope that the ferment will cool down and start behaving itself again. I've also been mashing down the cap regularly, with the long pole that looks like a giant potato masher. I was hoping this would cool it, but it hasn't.

The first time, standing on the edge of the tank pushing

down the skins, was terrifying, but the more I do it, the more I'm getting used to it.

As I walk, thinking about the juice, my phone rings. I pull it out, expecting it to be Dad. But it's Madame Beaumont.

'*Bonjour, Madame Beaumont*,' I say in delight.

'*Bonjour, Emmy*,' Madame Beaumont replies.

'*Comment allez-vous*?' I ask, smiling. She looks so much better.

Madame Beaumont rolls her head from side to side in a '*comme ci, comme ça*' way.

'They have moved me to a rehabilitation unit, to convalesce, they say. I want to come home but they think I am weak and need help to get back on my feet. But I will be home soon. But tell me, how's the juice?'

I take a deep breath. My flurry of happiness slips away and worry pushes its way back into my head.

'Actually, it's a little warm.'

'You could try pumping it over, get some air through it, if it's still warm,' she suggests. 'But if it's cooling off, leave it be. You'll be able to judge it.'

I wish I had her confidence.

I start to tell her about the harvest, the degustation and my family's visit.

'So you just have the last *parcelle* to pick?' she asks.

'*Oui*.'

'When you come to the final *parcelle* . . .' she has dropped her voice.

'Yes?' I frown a little, anticipating special instructions. Suddenly there seems to be an altercation at Madame Beaumont's end, possibly with a member of the nursing staff.

'Madame Beaumont? *Allo?*' I call at the screen. 'What is it? Madame Beaumont?' But the screen goes black. Not again! I think as I try to ring her back but get no reply. I sigh and shove the phone back into my pocket.

Back at the *chai* I start getting out the pump and pipes. I have no idea how to pump the wine over. Perhaps I could check on YouTube. There's no way I can ask Isaac because I can't tell him what I've done …

'Hey!' Isaac is standing in the doorway to the *chai* and he makes me jump. 'Sorry, didn't mean to scare you,' he grins.

'No, it's fine. I'm just . . . tired.' But my cheeks are burning with guilt. Should I tell him the temperature's rising? Or should I leave it, pump it over and hope that it settles down? I get a whiff of his aftershave, woody and lemony, taking me right back to that night of the mites. My insides lurch. It seems to happen every time I see him, reminding me of his touch. It stirs something in me. I have to get him to go. I can't let him know what I've done to the wine. I have to hope I can put it right on my own.

'How's the wine? Behaving itself?'

'Fine,' I say quickly but it comes out really high-pitched and doesn't sound like my invoice at all. 'Fine,' I lie again and hate myself for doing it.

'Thought I might pump it over,' I say as coolly as I can, turning on the hose and starting to hose down the floor, by way of keeping him at the door.

'Pumping it over? You shouldn't need to at this stage. Are you checking the temperature?' he calls over the sound of hosepipe.

'Uh-huh,' I say, turning away from him, hoping not to give anything away.

'Do you want me to check it—'

'No,' I cut across him, far more abruptly than I mean to, turning the hose in the direction of the door again. Then I stop, the water pouring away between us.

'Don't you trust me? I'm not lying,' my mouth suddenly charges off without taking my brain with it. 'I mean, check it if you want,' I wave a hand at the tanks at the far end of the *chai*, beyond the lake I'm creating, 'if you don't believe me.' I hate myself for calling his bluff, but if I can get this juice to calm down on my own he'll never know I went with the wild yeasts, and I will have done the best I can.

'No, no, I believe you.' He takes a step back. 'Sorry.' He holds up his hands. 'It's just I told Charlie I'd be overseeing this. He's the boss.'

'Yes, well, I'm sure you'll get your money when the wine's made,' I say, really not meaning to be so mean, but wishing he'd just go. I don't want to let him down – he's put his trust in me, leaving this wine to me – but if he does find out, he'll never speak to me again. That thought suddenly makes me feel really wretched. But I just want this wine to have the best possible chance of winning. It's a risk worth taking, I think, suddenly shocking myself. My mind flits back to that first day at the *gîte*, when I couldn't even choose which bedroom to have. I can hear Madame Beaumont's voice in my head telling me to trust my instincts, and I have, and I know Isaac will agree with what I've done when he tastes it, I think, suddenly feeling quietly confident.

'I just don't want you to think I've abandoned you, what

with all the wine we've had into the winery.'

'It's fine,' I say, feeling thoroughly ashamed of myself, not able to look him in the eye.

'I need to get back anyway. Just thought you might like the company now the others have gone.' I can feel him looking at me. 'But I can see I got it wrong. I'll come back tomorrow to taste the juice.' And with that, he turns and marches back to the van, getting into it with a slam of the door. Only when he's driving towards the gates do I look up at the back end of the van.

What am I doing? I need him to sort this out. 'No, wait!' I call, and I run into the yard, but the van pulls out on to the road with a spin of wheels on dirt.

'Isaac!' I call, and run down the track. But he's gone. The little tail-lights disappearing at speed.

'Bugger!' Now I really am on my own and I really do have to get this right. I'm going to have to pump it over. I head back to the *chai* and start to climb the ladder with the big, heavy pipe over my shoulder.

'*Bon nuit*,' I say quietly to the vats as they burble and bubble away that night, and I turn off the brown light switch with a *thunk*. I ache and am wet through from the pumping over. Every now and again the pipe attempted to flip out of the vat, spraying me with juice, but I managed to catch it in time and get it back in, with just a soaking for me.

It's colder tonight. I shiver, deciding to shut the big doors. The last thing I want now that the wine is nearly ready for barrelling, is for anything getting into the *chai*, like the wild boar that roam these parts.

Only a few more days to go and it'll be in the barrels, safe and sound. Isaac is coming up tomorrow to taste it and I need it to be behaving itself by then. I'm nearly home and dry. And I find myself drawing in a deep breath as I pull the doors shut and lock them. I look out at the clear moon throwing light right across the vineyard. It's definitely chillier tonight, which I hope means the wine will cool down, and a good dry day tomorrow will allow us to start the final *parcelle*. Exhausted but happy, I pull my hoodie around me and head for bed.

Chapter Thirty-five

The mist is twisting and weaving its way through the vines when I push back the shutters the next morning. The orange sun is creeping its way over the horizon and I feel a little jump of joy. I can harvest the final *parcelle.*

I dress quickly, pulling on my hoodie, which still has a faint trace of Isaac's aftershave. I catch myself smiling as I breathe it in. I just hope he's happy with the juice today. I'd hate for us to part on bad terms now. He was such a help when Madame Beaumont had her fall. But once this wine is barrelled and blended, he'll be on his way to his next job and I'll be back in the call centre. We'll probably never see each other again. Suddenly I have a strange feeling pulling at my stomach, twisting, like the feeling I had when I first arrived here. A feeling of homesickness only stronger, a yearning, only it's not home in the UK I'm thinking about. I take a deep breath and run downstairs. Isaac will be here soon and I want him to see how well the wine is doing.

I can smell it as soon as I reach the *chai* doors. It's way stronger than before. That must be a good sign. It smells like a summer pudding, all different red fruits, blackberries mostly. I yank back the door and the smell hits me right in the nostrils and eyes at the same time as juice hits my boots, gushing and pouring over and around them.

'Shit!'

The deep red juice, with its white foaming top, is cascading over the side of the tank like Niagara Falls, hitting the bottom and sending up waves of spray before spreading out across the uneven floor like the tide rolling in, fizzing with galloping and leaping white horses, filling rock pools and inlets in its unstoppable surge.

'Oh no, no, noooooooo,' I wail, and run to where the juice is cascading. I have no idea what to do!

I try to put the ladder against the tank but it's knocked this way and that as the juice tumbles out. My heart is racing, my breathing shallow and quick. I have to stop it. I shove the thermometer into my hoodie, push the ladder against the tidal wave, push my weight against it and begin to climb. It bounces away from the wall every now and again, but I manage to get myself to the top and lay against it, dangling the thermometer over the edge. It's the longest few seconds of my life for it to tell me what I already know. The temperature's way too high! It's completely out of control.

Quickly, I climb back down the ladder – well, half climb, half jump – and the ladder comes with me, hitting me hard on the shoulders and head.

'Ouch!' I bat it away and it falls into the sea of red around me. I run to open the doors at the far end of the *chai*, hoping the wind that has picked up will help cool the juice. It will certainly have dried off the final grapes ready for picking, I groan to myself. It's perfect picking weather.

Ridiculously, I try to sweep out the juice into the yard,

hoping it will slow down soon with the cooling air.

Why didn't I listen to Isaac? What made me think I knew best, an angry voice keeps shouting in my head.

I find a cardboard box – an empty wine box – and rip it up, then in desperation I try using it to fan the juice that's still bubbling over the edge.

It's no good. It's not working. I give up, exhausted. I have let everyone down. There's only one thing I can do. My hands are shaking, my throat tight and my eyes prickling as I dial the number.

The phone rings at the other end and the huge tennis ball in my throat moves into my mouth. My top lip is damp and there is a rushing noise in my ears that could be the runaway juice or plain fear.

'Hello?' answers a lazy voice, like he's just woken up, like on that first morning here. I desperately want reassurance but I know I have to enter the dragon's den.

'Isaac.' I swallow like I have a mouthful of sand.

'Emmy?'

'I think you'd better come . . . quick.'

Chapter Thirty-six

'What the . . . ?'

Even though I'm expecting Isaac he makes me jump right out of my skin when he arrives.

'It . . . the temperature went up,' I say, my back to him, hosing down the floor, adding water to juice. My sleeves are soaking and there are droplets of juice and water dripping from my fringe and earlobes.

'How?' He marches towards the tank, pushes the ladder against it and climbs it, ignoring the juice still rolling down the side and over him too now. He shoves the thermometer in and confirms that indeed, the temperature has risen.

'But you were checking it, weren't you?'

'Yes, three times a day, sometimes more.'

'Why didn't you say?'

'I thought it would go down, what with it being a cooler night.'

'You *thought it would go down*?' He laughs incredulously and it stings, like salt in a wound. 'It isn't a dolls' hospital; we're not playing here. This is science!' He quickly climbs down the ladder, tasting the juice off his finger. Then he looks around and grabs the old glass jug cafetière from the side, puts it in the flow of juice to fill it and then sips from it.

'This shouldn't have happened with the yeast mix I gave you. I've used it before. It should control even the trickiest of grapes. But this?' He sips again and I think my heart might actually burst out of my chest I'm so nervous. Then he looks at me, raising his dark eyebrows, and his eyes meet mine. He sips again, slowly.

'You did add the yeast, didn't you, Emmy?'

There's a long, painful silence, like I'm watching a silent movie: there's drama all around but no one's speaking. My stomach is swirling like a washing machine on spin cycle; the noise in my ears has turned to white noise.

I open my mouth to speak, but no sound comes out. I'm paralysed in his gaze, those big, brown eyes rendering me speechless.

'I . . . I . . .' I stutter, not able to pull away from his gaze. 'I . . . I . . .'

'You didn't, did you?' He sips at the juice again, shaking his head. 'You didn't add the goddam yeast!' he suddenly shouts. His face darkens even more. 'What did you do with it?'

'I, erm . . . I forgot about it. What with the excitement of my family being here and everything . . .'

'What did you do with it?' he repeats.

I swallow. 'I tipped it away.' I feel so stupid. I just want the floor to open up and swallow me. He tosses the jug of juice aside and then, his nostrils flaring widely, he glares at me once more and then storms out. I hear the car door open and slam shut and the wheels spinning as he tears out of the yard and down the lane.

As the car disappears from earshot, all I'm left with is the sound of running juice. Every glassful that tumbles over the edge is a glassful of Madame Beaumont's income from next year. How could I have been so stupid to risk that? And on top of that, I've lost Isaac's respect. Not that I realised I wanted it . . . until now. But all I can think about now is the anger in his eyes, and my own eyes well up with hot, angry, salty tears that begin to spill over. I brush them away with my sleeve. I have to do something.

Instinct, I hear Madame Beaumont's voice say. But right now I want to tell my instinct, which was so clearly wrong, to clear off and never come back again, and to tell Madame Beaumont to stop telling me I can do this when I clearly can't.

Just at that moment I spot the long stick with the potato masher on the end. Get air into it, my instinct is shouting. I have to do something. I grab the stick and climb the ladder; juice hitting me in the face, splashing my eyes and soaking me all over again. Despite the beautiful sunny, autumnal morning, I'm shivering. I stand on the concrete ledge, on the edge of the tank, the width of a breeze block. I lift the stick and begin to mash, plunging it in as deep as it will go and pulling it out again, hoping the air will cool it and stop it bubbling over and spilling away at least. As I'm mashing it Isaac's angry face keeps coming back to haunt me, and the more it does, the more I realise what I've lost. It was more than just desire, which I realise now has been growing like the slowly fermenting wine, now out of control and bubbling over; it was his trust, his respect.

I should never have come here. I should never have started this ridiculous attempt to save this vintage. I should certainly never have let it develop its own character. Look what good that did! I am shoving the stick in and out and my arms ache, my shoulders too. I change hands, straighten my back and then wipe away the tears with my sleeve again, which is wet and cold, like me. I sniff loudly, knowing there's no one to hear. There's no one at all. It's just me and I have never felt so alone in all my life. I feel a little light-headed and I wonder if it's the carbon dioxide the juice is giving off as it ferments.

I'm furious with myself. I mash harder. Furious for thinking I could do this and furious with Isaac for . . . being furious with me, but mostly for being right.

I keep mashing for what seems like an age, despite my arms aching and my eyes watering.

I brush away more tears with one arm and turn to move round the tank, but as I do, I catch the toe of my boot on the other and no matter how hard I try to correct myself, I wobble, left, right, my bum sticks out, I drop the pole and it crashes to the floor, I try and reach for it but my balance throws me backwards and with arms turning huge windmills backwards, I feel myself falling and there's nothing I can do to stop it.

'Jeez!' Isaac rolled his head, hearing the knots crunch, as he drove down the lane back in the direction of Petit Frère in the Featherstone's van, passing the field of sunflowers, no longer at their best.

'I cannot believe that woman!' He pushed his foot down hard on the accelerator, the little van whining with exertion. He swung it left and right with the bends in the road, as fast as he could.

Another car sounded its horn as it shaved past him, brushing the van against the grassy banks.

'What was she thinking?' He banged the steering wheel with the palm of his hand.

He looked at the vines in the fields either side of him as he neared town, now stripped bare of their fruit, naked, resting in the sun after the hard work of the summer.

How could she have let him down like this? He'd trusted her. He'd thought there was something between them; if he wasn't mistaken it had felt a lot like mutual attraction. Not the usual fast and furious attraction of short-lived relationships he was used to, something more was growing – an understanding . . . a connection. But clearly he had been mistaken. He knew better than this, he knew not to let down his guard. What had he been thinking? He shouldn't have let himself get too involved. He should have just done as Charlie asked and made the wine himself. The sooner he moved on now, the better. He'd make the calls this afternoon. He'd secure his next gig. He swung into the yard at Featherstone's, spraying white gravel as he braked hard, making Gloria and Candy jump as they made their way to the sales room, and pulled on the handbrake. The sooner he was out of here, the better, he thought as he stormed into the winery.

Chapter Thirty-seven

I hit the surface with a splash and then my head is totally submerged in the dark liquid and I'm falling and falling. I try to push open my eyes but I can't see a thing. It's dark and I'm disorientated, I can't tell which way is up. I try to push myself to the surface, my lungs begin to squeeze, searching for air. I don't know whether to swim up or down, but I'm being dragged downwards so I decide to swim the other way but my limbs won't work together. My clothes are heavy, making it hard; my lungs are feeling crushed. I need air, now! I push myself to what I can only hope is the surface but I have no idea. There's no light at all. I need to get out. Suddenly I can see my dad when I was young. We're on the beach and my sister and Mum are there, too. There's my sister and her boys in the vineyard and then there's my mum, driving in the pouring rain, having rowed with Dad, wanting to put it right, going out to buy sausages. Then the wreckage of the car. I have to get out, I have to put this right, I can't let it happen to me, too.

I give one final push and suddenly I can see light. I push my face towards it, my mouth before my eyes. I push up and open my mouth gasping for air, but taking in liquid, and I start to cough. I try throwing out an arm to the side but I don't make it and my hand slaps back down on the surface, disappearing into the liquid again, and my body follows. I'm not sure I have the energy to drag myself up again, against the pull of gravity. I try but the more I do, the more tired I'm getting and my head dips back down below the surface once more and darkness follows.

This is it, I'm drowning. Just like my mother who was trying to get back to her family and being ripped from them. One stupid mistake. I'm never going to see my family again . . . or Isaac, I realise, and my last thought is of Isaac before darkness draws me in once more, but deeper.

Just as consciousness is slipping from me I feel myself being dragged up through the surface. When I finally come round, Isaac's lips are on mine, filling me with life. He pulls away and with one almighty great cough I expel the fluid sitting on my lungs and drag in a huge mouthful of air. I realise I'm on the cold, wet floor and Isaac is kneeling over me. His shoulders droop. He blows out through his lips in what looks like relief. I'm gasping like a guppy and coughing so much I can't catch my breath.

'Sit up, gently,' he says, and helps me, one hand behind my back and the other on my shoulder as I wipe at my mouth, tasting of rich, ripe fruit, my lips tingling as if they've been brought back to life, which is quite possibly what just happened. There's a rasping noise that I realise is my breathing. I'm coughing and then the waves of dizziness come again.

'Thank you,' I manage to croak.

'No problem. I knew my lifeguard skills would come in useful one day, I just hadn't imagined it would be quite like this.' His smile pulls at one side of his mouth and my heart, despite nearly having all the life sucked out of it, still manages a somersault with pompom shakers.

'What happened?' he asks, looking back at the tank. 'What were you doing back up there?'

I shake my head.

'I was mashing down the cap. I thought it would cool the juice down,' I say, looking back up at the fluid still trickling over the top and down the wall.

Isaac is soaked through, his open shirt and T-shirt underneath clinging to his body, his slim but toned shoulders and chest. Red juice is running from his long wet hair over his shoulders, down his neck, separating at his Adam's apple before meeting again and sliding down the middle of his chest. He runs a hand over his dark hair, a handful of juice flying off it. I'm breathing heavily, my chest rising up and down, and it could be my lungs rejoicing in the air they can breathe easily or it could be that I'm watching Isaac's chest rise and fall too and he still hasn't moved away from me. He leans in and rests his forehead on the top of my head in relief and I can feel the heat of his breath on my cheek.

Slowly, I turn my face to his, his lips are up close to mine. I can hear him give a laugh, relief and desire making it low and guttural, and despite the cold, shivering floor a heat travels up through me and into my lips, burning and begging to be kissed.

'You came back,' I breathe heavily, and the sound of whooshing is no longer the fermenting juice filling my ears but the sound of blood rushing to my head.

He nods, his head still against mine, drips of juice

mingling and dripping from our foreheads as one. I lean forward and then, unable to help myself, I lean a little more and then my eyes close, my instincts take over and I kiss him; gently and softly on the lips. It feels like I'm drowning all over again, only this time it's heavenly and I don't want to be saved, and my insides explode like I've tasted the forbidden fruit. Then, slowly, and reluctantly, I draw back, opening my eyes. He doesn't move.

'I brought a cooler,' he says, breathing heavily. 'I went back to Featherstone's for it.' And we both look from each other's lips to our eyes and I know that if our lips meet again, I'm not sure it would stop at kissing. 'Thought it might help cool things down.' There's another splosh as more wine tumbles over the edge of the vat and splashes to the floor, making us both turn to look at it tumbling and splashing around us.

'Yes, of course,' I manage to say. I take another look back at Isaac and his lips, and drag myself to my feet and away from what might really have been the kiss of my life.

Isaac follows me, grabs the cooler to drop into the vat of wine and, despite our breathing still being out of time and still light-headed, I know he's right, we absolutely need to cool things down.

Chapter Thirty-eight

There is an awkwardness between us as we walk towards the furthest *parcelle*. I'm holding lightly on to Henri's head collar, using him as a shield between me and Isaac on the other side. With the cooler working wonders on the juice I've showered and changed, as has Isaac. He's now wearing one of my T-shirts – my Take That one, to be precise – and a pair of overalls that were in the van, tied at the waist, and that may belong to Jeff. He's rolled back the sleeves on the T-shirt, which shows off his biceps and the thick veins that run down them. The blue overalls keep slipping down his hips and he has to keep pulling them up and retying the sleeves. I look away every time he yanks the overalls up and find, infuriatingly, that I'm blushing each time. I can't believe what happened back there. I kissed him! It must have been the madness of the moment, gratitude, too, but still I'm finding it hard to make conversation, even bicker with him. Maybe if I just thank him for what he did it might explain it all away. I run my hands over the vine leaves as we walk.

'Um . . .'

He looks at me over Henri's neck.

'About back there,' I clear my throat and try to carry on. I can feel him looking at me, and again I reach out for the vines as we pick our way over the uneven path heading towards the château on the other side of the little valley where the Lavigne estate sits.

'Thank you for what you did, y'know, pulling me out.'

'No worries. Anyone would have done the same thing.'

Of course they would!

'You, um, probably saved my life.' I realise I'm shaking at the thought of what might of happened if Isaac hadn't come back with the cooler and rescued me.

'Like I say, anyone would have done the same.' He picks a vine leaf and is shredding it in his hands as we walk.

'But if you hadn't come back—'

He cuts across me and looks at me, dropping the remnants of the vine leaf.

'Let's not think about the "what if's".'

We fall back into silence and suddenly a creature darts across our path, followed by another.

'A hare!' he points out with delight, and I watch it go.

'They're always here,' I say, and we both look up at the call of a buzzard in the clear blue sky, with its mate, circling in the breeze, signalling it's going to be a glorious day. And I can't believe how very soon I'll be back home, catching the bus to work and spending all day in the office. The only mating couples I'll see will be those in the stationary cupboard after the Christmas party.

'About what happened back there . . .' I focus on the buzzards as I stumble over the rises and dips in the track, occasionally talking to Henri by making a *click, click* sounds in the side of my cheek. '*En avant*,' I tell him. 'Walk on.'

'Back where?' And I know he's now making this hard for

me, teasing me. He must be really laughing at me. The one man I said I'd never fall for, never be taken in by his charms, and there I go kissing him in a moment of madness and realising it never felt like that when I kissed Charlie. In fact, I've never felt like that before ever and maybe won't again. A little shiver runs up and down my spine.

'Oh, you mean when you kissed me?' He looks straight ahead, but there's a hint of a smile in the corner of his mouth.

'I think you'll find it was you who kissed me,' I try to bluff.

'Me? I think your memory's playing tricks on you. Mind you, I can't say I blame you,' and he's back to his usual joking, flirtatious self.

'Well, whatever it was,' I say quickly, flustered, 'I was confused, nearly drowned, probably drunk from the fermenting juice.'

'Ah, that old chestnut . . . "I didn't mean it, it was the wine I nearly drowned in."'

I can't help but burst out laughing, which I really didn't want to. Maybe I am drunk? I try to straighten my face. I snatch a quick sideways glance at him. He's smiling, not so much teasing, but kindly. I look away quickly and down at the fawn-brown earth.

'Look, I just want you to know that I'm really grateful for what you did, and I promise that won't ever happen again.'

'What? The drowning or the kissing?' He pauses and stops. 'Or the lying to me about yeast?'

I smart and stop too. 'Both, I mean, all of it. Isaac, I am sorry about the yeast. I was just trying to do what I thought was best for the wine – I thought I was doing the right thing.'

He says nothing.

'I'm sorry. I promise, no more lies and no more kissing.'

'Promise?'

'I promise. I've learned my lesson.' And I don't know if we're talking about the lying or the kissing now, because what I've learned about the kissing is that it was a kiss like no other and if I ever did it again there would be no way back from falling for this man. We start walking again, Henri moving slowly but steadily beside me.

'So, the wine seems stable again,' he says as if distancing himself from the conversation.

'Are you going to tell Charlie?' I have to know.

He stops and looks at me. I stop, too, and Henri snorts. Then Isaac shakes his head.

'About the wine or the kissing?' He raises an eyebrow and I blush. 'No, I'm not sure Charlie would be very pleased to hear about either. We'll have to keep going now and just hope that he doesn't realise.'

I let out a sigh of relief.

'I really am sorry, you know.'

We walk on in silence, just the sound of the buzzard and the slow pounding of Henri's hoofs, and the rattle of the crates in the trailer.

'If it's any consolation,' Isaac says quietly, 'the wine tastes fantastic. Much more complex than if it had had the yeast added. Full of character.'

'Really?' I'm suddenly pleased as Punch. 'I mean I know it's not what you were hoping for but, oh God . . . that's amazing.'

'Quit while you're ahead. Let me take it from here.'

'Absolutely,' I agree, and stop talking. But then, I have to ask, 'And it won't affect it? Y'know, with me having actually been in it?'

He laughs. 'No, it'll be fine,' he assures me. We walk on a little further in silence. He holds his face to the sun. Then he says, 'We need to get in the last of these grapes, get them into the tanks and start putting the fermented stuff into the barrels. That way the next fermentation can happen.'

'A second fermentation?'

'Uh-huh. The malolactic. It makes it . . . sort of creamier, smoother. After that we'll start tasting it and working out the blend, what percentage we want from each grape. When the malolactic is finished it's ready for its premier blending and tasting. All the wines at the competition will be infant wines, early blends, evolving. It's when the wine-makers see their toddlers take their first steps on the road to becoming fully formed wines. They will mature, of course, but it's their potential that's being assessed now.'

'I'm not sure Madame Beaumont is that scientific. She just goes with what works.'

'Hmm,' he says a little disapprovingly. 'And I still can't quite nail her blend. It's driving me nuts. There's a note in there I can't place,' he says, clearly frustrated.

I shrug. 'Maybe it's just down to Mother Nature.'

We're nearly at the final *parcelle*.

'And then once we settle on the blend we like, we can submit a sample to the judges for the wine medal.'

'Although I'm not sure what they'll make of it, seeing as it's not really what they're looking for.'

He looks at me and frowns.

'But it might win,' I say optimistically. Henri stops by the vines.

'Let's hope for all our sakes it does.' He follows me round to the back of the trailer where I get a bucket and pair of secateurs.

'And what will you do then?'

'Actually, I've just had an email.' His eyes light up. 'A big Australian wine-maker I wrote to has been in touch. I've told them I'm making a blend for Featherstone's and if this comes off they want me to go over and do the same for them, only on a much bigger scale. It's massive.'

I can tell this is everything he's wanted.

'They all want French-style wine . . . it's the granddaddy of wine.' His eyes are wide with excitement.

'It means a lot to you,' I say, standing next to him by the trailer, surrounded by vines, looking back at the Clos Beaumont farmhouse, the sun warming our faces.

'Everything. This is what I've been working towards for all these years.'

'Does that mean you'll stop being a travelling wine man, and put down roots?'

'Are you kidding? Nothing will stop me. I'll just fly to bigger and better places.'

'I'm not sure that there is anywhere better than this,' I say quietly, looking around.

'Careful, you sound as if you're starting to fall in love.'

'No, of course not.' I shake my head, trying to keep love at an arm's distance.

'So what will happen to you after the wine awards?' he asks.

'Me? Well, I'll go home. If we win the award, hopefully I'll hang on to my job at Cadwallader's call centre, get the bonus, keep trying to pay off the arrears on the mortgage, that kind of thing . . .' I hold out a bucket to him.

'That doesn't sound very exciting.'

'It isn't very exciting.' I hold out a pair of secateurs too and look at him. Henri snorts and shakes his mane. 'It's just . . . life.'

'Don't you want something more? Don't you want to spread your wings?' His brown eyes are looking right at me and I want to tell him, yes! Yes, I want so much more. But not a life without roots.

'Like what? A life like yours? No, thanks, I like to know where my home is.' I smile. He reaches out and I nearly drop the bucket as he puts his hand on mine to take it from me and a massive bolt of electricity passes straight through me.

'Won't you miss all this?' he asks.

This time I can't look at him. I look down at the ground. I can't tell him how much I'll miss it. I really will.

'I'll just be happy knowing that Madame Beaumont has got next year's vintage to sell.' My voice cracks a tiny bit.

'And if it wins the medal?'

'Well, then hopefully she'll make enough money to think about taking on some help.' I take a deep breath and look up.

'But surely, you don't want to just end up like your dad? I mean, don't you want to add a bit of spice to your life?'

I say nothing and I get the feeling he thinks he's overstepped the mark. I know he's right, but I can't see any way to change things.

'Tell you what,' he cuts across the awkward silence. 'You go one way and I'll go the other.'

I frown. He's smiling, teasing. He points to the vines.

'Race you, if you like. See who can make it home first.' Isaac is already unclipping the catch on his secateurs. 'Start on the outside and work in.'

'You're on,' I shout, and we both run to our vines at opposite edges of the *parcelle* and start cutting. I'll show him. I'll make it home first.

'I'm ahead,' I shout over the vines as we near the middle of the *parcelle*.

'I think you'll find it's me,' he shouts back.

There's no way I'm going to let him beat me.

We're neck and neck and as we race round the end of the row. There's only a few rows to go, right in the middle of the *parcelle*. We're nearly there and I'm enjoying myself, thrilled we're nearly at the end of the pick. We both empty our buckets and run to the new rows up the middle of the *parcelle*. Isaac is just in front of me. I go to dodge round him when suddenly he stops dead, right in front of me and I practically run into him. He doesn't move. I look in the direction that he's staring. Neither of us moves, we just stand and stare.

Isaac's the first to speak.

Chapter Thirty-nine

'Did you know about this?' The laughter has gone and although I don't know exactly what it means, I realise by the look on Isaac's face something is wrong.

I shake my head, put down my bucket and slide my secateurs in my pocket. I follow Isaac as he walks up to the next row of vines. He cuts off a bunch of grapes. They look different from others we've loaded on to the trailer. He takes one, pulls it in half, he sniffs it, puts the end of his tongue to it and tastes it, then he puts it in his mouth and chews, thoughtfully, and I sense not to interrupt. As he chews he begins to nod and his nodding gets bigger.

'What is it? Infection? Poisoned by insecticides?' I eventually can't help myself asking. I nod towards the château. To which he throws back his head, his dark hair shaking, and lets out a loud laugh.

'What? What is it?' I'm getting frustrated. I have no idea what's going on.

He shakes his head, but he's still tossing the grapes over in his hand and he throws another one into his mouth. He's grinning and shaking his head at the same time.

'Isaac, what's going on?'

'You tell me.' He raises an eyebrow.

'I have no idea. All I know is that these grapes and vines look really different from the others. Are they sick?'

He shakes his head and then says slowly, 'No wonder I couldn't work out what the "missing ingredient" was in Madame Beaumont's claret.' He puts up his fingers and makes inverted comma signs.

I shake my head, put out the palms of my hands and shrug, getting more and more frustrated by the moment.

'Here, taste this.' He hands me a grape. I take it. I'm pretty sure it won't poison me as I've just seen him eat one. I break it in half like he did and then sniff it and put it in my mouth. I chew.

'What are you getting?'

I shake my head and turn down my mouth and am just about to swallow, when ...'Wait! That's that . . .' I haven't got the words. 'I don't know, it's the other thing . . . the note.'

He nods and slowly smiles again, tossing the stalk to one side. The breeze seems to be much stronger here, whipping up through the valley to this high point, making my hair fly around.

'But I don't understand. This is a different grape, then?' I say above the wind.

'You're getting it. From what I can see, this is a totally different grape. If I'm not mistaken it's a really old variety. *La tendresse*. It means softness, heart. It marries really well with other grapes. Is great to blend with, from what I've read. These vines are pretty old, too. I thought this variety was wiped out in the great French wine blight in the 1850s.'

'A disease?'

He nods. 'France lost forty per cent of its vineyards because of it. This grape is found in other parts of the world now. But it's quite rare.'

They are short, with twisted trunks and much shorter branches than their neighbours. No wonder we didn't know they were here, tucked away.

'I couldn't work out the extra element in this wine, but it's this, this grape. *La tendresse*.' Isaac looks around.

Then he smiles. 'The wind, it must have kept the grapes safe from the blight.'

'And that's why Madame Beaumont doesn't want anyone on her land,' I say, understanding.

'These grapes aren't grown around here. The authorities could make her rip them up and replant.'

'What, like Charlie wants her to do?' I suddenly think.

Isaac nods.

'But why?'

'They're not grapes that are grown in this appellation, so it affects the taste of the other grapes.'

'But she doesn't register for the appellation. She hates rules and regulations.'

'And this is why. She's mixing this grape in with local grapes. That's what's giving it the twist, the edge, if you like.'

'How old are these vines?'

'I'd say about seventy years old, maybe more, some of them.' He lifts a bunch. 'They give a low yield at this age, but the flavour is much more intense.'

'Like they have gleaned wisdom and understanding on their way,' I say.

He smiles and nods as if accepting this explanation.

'Exactly. The thing is, the *terroir* over here is harder work, and the harder the roots have to work to find goodness . . .'

'. . . the better they fruit!' I finish for him.

He nods appreciatively and my heart lifts and begins to fly.

'Then this is exactly what we need,' I say, hope rising in my voice. 'I wonder how they got here.'

'But if the authorities or Featherstone's find out they won't let her sell this wine . . . it's against the regulations. It's why they're hidden.'

My heart crashes back down with a bump.

'And we won't be able to enter it for the wine medal,' I sigh, dropping my hands to my side.

'No,' he confirms.

'Or . . .' I say quietly. 'We could, if we don't tell them.'

'I can't do that, Emmy. It wouldn't be right. If I got found out . . .'

'You won't be doing it,' I take out my secateurs, 'I am.' I give him a hard stare, praying that he won't fight me on this. 'Without the grape, the wine's nothing special. You said so yourself. It's what gives it the edge. This way, you get your new job and Madame Beaumont gets to sell her vintage. Let's just say you knew nothing about the addition of the grapes, a bit like the yeast. It was all me. I didn't know any better.'

'Emmy, think about this. You could lose your job. You have to think of you, too. I can't let you do it.'

'You can,' I insist. 'And I am. Let's be honest, you were right. I do need to stick my neck out and get out there. I'll be as old as my dad before I've even started living, at this rate.

This could make the wine win! I can't go back not having tried.' We stare at each other and then I start to pick, slowly and carefully, and finally he follows behind me.

'If you don't pick them, we can say you had nothing to do with it. You hold the bucket, I'll pick,' I tell him.

And he does, but he's staring at me, head on one side.

'You are one hell of lady,' he says.

'Really, I'm not sure I am. I'm just like any other of the agents working in the office, except I'm not as good at selling as they are.'

'Maybe,' says Isaac, 'Madame Beaumont would say, that's because they're all supermarket blends . . . rolled out to taste the same, some better than others, but palatable blends all the same.'

'*Mais oui! Bien sûr!*' I say, giving him a stern look, through imaginary glasses, impersonating Madame Beaumont. And we both laugh.

'What does that make me then, vinegar?' I ask, turning back to the vines, working slowly, being careful not to damage the old vines.

'You, you're a single vintage,' he smiles.

'Oh, am I?' I can't help but smile back.

'Yes, you just haven't realised what kind of vintage you are yet.'

'Go on then, what kind of vintage am I?' I reach in for a small bunch of grapes in the middle of the vine and turn and place them in the bucket he's holding. But he's looking at me.

'Gutsy, bold, brave, I'd say you were a very rare, exceptional year. One that needed to mature to be fully appreciated.'

'Hey!' I make a swipe at him and he steps back, laughing.

'You're unique. Whereas your colleagues are more . . . last year's vintage. One that needs to be drunk quickly. You should be savoured.'

And I feel myself starting to tingle all over and need a distraction.

'Whereas you, you're like a *nouveau* wine. Here today, but gone tomorrow, doesn't hang around but is excellent in the moment!'

'Exactly! But with complicated depth,' he adds with a smile, 'that is only noticed by the discernible palate.'

'Discernible?'

'Yes, like yours. You have a very sophisticated palate, if only you'd let yourself believe it. You could do really well at this.'

I turn to put more grapes in the bucket, shielding my eyes from the sun. From here you can see fields and fields of vines rolling away down towards Petit Frère. The strong breeze carries the scent of rosemary and lavender to me.

'I couldn't do this,' I guffaw.

'Why not?'

'Well, for starters, I have a family that needs me back home.'

'I bet they'd love to see you do something other than work in that call centre. I could make some calls. You could think about coming with me, work in the winery.'

I stop. Did he just suggest I go with him? He must just mean as friends, and I'm not sure I could just be friends with Isaac any more.

'It's not that simple. I have responsibilities. I can't just fly off round the world working anywhere I want. Like you say, my roots go very deep.'

And if in some silly imaginary dream world, when I kissed Isaac I ever thought he and I could be more than this, I know now it could never happen. He's a free spirit, a rare 'here today, gone tomorrow' vintage and I'm one that needs to stay where it is to be enjoyed in years to come. Whereas Charlie? Charlie has potential. He'll mature with age – either that or turn sour! – but Charlie got Dad out here. He's looking to the future. His kiss may not have the effect that Isaac's did on me, but he's not going to be here today, gone tomorrow either. He knows what he wants and where he's going in life.

'Maybe one day I'll get to do something else, follow a dream. But not now.'

'Be careful you don't put it off too long, Emmy, or tomorrow might never happen.'

I carry on picking in silence, thinking about Mum, whose dreams of tomorrow never came. Of Dad, sitting in his chair, knowing tomorrow would be exactly the same as yesterday, and Jody, who has no idea what tomorrow will bring, but can be certain it will be very different from yesterday. And I think about Madame Beaumont. I have a feeling these vines are an integral part of her vintage, as I think about the photo and the silver badge by her bed, and I can't let her down.

Snip, snip. 'Come on, let's mix up some mischief.' I impersonate Madame Beaumont again and we laugh. It's all starting to make sense, her telling me how her father planted some of these vines. These must be the ones: they're part of who she is, and I swear I hear her laughter weaving through the vines.

Chapter Forty

'Oh, come on, at least let me crush them with you,' Isaac is pacing round the *chai* as I take my socks and boots off, ready to wash my feet.

'No! If you haven't touched them, you can't take any of the blame for this.'

'And what if you get found out, what if they disqualify the wine?' He throws up his hands.

'They won't find out. Madame Beaumont has kept it secret all these years. Why should that change?'

My phone vibrates in my pocket and I pull it out.

'Talking of which . . .' I look up and beam. 'She's messaged me!' I read the message. 'They've said she can do a home visit soon. And if she's well enough, leave the rehabilitation unit.'

'More like they're throwing her out for harassing the staff,' Isaac jokes, and I can't help but laugh. She's probably given them a really hard time and is desperate to get home.

'When she's coming?'

'She doesn't say. Would be lovely if she were there for the wine awards, though,' I say.

'Should be a big night. Charlie has you down as his guest.'

'Oh?' I say, washing and drying my feet. He didn't

mention it. But it just goes to show he's been thinking about me. But then again, I've hardly seen Charlie since my family's visit. Maybe if I'd seen more of him I wouldn't have been having such silly thoughts about me and Isaac. Isaac and I have just been spending way too much time together, that's all. This night out at the wine awards is just what Charlie and I need to start dating like a proper couple, now that our time here in France is nearly over. And any silly thoughts of going and working on vineyards with Isaac will be put to bed once and for all. My future is with Charlie, back at Cadwallader's. But my heart is taking a little time to catch up with my optimistic head.

'I'm taking Candy and Nick's partnered with Colette, God help him.'

'That's all a bit formal.' I put my phone on the side.

He shrugs. 'Jeff's coming with Gloria,' he says and we both laugh again, but the fact that Isaac is bringing Candy seems to be sitting in my brain and not shifting.

'Well, let's hope we can make Madame Beaumont proud then,' I say, distracting myself from the thought of Isaac kissing Candy and reminding myself of that kiss, his soft lips. 'If I can just get this vintage sold . . . give her enough money to see her through the winter, make some repairs to this place. Pay for her to have some help around the place. That's what she really needs: a helping hand.'

'That would be good. Someone to help out on the vines and do the manual work.'

I nod.

'OK, well, let's get this wine made. Now, once these few grapes ferment, get them into the barrel as quickly as possible.

Then you need to pump over the wine. Pump it out of the barrel, clean out the lees – the yeast at the bottom of the barrel – and pump it back in again.'

'Yes, I know what pumping over is,' I tut.

'I can help,' he offers.

'No! I've told you. You tell me what to do, and I'll do it, but the less you're involved the better.'

I climb into the barrel and Isaac holds out his hand to help me in and I take it, then wish I hadn't as I get a buzz going right through me, like I've grabbed hold of an electric fence. I pull my hand away, looking down at the grapes under my feet, feeling their wetness and the cold up through the gaps between my toes. I lift my foot to crush, then stop.

'I wonder if I have to do anything different with them.' I look back up at him. He's smiling at me and I feel a whoosh of excitement through my stomach and round my head again, making me feel a little light-headed. I have to stop this. I have to stop thinking about him. I have to put every spare thought I have into making this wine. Bringing in the grapes was one thing. I never expected to actually be making it.

Isaac shrugs. 'No idea. Never worked with this grape, but wine is wine essentially. Picked fruit, fermented, blended, bottled. Let's just keep going with how you've been doing it.'

I nod and start to tread up and down.

Isaac watches me for a while and I feel my breath quickening, like his eyes are on me and they shouldn't be. Then after a while I can tell he's frustrated as I load more grapes into the barrel and, like a child with nothing to do, he starts to wander to relieve his boredom. He inspects the juice in the tanks and the barrels waiting to be filled. He fiddles with the pump, checking it's in working order.

'When you're done, we need to get this wine into the barrels. We need to free up the tanks for this juice.' He points and I nod, puffing a little as I march up and down.

'Sure.'

Silence falls between us again, other than my breathing. *Stomp, stomp.* This is the best workout I've ever had. I can see why there's no need for gyms around here.

'You could go, if you like?' I suggest.

'Not likely, and leave you to cock up like you did with the yeast!' he half jokes.

Ouch. Point taken.

Stomp, stomp, squelch, squelch. My thigh muscles groan and my stomping slows.

'Sure you don't want me to take over?' he offers.

'No, I'm fine, honestly.'

Then he comes back to the barrel, reaches in and grabs a bunch.

'Hey!'

'Did you know that in Spain on New Year's Eve you have to put twelve grapes into your mouth on the stroke of midnight without crushing them? It's not easy.'

He starts putting grapes into his mouth, and I start to count, laughing.

'. . . ten, eleven . . .'

His cheeks are bulging and finally he cracks and he chews.

'Where did you learn that one? Have you worked in Spain?' I'm still crushing.

'Spanish girlfriend, years ago,' he grins, grape juice wetting his lips.

Spanish girlfriend, of course! 'You probably have a custom for New Year all over the world,' I blurt out. He looks at me and then slowly smiles, but with a hint of thoughtfulness.

'Actually I had a Spanish mother . . . hence the name Isaac, apparently.'

'Oh.' I feel my joke fall flat and then ask, 'Have you never wanted to settle anywhere?'

'Never found the right place.' He tosses another grape into his mouth.

'Or the right person, by the sounds of it.' I've spoken again without engaging my brain first. *Shut up, Emmy, for God's sake!*

'No, or the right person,' he surprises me by agreeing.

'What about your family? Brothers, sisters? Don't they wish you'd settle? I know I'd like to see more of my nephews.'

Oh good God, woman, what is wrong with you? I think crossly.

'Put it like this,' Isaac says, 'my name was about the only thing my mother ever did for me. She and my dad broke up when I was seven. I used to spend Wednesday nights with him, and every other weekend. Then he went to gaol and Mum took an overdose. I went into foster care and moved around. Different families, different bedrooms.'

'Oh God, how awful!' I think about my bedroom back home, the house I have lived in all my life, and can't imagine what it would have been like never knowing where my home really was. Just look at Jody now – even through all of this crisis she knew where home was when she needed it.

'But you didn't stay in foster care?' I ask.

He shakes his head, still tossing grapes in his mouth and wandering round like a kid who's been told he can't touch the bowl of sweets he's dying to get his hands on.

'I was a bit wayward at school. But my sports teacher and his wife adopted me. Like I said, they were older, but they bought me my first surf board and gave me an appreciation of wine. They encouraged me to go out and see the world, so that's what I did. I finished school and college, trained up and moved in with my girlfriend, set up home with her and started working as a travelling wine man, moving with the seasons and returning home in between jobs. What I didn't know was that my best friend at the time, a surfing buddy, was going to move in on my patch when I was away.'

I swallow. I have no idea what to say. I want to hug him tightly and tell him I know how it hurts to be feel your world has disappeared from under your feet. But I can't. I can't touch him because if I do, I realise, I may not ever want it to stop.

'I think they're ready,' is all I can think of saying, and he turns sharply, tossing a final grape into the air, catching it in his mouth and bowing as if to imaginary applause. His humour and his teasing are obviously the tools by which he's got by in life. Mine, I suppose, was to look out for others; that way I didn't have to think about myself.

Suddenly my phone rings on the side.

'Oh . . . er . . .' I go to climb out of the barrel, bare-footed, red stain to my calves and jeans rolled up with a hint of red grape juice around the bottoms where they've slipped down a few times.

''S OK, I'll get it,' Isaac says, looking pleased he can be useful.

'Thanks.'

I hold out my hand to take it from him and then watch as he swipes the screen, puts the phone to ear and says, 'Hello, Emmy Bridges' phone, who can I say is calling?' with a wicked grin and a wink. Honestly!

'Yes, she's just stomping the last of the grapes. Yes, then it goes into the tanks and we'll worry about them until we can finally barrel it. Yes, she's here now, I'll hand you over, no worries.'

I hold out my hand and cock my head on one side like I'm confiscating his ball.

He smiles, handing it over. 'It's your dad. I was just telling him where we were up to,' he smiles.

'Hi, Dad. Yes, that was Isaac. Yes, the one Candy has a crush on. Yes, they're going on a date soon, to the château for the wine medal ceremony. I'm going with Charlie.' Although I've only heard that through Isaac. 'Yes, Isaac's the one with long hair and the necklaces. Yes, in the bandana with the earring.' I roll my eyes and smile as Isaac waggles his hair. Then I listen . . . 'Really . . . ?' I'm still mulling over everything he's just told me as he goes on to tell me about what he's done since I saw him, and about Jody arranging to rent a small house down the road on the new estate, and about his new friends down the pub where he's been going for pensioner's dinner on a Friday. Reassured he's OK, I put down the phone. Isaac puts his hand out. I hand him the phone, staring at him, still replaying Dad's words.

'It was you, wasn't it?' I finally say.

'What?' He feigns innocence and turns away.

'It wasn't Charlie at all.' The information is slowly processing in my brain, turning it over. Everything in my head – and my heart – is shifting, like my whole world has just slipped on its axis. I don't know whether to be angry or ecstatic. I look at Isaac and say slowly, 'You spoke to my dad.' I swallow. 'You told him how much I'd like to see him and Jody. You even looked up the flights online for him,' I say to his back. He's tapping the phone in his hand and then puts it down on the side. 'You told them to come out and help me out with the harvest.' Tears prickle and sting my eyes as I stand up to my calves in cold grape juice. 'You did all that for me – not Charlie,' I say as the quiet realisation wraps itself around me. Isaac turns and looks, if I'm not mistaken, shy. He doesn't look me in the eye.

'Thought it would help . . . get the harvest in . . . thought you missed them. I know what it can feel like to be alone, without your family. I could see you were feeling it. He rang the office, couldn't get hold of you on your mobile . . . you were harvesting,' he says, still not looking at me. And finally when he does, slowly lifting his head and staring at me with his chocolate-brown eyes, I think my heart actually might burst, like a dam bursting, and I know I'm done for, there's no hope: I am seriously falling for this man, no matter how hard I try to stop myself.

'Come on, that juice can stay there happily for a while.' He points to the big stomping barrel and holds out a hand for me to get out of it. 'You need to get inside and have an early night and I have to be on my way.'

I take his hand as he steadies me getting out of the barrel.

'I'll just check the temperatures,' I say, pointing to the tanks.

'All done, now come on. Trust me, I'm the expert. You need to get in and get something to eat and go to bed.'

'Will you stay . . . I mean, eat with me.'

'I, er . . . I can't. I said I'd meet Candy, at the Le Papillon.' He looks away quickly, swallowing hard, and I wonder if he feels like I do but knows it can't happen. I may want him, but I can't have him. We could never be together. He'll be gone soon. This will just be another stamp in his passport. He's having fun with Candy, nothing serious, and that is all I think he'll ever want.

'Oh, of course, yes, I didn't think,' I say quickly, and we're back to being strangers, not sure how to be with each other. I finish up the *chai*, then quickly wish him a good evening and practically run into the house, feeling like a fool. But I find myself pulling on the sweatshirt, drenched in his aftershave, breathing him in and wishing his lips were on mine again, when what I really want, more than anything, is to never have to see him ever again, because that way it will be far less painful.

Chapter Forty-one

'That's it. Last one!' he calls.

Isaac has been here every day for the last ten days, whilst I have been pumping the wine into barrels from the tanks as it finishes its first fermentation.

'Once it stops bubbling and fermenting you have to get it into barrels, away from oxygen. This is when it's at risk. We don't want it turning to vinegar,' Isaac tells me.

'I thought it was at risk when it was fermenting?'

He laughs. 'There's always a risk with wine-making. Now for the second fermentation, the malo.'

And no matter how hard I've tried on my own, getting the wine into the barrels is a two-person job, with Isaac holding one end and me the other. I have to shout when the barrel is full and he turns off the tap. Sometimes he doesn't do it quick enough and I am regularly soaked, which I've come to realise is a hazard of the job.

And, even more infuriatingly, Isaac seems to find it funny most of the time. At least we both know where we stand now. He tells me about his dates with Candy. I tell him about my text messages from Charlie, but the truth is I've barely seen or heard from him in the past few weeks. I suppose the harvest is a busy time for everyone. *Hang on in there, you'll be home soon,* Dad texts me, and he senses how much I want that now. *I'm so proud of you.*

Once the juice is pumped into the barrels we press the skins. Isaac instructs me as we work the wooden press between us. My shoulders ache, as does my back, but it keeps my mind focused on the wine.

'Here, try it now . . .' Isaac encourages me to keep tasting the juice coming out of press. 'Stop when you think it's there. You don't want it to taste too green.' And I do, to his approval again.

I am washing clothes every day and hanging them out to dry on the line that is strung from the side of the house to Henri's field when the low autumn sun is out, and then in front of the log burner in the evenings. Cecil sits by the *chai* doors, occasionally barking to scare off the birds gathering on the overhead wires, this time preparing to leave for winter.

Henri seems content now that the harvest is over, although he still sometimes lifts his head to the air as if listening for the sound of Madame Beaumont's voice, '*Allez, allez!*' and I swear I hear it too.

For the next three weeks, as autumn rolls through into November, we fall into a pattern of Isaac coming up to check the wine on a daily basis, topping up the barrels and racking them with me, moving the wine from one barrel to another, separating it from the sediment. Each barrel is a little celebration for Isaac and me.

Then December rolls in, bringing winter with it. It's much colder – I'm wrapped up in a scarf and woolly hat from the market – and my cold breath forms smoke curls in the air in front of me in the early evening. It's the day before the wine medal ceremony at the château, where Selina and her team from Morgan's Supermarkets will choose their winning wine from the infant wines in the area, and I have to submit a blend of Clos Beaumont's wine for the judges to try. I'm so nervous, my stomach is a tight knot.

'Relax,' Isaac repeats. 'How does it taste now?' he asks, looking me in the eyes, then at my lips, and back to my eyes again. Our deadline is looming.

'Well . . .' I think, then say, rolling in my bottom lip, 'like ripe blackcurrants.'

'OK, what about if you add some of that now.' He points to another jug with wine from another barrel and I pour in a small measure. 'Too much or not enough?' he asks, and I taste it again.

'That's right, let it sit on your tongue. Are you getting any after-notes?' he asks as I spit. 'Think about which *parcelle* this wine has come from, decide which are your best *parcelles*, for sun and ripeness.'

I think about the ones near the boundary with the château and decide not to use them. I want this wine to tell us exactly where it came from.

For the next few hours I taste, point to the barrels I want more of or less of, taste again, write down which percentages I'm using from which *parcelle* and work out which blend works best.

Finally, I look up from the wine at Isaac, who bites at his bottom lip as I hold up the pipette and drip in a few drops of Madame Beaumont's secret grape juice. Isaac's eyes are wide and bright, as are mine. I'm feeling wild with excitement as I stir the blend gently with a long glass stick.

'Now,' he practically whispers, 'try it,' and he holds up the glass jar for me to try, moving it closer to my lips.

I hold my hand over his. The smell of the wine is full of ripe fruit and I breathe it in deeply and then slowly, sip the wine, pulling it back into my mouth and letting it sit on my tongue before finally swallowing.

'Well?' Delight is dancing across his face and I'm beginning to see why he loves this job so much. I think I do too . . . at least, I hope it's just the wine that's making me this excited.

'There's a full ripeness of the fruit and a hint of earthiness. It tastes of rolling hillsides, sunshine and a constant summer breeze,' I beam. It's like I've been transported back to the vineyard on a flying carpet on a hot summer's day. Nodding, Isaac grabs the notebook from the old wooden work bench and is writing it down.

'Good, good.' He's a scientist excited by the results of an experiment. 'Anything you think it needs more of, or less?'

I look at his dark head as he's writing by the light of the small lamp we've brought in from the house. He looks up at me, those dark eyes, the smudges under them. Oh God, I wish he didn't have this effect on me. Who'd've thought a few weeks ago we'd have rather done anything than spend time together. And now, well, I don't want this time to end. But he'll be gone in a week and so will I. This will all be just a distant dream, because however much I'd like to go with Isaac to the next job, I can't.

'It's just . . .'

'Yes?'

'Perfect,' I say quietly.

He smiles and then goes to take the tasting jug from me. I don't know if he's going to taste the wine or kiss me but: 'No,' I shake my head, pulling the tasting jug back towards me. He mustn't do either. 'You can't. This is my mistake to make. We agreed. It's too risky.' And, as he drops his hand, the bubble of excitement bursts.

'Now we have the blend just right, write it up, ready for Madame Beaumont when she comes out of hospital,' he says matter-of-factly, looking at the notebook and not at me, even though every bit of my body is shouting, look at me! It's hopeless.

'But who's going to make it for her? She needs help around her. She can't manage on her own.'

'You could . . .'

Just then my phone rings, heralding a message. Grateful for the interruption I fall on the phone.

'It's her!' I run to Isaac, forgetting about the professional boundaries we've set ourselves. 'They've said she can come out for a visit from the rehabilitation unit on Sunday. Oh my God! The day after tomorrow. She's coming home. We have to get everything ready.'

'The wine is ready, Emmy. You've done it. Now it just needs to make you proud tomorrow at the château,' he says, and adds, 'I know I am.'

And before I do something else I regret I tell him it's late, I need to sleep, and I run off into the house again where I wrap my sweatshirt smelling of his aftershave around me and curl up in bed for what may be the last time and listen to the big doors of the *chai* being closed and the van driving off into the night, wishing it wasn't.

Chapter Forty-two

The following morning, I'm up and at it early, dressed in hat, gloves, scarf and wellies. Cecil is barking for all he's worth, heralding someone arriving in the yard, as I'm busy trying to tidy up the *chai*, ready for Madame Beaumont's return. I stick my head out, hoping it isn't more tourists hoping for another degustation, a tasting session like last time. I just don't have time, especially not without Candy's help.

It's the Featherstone's van and my stomach makes an infuriating lurch. The door opens but instead of Isaac, it's Gloria getting out of the driver's seat, followed by Candy from the passenger seat and Nick from the back.

'*Bonjour!* We heard Madame Beaumont was coming home,' Gloria calls and waves.

'Yes, they're bringing her back tomorrow, and if she's happy, she'll stay.' I grin, feeling almost light-headed that I have got all the wine into the barrels, even if one naughty one does pop its cork every now and again. And we – or should I say I – have blended it and bottled two bottles ready for tonight's tasting at the château.

'We couldn't let you do it all on your own.' Gloria steps forward and kisses me on both cheeks, just like a French woman. Since taking over in the kitchen during the *vendange*,

Gloria seems to have transformed in front of our eyes. It's like she's lived here all her life. 'I thought we could help clean, get the house ready. I'll check over the books one last time and I could make a few more meals to put in the freezer for her. I bought some chestnuts and mushrooms too.' She lifts her heavy basket. 'Albert sells them from his garden gate on the other side of the river and Sophie on the flower stall outside the church gave me these.' She puts a bunch of roses in a jug. 'Said they were in full bloom and past their best, but they smell wonderful.' She puts her nose to them and I can't help but smile. If anyone is in full bloom, it's Gloria.

'I want to make sure we've got her page on the Featherstone's website and my blog pages looking their best too,' Candy joins in.

'And I'm going to finish the wood pile, but I picked up some new linen in the market, thought it'd look nice on the beds.' Nick waggles a blue plastic bag at me.

'Thank you so much, all of you. You are really good friends.' Suddenly, for no reason whatsoever, huge tears start to fall, and the three of them rush over and hug me and I really will be so sorry when we leave here and go back to being agents at Cadwallader's.

'Right come on, the quicker we get going, the more time we've got to get ready for tonight's big do at the château. Thought we could get changed here. Charlie says he'll pick you up at six. I have got a dress that is going to knock Isaac for six,' Candy instructs us.

I immediately look at Nick, who gives his head a little shake and looks to the floor. He hasn't told her how he feels and I wish he would. But then, I realise with a rush of blood to my cheeks, who am I to talk? I'm hardly being honest with myself. Then Candy's voice cuts across my thoughts.

'There's no way he'll be able to turn me down tonight,' she says with relish, and I blush some more. For a moment none of us says anything as Candy starts pulling out the huge bag from the back of the van.

'What you mean . . . you're not . . . ?' The words are out of my mouth before I've engaged my brain.

'Emmy!' Gloria chastises me good-humouredly.

'Sorry.' I hold up my hands. It's none of my business! But I can see Nick's spirits lifting from the floor, and my stomach has flipped over despite my telling it to behave, as if it were a lively toddler at a family dinner.

'Not yet. Honestly, at first I thought it was quite quaint but now, enough's enough! Tonight's the night,' she beams, pushing out her large bosom as Nick's spirits hit the floor again.

'Right, everyone, let's get cleaning,' Gloria rallies us, pulling out her yellow Marigolds from her basket, and we all follow her into the house.

'We should get that downstairs bedroom on the other side of the living room sorted for her,' she instructs, 'make up the bed. And then if she wants to move in there and out of this room she can.' I look around the one room that has been her home for so many years. I wonder what she'll think when she sees we've opened up the rest of the house, the facelift we've given it all. I get a pang of nerves. I hope she likes what we've done, I really do.

'I'll do that, and I thought more flowers, not just in here but in the bedroom too,' says Nick, pointing at the kitchen table, which is now back in its rightful place after the harvest.

'Oh, Nick, you're so thoughtful, you'll make some lucky man a very lovely husband one day. God, why can't you be straight?' Candy sighs and turns away to pull her computer from her bag.

I look at Nick, willing him to say something.

'Actually—' I say.

'Actually, you're right.' Nick gives me a warning look. He's worried that he'll lose her as a friend if he says anything, I know, and I should respect that, because I understand how he feels. And I want to hug him and for someone to hug me too. 'I hope to make someone a lovely husband one day,' he says as he stares at the back of her head in longing as she puts the laptop on the table and opens it.

'And I'll tidy up in here, leave all the paperwork in order, and then I can cook at the same time,' Gloria says, pulling out groceries from the basket.

'I'll finish in the *chai,* then start upstairs.' I clap my hands together and leave them to it. It's time I started packing too. I'll probably move back into the *gîte* tomorrow until we leave. I'm sure Madame Beaumont won't want me staying here once she's home.

For the next couple of hours we work away to the sound of Nick, chopping wood with every bit of frustration in his body. By lunchtime, when he arrives back in the kitchen, he's bright red, sleeves rolled up, hair dishevelled and sweating, an axe hanging by his side.

'Oh, Nick,' Candy's eyes widen in surprise. 'You look . . . ever so . . .'

'Knackered?' he finishes for her.

'Like Bear Grylls,' Candy corrects him, and I swear she gives a little shiver followed by a little laugh.

'*À table*,' Gloria calls us to the table she's laid up inside. Despite it being a glorious day out there, it's chilly, not eating-out weather. She's carrying over bowls of steaming soup.

'*Soupe de poisson*,' she announces. 'Hope you like it. And cassoulet to follow. That's sausage and beans, Candy.' Candy smiles and Gloria puts a basket of bread on the table.

She pulls up a chair and puts an open bottle of wine on the table.

'I think we should have a toast,' she says, and Nick joins us from having washed his hands and face and pours the wine into small tumblers.

'To Clos Beaumont and all it's given us.' Gloria beams as if she wants to say more but doesn't.

We all raise our glasses.

'To Clos Beaumont, where we all learned to be ourselves.' Candy holds up her glass and nods to me, and I quickly look at Nick.

'To us,' I say, and we all clink glasses and then tuck into our soup, followed by the wonderful cassoulet with thick sausages, lardons and fat, soft beans. I look at the dish and smile, remembering Mum, Dad and Jody and the stolen sausages had been meant for our tea. Then, I touch the necklace round my neck that Mum gave me, the curly E and think how proud she would be to see me here today.

'OK,' Candy instructs, after we've eaten a gorgeous Camembert, 'let's clear up and then we can use the other room for changing. It's exciting!' She claps her hands and my stomach twists with nerves as I stand to clear up our plates. I realise I'm straining to see out of the window into the yard. There's no sign of Isaac, and why should there be? His work here is done.

I'm so nervous, I need some fresh air. I decide to take a walk up to the churchyard to check on the grave while the others start getting ready for tonight, when the judges will taste the two bottles of wine I've blended. It won't be the finished product but it'll give them a good idea. If they like it, and it wins, it'll cause a real buzz. Charlie will be delighted.

Charlie . . . I think as I walk. But my mind keeps flipping back to Isaac, his excited eyes as we blended the wine, and that kiss. Did it mean anything or was it just a moment of madness?

Back at the farmhouse, after my walk, Candy has turned the middle living room into a changing room, with her dress draped over one chair, a big make-up box, a selection of shoes, and heated rollers on the windowsill and in her hair.

'Now if you can just lower this mirror,' she's telling Nick. 'If we push the clock along, I can rest it on the mantelpiece.'

He does and as he moves it, all of a sudden the clock strikes the hour. We all look at each other. And then it strikes the hour again.

'Wow! That clock hasn't worked since I've been staying here, and who knows how long before that?' I tell him.

'Looks like it just needed bringing back to life,' Nick says, looking at it. 'It's beautiful. Could be worth a bit, too.' He picks it up and Candy takes it off him.

'I could look it up on eBay,' she says, turning it upside

down and looking underneath. 'Just need a date or a make.' As she turns it upside down, a yellowing folded piece of paper falls from the back of the clock and flutters down in front of the old black fireplace.

We all look at it, and both Nick and Candy nod to me to pick it up. It smells . . . musty, like a second-hand bookshop. I look at them then, take the paper to the window and carefully unfold it and start to read.

'*Chère Nancy*, my dearest Nancy,' it says in simple French. 'I know you wind the clock every day and so that's why I'm leaving this note here . . .' My French is improved but not good enough yet. I hand the note to Gloria, who carries on translating, reading aloud slowly.

> As you know this year's vintage has gone from the chai. It has not been taken by my officers; rather, I have made sure they don't get it. It is safe in the cellar. You can sell it. It will keep you and your family going until I can return and be with you once this awful war is over. Let the new tendresse vines we have grafted and planted be a reminder that I will get back to you, soon. Keep them well.
>
> Stay safe, keep our little one safe too until I am back with you once more. I will love you for ever. Always tell our daughter that her daddy loves her too. Tell her to be proud of who she is.
>
> Yours forever, Frederic x

When I look around there isn't a dry eye. Each of us is sniffing, red-eyed, tears rolling down our cheeks.

'That's why there's no gravestone for him,' I say hoarsely. 'Those vines are his legacy.'

'What?' Candy blows her nose on the big spotted hankie Nick has handed her, and then hands it back to him. He pockets it without a second thought. 'Who's Frederic?'

'Wait.' I run into the kitchen and pick up the picture by Madame Beaumont's bed, and the silver badge, and take them back to show the others.

'I think it's Madame Beaumont's father.' I pass round the picture. 'He was a young German soldier. They were very much in love. But he returned to Germany and never came back.'

Gloria is still blowing her red nose on a small tissue and I nod.

'The vines are really rare, practically wiped out from this area in the mid-eighteen hundreds. He must have replanted them from a surviving vine.'

'In which case, if this note hasn't been read before, and it doesn't look as if it has . . .' Nick says.

'The wine must be in the cellar!' Candy suddenly jumps up and down with excitement and we all run to the door leading down to the cellar, somewhere even I haven't ventured before. We push it open. It's dark, there are cobwebs hanging all around and there is a wooden staircase.

This could be the answer to all Madame Beaumont's financial worries.

Chapter Forty-three

'I can't believe I actually thought it might be there.' I rub my hair vigorously after a quick shower, feeling foolish, having got carried away with the romance of it all, as if I was in some episode of *Scooby-Doo* and everything was going to come right.

The cellar door is very firmly shut again. There was nothing there, nothing but empty crates, dustsheets and empty wine bottles.

'And now I've got cobwebs in my rollers,' Candy squeaks.

'We have to hurry, we have to be at the château by six thirty,' Gloria rallies us, and we all disappear to different corners of the house to dress.

I put on my other dress, bought from the market – a straight, simple yellow cotton halter neck – wrap a cream scarf around my shoulders and borrow some high heels from Candy. Then I pin up my hair in a French pleat with Candy's help and dress it up with jewellery, and for the first time in weeks put on foundation, mascara, blusher and, finally, a lick of lip gloss.

When we're dressed we join Gloria in the kitchen. She's looking fabulous in smart wide-leg trousers and an elegant top. She looks a completely different woman from when she arrived, and not a fan in sight.

'You look amazing. New clothes, and is that a new scarf, too?' I ask, and she smiles.

'Jeff bought it for me, in the market,' and at first none of us says anything but we all smile.

'I didn't know you and Jeff had been to the market together.' Candy can't help herself.

'We didn't. But he did take me to the tea dance last Sunday.'

'Really?'

'Well, as we're leaving next week, I thought, why not?' Gloria throws the brightly coloured scarf around her neck with a flourish.

'Quite right,' I say, and hug her. 'So are you and Jeff . . . ?'

'Oh, no, nothing like that,' she says seriously, and I feel myself dip a little. It would have been lovely if Gloria had found a little happiness for herself. 'We're just friends. Good friends. But it was lovely to be taken out. Made me feel . . . well . . . less invisible, I suppose.'

'Well, you're certainly not that in that outfit and scarf,' Nick says, coming into the room in smart blue trousers, a white shirt, a change from his usual pink choices. 'You look gorgeous.'

'You look lovely yourself,' Gloria smiles up at him. And he does.

'Thought I'd give the pink a miss. Don't want to give out the wrong signals.' He smiles at me and I return it, but Candy's not listening.

'Nick, do me up, would you?' Candy turns her back to Nick.

'Way too subtle,' I whisper to him, and he coughs to clear his throat.

'Actually, perhaps you could, Emmy?' and he goes out, much to Candy's chagrin.

'I have no idea what's got in to him today. He's being so moody,' she complains.

'Maybe there's something on his mind . . . or someone,' I say as I zip her into her tight, floral dress.

'Uh?' She takes a sharp intake of breath and turns to me.

'You don't think . . .' she gasps, her hand over her mouth.

'Yes?' I nod and smile.

'You don't think he fancies . . .'

I raise my eyebrows and nod more.

'You don't think he fancies Isaac, do you?'

I drop my head in despair.

'Who wouldn't?' I hear myself saying flippantly, feeling foolish at the same time.

'Come on, guys, time to go.' Nick comes in and hurries Candy out. 'Do you want to come with us?' he asks me.

'No, I'll hang on for Charlie. I'm sure he'll be here soon,' I say, deep down wishing I was going with them. I wave them off and then I wait, sitting at the table and chairs, looking out over the vines, a wrap around me for warmth, clutching the two bottles of Clos Beaumont I've made. Anxiously, I watch the sun starting to set and wish that this wasn't the last time I was going to see it here.

By the time Charlie arrives, my heart is beating so fast and I'm not sure if it's because I haven't seen him in so long and am nervous about the date, or that I'm just terrified we're going to miss the judging, or that I know I'm harbouring a secret in these bottles and am terrified of being found out.

'Sorry, got held up . . .'

He looks freshly showered and cool in his suit. He leans in to kiss me and I quickly turn my head so he kisses my cheek, and I get into the car.

'OK, let's go. Finally, I get to go on a date with you,' he says smiling, and he spins off towards the château. I clutch the two bottles as if my life depends on them.

'What's the news on Madame Beaumont?' Charlie asks, and I'm pleased about that.

'She's coming home, tomorrow. If she's happy, they'll let her stay.' I feel like I've done my job. Looked after everything while she was away.

'Tomorrow? Really? I didn't know,' Charlie says, interested.

'She only rang yesterday, when we were . . .' I stop. 'When Isaac was up blending the wine. Completely forgot to tell you. Sorry.' Although why I'm apologising I have no idea. We fall into silence for the rest of the way up the hill to the château.

Charlie pulls up, spraying gravel, in the busy car park. I get out with the precious bottles and he bleeps the car shut, doing up his jacket button as we walk through a stone archway. As I step through it I catch my breath. On the other side there are long flaming bamboo torches all the way down the path to the stone building, lighting the way and the stone walls behind it.

As we reach the door, there is a maître d', wishing us '*Bonsoir*' and guiding us through the low doorway, down a corridor with worn flagstones on the floor, past two large rooms with dark panelling on the walls and big fireplaces. In the first room there is a small group standing round, mostly speaking French. They're not drinking, I notice. But I recognise the château owner, Monsieur Lavigne, who turns and raises a hand at Charlie, who returns the wave and hurries me along.

'The judges,' Charlie whispers, and takes hold of my elbow, guiding me up the hall. The walls are covered with thick tapestries. In the next room I can see a long table with bottles of wine in pairs and an envelope under each, which will have the maker's name on it. We stop and Charlie shakes hands with the man in there, putting out bottles of water and glasses.

'*Je vous présente Emmy Bridges.*' Charlie holds out a hand to me by way of introduction but I can't shake hands because I have a bottle in each. Charlie switches into English. 'She has been helping my wine-maker, Isaac Allen.'

'*Enchanté.*' The man nods his head by way of hello. 'I have heard of your wine-maker. Here,' he takes the bottles from me and the envelope with Clos Beaumont's name on it. I recognise him now as the château's *vigneron*, the one driving the tractor in the fields. The one Madame Beaumont steadfastly ignores. He holds out his hands to take my infant wine, ready for its premier tasting. But I clutch the bottles, reluctant to let them go.

'I can take these from you. They will be safe with me,' he smiles, the same smile he gave Madame Beaumont on that first day, spraying the vines. It feels a bit like how I imagine it would leaving your child at nursery for the first time with bigger kids. I watch as he puts the bottles on the red tablecloth next to the other wines and tucks the envelope underneath.

'Bernard, I need a word . . . erm, your advice in a while. When you're free,' Charlie smiles at him then back at me.

'*Bien sûr, monsieur.*' He nods and Charlie ushers me quickly along the hall but I'm trying to hang back, craning my neck, like a worried mum trying to watch the playground from a distance. But then I see a waitress in short black dress, pearl earrings and flat shoes make her way along the passage and turn into the room, holding large jugs of water, and I decide I can leave.

We follow the sound of chatter and laughter to the end of the corridor, where it opens out into a massive, high-ceilinged room. There is a huge stone fireplace and a roaring fire. There are large windows down one side, with big glass doors. Outside there are high tables, with flaming patio heaters, more flaming bamboo torches and people standing around, blowing smoke into the air, whilst holding glasses in their other hand. Monsieur and Madame Obels from the shop are there tucking into the tray of *amuse-bouches* as the waitress passes. As is the mayor. They raise their glasses and wave, then call the waitress back for another morsel from the tray. I'm sure that I can see our degustation guests too, our second home owners, who also turn and wave across the crowded room.

A waitress holds out a silver tray with slim glasses of sparkling wine and tells us it's the château's own '*méthode champenoise*'. I smile, take a glass but I'm too nervous to drink. I'm drawn to the window. Beyond the patio and the heaters are the vines, floodlit at this top end, making a fantastic dramatic backdrop. But beyond it, I can just make out Clos Beaumont.

'You made it!'

I turn round. Nick is excitedly holding his glass by the stem whilst Candy is knocking back the last of hers and looking around.

'You had us worried. You're late! Is it here, the Clos Beaumont wine?'

'Safely delivered,' I smile, and then realise I'm scanning the room too.

'Excuse me a moment. There's someone I must see.' Charlie puts his hand in the small of my back, then steps away and moves across the room. I follow him with my eyes and then I see her, dressed all in red. Selina. He kisses her on both cheeks, whispering something into her ear and as he does, she tosses her head back and laughs. Am I really pinning my future hopes on a man I don't really know at all? After all, he never said it was Isaac who organised for my family to come over. Just took the credit. I look at him again. He looks smart. Blue suit, fitted shirt, silver cufflinks. He's tall, smells expensive, keeps himself fit. Why then have I got this niggling feeling that something doesn't quite fit? Was I right not to sleep with him that night in Saint Enrique? I take a sip of my drink. Something in my head, my gut . . . instinct! I hear Madame Beaumont's voice and I practically laugh out loud, choking on my drink, the bubbles going up my nose.

'You all right?' A voice behind me says. Candy spins round and her face lights up. It's Isaac. My eyes water, and I hold my hand over my mouth, trying not to choke some more. But my ridiculous heart still flips over and back again as I take him in. He's wearing a long white linen shirt, open at the neck, showing off his leather necklaces, still entwined, a soft leather jacket and dark blue jeans. One hand is shoved into his pocket, his leather friendship bracelets poking over the top. And on his feet, chunky, black biker boots. He smells familiar, of forests and lemon. A smell I have come to know so well and that sets a fire burning in my belly and makes my body start to ache with a longing, drawing me in. I seem to have stopped breathing altogether.

'No bandana,' I croak stupidly through my tight throat. The last thing I want is for Isaac to have to save my life again and I take another sip of fizz, hoping it'll clear my airways.

'No,' he laughs. 'No bandana. And no red wine stains,' he retorts, referring to my many soakings, and try as I might I can't help but laugh, and Candy pouts.

A bell rings.

'Dinner.' Isaac smiles, and Candy muscles in beside him and slides her arm through his. I step back to let her through.

Nick pulls himself up from his chest, where his shoulders had just drooped and holds his arm out gallantly to Gloria. Charlie finally joins us and puts his hand in the small of my back again, guiding me into dinner, nodding and smiling, shaking hands and kissing people on both cheeks on the way.

'Sorry, just some business I needed to address. But I'm all yours now. Let's finally enjoy an evening out together,' he smiles, and I wish I could, but I'm way too nervous.

It's a glorious meal. Wonderful orange charentais melon draped with soft pink smoked ham or *terrine de campagne*, a local pâté, with baskets of still-warm sliced bread. Then *filet de boeuf*, pink on the inside, brown around the edges, wrapped in soft, flaky pastry with *gratin dauphinois* potatoes and roasted vegetables. There is *tarte tatin*, golden on the top, and big cheese boards placed down the table for us to dip into with more baskets of bread. But it's more like a game of wink, wink, murder, than a dinner party. Nick is snatching glances at Candy, Candy is drinking in Isaac, Isaac I swear is taking sideways glances at me, and Charlie is gazing over at Selina, who keeps smiling back. Gloria, on the other hand, is sitting next to someone I've never met, chatting and smiling. They talk and listen to each other intently throughout the meal. I barely eat or drink, I'm so nervous, despite the wonderful food and offering of wine.

I do have coffee, and the judges are starting to gather. I take the coffee to my lips and catch Isaac's eye. I swear he gives me a little wink and a tiny smile from the corner of his mouth. Candy has her head now leaning against his arm, staring up at him with unconcealed adoration.

'Think I'll get some air.' He raises his eyebrows and motions to me to follow. I go to stand.

'Oh, smashing, yes . . .' Candy staggers to her feet. I'm midway standing and not sure what to do. I go to sit back down and feel Nick tense up beside me. Isaac marches outside followed by a tottering Candy.

'You have to say something, tell her how you feel,' I tell Nick.

'I can't.' He looks pained. 'I'm never going to be the sort of guy she'll go for. She thinks I'm gay, for God's sake! She'll hate me for telling her.'

I pat his arm and Gloria pats the other. My stomach is a tight ball and I wish they'd get the judging over and done with so I can go home. I look around for Charlie, who is talking with Bernard, getting his advice, no doubt. I wonder if Charlie is always working. Was that why his marriage broke down? I watch him looking at his watch, as does Bernard. It seems quite an intense conversation considering Charlie's asking his advice. Suddenly, Candy comes pushing past them, back to the table, sobbing.

'Candy?' Nick jumps to his feet and puts an arm round her, guiding her to a chair, looking round for Isaac.

'What did he do?' Nick demands.

'Nothing,' she wails.

'Nothing?' Nick frowns.

She shakes her head. Nick pulls out a hankie for her, she takes it and blows on it very loudly, leaving her nose red and her eyes sore and puffy.

'I asked him to kiss me and he . . . he . . . he said no. That he was very fond of me, but he didn't want me in that way. I thought . . . I thought . . .'

She blows her nose again and looks up at Nick.

'What's wrong with me? Wouldn't you kiss me if you were—'

She doesn't have time to finish her sentence because Nick lifts her to her feet, takes her head in one hand, the other behind her neck and bends down and kisses her very thoroughly indeed.

'Oh, Nick,' Candy finally says as they come up for air, looking like both of them have had their breath taken away.

'I have wanted to do that for so long,' he beams.

'In that case, I think we'd better try it again,' says Candy, grabbing her man and pulling him to her like a praying mantis ready to devour him.

A chink on the side of a glass with a knife and the room falls silent.

'Time for the judging,' Gloria whispers with an excited squeak.

'Gloria, who was that man you've been talking to all night?'

'I'll tell you later.' She squeezes my shoulder and looks across at Monsieur Lavigne, who is holding three envelopes in his hand.

The atmosphere in the room is electric. There's the occasional excited whisper as wine-makers and sellers shuffle forward to stand shoulder to shoulder in front of Monsieur Lavigne and his table, where a glass, silver-topped decanter is sitting. I close my eyes, feeling the anticipation in the air. This announcement could change a wine-maker's life. We are all standing in the middle of the crossroads.

'*Mesdames et Messieurs* . . . Ladies and gentlemen. This award is for an infant wine, a new wine in which we see great potential,' says Monsieur Lavigne.

I hold my breath and hold the curly E of my necklace to my lips.

'We have tasted for aroma, texture and the balance of tannins and acidity,' he continues, and my legs start to jiggle. Get on with it, I think, my eyes screwed up tight.

'The winner will take home the medal and also a contract to supply Morgan's Supermarkets back in the UK.' The room falls silent as he struggles to open the envelope with a glass in one hand and trying to put his spectacles on his nose from round his neck.

'And the winner of the Morgan's Supermarkets wine medal for this new vintage, is . . . Featherstone's Wines for their Clos Beaumont wine!' he says loudly but with a hint of surprise in his voice.

'We won! Clos Beaumont won!' I hear a voice telling me, and I'm being bounced around from neighbouring shoulders.

I force my eyes open. Gloria is hugging me, as are Jeff and Colette. Someone shoves a glass of fizz into my hand, I'm not sure who, but it slops everywhere with the hugging and shoulder pattering. Charlie's up with Monsieur Lavigne accepting the silver-topped crystal decanter trophy, shaking hands and posing for photographs.

I am stunned; I can't even speak. We did it. I stand on tiptoes and look around for Isaac. I just want to share this moment with him. It's as much his celebration as it is mine. But he's not anywhere to be seen. At least he'll get his new job now. He'll be able to go, I think with a mix of pride and overwhelming sadness. Then I spot him. He too is now being congratulated by Monsieur Lavigne. He's nodding but not saying much, he's looking around too and then our eyes meet and hold each other's gaze. He smiles and I smile back. We did it.

Everyone is congratulating us. Local wine-makers I've never met, shaking my hand and patting me on the back. It's hot and I start to move towards the long French windows where it may be cooler, away from the throng around Charlie and the Featherstone's gang. We did it, I think again, exhilarated. I realise I've never felt anything like this: as if anything is possible now.

I turn to look out on the valley below, back towards Clos Beaumont. I can barely see it but I know it's there.

I did it, Madame Beaumont, I did it . . . I look out on the lights moving down in the valley. It almost looks like they belong to a tractor. And, if I'm not mistaken, they're heading towards the Clos Beaumont vines. Why would there be lights down in the valley at this time of night? Suddenly my blood runs very cold.

Chapter Forty-four

'No!' I grab and turn the handles to the big double doors and push them wide open. The thin, white voile curtains fly up in the wind and the partygoers all turn in the direction of the wind, their hair, jacket tails and skirt hems lifting. I run out on to the patio, to the surprise of the smokers there, and Nick and Candy who are still practising their kissing.

'This was all planned to get me out of the way!' I say to Charlie, who has followed me out. The smile slips from his lips and he starts to look uncomfortable.

'It wasn't planned, Emmy, but it's what we agreed: that Featherstone's would take over the running of the vineyard.'

'No! We didn't agree it. It's what you wanted but it was never agreed. I'm just here as your date to keep me out the way. You're not interested in me, you just want to get your hands on those vines.'

'That's not true. Look, Emmy, calm down. Have another drink.' He holds out a glass of fizz, which I push back at him, spilling it over his blue suit.

'I don't want a drink,' I say firmly. 'I want you to stop. Stop that now!' I point towards Clos Beaumont.

I look out across the patio. It's very dark out there. Then

big blobs of rain start to fall, just occasionally at first, plip, plop over the terrace paving slabs, like bullets, hitting the ground, creating little craters of water where they fall. The onlookers move inside until it's just me and Charlie here. Ripping my gaze away from the trundling tractor, and glare at him, fury tumbling through my veins.

'Why today?' I practically growl. 'Why now?'

'Well, since Madame Beaumont is due home tomorrow, I thought it best to get started. No need to upset her any more than necessary. This way, we'll get the new vines in and take over on all the grape growing and harvesting. She'll be paid for her wine.'

'You mean your wine, the one you want her to make! Your bland blend wouldn't win medals.'

'Well, I think you'll find it just has,' Charlie smiles smugly.

'Everything all right out here?' Isaac appears in the doorway, framed by two floating curtains.

'Fine, Isaac, yes, nothing to worry about. Oh, by the way,' Charlie turns to him and pulls an envelope out of his inside pocket. 'As promised, a cheque and a reference. Well done.' He slaps him on the shoulder. Isaac stares at the envelope and then at me, and I turn away. How could he take it? Did he know about this too?

'No, everything is not all right,' I spin back. 'He's about to rip out Madame Beaumont's vines! Isaac, can I have the van keys, please?' I hold out my hand. More rain starts to fall, soaking my palm. The wind whips higher and I shiver.

'The keys?' he asks.

Suddenly there's a rumble down below: the tractor has made it to the *parcelle* below us.

'Now, Isaac!' I shout.

'But you can't drive.'

'I just said I didn't drive.' I thrust my hand towards him and he reaches into his pocket, pulls out the keys and drops them into my hand.

'Look, I can—' He goes to step forward.

'No, I don't think so! And anyway, you've been drinking.'

'Look, Emmy, let's go inside and let them do what they've got to do,' says Charlie. 'You've done well. We've got your future to plan with Featherstone's. I think we can announce that team leader's job is yours now and perhaps finally take that weekend away, for you and me; finally get this relationship started, anywhere you fancy. Paris?'

I look down at the keys in my hand. My hair is getting plastered to the side of my face. Just like the night my mother left.

'Come on, let's go inside.' Charlie is trying to usher me, just like my father did that night, ushering me back inside, telling me everything will be all right.

I take a deep breath. 'Y'know what, Charlie?'

'No, Emmy, I don't know "what"?' He smiles, one of his full, pulled-back-to-the-ears smiles. 'But I'm glad you're seeing sense. We're going to make a great team, you and I.'

'Charlie? What's going on, honey?' Selina is at the doorway, holding on to the frame, looking out into the now heavy driving rain.

The fury in me bubbles over like the fermenting grape juice, red, angry and ready to explode.

'You know what, Charlie? You really are a pillock! An absolute pillock!'

And with the rain flying in my face I put my hand up to cover my eyes and run through the puddles towards the car park, as fast as I can, until, like Cinderella running from the ball, I ditch the high heels and run barefoot to the van.

'Emmy!' I hear Isaac's voice behind me but I don't turn round. He's got what he wanted – his cheque and his reference – but all I know is I have to try to stop them ripping up those vines.

Chapter Forty-five

'Come on, come on!'

The key is slipping and sliding in my shaking hands and I can't get it into the ignition. But at least I am now sitting in the correct side of the car. In my rush, I'd opened the car door, got in and realised there was no steering wheel. Now I'm locked in and trying to start it. I've never driven abroad, but I'll just point and drive. What else can I do? I can't sit back and do nothing! The key is still slipping and sliding as the rain falls hard, and suddenly the image of my mum running to the car and starting the engine comes back to me. Her face, as clear as if it was yesterday at the wheel of the car, smiling, telling me everything would be fine. She'd be back soon and starting the engine in haste. My hands are shaking. My heart is thundering; I'm right back there. I can't do this! I drop the keys in the footwell. Stop! I tell myself. Enough! I take a deep breath, reach for the keys and then, breathing deeply, try again. It's time to step forward.

'Yes!' The key slides in and I turn it.

Brrrrr, brrrrr, and then nothing. Isaac is banging on the bonnet, hair soaked, shouting at me to stop.

'Come on!' I shout, this time turning the key and standing on the accelerator – at least I think that's it – and the engine roars into life. 'Yes.' I touch my necklace again. 'Thank you.' I raise my eyes briefly to the skies. Then I look down at the gear stick. In addition to its being on the wrong side, I've never seen one like it. The wind and rain is pelting against the window and there's a loud rubble of thunder, only I'm too busy trying to work out which gear reverse is, lurching the car forward and backwards, to worry about how many elephants to count.

Finally with a grind and a crunch I find reverse again just as a huge lightning bolt cracks across the sky. But the lights on the tractor in the valley below are still moving slowly forwards.

I spin the van backwards and then, with another crunch and grind, let it lurch forwards. This time instead of counting elephants as another clap of thunder bangs overhead, I'm kangarooing down the road, throwing me forwards and back. Isaac is behind me in the rear-view mirror.

'Come on, Emmy, you can do this,' I say out loud. I have to get to the vines!

Suddenly I put my foot down on the accelerator and the van shoots forwards, whining for me to change gear. I pick a gear and press on the accelerator again. I'm careering down the road, turning a corner, this way and that. I'm doing it. I'm actually doing it. As I turn another corner, a small car is coming in the opposite direction. I swerve left.

The driver lets out a blast on the horn.

'Argh!' I swerve really hard back the other way. Wrong side of the road! The other driver honks again as the car passes me. I hit the accelerator, panic pushing me to drive ever faster. I don't even think I've remembered to breathe until I see the turning into Clos Beaumont and I take a huge gulp of air as I swing into the yard and slam on the brakes.

Cecil is there, barking like crazy.

'*Doucement, doucement*,' I tell him, getting out of the car in bare feet in the wind and rain. 'Steady, lad,' and I bend to pat his head to let him know it's me.

Henri is thundering up and down his field, dipping his head, matted mane flying and then kicking out with both front feet, first one side and then the other.

I run to the French doors where my wellies are upside down on sticks. One of Nick's inventions. He really has turned out to be the Linda Barker of Petit Frère. I hope he and Candy are finally telling each other how they feel, I think quickly as I pull on the boots, grab the big torch from the *chai*, hike up my dress and begin running down through the vines, stumbling and slipping now over the wet clods of earth and stones. Through the first *parcelle* and into the next. The vines seem to be leading me, pushing me back on track as my wellies gather clods of earth, slowing me down, and my breathing gets heavier. The smell from the soil is like nothing I've ever smelled before: a rich mix of nutrients, minerals, vitamins and herbs. I suck it up to keep me going. I can see the lights of the tractor and I pick up speed, trying to push my arms faster and faster, punching through the air in front of me, urging my lagging legs to follow suit.

The wind is whipping my eyes as I'm blinking against the rain. My hair has fallen from its hairpins, and my French pleat is no longer. My lungs are hurting as I run from side to side across the worn path, despite trying to drive myself forward.

I think the rain may actually be easing up, thank God, and the thunderstorm passing. I take a big breath of relief, just as I hear the sound that makes my blood run cold once more. The sound of a tractor's roar and ripping roots.

'*Arrêtez! Arrêtez!* Stop!' I shout, waving my arms, and I'm running towards the big round lights of the tractor. But it isn't stopping. I have to make it stop and I run even closer, throwing myself in front of the next couple of vines into its sights. I look up like I'm staring into the mouth of a hungry tiger, hoping it'll stop and find another prey, but instead this one just keeps rumbling forward.

'Oomph!' Suddenly all the wind is knocked out of me as I'm barged off my feet and clear of the vine, only not by the tractor coming towards me, but by a blow to my side. I'm thrown to the ground with a thud and there's breathing as heavy as mine beside me.

'Isaac? What the hell are you doing? How did you get here?'

'Ran down through the château vines . . .' he pants, standing in front of me, bent over and holding his knees. 'And what do you mean, what the hell am I doing? What the hell are *you* doing? You could get yourself killed!' he suddenly roars at me.

I stagger to my feet, glaring at him, then dodge him and run back in between the vines.

'He's not doing this. He's not ripping up the vines! Not the *tendresse* vines! Did you know about this? Was it all part of the plan?' I shout.

'Emmy,' he grabs hold of both my arms, 'I swear, I knew nothing about this. You have to believe me.' He looks right at me and I know he's telling the truth. Then I shrug him off and start to wave my hands in the air just like I was on that first day trying to get Madame Beaumont's attention to give her back her purse, only this time I fighting for so much more – her history, everything she stands for – and maybe what I do too now, I realise. I don't want these vines to go any more than she does.

'*Arrêtez!*' I shout. 'You're not taking them, you big bully! They belong here! You're not hurting them. Take me first!'

'Oh, for God's sake,' I hear Isaac say and then he's right beside me as he begins to wave and shout too.

'*Arrêtez!*' he yells. 'Stop!'

Suddenly the tractor's engine cuts out and the lights dim. It takes a moment for my eyes to readjust. Then I hear Charlie's voice. He must have come through the château vines too. Why didn't I think of that?

'What on earth are you doing?' he asks evenly, though I can't see him as my eyes are still blinded by the headlights.

'I'm stopping this vandalism!' I shout in his direction.

'These are old vines. They need to go.'

'Yes, they're old. Their yield might be low, but it has so much more character, depth. It's . . . what makes Clos Beaumont a medal-winning wine.' My eyes start to make out his figure beside the tractor with Bernard at the wheel.

'We can recreate it, can't we, Isaac?' Charlie asks smoothly, turning to Isaac, as I do. Now covered in mud splashes, his hair wet and pushed back off his face, Isaac is looking much more like his usual self than he was earlier.

'Actually—' he starts.

'Actually, you can't,' I cut across him. I can't let him take any of the blame for this.

'Emmy—' he tries.

'You can't recreate it, because first, new vines will never give you the character like the wine we've just made. And—'

'Emmy—' Isaac warns again.

'The reason it tastes like it does is because of these vines.' I point to the vines to my right, not yet touched by the tractor, but practically kissing it.

'What are you talking about? Isaac?' Charlie looks at me as if I'm mad.

'Isaac had nothing to do with this wine. I made it,' I announce, and there's a gasp from the wine-makers who have also gathered in the vineyard and are muttering in French in surprise and then, '*Bravo*' rustles in amongst the growing group.

'Hear, hear!' I hear Candy and Nick's voices and they lifts my spirits.

'And the reason I made it is because it's not the claret you asked for. It's not a blend to roll out. It is as individual as Madame Beaumont. It is full of life and vitality. It tells you about the soil it was grown in, the love it's nurtured with. It tells so much more than your supermarket blend, it is a story, a story of a woman's life.'

'Hear, hear!' I hear again, and a sniff or two. And a whoop this time, the loudest from Isaac beside me, clapping.

'That's great and we'll use it in the marketing.' Charlie is now trying to guide me away from the vines by putting his hand in the small of my back again. This time I shake him off. 'Selina is here and I'd really like to get this deal in the bag.'

'But that's the thing, Charlie. There is no deal, because Selina wants you to recreate a good, honest claret. This isn't a good, honest claret. Far from it. It's a unique wine. A breed all of its own.'

'A what?'

The moon suddenly appears from behind the dark clouds, which are rolling off into the distance, and throws a silver sliver across the vines.

'These grapes,' I point. 'They're not part of the blend. That's why Madame Beaumont never conformed to the AOC labelling, because her wine has a hint of something else in it . . . something from her past, which makes it special. These are grapes,' I point again, 'very old *tendresse* grapes. Her wine is a one-off.'

There is a silence around the gathered throng, finally broken by Charlie swearing loudly and then the stomping off back to the château and the metaphorical sound of a medal being stripped from round his neck. Then we watch as the tractor starts up and begins to reverse out of the vines.

Isaac scoops me in his arms.

'I am so proud of you,' he smiles, and kisses me all over again in the silver moonlight, in amongst the vines, who I swear are whispering a sigh of relief, 'for so many reasons. You are a one-off vintage, Emmy Bridges.'

Then we walk back together through the vines. He slips off his jacket and puts it round my shoulders, leaving his arm around me too, and we make our way back through the vines in the silver shard of moonlight, to the farmhouse, euphoric, reckless and neither of us knowing what tomorrow will bring.

'Wait!' I suddenly stop him. 'What about you and Candy?'

'Candy and I . . . she's great but we're just friends. I never . . . I didn't want to fall in love with you. I tried to distract myself. I thought you were falling for Charlie and his charms!' We both manage a little laugh. 'I think Candy's found someone far more deserving of her affections than me.' He smiles and puts his finger to my chin. I smile back as he pulls me closer and kisses me again, making me feel as though the missing piece in the jigsaw of my life has finally been found.

That night, back in Clos Beaumont, on my last night there, I take Isaac by the hand and lead him to join me in my bed, where he kisses every part of my body and tells me time after time how proud he is of me, and this time I follow my instincts, give in to my feelings, and our bodies finally join as one, as the moonlight rises over the vines, and I know this night will stay with me for ever. If only I didn't feel this was goodbye. And finally, our bodies entwined, like the roots of the vines I've come to care for, I fall into the deepest sleep, knowing I'm also falling in love.

Chapter Forty-six

The next morning, although I've hardly slept, I'm awake early. I turn gently to look at Isaac's sleeping face, drinking him in. Fighting the urge to wake him and pick up from where we left off last night, I slide from under the covers. Madame Beaumont is coming home today for a visit and if she feels she can cope they'll let her out. I have to check everything is as organised as it can be.

I pull on my sweatshirt, breathing in Isaac's smell, letting it fill my lungs and make my body feel alive all over again. I wonder how long the smell will stay with me after he's gone. Quickly I push the thought away, putting it into a little box in my head and closing the lid. I'll take it out and think about it later, after today is over.

I creep downstairs and into the newly painted and redesigned living room. Nick worked really hard to get this looking gorgeous. And the lilies are doing a great job of taking away the smell of paint. The heavily embossed wall-paper looks so striking, as does the green wing-back chair by the fire.

I poke my head into the downstairs bedroom. The bed is made up with new linen and again, a bunch of flowers scents the room. As well as a light by the bed, there is a jug and glass. He's thought of everything. I briefly think about him and Candy and feel so pleased for them. Then I remember Gloria last night. Who was that man she was with?

I use the downstairs bathroom and shower with the hand attachment over the bath, holding the end on to the tap to stop it spraying everywhere. It's a knack I've acquired over these past few weeks and I wonder why I ever complained that the one at home was old and useless. It's luxury compared to this.

I make coffee and take one up to Isaac, waking him by gently saying, 'Good morning,' and putting the coffee on the wrought-iron table by the bed.

He opens his eyes sleepily and just for a moment I panic, wondering what his reaction will be. Then, seeing me, he smiles and I know he feels like I do. I break into a smile too, thankful it wasn't all a big mistake. He reaches up, pulls my head to him and kisses me softly, making me dissolve into the covers with him. Then he wraps his arms around me, pulling me in all over again. But thankfully I have the resolve to pull away, or Madame Beaumont will arrive and I'll still be in bed!

'I have to go and check the barrels,' I groan.

Reluctantly, he lets me go. Saying goodbye is going to be one of the hardest things I've ever done, to Isaac and to here. I'm just going to enjoy the time we have together, I think to myself.

'I'll come and help,' he says, sitting up. I take in his smooth chest and rounded shoulders and the tattoo on his shoulder. I reach out and touch it.

'What is it?' I run my finger over it.

'It's a hawk. A Swainson's hawk. A migratory bird,' he pauses. 'California is the Pacific highway for migrating birds, y'know,' he adds, trying to brighten things. 'It's like the superhighway for birds travelling between Alaska and Patagonia.' He looks at the tattoo. 'It gives me wings.' He doesn't look at me but I know what he means. Just like a migratory bird that leaves when the season changes, so is Isaac getting ready to leave. He pulls his knees up and sips his coffee.

'Come on,' he suddenly says, 'we have wine to check.' He tugs at the corner of the bedclothes that I'm sitting on, just like on his first day, but this time I'm the one who laughs.

'Go on then!' I goad him, and suddenly he yanks back the covers playfully and I rush out, shrieking with laughter and excitement, running downstairs or I'll never get out of there.

I put the oven on to warm through yesterday's croissants, go to the back door and open it. It's cold, and I wrap my arms around myself and make my way across the yard, to where Cecil is sleeping in his kennel.

'*Bonjour, Cecil.*' He raises his head and give a deep 'woof' then lumbers to his feet. I go to the shed on the far side of the yard to get his feed. There is a wonderful smell of fruit in the air, coming from the *chai*, and if nothing else I know that I have got Madame Beaumont's wine safe. It may not be worthy of a medal any more, but word'll get around that it's a great vintage. Monsieur and Madame Obels from the shop will be passing it on by now, after our degustation guests were so grateful to them, and Candy's blog is getting loads of hits, so maybe she could sell it online. But I must talk to her about getting some help with the vines, pruning and harvesting.

I feed Cecil and Henri.

'She'll be home today, Henri,' I tell him and pat his neck. Then, seeing the sheep there, I realise it's probably time for them to get to work in the vineyard, keeping down the weeds that are starting to sprout so I open up the gate to let them out. They tumble and bounce off each other, playing follow my leader as I shoo them away from the yard and down into the vineyard. After a while they stop running and jumping over each other and drop their heads to grass that's grown between the vines during the harvest.

I stand and stare as the sun starts to make its way up the sky and that low mist I have come to know weaves its way through the vines on its early morning meander.

It is going to be so hard to say goodbye. I wrap my arms around myself as I stare out over the vines across the valley. My heart squeezes.

Suddenly a kiss is planted on the back of my neck and I lean in to him, breathing him in before turning to face him, still wrapped in his arms.

'Hello,' he smiles down at me.

'Hello,' I smile back.

'Everything OK?'

'Yup, I'm just going to check the barrels but it's all good out here.'

'Look, Emmy, about me going . . .'

'Let's not. Not today.' I can't bear to talk about it now.

'But you could come with me, we could travel together. Please, think about it.' He stares at me with those dark eyes.

I shake my head. I wish we could, with every bit of my body aching to say yes, but I can't. I have to go home.

'I have people that need me.' I turn to go but he holds my elbows.

'What about what you need? Your sister is there. She could look out for your dad. We could visit, maybe even look at getting a season on an English vineyard. I've heard they have them.'

I let out a laugh.

'I have never met anyone like you and I know I never will again. I've finally found what it means to belong. I want to belong to you.' He takes both my hands and I can't speak.

The lid of the box is finally being forced fully open in my head and I really don't want it to. I slam it shut. I don't want to think about it. I swallow and blink back the tears that are threatening to fall.

'I'll have to check the barrels. We'll talk later,' I say through my tight throat, and go to turn and leave quickly before he sees that my eyes are filling again with little pools of salty tears.

'I'm going up to check the vines,' says Isaac. 'See what damage was done last night, see if we can save the ones that did get pulled up.'

I nod. He places a long kiss on my forehead that seems to give me strength, and then puts his hands in his pockets and starts walking through the vines, silhouetted in the early morning mist. Cecil follows him and he leans over and gives him a reassuring pat on the head. I watch the two of them go, then I turn towards the *chai*.

The padlock's swinging free on the barn lock. I must have

forgotten to lock it up last night, what with . . . well, everything that happened, and I realise that at some point I'm going to have to explain myself to Charlie, tell him why I did what I did and hope that it doesn't affect my job at Cadwallader's. He won't promote me now, but I do still need my job. And it's not like I don't know about wine now.

I can smell the fruit really strongly now I'm by the door. It's never smelled like this before. I go to pull the door back. Oh God, what if one of the barrels has popped a cork? I can hear it, smell it. It sounds like a waterfall. I yank open the door and flick on the light. It crackles, spits and fuses with a bang. I grab the big torch but I don't need it to know what's happened. The *chai* is awash, like a lake of deep red blood. I run the torch along the barrels. Every single one of them is spewing out its juice. It's like a car crash that's already happened.

'Noooooo!' I run to turn off the taps but there's so much liquid I can't get to them. I grab at the first ones I can see, turning them but it's too late: the barrels are practically empty. I slosh through the wine until I get to the double doors at the back of the *chai* and pull back the stiff bolt. I push open the double doors and watch as the wine spills, tumbles, pours over the stones like a river making its way back to the sea where it belongs.

'Isaac!' I scream, but Isaac is too far away to hear me.

I try to run to each of the barrels, slipping and sliding, but it's too late, most of the barrels are all but empty now. It's all gone . . . all the wine is gone. How can this have happened? The floor is now ankle-deep in rich, fabulous-smelling red wine. None of it ever going to be drunk.

I hold my head and fall to my knees. 'It's gone, gone,' I say quietly, and tears pour down my face. I couldn't save it. I feel utterly, utterly drained. As empty as one of the barrels. I couldn't do anything to stop it.

Chapter Forty-seven

'You'll catch your death down there.' I snap my head up. My racking sobs slow to hiccups. Charlie is standing in the doorway, holding a bag.

'Oh God, Charlie! Thank goodness! Look what's happened. It can't have been an accident. Every single one of the barrels has had its taps opened. I can't believe someone would do this. It's all gone.' I stagger to my feet, grateful for the help.

'So I see.' He looks around. 'A shame . . . it smells,' he takes a deep breath, 'really good.'

'I don't know what to do! Madame Beaumont will be home any time now.'

'Good,' he nods.

'Good? What's good about any of this?' I turn around holding my hands open to indicate the devastation around me, like Noah in the flood.

'Well, let's be honest, the wine couldn't be sold now. It's got a dodgy grape in it.'

'But that's what made it special, don't you see?' I start to frown.

'Not if you want to run a business.' He looks round idly.

I stare at him. His eyes are dark now, like stormy waters.

The cogs in my mind are slowly whirring and then picking up speed.

'I brought the rest of your things from the *gîte*. Suits, shoes, that kind of thing.' He looks in the carrier bag and then holds it out to me. 'Oh, and I've booked you a flight home. No need for you to stay on now. Featherstone's doesn't require your services.' He holds out an envelope with the other hand. I stare at it and then slowly back at him. He's sending me home.

'You're sacking me?' I say, stunned, and then I begin to panic. Dad will lose the house for sure now. What am I going to do? 'I did what I thought was best . . . for everyone. You can't sack me for that! I need this job. My dad will lose his home.'

'Sacking? Call it what you like, I think it's best you go. Don't want this causing too much of a fuss with the others. The flight's for this afternoon. I've told Trevor back at Cadwallader's.'

'This was my last chance. My last chance to get something right,' I manage to croak.

'Well, maybe then you should have done as you were told. Maybe you're not in the right line of work. Maybe you should look for a change of direction.'

'Oh, I was in exactly the right line of work. I had finally found something I was really good at. Not sitting at a desk, reading and learning scripts or pushing up sales figures. But I was good at this. This is real.' I hold my hands out to the wine. 'This was a really good vintage. A classic, unique. It didn't just stand in line with the other supermarket wines. It stood out. It said, "Look at me I'm special."'

'Well, maybe it should have just stood in line with the others and it might still have had a job.' He's holding out the bag and envelope again when reality hits me like a surfer being swept off her feet by a massive wave, suddenly everything going fuzzy like the drowning feeling I felt in the tank. And then all becomes clear.

'You . . . did . . . this . . .' I say really slowly, my eyes widening with each syllable.

'I didn't exactly do it,' Charlie smiles. 'Just between you and me. But I did get someone to do it.'

'Who?'

'My staff are very loyal and well rewarded for their efforts.'

'Was it Isaac?' My head spins and dips.

Charlie throws his head back and laughs. 'Now, that would be a turn-up for the books, if your boyfriend had been the one. He doesn't have a loyal bone in his body. He'll do whatever he's paid to do, go wherever he's paid to go. That's a soul up for hire, if ever I saw one.'

Suddenly, Isaac appears behind Charlie.

'Say that again,' he growls.

Charlie turns to look at him. 'I said you're a soul for hire. You're not interested in how the wine tastes, you just want your cheque. You want the next gig, the bigger wine house. You're as mercenary as I am.'

Isaac looks around horrified at the wine lake in the *chai* and I know in my heart it wasn't his work. It came to mean as much to him as it did to me.

'Why? Why would you do this?' I shake my head, incredulously.

Charlie shrugs. 'Well, if I can't run the vineyard my way,

Madame Beaumont will have no choice but to sell it to me now. She won't want the château taking it over, so really, I'm her guardian angel. At least this way, I may still have a job for you next season, and Selina is still happy for us to get into bed together,' he says to Isaac.

'From what I've heard, that happened a long time ago.' Isaac's face darkens further.

'Well, I couldn't very well wait for Miss Prim-and-Proper here, could I? Although by the looks of it you've succeeded where I've failed.' Charlie grins grotesquely and I have no idea what I ever found attractive about him.

Blood rages through my body but before I have time to wade over to Charlie and put my knee exactly where it will hurt, Isaac pulls back his arm as far as it will go, makes a fist and thrusts it right on to Charlie's cheek, sending him, the bag of my possessions and the envelope with the flight details in it flying backwards into the calf-deep wine. Charlie lands with an almighty splash and an 'oomph'. The suits and shoes scatter and the envelope floats off towards the door with the wasted wine.

'And while you're at it, have this.' Isaac pulls out his own envelope from his jacket pocket and drops it on top of Charlie, writhing about in the wine to right himself.

Charlie staggers to his feet, grabbing the envelope with the bonus in it, pulls back his big arm and throws a punch back at Isaac, landing it on Isaac's cheek.

'Never underestimate a rugby boy,' Charlie smiles, panting for breath, as Isaac staggers back.

'Isaac!' I scream.

'And never underestimate how much I hate you and what

you've done here!' Isaac launches himself at Charlie, grabbing him round the neck. They both fall back into the wine, flaying and throwing punches.

'Stop it, both of you!' I shout. Cecil starts to bark. 'Stop it!' But the two are wrestling around in what looks like a blood bath, gasping for air, throwing punches that barely come close to their target. They stagger to stand and then send each other flying all over again.

'Stop!' I shout.

Suddenly a shadow appears beside me and I turn, desperately hoping help is at hand, but my mouth just waggles open and shut.

'Madame Beaumont?' I finally manage to say.

Chapter Forty-eight

She is leaning heavily on a crutch. She's smaller and paler than when she was last stood here. But when she was last here, she had a vineyard, a harvest to come in and a vintage to sell.

Now there is just devastation all around her.

Charlie and Isaac stagger to their feet, dripping red wine from their hair, hands and faces. Isaac pushes his hair back and a slick of wine flies off it. His shirt and T-shirt are clinging to his chest and flat stomach. He catches his breath.

Charlie, on the other hand, is panting. But he attempts one of his killer smiles, and sticks out his hand.

'Madame Beaumont, Charlie Featherstone, Featherstone's Wines. Just . . . um,' he barely misses a beat, 'just finding out what's gone on here. Terrible, just terrible.' He shakes his head and extends his hand further towards Madame Beaumont. Madame Beaumont does not shake his hand or respond.

She turns slowly to me.

'Walk with me,' she instructs and, leaning heavily on a stick, starts to limp towards the vines and to Henri's gate where he is neighing and stomping. I follow, feeling like a child trailing off to the headmaster's office.

When we reach Henri's gate and he has sniffed her hands and pushed at her and nudged her and greeted her like a soldier returning from war, I try to steady him but she seems unfazed.

'Madame Beaumont. I'm so sorry. I really . . . you see, last night, the wine won a medal and then I saw the tractor in the vines and well . . .'

She puts up her free hand, the other still holding tightly to the stick she's leaning on.

'Get me a chair,' she says, and I run to get the deckchair Dad sat in. I put it down in Dad's spot, overlooking the vines and she lets me help her into it and put her crutch down by her side.

'Now, start from the beginning.'

And I take a deep breath and do just that.

In the yard behind me, an ambulance and its driver wait, as do Charlie and Isaac.

'. . . The pickers didn't show up. Had been paid more to go to the château . . . And then Candy stood on a wasp and had an allergic reaction.'

She listens and nods as I pour out the events of the last few weeks.

'. . . And then I didn't use the yeast, I went with the wild yeast . . .'

I turn and see the Featherstone's van pull into the yard, and Gloria, Nick and Candy get out, carrying flowers and wine. I turn back to Madame Beaumont.

'. . . And if he hadn't come back I'd have drowned . . .'

She says nothing. Just listens. When I finish telling her what just happened in the *chai*, she nods slowly.

'I'm so sorry.' I drop my head and she puts her hand on it.

'You did your best and no one can ask for more. *Merci, Emmy.*'

I look up at her, but can't smile.

'Now, it looks like you've been working hard on the house too. Show me . . .'

I help her with her stick, just hoping she's going to be able to manage the steps.

I show her the log pile, ready so that she'll have plenty of wood. The meals in the freezer, the living room – or *salon*, she corrects me – and the bedroom. She declines to go upstairs but instead comes and sits in her chair and the cat jumps on to her lap.

'And Isaac, your good friend, he helped with all this?'

I nod.

'He was repairing the vines when Charlie arrived.'

'My father planted those vines. He grafted them from a few surviving plants. Told my mother to look after them until he returned to be with her. But . . . he never came. He was killed on his return to Germany, a stray unexploded bomb. The village, of course, shunned my mother once they discovered she was pregnant, out of wedlock and by a German soldier. But my family were determined I would always be proud of who I was. Individual. Just like the vines have survived and thrived, so have I.' She turns to me. 'Please, thank your friend for saving them.'

'About that . . . see . . .' I look out to the yard. Charlie's car has gone and Isaac is nowhere to be seen. The ambulance men have finished their glasses of wine that Candy has offered them and are beginning to look at their watches. I see her offer to top them up, pacifying them, working her charm.

Madame Beaumont raises her eyebrows and looks at me.

'He's not my friend. Never was. Well, not then, anyway. He was working for Charlie, they wanted . . . well . . . an in with you.'

'I see. Not your close friend?' She nods sagely, looking down at her hands in her lap.

I shake my head then she looks straight back at me.

'But you love him now, *non*?'

I nod and tears start to slide down my face. And I wish with all my heart I could go with him, wherever that may be, although it sure as hell won't be the big wine house in Australia now, for which Charlie was giving him a reference.

'Then you should follow your heart. Be with him.'

'I can't. I have to go home. I have to look after my dad. He just hasn't coped since Mum died.' It's my turn to look down.

'Maybe . . . maybe now, it is you who can't move on,' she says quietly.

My head snaps up again and I wipe my nose.

'I'll tell the ambulance men to go,' I say, distracting myself from what may well be the painful truth, and start towards the door. Of course I miss my mum, but perhaps Madame Beaumont is right – perhaps it's me that hasn't been able to move on. 'I'll tell them that you're happy.'

'You have done wonders here. The loss of the wine wasn't your fault. That was just malicious. There will be next year. It looks like new life has been breathed into the place.'

I smile, pleased that I've at least managed to make her home nice for her.

'But actually, I'm afraid I don't feel too well. I would like to be taken back to the rehabilitation unit now,' Madame Beaumont announces, and attempts to rise from her chair.

'You can't go. Who will look after this place? The vines?'

'I will have to sell it. I cannot run it on my own. And without this year's vintage I cannot afford to pay for help.' She dips her head.

'But there must be something we can do! Madame Beaumont, you are the strongest person I have ever met. You can't walk away now.'

'We cannot stop time. I'm getting old. My bones are brittle. I don't have the same . . . confidence. We can only make the most of the time we have here. Take opportunities when they come and don't let the good ones get away.' I see a glimmer of the old twinkle in her eyes. 'In life there is a time to arrive and a time to leave, *chérie*.' She puts a bony hand to my cheek and I feel finally defeated, beaten.

'Now then, please tell the ambulance driver I would like to leave. Please, stay until the sale is agreed, for Henri and Cecil.'

'It's the very least I can do.'

'I will talk to Monsieur Lavigne at the château,' she says, resigned.

Chapter Forty-nine

'I'll come and see you, tomorrow,' I shout after the ambulance, and realise I'll have to catch the train from town now that the van will be out of bounds to me.

'I can't believe she went back,' Candy wails.

'Come on, let's all have a drink,' I say, and guide them all into the kitchen.

Isaac appears from the *chai* where he's been sweeping and hosing out the spilled wine. He props the broom against the door frame, and just for a moment I allow myself the little fantasy that he and I really could work together.

My phone rings.

'Hi, Dad.' I know I sound weary, though when he phoned a few hours ago I was the happiest woman on the planet.

'So, how did it go, love?' he asks expectantly. 'Did you win? Did you get the job?'

I take a deep breath. 'No. Dad, I didn't, I didn't get it. I messed up, I'm afraid, Dad. I'm so sorry.'

'You didn't get it?' he pauses. 'Oh, I'm sorry, love.' He pauses again. Then, putting in huge amounts of effort to be positive, he says, 'Well, no worries. Something'll turn up.' There's a tiny crack in his voice.

'No, Dad, I just don't think it will. I'm so sorry. We're going to lose the house, aren't we?'

'Really, love, don't worry. We'll just carry on as we always have. Getting by. Don't you worry. Your home is here with me, as long as we can keep it. We'll be fine, especially now I'll be working at the DIY superstore,' he tries to say brightly.

'I feel I've let you down,' I say. 'There's no way we can pay off the arrears. We're going to lose it, Dad!'

'You haven't let me down, love. I'm gutted for you not getting the job. But if anything, these weeks with you away have done me a favour. It was about time I got off my backside and out into the world again. We'll cope,' he says. 'In fact, love, I do have an idea . . .'

When he's told me I end the call, dropping my hand with the phone in it by my side.

'Everything all right?' Isaac comes to join me and slides an arm around my shoulders.

'My dad. He wants to put the house on the market, move on,' I say stunned. 'Downsize.'

'That's great news.'

'Says he's realised it's too big for him and that I won't want to be there for ever. He's looked at sheltered accommodation in town, close to the DIY store where he's got a job.'

'That's brilliant! You don't need to stay where you are for him any more. You're free to finally spread your wings.'

'Is it? Maybe a few hours ago, when there was a chance of me packing a rucksack and coming with you. But that can't happen now, can it?' I look at him and slowly he shakes his head.

'Charlie'll withdraw his reference. That'll tell the wine houses everything they need to know.'

'What will you do?' I want to wail, but don't.

He shrugs. 'Start phoning round, see if there's anything going. Go back and stay on some friends' sofas in California. I can phone you when I find something. You could join me.'

'We both know that's not going to work.' The tears spill down my cheeks.

We walk slowly back to the kitchen, our heads tipped and touching each other's. Gloria has the wine open and glasses poured, and hands one to each of us, feeling for us.

'Well, at least you two have finally got together, that's some good news,' I say, trying to lift our spirits as Candy snuggles into Nick.

'Who'd've thought? I didn't realise he was interested in me . . . or into any girls, actually,' Candy giggles.

'Oh, Candy, Nick's been in love with you since we got here,' I say fondly but exasperated.

'What?' She sits up straight and gapes at Nick. 'And you never let on? I let you undo my bra when I was sunburned and told you how I felt about . . . everything!'

'There never seemed to be the right time to tell you.' Nick holds out his palms.

'Well!' Candy harrumphs and turns away from him.

There's an uncomfortable silence.

'So what will you do now?' Gloria asks me.

'Go back home. Look for another job, I suppose. Look for a room to rent. Stay with my sister for while, maybe.' It's a long way from what I've always dreamed of.

'Isaac?' Gloria has pain in her eyes.

'Same. Back to where I started and see if I can pick up some work. It won't be as a wine-maker, though, not if Charlie's done his work well, which I'm sure he will have.' Isaac stretches out his hand, red and painful from landing a punch on Charlie.

'And there's no way either of you can stay on here?'

I shake my head. 'Madame Beaumont has to sell this place. She needs to pay for somewhere to live. Probably in town would be best, and with a lift. A retirement block.'

'Overlooking the river,' Nick adds dreamily.

'What about you, Nick? Are you looking forward to going back to Featherstone's?'

'Actually, I've been thinking about starting up my own business. Buying and selling French *brocante*. Thought I'd come over and do a buying trip. Do up a few pieces and sell them on eBay. Candy said she'd help me.'

Candy harrumphs again and folds her arms and crosses her legs.

'Looks like the team leader's job comes down to you two then?' I smile at Candy and Gloria. I'm happy for both of them.

'Oh, I'm not going back to England,' Gloria says matter-of-factly. 'Well, I am just for a while and then I'll be coming back out here.'

'What?' we all say together.

'Has this got something to do with that man you were with at the wine medal ceremony?'

She nods and can't hold in her news any more. She's smiling like she's about to burst.

'There's a café down by the river. Le Phénix. It's been

closed after a fire. But it's been repainted. It's only small. And, well, Jeff introduced me to the owner.' She pauses. 'I'm signing for the lease. Going to have my own café bar. I'll do a set menu every day, that kind of thing . . .' She runs out of breath and we all shriek and hug her.

'Glasses, quick!' Candy shrieks, and we each grab a glass.

'To the Phoenix!'

And then Nick starts to sing, 'From the ashes of disaster grow the roses of success...' and we all join in, apart from Isaac, who looks completely baffled.

'Is that like an English traditional song?'

'Sort of . . . it's from *Chitty Chitty Bang Bang*,' and we all sing it again and then sit down and sip our wine.

'If only there had been wine in the cellar,' Candy says, and we all nod and agree.

'What wine in the cellar?' asks Isaac.

'Like it said in the letter.' Candy stands and goes to get it from behind the clock that is still working and ringing the hour, twice every hour.

She shows it to Isaac. He reads it, then puts it down.

'Show me.'

'It's no good, it's not there. We looked everywhere,' Candy says.

'Show me,' he repeats, and we all traipse back down to the empty cellar holding our wine glasses.

Isaac looks around. Then runs his hand over the brick wall, this way and then that, putting his fingers into the mortar between the bricks. Nodding briefly, he then disappears up the wooden stairs again. We look at each other, shrug and go to follow, but he's coming back down with what looks like the sledgehammer from the *chai*.

'Isaac, dear God! What are you doing?'

'I may not have seen *Chitty Chitty Bang Bang*, but I have seen *The Secret of Santa Vittoria*, with Anthony Quinn, which evidently you guys never have. Part of my childhood, watching that video, with my new dad. And where my love of wine started.' He looks at me with a smile. 'Now,' he nods. 'Stand back.'

And with that he swings the sledgehammer back and whacks it into the stone wall.

'Isaac!' I cry as he does it again and the wall starts to crumble and fall. 'Have you gone mad?'

Chapter Fifty

'It was Isaac . . .' Candy's explaining.

We're all standing round Madame Beaumont, who is sitting in a chair in the day room of the convalescent home, looking out on the garden and seeming much better.

'Well, it was you really, Candy,' I interrupt.

'Wait, wait, what are you talking about? One at a time. Emmy, slow down and explain what has happened now,' Madame Beaumont instructs.

We all stop talking and I reach into my bag and pull out the bottle I have carried all the way here on the train.

'This . . .' I announce, handing the dusty bottle to her. She reaches out with shaking hands for her small, wire-framed glasses from the side table. She puts them on her nose and they slip this way and that. She reads the label, slowly. Then she looks at me.

'*C'est vrai?*' Her voice cracks, her eyes fill with tears.

I nod, lots of tiny little nods and can barely contain myself.

'Candy looked it up online. A bottle like this from 1945 will fetch at least five hundred pounds at auction.'

Madame Beaumont smiles a watery smile.

'But where did you find it?'

'In the cellar,' I tell her, enjoying watching her run her hand over the faded label and the wax covering the cork. 'It had been bricked over, to keep it safe for your mother.'

'This,' she points to the writing on the label, 'this is the best news of all.'

I bite my bottom lip. 'I know.'

'*AOC Appellation Clos Beaumont*,' she reads through misty eyes, the last words catching in her throat. 'The vineyard had its own appellation.'

'What is that? I've never understood it.' Candy screws up her nose.

'It means that the vineyard has its own recipe for wine. It's not ruled by the same regulations as Petit Frère or Saint Enrique. Clos Beaumont has the right to call itself an AOC wine, *Appellation d'Origine Contrôlée*.'

'It's a way . . .' Isaac starts, and then laughs and holds out a hand to me to carry on.

'It's a way of identifying the geographical origin of the wine, the quality and style of the wine,' I tell Candy. Then sigh. 'In other words, Madame Beaumont's doesn't have to be a *Vin de France* any more. It's a unique, recognised wine and she can get more money for it.'

'The appellation must have been lost after the war. My family . . . there were a lot of people who shunned them. They wanted just to live peacefully but with dignity. Maybe hanging on to the appellation was a fight too far.'

'But now we know. It's here and next year's vintage will be able to use this appellation. You won't have to move after all.' I beam, wishing I could hug her.

'I'm afraid five hundred euros or pounds won't be able to

keep me at the vineyard.' Madame Beaumont slips off her glasses and puts them back on the table.

Isaac nudges me.

'Oh, yes, of course.' I'm so caught up in the excitement I'm missing bits out. 'Madame Beaumont, there isn't just one bottle we found behind the bricked-up cellar. There were loads of bottles. It was the whole year's vintage, in fact.'

There is silence while we allow Madame Beaumont to digest the information and then, looking up from her chair in the sunny lounge, she says to me, 'I think I would like to see those bottles for myself. Tell the nurse I want to discharge myself. I will go with my friends. I have business to attend to.'

The nurses look as if they're breathing a sigh of relief and have her belongings packed in no time and produce forms for her to sign.

Back at Clos Beaumont, Madame Beaumont insists on coming down to the cellar. There are broken bricks and dust everywhere. A far cry from the neat and tidy home I wanted her to come back to. But she doesn't seem to care.

Leaning heavily on Isaac and her stick, she picks her way over to the crates of wine behind the smashed-through wall, holding on to crumbling bits of red rubble for support in the dim cellar, lit by a single bare bulb hanging from a long wire.

She reaches down and picks up one of the bottles. It's covered in thick dust, old and new.

'Here, I say,' and hand her one of her tea towels that I'm carrying.

She reaches into her pocket and pulls out the small wire glasses and reads the label all over again. Then, looking round the small annexed part of the cellar as if breathing in the fact her father was the last one here before today, she nods, sniffs and holds out a bottle for me to carry.

'We will drink it when we have something to celebrate,' she says to me. Frankly I'd've thought discovering you had thousands of pounds worth of wine in your cellar was a good enough reason to celebrate. On the other hand, I'm not sure I'd be able to drink a bottle of wine that could pay my mortgage this month.

'What about the vines, how are they?' she asks as Isaac guides her away from the bottles.

'Well, we lost a couple to the tractor. Not the *tendresse* ones,' he says.

'Isaac has replanted them and we're keeping a close eye on them, but . . .' I tell her.

'They are old, like me.'

'In that case I'm sure they'll keep fighting,' I reassure her with a smile.

She puts out her hand for Isaac to help her again and stiffly makes her way back over towards the stairs, which she insists on climbing by sitting on one and going up on her bottom, backwards. I watch her slowly and stiffly make her way up them, wincing with every step.

Back in the kitchen, Monsieur Lavigne from the château is there, holding flowers and a bottle out to Madame Beaumont.

'Madame Beaumont, we are all so pleased to have you home. I hope it's for good now.'

'Really? I thought you wanted to buy my vineyard when you thought I couldn't manage it any more,' she says, not accepting the extended bouquet of flowers.

'I just wanted to help you out. After all, we have been neighbours for years, as our families were before us.'

'Here,' she points to the bottle of wine that I'm carrying and I show it to him. He reads the label, strokes the bottle and is practically salivating and grinning.

'This is fantastic news!' he beams.

'It is. My wine is worth a lot more as a result of it. As is my vineyard,' Madame Beaumont tells him.

'Of course,' he agrees.

'But what is more important is that my family's name will be remembered around here. This is my father's legacy. I can die knowing it wasn't all for nothing.'

Monsieur Lavigne is not smiling now.

'From now on, *monsieur*, I'd be grateful if you'd keep your spraying away from my vines. Respect them as I respect yours.'

He nods.

'And then there's the medal.' I step forward. 'Now that the vineyard has official status, perhaps the judges would like to reconsider their decision. It's a worthy winner, with its own appellation.'

Monsieur Lavigne smiles and nods. 'Of course. This is very good news for the area.'

'And for me and my family name,' Madame Beaumont adds, leaning on her stick.

'But it is too much work for you. I want you to know we will respect the appellation and your family name. And of course, there will be a new price to reflect this development.'

'Some things are worth more than high profit margins,'

she says crisply, and makes for her chair by the wood burner, which is burning merrily. Isaac guides her into her seat.

'Thank you, Monsieur Lavigne,' Madame Beaumont says as she sits. 'I will be in touch when my affairs are settled.' She dismisses him and he nods, smiles and turns to leave but then turns back to Isaac.

'Isaac, may I speak with you?'

'Sure.' He looks to me, I nod that he should go and he follows Monsieur Lavigne out into the yard.

'Now I will message my solicitor and tell him to meet me here. May I?' Madame Beaumont picks up my phone. I nod and she starts tapping away like a teenager.

'I'm glad you're pulling out of the sale. I can't imagine you living anywhere else.' I smile warmly.

'Oh, I'm not going to live at Clos Beaumont but I am pulling out of the sale.' She stops typing and looks at me over her glasses.

'What?' I'm confused.

'I want you to live here,' she says matter-of-factly.

'I can't buy this place and I have to go home.'

'How is your father?' she asks over her glasses.

'Actually he's good, really good. He wants to sell the house,' I tell her. 'My sister is settled nearby, too.'

'That's good. Then your father is ready to move on. The question is, are you? What's to stop you living here, caring for the vines? It looks like this place is your home too now. You and your good friend. He may look a mess, and need to learn some manners, but he is trustworthy. He has shown that.'

'But, but . . . I couldn't buy this place?'

'I'm not asking you to buy it. Think about it. I cannot stay here. But I do not want to sell to Mr Featherstone or the château.'

Outside Isaac is smiling and shaking Monsieur Lavigne warmly by the hand.

Chapter Fifty-one

Crisp, winter sunshine is pouring in through the glass panes in the French doors. Everything seems to be happening so quickly. Isaac has made himself scarce walking Cecil up to the damaged vines.

The document is on the table. The solicitor does up his briefcase and shakes Madame Beaumont by the hand. She insists on standing to see him out.

'So you see, there it is. I am going to move into one of the retirement properties by the river. I will have views of the vines every day, but I cannot work them any more. I want you to have this place. Rent it from me for a . . . how do you say? . . . a peppercorn rent, until it starts to make money, and when you are ready you can buy it. It's all written down. No one will be able to take it from you, even if I die.'

'But . . .' I don't know what to say.

'Say yes. Or perhaps you'd rather move home and go back to your old job in the call centre?'

Suddenly the thought fills me with dread.

This could be everything I've dreamed of. I'm not an office worker or a salesperson. That's Candy, not me. But I think I could be good at this. And if Isaac and I were to work at it together . . . Is it really possible?

I need some time to think and I go out to the vines where Isaac is walking back into the yard, smiling and sending text messages. It is a stunning winter afternoon. The sun is low and bright in the sky.

'Great news!' he beams, and I can't help but beam back.

'I know!' I'm holding in my excitement but I think I may explode at any moment.

'Monsieur Lavigne, he's offered me a job. Wants me to start straight away,' he practically yells with excitement.

'What? That's fantastic!' I join in.

'He loved the wine and even though I told him you made it, he's offered me a wine-making job.'

'What, here at the château?' I can't believe it: how perfect!

'No, he has vineyards all over the world. He has one in South Africa. His wine man has let him down. Wants me to start straight away. Now. South Africa, Emmy!'

'Oh, right.' I try to sound happy, I really do.

'Wooohooo!' He throws his hands in the air and then hugs me and picks me up and swings me round.

'Come with me, Emmy! Come away with me. It's gonna be fantastic.'

I smile but this time it's me that has the watery smile and then I look away so he can't see the tears and shake my head.

'I can't do that.' I hold my hand to my tingling nose.

'What? Why? Why can't you? Even you said your dad wants to sell the house now.'

'I need to make a home of my own,' I say, despite my throat squeezing and getting tighter and tighter. 'I don't want to just keep avoiding making a life for myself. I have to find my own place in the world, and I think that might be here,' I look out over the valley in front of me and let its beauty wash over me all over again, 'with Cecil and Henri and the sheep.'

He looks at me crestfallen.

'And your place is wherever the next job is. You're a travelling wine man.' I feel the hot tears rolling down my face. 'Look, this is everything you wanted.'

His phone beeps into life. He looks at it.

'He's sending a car from the château, now, to take me back to the *gîte* and pack,' he says, dazed. 'Then I'll be on my way. He wants me out there as soon as possible. There's a plane in a few hours.'

'This is your world, your life. You have to go.'

'We could make it work.' He holds my face in his hands. 'Long-distance relationships do work.'

I shake my head and now the tears are flowing freely.

'It won't, and I won't ask you to give it up. It's what you live for, to be free of any roots. But me, I need to start putting down some of my own, not getting choked by those of the past. I can't live waiting to start my life in the future, wondering if there's something better round the corner, waiting for you to come home. I need to live for the now and make every day count.'

He is holding my face, tears are escaping and sliding down his cheeks. There is nothing more to be said. He must go his way and I must stay, we both know that. He pulls me towards him and kisses the top of my head over and over. Then he draws back and pulls off one of the leather bracelets from around his wrist and ties it on mine. We both laugh through our tears.

'Never, ever, take it off. Promise me,' he says hoarsely.

'I won't. Ever.'

'You are going to be a fantastic wine-maker, Emmy Bridges. I'm going to read about you. One of the new wave of women making wine with love and nurturing. "The Tinker Bells of French wine-making" they're calling them in the press, making Old World French wines fantastically.'

'And you are to be a top wine-maker in a top New World winery, Isaac.' Then I drop my head. 'I'm just not sure I can do this on my own.'

'But you did it. And what's more, you did it your way. You followed your instincts and you must do that now.'

There is a honk of a horn as I turn. A silver Mercedes turns into the yard.

'That's for me. It'll take me back to the *gîte* and then to the airport. I'm leaving now, Emmy. You could still come . . . be impetuous.'

I sniff and shake my head.

'You could ask me to stay,' he says quietly.

I shake my head again.

'I couldn't do that. I couldn't ask you to give up everything you've dreamed of. You have to want it for you. Besides, we'd be a nightmare together. You'd want to bring in all your modern wine-making techniques.' I try to laugh through the tears.

The driver beeps again.

'Go! You have to go!'

Isaac takes my face and kisses me like I've never been kissed before. Then he turns and runs to the car without looking round, gets in and the car spins out of the yard and off down the lane.

Madame Beaumont is there behind me, holding the bottle.

'Put the table and chairs over there, where I can see the vines,' she says, and I make big sweeping arm movements and wipe away the tears, then move the table and two chairs.

'Bring another,' she says, pointing to a chair.

'Oh, Isaac's gone,' I say through my tight throat. 'He, erm, Monsieur Lavigne offered him a job in South Africa,' I say. 'It's a great opportunity for him to be part of a big cooperation.

'Yes, bring the chair anyway,' she nods. Then with her gnarled fingers she starts to open the wine before handing it to me to pull the cork. Henri's head is hanging contentedly over the gate and Cecil lies down with an 'oomph' just beside us.

The wine is poured into three glasses as she insists, even though I tell her again that Isaac's gone. And then I sit and look out at the vines.

'To new beginnings.' Madame Beaumont raises her glass to the vines and then to me. Then she sits back and sips, her face beaming with pride and pleasure.

'So you'll stay? You'll take over, look after them?'

'Yes.' I am crying and smiling all at the same time. 'I'll stay. I'm ready. I know my mum is with me wherever I am, not just in that house. I'm going to tell Dad to go ahead and sell it. It's time we both spread our wings.'

'And now a family of your own to look after.' She looks at the vines.

'I think I started putting down my roots here some time ago. But it'll just be me. I'll take over the vineyard,' I say.

Madame Beaumont says nothing, then: 'Just wait.' She continues to look out over the vines, her glass held to her chest. 'Sometimes the naughtiest and wildest of grapes take a while to understand what they need to do next.'

I frown and she sips her wine, closing her eyes with absolute contentment. I follow her and look out too, imagining my dad and sister and my best friend, Layla, coming to visit next summer. Who knows, maybe Isaac will drop by on his way again someday? I shut my eyes and let the winter sun warm my face.

'Of course, you could turn that big barn into a new winery. And there would have to be new tanks and a destemmer crusher. And then there's the yeast. We'd need proper cooling systems,' I can hear him saying. 'Emmy? Emmy?'

My eyes spring open and I turn round. Isaac is standing there. I look for a silver Mercedes.

'He's gone. Got him to drop me off at the end of the drive. Realised it's time I stopped running and put down some roots too . . . so, I'm not asking if you'll have me, I'm telling you, I've decided to stay.'

I jump up and run at him, wrapping my arms round his, his head burying in my neck, entwined, like we're putting down roots together.

Madame Beaumont is smiling to herself.

'Like all good wine, sometimes the most unlikely of grapes can make the most characterful wines together.' Madame Beaumont is talking to her vines as if telling the children about their new family. Then she turns to Isaac and me.

'That's not to say there won't be a few explosive chemical reactions along the way. Old methods and new ones. But the harder you work, the deeper your roots will go and the more rewarding and colourful the taste will be.'

She laughs to herself and Isaac reaches out to the table and picks up a glass. I do too, but neither of us is letting go of the other now.

'To a classic vintage, individual in every way,' Madame Beaumont says, and we all raise our glasses, Isaac to me, me to Madame Beaumont and Madame Beaumont to the vines, and Cecil stands up and joins in with a 'whoo, whoo, whooo', too.

Epilogue

I have new boots just for the occasion, and a new spade, with a pink ribbon round it. A present from my dad when he arrived yesterday with Jody and the boys. Dad stopped off in town to buy it. He's really starting to find his way around, he's been out so many times now.

'OK? Ready?' Isaac slips an arm round me and we all begin to walk out of the yard and up the lane, towards the new *parcelle* of land that now belongs to Clos Beaumont after the former owners decided to retire, and we were given first refusal. We've called this *parcelle* 'Dad's Lot', because Dad put up the money for it after selling the house.

Just as we're about to leave, a white van pulls into the busy car park and Cecil feels it's his duty to get up and 'woof'. It's a British van and down the side of it, in purple writing is 'French Affairs'. The door opens and out jumps Candy from the driver's seat, and Nick from the passenger's. 'It's not like my old soft top,' she says, and I shriek and hug them both.

'You made it!'

'You don't think we'd let you mark today without us being here too, do you?' Nick says, smiling.

'We were on a buying trip for antiques for Nick's new shop.' Candy points to the van.

'Or some stuff we bought second-hand in France and fancied up!' we all say together, and laugh.

'We wouldn't have missed it for the world. Besides, I'm writing a piece for *Wine Magazine* all about it, and on my blog, of course. Who'd've thought it would have got me so much feature writing work?'

'OK, now I'm ready.' I smile at Isaac, and we make our way up the lane in the glorious spring sunshine, looking out over the pruned vines. The buds are just starting to burst with green leaves.

'Here we go again. A new vintage,' I say to Isaac as we walk arm in arm. It's been a busy winter, some changes, a blend of old and new. We bought new tanks and a new destemmer crusher, but we've agreed to stick with the wild yeasts and the original vines. But we've taken cuttings and are growing new ones from the old. Isaac and I have spent the winter pruning, putting in new trellis systems, wires along the ground that we will lift on to wooden stakes as the vines start to grow, to help the grapes grow off the ground. Easier for picking, too.

At the entrance to the new vineyard, everyone is there. Monsieur le Maire, Monsieur Lavigne and Bernard, Jeff and Gloria, the Obels, and our second home owners who have already booked to help with the grape harvest again. Cecil is standing beside Isaac and in the distance I can see Madame Beaumont's black and white cat inquisitively following up the road. Henri is there, too, lifting his head and sniffing the air in the new vineyard. Colette is trying out her English from her new English classes on Dad, who is there with his new friend from the DIY store, Shirley. She helped him pick out the colour scheme for his new flat, apparently. Jody is there with the boys, whom Jeff is chasing around in the newly ploughed field. Mr and Mrs Featherstone are there, on their own. Charlie is away, exploring new business opportunities, Mr Featherstone tells me, whatever that might mean. But Mr Featherstone is back at the wheel of Featherstone's Wines, with Lena by his side. He's downsized, only taking small, exclusive artisan vineyards on.

'*Bienvenue, tout le monde*,' says the mayor.

'Wait!' I put up a hand. 'Madame Beaumont?' I look around and down the road and then I see her, following us up the hill, on her new red mobility buggy, filming everything on her new iPad, and I smile with relief.

'OK, we can start.' I turn back to the mayor, and Madame Beaumont arrives and parks next to me.

'*Vous êtes arrivé à votre destination*,' says the sat-nav on her iPad in a deep, sexy French voice.

'We are here today to celebrate new beginnings, but also to remember the past,' he nods to Madame Beaumont. 'Isaac?'

Isaac steps forward and with the new spade digs a hole, and then I step forward and put in a rosebush next to the first of our new vines.

'This rosebush is being planted to honour those that fought and fell in love during the war. We want to honour their memory and their legacy. For those that made us who we are today,' Isaac says, and digs in the rose bush.

'The first of many,' I say, and everyone cheers and claps.

Gloria steps forward and hands round a tray of sparkling white wine. We all take a glass.

'To Clos Beaumont,' I say, and we all raise our glasses.

'And,' says the mayor, 'a toast to the future, for Petit Frère, no longer living in the shadows of our bigger neighbour, Saint Enrique, proud that we can stand up and be who we are. No longer the poor relation but a rapidly growing wine region in our own right, thanks to the word on the net.' And we toast Candy, who blushes. 'And to new winemakers.' They all turn and toast me, and I blush too.

Just then Isaac's phone rings. He looks apologetically at me. I shrug and nod for him to answer it.

'Nope, sorry, mate, can't help you. I'm staying put in France now. Yes, take me off your list.' He finishes the call and hangs up. 'Australia,' he tells me, shoving his phone back into his pockets. And for a moment I wonder if he wishes he was moving on now the seasons are changing again. He wraps an arm around me.

'I'm not going anywhere,' he laughs. 'Well, someone needs to be around in case you fall in the wine tank again.'

'To individuality and uniqueness,' says Madame Beaumont. 'It's the rich mix that makes Clos Beaumont truly special.' And we all raise our glasses and drink to that.

'Oh, and by the way, I have you all down for picking at the harvest again this year,' I say beaming, pointing round the group, and everyone laughs and agrees, and raises their glasses once again.

As the sun begins to set over Clos Beaumont and its new family members, the little vines that will need caring for, I photograph them.

New beginnings, I type and send to Layla. She sends back a text straight away. *And here, Auntie Emmy!!* And sends me a blurry, black-and-white photo of what appears to be . . . her twelve-week scan.

I'm beaming from ear to ear as we walk back down the hill, to Le Phénix, Gloria's new café and bar, where we toast new beginnings and putting down roots all over again. Because I know my roots are very firmly here with Isaac for as long as these vines need me.

'Just one thing,' Isaac whispers in my ear as we sit looking out over the wide river, back towards the humpback stone bridge. Ducks are paddling by the edges, a fish jumps and lands with a splash, and those big white birds are still honking their way down the river, low along the water. The rowers pass, followed by the little motor boat with the coach shouting instructions through a loud-hailer. There are fairy lights in the trees around us, and Gloria switches them on to celebrate the opening of her new business.

'Yes?' I say to Isaac.

'Y'know that you're supposed to be my close friend, like I told Madame Beaumont?' His face is up close to mine and I laugh.

'Yes, well, that was when we hardly knew each other,' I joke.

'Well, now that we do know each other,' he reaches into his jacket pocket and pulls out a small blue velvet box, 'do you think I could be your fiancé even?'

I look down at the little ruby ring and back at him as he pulls it out of the box and holds it to my finger.

'Will you be with me for ever?' He looks slightly nervous.

'What do you say, Goldy?' I reach out and hug him, my wild, curly blond hair falling over my face, feeling like all my vintages have come at once, but this is the going to be the best vintage yet.

Bonus Material

Jo Thomas's Guide to France

Jo Thomas takes us on a mouth-watering journey through her favourite French food.

1. Oysters – Arcachon

Whilst I was writing *The Oyster Catcher*, I stayed at a writing retreat in France. Every Sunday morning, as the church bells rang out, the Arcachon oyster men would arrive in the town square and set up stall. People would arrive with big plates ready to be loaded up for their Sunday lunch. And so I did the same thing. They were wonderful.

2. Sweet Chestnuts (*châtaigne*) – the Ardeche

My family and I holidayed in France when I was a child, and we would always camp in the same place every year – a forest in the Ardeche called La Châtaigneraie. We were surrounded by tall chestnut trees and prickly husks on the ground: a good reminder to always wear something on your feet! Recently, I discovered Châtaigne liqueur, which inspired my novella, *The Chestnut Tree*. You can add it to white or sparkling wine as you would crème de cassis in a Kir or Kir Royale. Just gorgeous.

3. Rosé wine – Provence

I have been told that the best rosé comes from Provence. One of the things I love most about writing in France is the *petit rosé* regularly offered to me by the wonderful local bar owner, as though it is as simple as having a glass of water or a coffee. It seems to be part of the fabric of everyday life. I adore this light, dry, aromatic wine, which reminds me of the lavender-covered hills of Provence – perfection.

4. Camembert – Normandy

I love cheese! But I *really* love Camembert – the softer and creamier the better. Before serving, I take it out of the fridge and let it stand until the smell lets me know it's ripe and ready to be cut, scooped on to the plate and eaten with crusty French bread and big, fat beefsteak tomatoes.

5. A really good steak – near Bordeaux

When I visit the region of France just outside Bordeaux, the one thing I really want is a good *entrecôte*. We go to a restaurant across the Dordogne River and sit outside in the open air, looking over the river, under strings of coloured lights that hang from tall trees. The steaks are cooked outside on hot grills, sizzling and spitting, dark brown on the outside and pink in the middle. They are best served with *frites* and salad, of course! Add a sauce made from shallots and Bordeaux red wine and you have *steak bordelaise*.

6. Charentais melon – Poitou-Charentes, western France

To finish a meal, I like nothing better than a gorgeous small charentais melon – like a cantaloupe – light green and striped on the outside with sweet, orange flesh inside. I could eat these for breakfast, for lunch with charcuterie, and for dinner as dessert. And I often do! When I buy them at the market I love to pick them up and smell them. If they smell fragrant and floral, they're ripe and ready to eat.

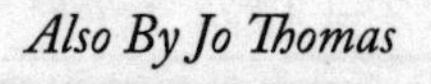
Also By Jo Thomas

'A world you long to live in with characters you love' Katie Fforde

Dooleybridge, County Galway: the last place Fiona Clutterbuck expects to end up, alone, on her wedding night.

But after the words 'I do' have barely left her mouth, that's exactly where she is – with only her sequined shoes and a crashed camper van for company.

One thing is certain: Fi can't go back. So when the opportunity arises to work for brooding local oyster farmer, Sean Thornton, she jumps at the chance. Now Fi must navigate suspicious locals, jealous rivals and an unpredictable boss if she's to find a new life, and love, on the Irish coast. And nothing – not even a chronic fear of water – is going to hold her back.

Join Fi as she learns the rules of the ocean – and picks up a few pearls of Irish wisdom along the way . . .

Also By Jo Thomas

'Sun, good food and romance, what more could you want?' ***Heat***

You can buy almost anything online these days. For Ruthie Collins, it was an Italian farmhouse.

Yet as she battles with a territorial goat and torrential rain just to get through the door of her new Italian home, the words of Ed, her ex, are ringing in her ears. She is daft, impetuous and irresponsible.

But Ruthie is determined to turn things around and live the dream.

First, though, she must win over her fiery neighbour, Marco Bellanouvo, and his family . . . Then there's the small matter of running an olive farm.

As the seasons change and new roots are put down, olives and romance might just flourish in the warmth of the Mediterranean sun.

Escape to happy ever after with

Jo Thomas

Step into Jo's world of books, food, and travelling
There's no better place to be

Find Jo on:

/JoThomasAuthor

@Jo_Thomas01

Or browse her scrapbook at
www.jothomasauthor.co.uk